MALTA INFERNO

Jack Pembroke Thrillers Book Four

Justin Fox

Also in the Jack Pembroke series

The Cape Raider

The Wolf Hunt

Hell Run Tobruk

MALTA
INFERNO

Published by Sapere Books.

24 Trafalgar Road, Ilkley, LS29 8HH,
United Kingdom

saperebooks.com

ISBN: 978-0-85495-864-1

In loving memory of my father, Revel Fox (Sherman tank gunner), and my four uncles and two aunts — Bokkie Krige (South African Air Force pilot), Uys Krige (war correspondent and POW, captured at Sidi Rezegh), Arnold Krige (intelligence officer, wounded at El Alamein), François Krige (official war artist), as well as Lydia Krige (née Lindeque) and Mizzi Krige (both in the Union Defence Force entertainment unit) — who all served in Egypt and the eastern Mediterranean during World War II.

No crosses mark the ocean waves,
No monuments of stone.
No roses grow on sailors' graves,
The sailor rests alone.
His tributes are the seagulls' sweeps,
Forever wild and free,
And teardrops that his sweetheart weeps
To mingle with the sea.

— Naval ode, author unknown

ACKNOWLEDGEMENTS

I would like to offer my sincere thanks to the Artists in Residence programme of the University of Johannesburg for granting me the support, time and space to complete this novel. I was greatly assisted in Alexandria by Isabella Morris and Mohamed Kamal and in Malta by Marcus Brewster, Mark Leach and Annelie Roux, as well as Keith Gatt of the Malta Maritime Museum, who kindly gave me a copy of his unpublished master's thesis, *The Unsinkable Aircraft Carrier* (University of Malta). Thank you also to the helpful staff at the National Library of Malta and the National Archives of Malta.

I was generously hosted for long periods by Gillian and Alec Foster in London, where I spent many happy hours in the British National Archives, British Library and the archives of the Imperial War Museum. The Simon's Town Museum, SA Navy Museum and the Naval Heritage Trust (especially its meticulously recorded personal accounts of South Africans who served at sea during the war), provided invaluable material. I would also like to thank my talented editors Amy Durant and Rear Admiral Arnè Söderlund (Rtd), as well as those who generously gave of their time to read the manuscript, offered advice or helped with research: David Attwell, Cameron Ewart-Smith, Bruce Jack, James Holland, David Krut, Gill Moodie, Paul Morris, Don Pinnock, Luke Stevens, Commander Leon Steyn, Stephen Symons, Alexander Sceberras Trigona, James van Helsdingen, Gillian Warren-Brown and Tracey Younghusband. A special thank you to the Sapere Books team, and to my tireless agent and friend, Aoife Lennon-Ritchie. The principal ships and characters of this tale are entirely fictitious.

FOREWORD

When South Africa declared war on Germany on 6 September 1939, the Union's permanent naval force consisted of only two officers and three ratings. The Cape of Good Hope was a critical strategic point on the sea route around the continent and would be vital in the coming North African and Asian campaigns. When Italy entered the war in 1940, the Mediterranean became extremely hazardous for Allied convoys and most were rerouted around the Cape. The Royal Navy base in Simonstown (the 1940s spelling, versus today's Simon's Town) had to be expanded and reinforced, and a fledgling South African navy created almost from scratch.

Enemy action off the South African coast accounted for more than 150 vessels sunk and nearly a million tons of shipping lost. Further north, as the toll on Allied ships in the Mediterranean increased, the Royal Navy requested that South African ships be sent to help with anti-submarine, escort and minesweeping work. As the war expanded, South African vessels did service throughout the Mediterranean.

These episodes in the country's history went largely unheralded. During the war, this was justified given the need to keep ship movements secret. After coming to power in 1948, the Nazi-sympathising Nationalist Party did not wish to celebrate, or even acknowledge, South Africa's war achievements, particularly those that involved the Royal Navy. For them, the future of the country looked not dissimilar to Hitler's Germany, with racial segregation being central to their post-war plans.

Defending against the U-boat threat and protecting convoys around the Union's coast fell to the Royal Navy — mostly ships based in Simonstown — and to the new South African Navy, initially named the Seaward Defence Force (SDF). In 1940, some of the focus shifted to North Africa and by the end of 1941, there were some 60,000 South African troops serving in the Western Desert. By the time Rommel reached El Alamein, poised to take Cairo and the Suez Canal, most of the Royal Navy had been evacuated from Alexandria, leaving little more substantial than a few (mostly South African) minesweepers and anti-submarine whalers to hold the line and run perilous convoys to and from Allied ports. During 1942, the deadliest shipping route of all was to the besieged island of Malta.

For many 'Springboks', as South African sailors were called, their life's greatest adventure was the time spent in the Mediterranean taking part in some of the most hazardous small-ship work of the war. This is the story of one such vessel, HMSAS *Southern Gannet*, commanded by a British lieutenant, Jack Pembroke DSO RNVR, operating in those deadly waters during the summer of 1942.

CHAPTER 1

Jack stood behind Alana, inhaling the jasmine scent of her hair as she leant against him. He ran his fingers lightly along her darkly tanned shoulder and down her arm, feeling a quiver to his touch. She turned, entwining her arms about his neck.

'*Mi amor*, that frown,' she whispered, gently kissing his cheek. 'You are troubled.'

'Preparations for sea, everything stretched to breaking point, nothing new,' he muttered.

'Another convoy?'

'I am not permitted to say —'

'Captain Jack, I have eyes.' The beautiful Spaniard freed a hand and swept it across the harbour. Their sunset vantage on the terrace of the yacht club presented a vast panorama of ships. Since the previous month's Alexandria Flap — when Rommel had come within spitting distance of the city and only been stopped by a last stand at a nondescript railway siding called El Alamein — things had settled into an attritional struggle along a line stretching south into the desert.

Somehow, the Allied defences had held and, in due course, the Eighth Army would attempt to strike back. During the past few, volatile weeks, HMSAS *Southern Gannet* had been busily employed patrolling the western approaches to Alexandria with her captain, Lieutenant Jack Pembroke, never quite knowing what the enemy might be sending his way, a situation aggravated by the Royal Navy having all but fled to safer ports to the east.

Meanwhile, a daring — some would say foolhardy — convoy was secretly being prepared in a last-ditch attempt to send supplies to save Malta, the only pinprick of British soil left in the central Mediterranean. And Jack's *Gannet* was to be one of its escorts.

'Alana, please —'

'After everything, I cannot lose you. I need to know.'

Jack sighed. 'All right, yes, there is a convoy, soon. But I cannot say more.'

'And you, *mi amor*, are in this convoy?' Alana's eyes clouded.

His silence and the busy scene before them were proof enough. The harbour throbbed and smoked with activity around the newly arrived cruisers and destroyers, its water agitated by the wakes of liberty boats passing in and out of Arsenal Basin, while small craft, feluccas and picket boats cut back and forth between the moorings. Among the newcomers was the ageing aircraft carrier, HMS *Vulture*, on loan from the Royal Navy's Far Eastern Fleet, lately based in Mombasa due to Japanese advances in the Indian Ocean. She occupied the berth vacated by the damaged battleship HMS *Queen Elizabeth*, which had been hastily withdrawn to the Suez Canal during Rommel's advance.

The ships appeared gold-plated by the sun's last rays as bugle calls echoed through the harbour, Royal Marine guards presented arms and the ensigns on every ship slid to the deck. Across the city, silver barrage balloons jerked skyward on their wires like thought bubbles and anti-aircraft batteries prepared for the ubiquitous nocturnal intruders.

On the opposite shore, to the left of the coaling quay, Jack could just make out his *Gannet* amid a pod of other whalers and trawlers that had been employed in the coastal 'spud run' to Tobruk for the past year, keeping the town supplied until its sudden and calamitous fall the previous month. *Gannet* had been the last ship to leave before Rommel's panzers overran the port, taking more than 30,000 prisoners, many of them South Africans.

The sun dipped behind the breakwater and the harbour was bathed in pastel shades, but the masts and minarets still reflected the last honeyed rays. Alexandria was a city on edge and braced for attack, yet somehow it remained so beguiling, so freighted with history. Jack pulled his lover closer and kissed the top of her head, his thoughts turning to the heartbreak she'd endured. Alana hailed from a family of anti-fascists and had escaped with her father just before the fall of Barcelona in 1939. He remembered how, during their first dance on the night they met, her face had clouded when she'd told him about her husband, Hernando Vilar, being killed near Tarragona while fighting for the Republicans. He well understood her anxiety at the prospect of losing him too. Jack couldn't bear the thought of losing her either: during the rapid Axis advance across the desert, he'd insisted that Alana be evacuated by train to Palestine, but with the front having stabilised, she'd returned to the city to be near him.

Air-raid sirens interrupted his thoughts, beginning their mournful wailing across the city, followed soon after by the unsynchronised drone of aero engines.

'The Luftwaffe is early this evening,' said Alana, looking up at her handsome paramour with his chestnut hair, steel-blue eyes and scar on his temple.

'The bastards can't wait to get at all these juicy targets,' replied Jack.

The couple lingered until the city's western batteries began their heavy bass drumming and the glitter of flak sparkled in the dusky sky.

'To the shelter, my love,' said Jack.

'*Sí*.'

But still, they did not move, locked in a tight embrace as the first bombs began to fall.

'Jack, we must share *todo*, everything, you understand this?' she whispered.

'Yes.'

'We are as one, *mi amor*.'

'We are.'

When the dockyard Bofors guns opened up with their rhythmical beat, the lovers made their way hand in hand down the steps to the yacht club's makeshift bunker.

The convoy conference had taken place the previous day in the expansive wardroom of the aircraft carrier HMS *Vulture*. Jack had found a seat at the back of the large gathering of all the captains of the escorts and freighters, accompanied by their navy liaison officers, as well as a number of representatives of the air force and army. Among the merchantmen were Greek, Dutch, French and Norwegian masters — all of them with families suffering under Nazi occupation in their home countries. Brave men, each carrying an even heavier load than the command of his own ship.

A short, balding figure in immaculate whites, his breast adorned with four ribbons from the Great War, stood before a mounted chart of the eastern Mediterranean covered by a curtain. Rear Admiral Somerset was a much-admired officer, experienced and dependable, but even he had grave doubts about the proposed operation.

'To put you out of your misery, gentlemen: we are indeed going to Malta.' The admiral's voice was clipped, his words hard and precise as he drew back the curtain to a swell of muttering and a few exclamations. Like most of those gathered, Jack had surmised their destination, but now that the island's talismanic name had been uttered, he felt a constriction in his chest. Malta. An isle more sinned against than Rotterdam, Warsaw or London. The most bombed place on earth.

The admiral waited until silence was restored. 'There's no need for me to stress the importance of this convoy, codenamed Operation Assegai. You all know what Malta means to the Empire and to the war effort. It is the thorn in Hitler and Mussolini's side. As long as we hold Malta, we retain the ability to strike at Rommel's supply routes from Italy. If Malta falls, the Mediterranean could follow suit, and the domino effect might skittle us out of Egypt and the Middle East, allowing Axis powers to link up in the Indian Ocean and that, gentlemen, might be game, set and match.'

There were uneasy murmurs. Jack stared at the proposed route drawn in blue on the chart, almost every mile of it through enemy-held waters. Dotted arcs marked the range of Axis and Allied aircraft, black crosses denoted enemy harbours, shaded areas warned of minefields. It looked like an obstacle course devised by a sadist: as the convoy travelled westward, further from Allied air support, so the snares and pitfalls multiplied. *Another* Malta attempt, especially at this desperate stage in the fight. It was, surely, madness.

'The brave little island is on its knees, the inhabitants and the garrison on starvation rations,' Somerset continued. 'The new governor, Lord Gort, has given me some idea of their privations. Present stocks of wheat and flour, Malta's staple, will last no more than another month; fuel and coal, possibly six weeks; ammunition, perhaps five weeks, but they're already having to ration their anti-aircraft shells. As you will appreciate, it is down to the proverbial wire and only a substantial convoy can save that Promethean rock. It is Prime Minister Churchill's ardent and expressed wish that such a convoy be pressed through, come hell or high water. We should expect both.'

The admiral paused to allow the tense chuckles, then continued: 'A trickle of supplies has been reaching the island thanks to the "Magic Carpet Service" provided by our large Thames-class submarines, and the fast minelayers, *Welshman* and *Manxman*, that have been making the perilous run. But this slender lifeline has not been enough. Now there is a target date, not much more than a month away, when Lord Gort tells me he will be forced to surrender. It is our task to make sure this does not happen.

'Ours will be a fast convoy of fourteen knots. Laggards will be left behind ... and might have to be scuttled.' The wardroom was silent as Somerset cleared his throat and glanced around at the grave, attentive faces. 'Operation Assegai will comprise ten fast, modern merchantmen and a strong escort force of one flat top and seven cruisers, as well as thirty-two destroyers and smaller craft, including two MTBs and one MGB, each towed by a merchantman.'

Jack ran his eye over the list of warships in his docket. Four of the cruisers were Dido class, thinly armoured but fast, with a complement of nearly 500 men, a good anti-aircraft armament and six 21-inch torpedo tubes. The three heavier cruisers would be led by HMS *Rhodesia*, wearing Admiral Somerset's flag. Capable of thirty-two knots and with a displacement of about 7,000 tons, the heavies carried more than 600 men and had up to twelve 6-inch and twelve 4-inch anti-aircraft guns. To ensure close co-operation with Malta-based aircraft, *Rhodesia* was fitted with very high frequency radio telephony to communicate with Allied pilots.

The cruiser flotilla would provide their principal defence if the Regia Marina dispatched its own heavy units, but the convoy's workhorses would be the destroyers and smaller escorts, keeping U-boats and E-boats at bay, as well as providing the bulk of the anti-aircraft protection. The destroyers were a mix of big, modern, 1,800-ton Tribal-class vessels, along with J, K and L class, forming an outer screen, and slower Hunt-class destroyers forming an inner screen. The Hunts were small, mass-produced vessels with six high-angle 4-inch guns housed in twin mountings and had become the stalwart escort of Mediterranean convoys. There were also a handful of corvettes, mostly Flower class, two fleet minesweepers to help clear the heavily mined approaches to Malta, and the minnow of the fleet, the South African whale catcher HMSAS *Southern Gannet*, designated as one of the rescue ships.

The air defences of all the merchantmen had been greatly strengthened with the addition of 40-mm Swedish-designed Bofors guns, as well as British pom-poms firing low-velocity two-pound shells, and Swiss-designed 20-mm Oerlikons fitted with sixty-round drum magazines and operated by a gunner strapped into a shoulder harness. The merchantmen had acquired extra Royal Navy and Maritime Regiment gunners to man the plethora of newly added weapons that now bristled about their superstructures.

The admiral continued: 'Each freighter will be loaded with a wide range of supplies — drums of aviation spirit, cooking kerosene, coal, ammunition, flour, medical equipment and the like — so that even if only a handful of you get through, the island will have some emergency rations of everything. We will also be ferrying a contingent of anti-aircraft gunners of the Cheshire Regiment to bolster Malta's defences.'

Jack wondered about the myriad scenarios that must be running through each captain's mind at that moment. Every merchant ship would be loaded with highly flammable fuel and tons of ammunition on the most dangerous convoy route in the world. Every one of them would be a floating bomb.

'However, the crown jewel in our little armada will be the spanking new American tanker, SS *Lexington*, of the Eagle Oil and Shipping Company. Upon her shoulders rests the hope of a fuel-starved Malta. She will sail in the centre of the convoy.'

Whenever Jack heard the word 'tanker', he pictured the horror of the mined Norwegian sinking off the Cape of Good Hope and how he'd witnessed men on fire for the first time, living faggots kept afloat by their lifejackets, dying the most horrific of deaths, their screams echoing across the water to *Gannet* as his men tried to rescue a handful of survivors.

The admiral's voice cut into his thoughts: 'We must expect molestation by the enemy from the moment we leave Alex. A major combined land and air assault on the El Alamein line has been planned to coincide with our departure, which should keep the enemy air forces distracted. In addition, there will be another convoy to coincide with ours, codenamed Operation Fortress, comprising ten merchantmen with a strong escort departing from Gibraltar, also bound for Malta. In this manner, it is hoped that the enemy will be compelled to divide his attacks between the eastbound and westbound convoys.

'It goes without saying that our air forces in Egypt, Cyprus and Malta will not only provide as much cover as possible but will also be plastering enemy airfields and harbours over the coming days. A long-range desert force and commando units, including the SAS and SBS, will be doing the same to coastal and island ports and airfields.

'When we reach the Mediterranean basin, there is a chance the Italian battlefleet will put in an appearance. To this end, a diversionary convoy will depart from Port Suez before us to try to draw the battleships out prematurely. It is hoped this feint will expose them to attack by our submarines and aircraft, and use up their precious fuel.

'An added fly in the ointment, and still rather hush-hush, is the possibility that the Germans have established a powerful RDF station on one of the islands along our route. If this is found to be true, it will enable the enemy to track our progress in the central basin better than any reconnaissance.

'In your dockets, you'll find detailed instructions as to how the convoy will react in each eventuality. But for the merchantmen, as always, the old maxims apply: don't make smoke, don't show any light at night, keep good station and, if you're hit, try to keep going at your best possible speed. This convoy, gentlemen, *will* prevail.'

Jack thought he could detect anxiety, perhaps even doubt, in the admiral's voice. The previous month's attempt to get supplies through to Malta, codenamed Operation Vigorous, had been a disaster. The convoy had received such a beating and expended so much ammunition that it was forced to turn back before reaching the island, and had left many fine ships, including a cruiser and three destroyers, on the Mediterranean floor.

Jack could not think of a single reason why this convoy could expect a different outcome. If anything, the enemy had grown stronger in the interim and learnt from any mistakes made during its attacks on Vigorous. What's more, the African frontline had shifted hundreds of miles eastward, to the very gates of Alexandria, which meant the convoy would have far less air cover, and be subject to enemy air attack for much longer than the previous attempt. In the interim, Axis forces had also extended and improved their bomber, U-boat and E-boat bases on Crete and along the shores of Cyrenaica and

Egypt. Field Marshall Kesselring now had more than 1,300 aircraft at his disposal. Each day, the noose had been tightening, and now it was their singular responsibility to run the gauntlet to Malta.

As the admiral continued, Jack felt an increasing weight bearing down on his shoulders. He looked around at the serious faces: merchant masters, RN and RNVR escort commanders, Australians, Americans, Canadians. How many of them would reach Malta … and how many would make it back? Jack pictured the carnage of the Tobruk convoys: sinking freighters, desperate survivors in the water, escorts assaulted from above and below. The agonising decisions of whether to attack or defend, whether to rescue the drowning or stick with the convoy.

Somerset was reaching the end of his address. 'With the Japanese threatening the western Indian Ocean, we have not been able to release any battleships for this convoy, and you all know the fate of *Queen Elizabeth* and *Valiant*, but we *are* fortunate to have the services of HMS *Vulture*, which will provide essential air cover. My intention is to get the convoy to within easy reach of Malta on the fourth night, when the heavy units will retire eastward and the freighters will slip into Grand Harbour under the cover of darkness.'

The admiral then took questions and a discussion ensued concerning procedures to be followed when the enemy was sighted, screening dispositions, fuel endurance, signal codes, and the like. The instructions in their dockets already covered much of this and Jack had heard a lot of it in one form or another before. His thoughts drifted to the voyage at hand. Given the failure of Vigorous, he tried to weigh the chances of Operation Assegai's success. Less than even was his considered guess.

'The convoy will assemble during the forenoon on Tuesday.' Loud rumblings from the assembled. 'Yes, yes, not much time, I know. Although Alexandria's spies will be keenly watching our preparations and drawing their own conclusions, I must stress the absolute necessity of secrecy as to our destination, time of departure and details of this operation. Again, I need not tell you how high the stakes are. The survival of Malta and, perhaps in some small measure, the outcome of this war, depends on us … depends on you. That is all. Godspeed.'

It was in a dark mood of foreboding that the captains and officers — some talking in low, earnest voices, most of them silent — took their leave. Across the wardroom, Jack spotted Captain Pierre Marais among the pale blue uniforms of the SAAF and RAF representatives. Pierre was a pilot friend from Cape Town and the brother of Clara, Jack's former lover. The two officers shook hands warmly.

'A big one,' said Pierre.

'Aye, feels a bit do or die, doesn't it?' Jack replied.

'Derring-do on the high seas — just your sort of thing, I'd have thought.'

'You insist on confusing me with my father.'

Pierre chuckled. 'At least you'll have our chaps providing you with a brolly for the first leg.'

'But not in Bomb Alley between Crete and Cyrenaica, where the Luftwaffe has doubled its strength.'

'You'll have *Vulture*'s birds.'

'A handful against hundreds, but you're right, it is a comfort. How goes the bombing caper?'

Pierre was the pilot of a Boston light bomber employed in daily raids on the Afrika Korps' supply lines, which had been severely stretched due to Rommel's lightning advance.

'We're playing havoc: fish in a barrel,' said Pierre. 'I like to think the SAAF is severely hampering Jerry's ability to launch the next offensive.'

'That's jolly good to hear.'

'By the way, I have an airy-fairy chum on board: Flight Lieutenant Grayson Douglas, bloody decent chap, Canadian, fought in the Battle of Britain, then switched to flat tops. I think you should meet him.'

The pair were directed to the pilots' wardroom, where they found Douglas sprawled in an armchair reading the *Egyptian Mail.*

'Pierre, old sock, what a splendid surprise!' said Douglas, bounding from his chair. As the pilot turned his head, Jack was shocked by the young man's face: one half handsome as a Hollywood star, the other badly disfigured by burns sustained, he later discovered, in a dogfight above the fields of Kent. Recovering from the initial surprise, Jack's next impression was of a serious young man of purpose, but with a twinkle in his eye that suggested a refined sense of humour.

After the introductions, Douglas offered to take them on a tour of the ship. *Vulture* was an elderly escort carrier whose mix of aircraft — thirteen Sea Hurricanes, nine Fairey Fulmars and six torpedo-carrying Fairey Albacores — would scout ahead of the convoy and try to keep the enemy at bay, with the Albacores being deployed in the event of an encounter with the Italian battlefleet.

The three officers stepped through a doorway and entered the hangar beneath the flight deck, a cavernous, echoing space filled with noise and industry. Riggers and fitters were everywhere, probing with tools and powerful lights under and about the aircraft like Lilliputian surgeons. Bold signs adorned the bulkheads, warning against smoking and the danger of fuel leaks.

'This is my baby, a Mark IB,' said Douglas, running an affectionate hand along the rounded wingtip of a Sea Hurricane — a squat, hunchbacked fighter in grey-blue and dark green camouflage with an arrester hook for carrier landing. Jack noticed a winged cheetah painted on the cowling — the pilot's personal emblem.

'Such a joy to fly,' said Douglas. 'She's had her Merlin III modified to accept sixteen pounds of boost and can generate more than 1,400 horsepower at low altitude. And my eight Brownings pack a pretty decent punch.'

'You might have your work cut out on this run,' said Jack.

'We serve to please,' said Douglas, smiling.

They climbed a companionway and emerged into the dazzling white sunshine and wobbling heat of the flight deck. It was vast, just like a planked airfield, though Jack knew *Vulture* was much smaller than fleet carriers such as *Ark Royal* and much, much slower. But the dear old *Ark* — for so long the navy's 'lucky ship' — lay broken on the bed of the Mediterranean, and beggars could not be choosers.

'It's like landing on a postage stamp, a bucking and bronking one at that,' said Douglas, seeing Jack's eyes measuring the flight deck.

'I've always been somewhat enamoured with this combination of navy and air power, but by God, rather you than me,' said Jack.

'Given what's coming our way, I'm not sure in whose shoes I'd rather be,' Douglas replied.

CHAPTER 2

The sailors of HMSAS *Southern Gannet* were determined to make the most of their last shore leave. A boisterous troop poured out of Number Twenty-Two Gate and climbed aboard the waiting horse-drawn gharries. With a cracking of whips, the carriages set off for the city centre, where most sailors were dropped off at the Fleet Club on Rue de l'Hôpital Grec, a home from home for Allied ratings in Alexandria. They made straight for the beer garden, where a small stage offered non-stop entertainment, most of it provided by inebriated seamen telling crude jokes or initiating singalongs. With so many ships in port, there was also an enormous game of housey-housey on the go with a substantial pot of prize money.

After downing a few pints of 'gnat's piss' — the local Stella — the Gannets spilled back out onto the street and broke up in search of more spicy entertainment. Some ended up at the Top Hat Cabaret, a few had their logbooks stamped at the official army brothel on Sisters' Street, and others chose the marginally more refined naval bag shanty at Number Fourteen Gate, where the queues were shorter but the women dearer.

Gannet's officers were also bent on enjoying their last day in port. Sub-lieutenant Tom Fletcher, Gannet's dandy new officer and Oxford history graduate with a passion for the theatre, made for Mary's House where a sinuous Lebanese had been demanding a great deal of attention, resulting in a pronounced shrinking of his wallet. After a bad first impression, Jack had grown fond of the rather flamboyant Fletcher during their perilous months of Tobruk convoys. The young sub had quickly acquired the ship's arcane — often South African —

jargon, mastered the art of good station keeping, and at long last learnt when to rouse his captain and when to let him sleep. Despite Jack's initial reservations, Fletcher had become a valued, dyed-in-the-wool Gannet.

Sub-lieutenant Geoffrey Robinson, the whaler's navigator and aspirant architect from Cape Town, managed to arrange a clandestine meeting with Charlotte, a winsome teenager from a well-to-do French-Lebanese family determined to shield their daughter from the attentions of the foreign officers thronging Alexandria. She would be meeting a 'friend from the lycée' at Stanley Beach.

Gannet's dependable Number One, Sub-lieutenant Jannie van Zyl, was a law student from Stellenbosch who had recently lost a friend to suicide. The Jewish writer Stavros Davison had become a mentor to Jannie, helping him with his own poetry, but the cultivated gentleman had refused to flee his beloved Alexandria and, fearful of his fate at the hands of the advancing Nazis, had taken his own life during The Flap.

Van Zyl returned to Grammata, the bookshop on Rue Debanne where he'd first met Stavros, and once again stocked up on reading matter for the wardroom. As *Gannet*'s unofficial librarian, the young Afrikaner bought books that catered to the officers' varying penchants — natural history for Jack, architecture for Robinson, popular fiction for Fletcher — but always added a few to his own, often poetic, taste. Today's haul included William Grant's *Birds Found in Malta and Gozo*, Edward Bell's *The Architecture of Ancient Egypt*, Graham Greene's *Brighton Rock*, Ernest Hemingway's *For Whom the Bell Tolls*, Dylan Thomas's *Portrait of the Artist as a Young Dog* and another anthology by Constantine Cavafy, bard of Alexandria and, thanks to Stavros, Van Zyl's new favourite poet.

That evening, Jack also managed to escape the needy clutches of *Gannet.* Dismounting from his gharry on a thronging Saad Zaghloul Square, he stepped into Hotel Cecil's tranquil lobby. The Moorish-style establishment on the promenade was popular with officers and had become a regular of Jack's. He walked through the mirrored vestibule with its dusty palms, lazily ticking fans and alcoves filled with robed men bent to their chessboards. He spotted Alana seated at a window table, looking ravishing in a low-cut emerald dress, a tiny diamond suspended from each earlobe and serpents of hair loosely impaled with something lethal on top of her head to accentuate her Pharaonic neck.

'My Cleopatra,' he whispered, kissing both her cheeks. 'Sorry I'm late. Have you been up to the room?'

'My valise, yes. Me, no. I waited for you.'

'Let's go straight through to dinner, shall we?' His eyes revelled in her dark beauty. 'Then after, we can be alone.'

'You want to eat early and fast?'

'No … er, yes.'

'Not very Spanish.'

'I suppose not, sorry.' He looked a little crestfallen. She giggled deliciously.

'Let us eat fast then, *mi amor*.'

Not very much later, they sat smoking on their room's tiny balcony. The dusky city still exhaled the dry heat of the day, but a zephyr off the sea breathed among the buildings, offering moments of damp, salty coolth. From the west came the distant rumbling of a barrage, the flashes of an artillery exchange reflecting off the clouds.

'Out there in the desert, the fate of Egypt is perhaps being decided, no?' said Alana.

'I think the lines will remain pretty static while the two armies gather their strength for the next push.'

'Alexandria is safe for now, you think?'

'Yes, I do.'

'And you, are you safe? This journey, this convoy, when is it? Where are you going?'

'Too many questions, Alana.'

She leant forward and kissed his neck, her fingers toying with the buckle of his belt. '*Mi amor*, it is just that I cannot lose you. Not again. Not after everything that was taken from me in Spain. I need to know.'

They were kissing, ravenously now, the clips of a silky bra coming undone between his fingers, her breasts full and warm in his hands.

'I love you, Jack. I have never before felt this way, but I am so very scared. Every minute you are gone from me, it hurts very, very much.'

They stood up and, still holding each other, moved towards the bed, clothing items coming adrift to mark their progress. They fell among the pillows, naked now, clutching at each other with a desire tainted with dread for what lay ahead. Unspoken was the spectre, the terrible possibility that there may never be another night like this. Jack could almost taste the potent cocktail of lust, foreboding and overpowering love.

'When are you leaving?' she whispered.

'Alana —'

'When, *per la merda*?'

'Tomorrow, my love, tomorrow.'

'Where to? Where to?'

'Malta.'

'Oh no, Jack, *Dios mío*, no! Just hold me.'

*

Pale sunlight fingered a gap in the curtains, the morning already hot and demanding. Jack lay perfectly still, admiring the sinuous curves of the woman beside him, one brown leg thrown casually over his, hair strung across her face in burnt-umber ropes. A muezzin's call to prayer echoed across the rooftops, followed by the soft clatter and squeal of a tram leaving Ramleh station. Alana's scent was heady in his nostrils.

What if Malta was a mountain too high and this convoy, like so many before it, doomed? Never to see Alana again — a prospect too appalling to countenance, beyond the pale of despair. He would have to make sure he survived. He would have to bring *Gannet* back to this port, this Alexandria, to the landfall that was Alana.

Jack thought, too, of everything he and his men had endured, the incessant aerial attacks of the Tobruk runs, how his nerves had been stretched to breaking … at times, even, beyond breaking, and only a tremendous force of will had saved him. Memories of his own terror, his earlier paralysis and shame at Dunkirk, still tarried in his mind's recesses. How he had been unworthy of his former ship, HMS *Havoc*, and how her sinking beneath his feet, his feet of clay, was an enduring stain on his conscience. Ahead of him lay a voyage far more perilous than any Tobruk run, a convoy with the slimmest chance of success and his dear *Gannet* in the thick of it.

His alarm clock began its loud clamouring, followed by a scramble to get dressed, hasty and miserable goodbyes, Alana's tears wet on his uniform, and the hailing of a gharry back to the harbour and through the dockyard gates. A rickety wooden gangplank led down to *Gannet*, snug against the wharf beside Number Forty-Four Shed, home to the SDF in Alexandria. He saluted the quartermaster, a grim-faced Able Seaman Behardien standing to attention at the brow, wearing faded work overalls with a revolver at his waist. No turning back, no time to reflect — the departure was upon him.

The previous day, fleet auxiliaries had come alongside to prepare *Gannet* for sea: a water barge to fill her tanks, then a lighter with ammunition. Stores of all kinds had streamed aboard, including jam from the Boland, crates of tinned milk, paint, rum, canvas, wire hawsers, cigarettes — all of it needing to be fitted into already crammed stowage spaces. Under the direction of PO Combrink, ammo boxes by the dozen had come aboard, with sailors hauling out the 4-inch HE — high-explosive — and armour-piercing shells and carrying them to the store beneath the ratings' accommodation. *Gannet* had then paid a visit to the coaling arm and gone alongside an oiler to top up her fuel tanks.

Seated at his desk in the sanctity of his cabin, Jack was peripherally aware of the industry above and below decks as he worked his way through last-minute paperwork. Then he climbed to the bridge and stood surveying the scene. Only weeks before, Alexandria had been in the grip of The Flap, the harbour emptied of ships on the assumption that Rommel's tanks were about to roll down the boulevards. In those days of turmoil, it was said that the portraits of Churchill and Roosevelt displayed in cafés had images of Hitler and Mussolini on the back, ready to be reversed.

The Flap culminated in what became known as 'Ash Wednesday', when a funereal pall of smoke hung over the city and the grey snow of charred paper rained down as British officials burnt documents. Rumour in the bazaars and back alleys had it that the Allies had already lost Egypt, and thousands fled to the east and south amid widespread panic and looting. But the defensive line had held — just — and the top brass, in their wisdom, were now dead set on wrestling a convoy through to Malta.

An air of resignation hung about the crew and nerves grew taut as the time for sailing drew nearer. Ratings performed their tasks in silence with none of the usual joshing and jesting. Just before departure, *Gannet*'s captain asked that his crew be mustered on the foredeck. After so many months of convoy duty, this was unusual, but Jack wanted to offer some words of encouragement, and a prayer, not because he was religious — his Christian faith had fallen by the wayside during his Oxford years — but because he thought his men and the moment warranted it.

He looked around at the anxious, upturned faces, cleared his throat, and began: 'Most of you will doubtless have already guessed our destination. The time has arrived for us to take part in a great venture to help save the courageous people of Malta from starvation and capitulation. It is up to each one of us to do our utmost to make sure this convoy reaches the island. You may be assured that the enemy will do everything in his power to prevent us from achieving our mission and it will require every exertion on our part to see that he fails.' He paused, registering his men's breathless silence.

'Over the coming days, *Gannet* will need to be in the first degree of readiness for long periods. When you are on watch, you must be especially vigilant, and when you are off duty, get all the sleep you can. I have no doubt each and every one of you will give of your best. When you are dismissed from here, you will go directly to your stations for leaving harbour.'

Jack concluded by reading the Royal Navy prayer, adapted to the occasion: '*Preserve us from the dangers of the sea, and from the violence of the enemy; that we may be a safeguard unto our most gracious sovereign lord, King George, and his Dominions and Unions, and a security for such as pass on the seas upon their lawful occasions; that the inhabitants of our Empire, and of the little island of Malta for which we are bound, may in peace and quietness serve thee our God; and that we may return in safety to enjoy the blessings of the land, with the fruits of our labours; and with a thankful remembrance of thy mercies to praise and glorify thy holy Name; through Jesus Christ our Lord. Amen.*'

A heartfelt 'Amen' rang out from the crew.

'And so, brave Gannets, to sea once more. Carry on.'

CHAPTER 3

Jack scanned the harbour, his nostrils alive to the pungent smells of garbage, rotting fish, coal and a hint of horse manure wafting from the gates. Special sea dutymen were being piped throughout the escorts, cable and side parties closed up, and a handful of merchantmen were preparing to cast off. One by one the ships let go mooring lines and eased their way across the enormous harbour, passing through the boom gate, rounding the breakwater and sailing to the end of the swept channel where they would begin the laborious process of assembling into convoy formation.

'Hello tower, hello tower, hello tower, this is *Gannet* calling tower, request permission to leave harbour, over,' came the voice of Leading Seaman 'Sparks' Thomas from the wireless cabin.

'Hello *Gannet*, this is Ras el-Tin, you are clear to leave harbour, over.'

Thomas cut the power to the transmitter, opened the voicepipe cover and called up to the bridge: 'We have permission to leave harbour, sir.'

Jack leant towards the voicepipe's trumpet mouth and said, 'Very good, thank you, Sparks.'

'Main engine rung on, sir,' came the voice of Chief McEwan from the engine room. Jack pictured the old Scot and his grease-smeared stokers tending to their machinery in the gleaming world of dials and gauges far below.

'Let go aft.' Then, a few moments later, 'Let go for'ard, but hold on to the bow spring. Slow ahead.'

Gannet's fo'c'sle and quarterdeck men hauled in the berthing wires as the propeller churned milky water and the whaler went forward, straining against the spring and pressing her bow against the heavy fenders until her stern edged away and she lay at forty-five degrees to the wharf.

'Stop engine. Let go bow spring.' Jack gave an involuntary sigh as *Gannet* released herself from the land. 'Slow astern.'

The whaler backed into open water, turned to aim at the corner of the coaling elbow, and stopped her engine once more.

'Slow ahead.'

His heart heavy, Jack glanced over to starboard at the submarine trots, all empty save for one T-class boat undergoing repairs. The rest of the flotilla was already in the Ionian Sea, preparing a picket line to waylay the Italian battlefleet should it venture out.

Gathering way, *Gannet* passed the dormant hulks of Force X, the interned Vichy French men-of-war that included the old battleship *Lorraine* with her four cruisers and three destroyers. Over to port, a shoreline of wharves, cranes and godowns; beyond them, half a mile inland, Lake Maryut, where Jack had gone birding and added a handful of new fowl to his Egyptian list. And beyond Maryut, sixty miles to the west, lay the uneasy defensive lines of El Alamein, some days broodily silent, other days seething with rancour.

Gannet's crew closed up at action stations as she passed through the boom gate. PO Combrink did his rounds, inspecting the guns, ready-use ammunition and fuses. Pickles Brooke checked his ammunition belts, then trained and elevated his pom-pom through its full limits; Behardien and Malan did the same to their Lewis guns; Jonas and Levy to the

Oerlikons and drum magazines, Lister and Johnson to their captured Breda guns.

Gannet exchanged greetings with two South African minesweepers, *Weenen* and *Saxonwold*, returning to their berths after a sweep of the channel. She sailed down the Great Pass and, rounding the beacon at the end of the channel, turned northwest, bound for a small, besieged island more than 900 miles away. Spread out ahead of her lay a vast armada, shimmering and distorting in the heat haze, its many wakes churning the ocean as vessels took up their stations and friendly fighter planes circled overhead.

Jack pictured the nautical chessboard from above, his own ship attaching herself to the tail of this great leviathan. Apart from the three motorboats under tow, *Gannet* was the smallest vessel in the fleet, but a pugnacious terrier nonetheless, her decks bristling with armaments. To Jack's eye, she was a thing of petite beauty, handsome in her light-and-dark disruptive camouflage, from flaring whale catcher bows along a low waist that toyed with the waterline to her graceful cruiser stern packed with depth-charging paraphernalia. Jack knew, too, that she looked hard-used and rust-streaked, sporting shrapnel scars and torn splinter mats from her months of convoy work. A nuggety, bantam fighting ship. His ship.

Gannet took up her allotted station astern of the convoy's main body, behind a minesweeper in the middle ring of escorts but inside the outer destroyer screen. She was designated as a 'death ship', charged with picking up survivors in the event of a sinking, but would also offer supplementary anti-aircraft and anti-submarine defences.

'Tail-end Charlie once again, sir,' said Van Zyl.

'Aye, Number One, forever wiping the merchants' arses,' said Jack.

HMS *Rhodesia* soon had the 'commence zigzag' signal flying. Leading Seaman 'Bunts' Gilbert hoisted the red-and-white answering pennant, pausing momentarily at the dip, in acknowledgement. When all ships had replied, Rhodesia's flags came down, signalling 'execute'. Jack leant towards the voicepipe and called down: 'Port ten and continue with the ordered zigzag.'

'Aye aye, Cap'n,' came Coxswain February's gruff reply.

Both the convoy commodore, whose broad pennant flew at the tanker's yardarm, and the admiral as escort commander aboard *Rhodesia*, closely scrutinised the first manoeuvre. But these merchant captains were highly experienced and their ships modern and fast, so the operation progressed without a hitch, one wing of the convoy maintaining speed while the other slowed as they swung through the turns of the prescribed zigzag, at all times maintaining the correct following distance.

The turn completed, Jack lifted his binoculars and panned across the awe-inspiring sight of the convoy with its three defensive rings: fifty-odd ships covering an area of more than ten square miles. Forming the outer ring, at a distance of 5,000 yards from the centre, were the big fleet destroyers or 'Fleets', mostly Tribal class with their hungry grace, uneven funnels, powerful armament of eight 4.7-inch guns and speed of 36 knots. The middle ring, 3,000 yards from the centre, comprised mostly small Hunt-class destroyers, while the inner screen held the seven cruisers, resplendent in the warm grey of their Mediterranean camouflage, with HMS *Rhodesia* in the van.

Inside this triple cordon, like a small herd of cattle, lay the ten merchantmen, two of them towing MTBs and one an MGB. The speedy craft would increase the convoy's strike power should a surface action develop, especially if E-boats joined the fray and, upon reaching Malta, the three boats would remain behind to supplement the island's much-depleted light forces. Jack felt for the sailors in those tiny vessels, dancing and corkscrewing horribly as they were dragged along in the churned-up wakes. He wouldn't be surprised if their crews were already sick as dogs.

Jack took a closer look at the merchantmen, sailing in four columns, six cables apart, each one with lifeboats slung out on davits, ready for lowering. He tried to match the ships to the manifest in his docket. SS *Calcutta* and SS *City of Durban* were British, SS *Zevenaar* was Dutch and MV *Hovden* Norwegian; the tall-funnelled, three-island freighter SS *Callisto* was Greek, and the modern, black-hulled MV *Fontannes* was Free French. MV *Rangatira* was a Shaw Savill cargo-liner and regular of the Australia to New Zealand route, while *Kimberley Castle* was an elegant, Union-Castle refrigerated-fruit and mail ship from the South Africa run. The Grace Line's *Santa Almeria* hailed from the United States, as did the tanker *Lexington*, taking pride of place in the centre of the convoy. The latter had a Texan master, the whiskered, pipe-smoking, bourbon-swilling Captain Johnson. Aboard her was the convoy commodore, an elderly, teetotal British rear admiral recalled from retirement whose job it was to keep the merchantmen in order. He and Captain Johnson had struck up an odd friendship, adjourning to the bridgewing to talk philosophy whenever opportunity allowed.

Lexington had good lines for a tanker with a high bridge amidships and a squat funnel aft, while her upper works bristled with anti-aircraft weapons that required a large additional complement of navy and army gunners. Jack glanced down at the manifest, noting that her cargo comprised 8,703 tons of fuel oils, 1,893 tons of paraffin, 1,710 tons of diesel, 1,295 tons of bunker fuel and 16 tons of lubricating oils. What an irresistible target she made. Captain Johnson and his crew would need nerves of steel in the forthcoming days.

This small flotilla of merchantmen carried salvation in their bellies for 300,000 Maltese: rice, beans and coffee, tinned meat and tinned milk, soap, forage for livestock, babies' napkins and dummies, spare gun barrels and ammunition, lorries, nails and screws, Spitfire engines … and two Matilda tanks. It carried lifeblood for the island's every artery and limb. To Jack, the whole enterprise embodied a profound sense of purpose, possibly even some form of higher purpose, although he preferred not to think in such terms. But this was certainly no ordinary voyage. In the coming days, his men — every man in the convoy — would be pushed to the limit of endurance. On long ocean passages, there were often singsongs, BBC radio programmes or the wail of a mouth organ to punctuate the daily round. Jack knew there'd be little such diversion this time.

News of the assembly of a large convoy in Alexandria had long since reached the enemy via its varied sources and spies. To meet the challenge, hundreds of German and Italian bombers, dive bombers, torpedo aircraft and fighters were being prepared in Greece, North Africa and Sicily. More than a dozen U-boats had been redirected to intercept the convoy, while fast German E-boats and Italian MAS boats had received instructions to lie in wait at strategic points and a new minefield was being laid in the Malta approaches.

The flat-topped bulk of HMS *Vulture* and her destroyer escort appeared out of the haze astern of the convoy, passed through the outer screen and took up loose station abeam and to starboard of the inner ring, where they would operate independently. If the carrier needed to leave the screen to fly off or take in aircraft according to the dictates of the wind, she would be joined by the two nearest destroyers. Jack found comfort in *Vulture*'s boxy shape, knowing that it was upon her broad shoulders, and pilots like Grayson Douglas, that much of the convoy's protection would fall.

Gannet's first task was to pass verbal messages by loudhailer to each merchantman about course alterations planned for the first night. The job took a couple of nerve-wracking hours until, finally, the whaler could return to her designated anti-submarine station. It was a windless summer's afternoon off the Egyptian coast with the ships spread out like toys on an endless blue carpet. The iron plates of *Gannet*'s deck were hot underfoot and even in the white shorts and shirtsleeves of his tropical uniform, Jack was sweating prodigiously. The arrow-like V of their wake spread out astern, while the Asdic's regular ping was an ever-present reminder of dangers lurking below. Albacore biplanes had been flown off *Vulture* to conduct anti-submarine patrols, while high above them, the convoy was still being covered by fighters of the DAF, flying in relays from their Egyptian bases.

Gannet's captain remained on the bridge, surveying the armada, now coated in soft light as a buttery sun slid towards the horizon. Just before sunset, when the Hurricanes and Kittyhawks turned back towards their aerodromes around Alexandria, Jack felt a pang at their departure. He knew that by morning the convoy would be too far west to receive land-based cover, save for a few long-range Beaufighters. The clatter of the whaler's Aldis lamp was almost continuous until dusk as signals passed to and fro, after which it was replaced by the muffled slapping of the blue night lamp.

'Enemy aircraft, sir, bearing green eight-oh!' yelled Behardien from the bridgewing, his high-pitched voice betraying his nerves.

'Thank you, AB, must be a shitehawk.'

The reconnaissance aircraft — a vague dot above the northern horizon — was probably a high-flying Ju-86 and had doubtless begun to transmit position reports. Two Sea Hurricanes were scrambled to chase the snooper away, Jack watching closely as the little aircraft lifted off *Vulture*'s deck. But the fighters were unable to climb to the impossible height of 40,000 feet and returned to the carrier in near darkness. There would be no further attempts at interception until dawn.

By now, all ports and deadlights throughout the convoy had been clamped down so that not a glimmer of light was showing. As night descended, Jack watched the leading destroyers slowly dissolve from view, then the cruisers, then the merchantmen, until only a few smudges remained visible ahead, adorned with shaded blue stern lanterns for station keeping. Now came the ticklish business of maintaining the correct zigzag, not getting too close to a consort or losing the convoy altogether.

A breathless tension hung about the ships. Asdic operators bent over their sets, listening intently for a U-boat's echo, lookouts scanning every quadrant of the sky for night bombers. Nerves stretched like elastic bands, waiting for the axe to fall. It was surely only a matter of time.

But despite the enemy snooper, the situation remained mercifully quiet and Jack went below for a hasty supper in his cabin. On his cot lay an envelope marked 'Not to be read until at sea'. Using his brass opener, he took out the letter from Vice Admiral Sir Henry Harwood, Commander-in-Chief of the Mediterranean Fleet, and read:

I would like you to know how grateful the Board of Admiralty and I are to you for undertaking this difficult task. Malta has for some time been in grave danger and it is imperative that she should be kept supplied. These are critical months and we cannot fail her. She has stood up to the most violent attack from the air that has ever been made, and now she needs our help in continuing the battle. Her courage is worthy of yours. Remember the watchword: the convoy must go through*!*

Back on the bridge, the night was balmy and bright with the glitter of starlight, the Admiralty having chosen a moonless period for their passage. Phosphorescence fizzed around the whaler's prow and coiled in her luminescent wake. The convoy was maintaining good formation and there had been no chivvying signal from either commodore or escort commander for some time. Jack heard the chime of the zigzag clock and noted the dim compass-card wobbling around within its orb, the deck tilting as *Gannet* swung onto her next leg. He listened to the crisp threshing of the bow waves and felt the deck pulsing beneath his feet as he watched the faint stern lights and their attendant shadows rocking in the darkness ahead. Inside those shadowy shapes, there was light and life, mealtimes, banter and card games, and the Andrew's many timeworn rituals. Another brassy chime from the Asdic interrupted his thoughts, each ping a pebble dropped in the water, transmitting its heartbeat, searching for a mate.

Despite the undercurrent of menace, the night's lusciousness helped soothe his anxiety. Jack heard Porky Louw, the cook, moving about the boat deck with a tray of steaming kye for the men on watch. Fido, the ship's incongruously named female marmalade cat, put in a rare appearance on the bridge with what looked like a balloon tied to her collar. Everyone on *Gannet* wore a lifejacket at sea, except Fido, and Hendricks the steward had decided this was neither right nor fair. He'd come up with a makeshift solution, inflating a Durex and tying it to the cat's collar, where it was set to remain until they reached Malta.

Another ping from the Asdic, like the beat in his own chest, sent a pulse that sought only Alana's, his heart's sonar probing the night's depths for hers. How he longed for an echo. Sitting in his upright bridge chair, Jack was close to dozing, his mind arcing back to their last night at the Cecil: Alana asleep in his arms, strands of her hair snared in his stubble, her dark-olive skin, the curve of her tiny body against his flank, a nipple hardening, even in sleep, at the stroke of his thumb. And her despair at the prospect of his departure, that look of ... what was it ... desolation? The hunger in her eyes for ... for ... he could not quite put a finger on it. Yet his ache for Alana, at this moment, on a ship sailing away from her into the infinite darkness of the west, was like a raging thirst.

Later that night in the wireless cabin, LS Thomas tuned his set to Radio Rome, whose music programme was interrupted for a message from Il Duce, which Sparks relayed to Jack. Mussolini boastfully announced the size, route, timing and destination of the Allied convoy, and the ambush his Regia Marina and Regia Aeronautica, along with their Kriegsmarine and Luftwaffe brothers, were laying in store. Sailing 1,000 yards astern of the middle screen, and 1,500 yards ahead of the outer cordon, Jack felt their isolation most keenly as the darkness and danger, heightened by Mussolini's menacing voice, pressed closer.

'I've been reading the Greek bloke again.' Van Zyl's voice was a ray of light.

'Cavafy, your new fixation?' asked Jack.

'Negative, sir, the other one.'

'Homer?'

'Aye, him.'

'What of him?'

'I've been thinking this Malta lark feels a bit like the Odyssey — trials, tribulations, monsters of the deep.'

'I suppose, if you put it that way.'

There was a long pause.

'I've been thinking of penning my own poem, in the spirit of Homer.'

'Oh yes? "There was an old Itie from Sicily, who wouldn't stop biting his —"'

'No, sir, not exactly.'

'You'll let me have a read, won't you?'

'Aye, sir, of course. You can wield your red pen.'

They both looked up as a parachute flare dropped by a bomber burst in the sky some miles to the north, then more flares, closer, flooded the sea with a sickly yellow light and silhouetted the vessels for agonising moments. Admiral Somerset had ordered a policy of evasion and forbade any ship to open fire. For a while, this tactic succeeded, until a flare erupted directly above the merchantmen and a bomber swooped out of the darkness, briefly illuminating itself in the glow, and released a stick of bombs that fell harmlessly over to port. Then merciful darkness once again, with more hide and seek.

Unseen bombers shadowed the convoy, dropping occasional flares and bombs and making sure that all ships remained permanently at action stations and no-one got any rest. Least of all Jack, who remained topside, either seated in his high wooden chair or pacing restlessly between the bridgewings. In the morning's early hours, the situation quietened and Jack called for a defence watch, allowing some men to go below and try, fully clothed, to get some sleep. Minutes later, the peace was shattered.

'Torpedo tracks, starboard beam!' screamed Behardien, his voice hoarse with terror.

CHAPTER 4

A single leap brought Jack to the brass mouth of the voicepipe, bellowing: 'Full ahead, hard a-starboard!'

Two frothing trails streaked towards *Gannet* just below the surface. Heart in his mouth, Jack called down an order for February to steer between them, but the ship's head was coming round too slowly. Jack held his breath, mesmerised by the bubbling tracks, now only 200 feet away. The projectiles appeared to follow *Gannet*'s turn, closer still, as the bows swung agonisingly slowly … then the torpedoes were past, lancing down either flank and into the night. In the heat of the crisis, Jack had forgotten to sound the alarm.

'Hands to action stations, Number One.' He tried to keep his voice even.

Bells clanged throughout the ship, boots drumming on decks and ladders as the off-watch scrambled to their posts. Moments later, the various positions reported through the voicepipes.

'Depth-charge crew closed up,' called Combrink from aft, where his team had removed the safety lashings from their precious ordinance.

'Boat-deck guns closed up,' came the high-pitched voice of Pickles Brooke, the seventeen-year-old from Benoni.

'Gun's crew closed up!' sang out Fletcher from the fo'c'sle.

'Action steaming stations!' called Chief McEwan from the engine room.

And from the wheelhouse, waiting till last, PO February: 'Coxswain at the wheel, sir.'

Jack glanced around the bridge: Behardien and Malan were at their Lewis machine guns, 'Bunts' Gilbert beside his Aldis lamp.

'Action stations closed up, sir,' announced Van Zyl.

'Very good.'

In the meantime, HMS *Rhodesia* had sounded the three sonorous blasts of a U-boat alarm, taken up by the horns and sirens of other ships as the convoy performed an emergency turn away from the danger. The two fleet destroyers nearest the threat swung towards it and began to lace the sea with depth charges — flashes of incandescence beneath the surface, followed by tall mushrooms of atomised water, luridly green with phosphorescence, then a low rumbling that rolled across the wave crests.

'Looks like they might have a firm contact,' said Van Zyl.

'Aye, let's hope they nail the bastard,' said Jack, eager to join the hunt but knowing that *Gannet* must keep her station. He watched the destroyers turn in unison, like dancers, then race back over a patch of agitated water to drop more charges, the sea roiling and cascading in their wake. Jack knew the Mediterranean was not a good place for Asdic, with temperature layers and salinity producing hydrophonic anomalies and false echoes to throw off attackers. The recent loss to submarines of the aircraft-carrier *Ark Royal* and battleship *Barham* in these waters underlined the convoy's vulnerability, but perhaps these two destroyers had a decent echo.

Jack's eyes strained at the darkness, yearning for U-boat debris or, better still, streaks of tracer indicating a surface contact. However, it was not long before a lamp on one of the destroyers flashed the signal: 'Contact lost. Water conditions poor.'

The pair were already five miles away and a continued search would leave gaps in the screen that could be exploited by other U-boats. From grim experience in South African waters, Jack knew exactly the conundrum Admiral Somerset faced: allow the destroyers to keep hunting with the slim chance of a kill or recall them. Protection of the convoy had to remain his top priority. Besides, the destroyers' action had already prevented the U-boat from a repeat attack and, given the approaching dawn and speed of the convoy, had most probably held it down long enough to make another strike impossible. Both hunters were ordered to rejoin the screen with all despatch.

A moment later, a blinding flash rent the night sky. The report seemed to bounce off the surface of the water and punch *Gannet* with a thunderous blow. Jack saw a milky tower rise high above the second merchantman in the starboard column, followed by a flaming orange mushroom, snakes of fire writhing about themselves as they climbed skyward. The torpedo had detonated in the freighter's number three cargo hold, blowing off the hatch and opening a tear in the ship's side that let in hundreds of tons of water. The hold was filled with sacks of flour whose contents billowed into the air like faux smoke, coating the decks with fine powder. Jack watched in despair as the adjacent cargo of cased aviation petrol in number two hold caught fire, leaking over the side and igniting the sea. Next came a series of small eruptions as burning fuel rained down on the freighter.

Gannet was ordered to stand by one of the minesweepers acting as rescue ship. Jack conned *Gannet* towards the stricken merchant as the sweeper peeled away and slowly approached the scene to gather up the survivors. A signal flashed from the bridge of *Rhodesia*: 'Convoy will alter course fifty degrees to port on the executive and steer two-six-oh degrees until further orders.'

The doomed ship was the Dutchman, *Zevenaar*, now listing heavily to starboard as her superstructure was licked by flames, accompanied by the hissing of steam and booming of internal explosions. Some of her crew were abandoning ship into a lifeboat and two rafts; others jumped into the sea and swam towards the minesweeper.

Jack watched as *Zevenaar* sank by the bows, her stern rising into the air to expose a rust-streaked bottom covered in slime and a propeller still slowly threshing like a perverted windmill. She hung there, seemingly suspended, groaning to the sound of rending metal, then slid towards the seafloor in a storm of frothing water and oily bubbles bursting on the surface. *Gannet* circled the sweeper in the darkness, pinging her Asdic in every direction as the last survivors were plucked from the waves. Task completed, the two ships returned to the convoy at their best speed, leaving only burning debris and corpses bobbing on the black skin of the sea.

CHAPTER 5

Dawn was always a perilous time. Jack searched the sea and sky with his binoculars, inching along the horizon and between the fading stars, probing, probing. The east had acquired its first blush of colour as the firmament slowly brightened, rinsing itself in shades of pink. All about the ship, men in tin hats studied the quadrants with the diligence of examination students. With all his heart, Jack did not want this day to dawn, and yet here it was, bringing with it the certainty of renewed attack.

Even before the sun had risen from the sea, the stalker was back, a pestilential speck tracking their progress from the northern horizon. Jack felt sick at the thought of aero engines warming up to the north and south, on Egyptian, Cretan and Dodecanese airfields, of bombers lifting into the clear morning sky and heading inexorably their way.

The aircraft carrier was responsible for fighter protection during daylight hours, which took the form of slower Fulmars providing low cover and more nimble Sea Hurricanes flying high cover at about 20,000 feet. Jack watched the feverish activity on *Vulture*'s deck.

'D'ye hear there? D'ye hear there? Hands to flying stations!' came the faint, echoing call from the carrier's tannoy. Signal flags jerked to the yardarm as the flat top turned ponderously into the wind and began working up to full speed. Through his binoculars, Jack saw four figures running towards aircraft parked near the aft end of the flight deck. He thought he could make out a winged cheetah on the cowling of one and the stocky figure of Grayson Douglas climbing into the cockpit.

Men stood at the lanyards that secured the wingtips of each aircraft; others lay beside the chocks.

'Stand by to fly off aircraft!'

A fitter gave the thumbs-up as Douglas ran his eye over the instrument panel. He tightened his harness and adjusted the awkward bulge of the parachute beneath his buttocks. Goggles and microphone in place, he was ready. The Hurricane's propeller turned stiffly then jerked abruptly into life, accompanied by a cough of smoke. Douglas slid the canopy closed, waved the chocks away and taxied to the end of the flight deck, guided by ratings holding onto the wings. He received clearance for take-off just as a flare was fired from the island and arced away downwind. The flight-deck officer began to rotate the green flag in his right hand while giving a thumbs-up with his left. Douglas returned the thumbs-up and gradually opened the throttle without releasing the brakes. The green flag rotated faster and the fighter was given more juice, straining to be set free. Mouth dry, heart pounding, the old butterflies never went away. His Hurricane started to buck and strain, its tailplane trying to lift.

The flag fell; Douglas released the brakes and eased the stick forward, applying full throttle. There was a loud roar from his Rolls Royce Merlin engine as the fighter set off down the white centre line, at walking pace at first … now gathering speed, the island slipping by and his stick pulled back, followed immediately by a weightless, heart-in-the-mouth drop … then merciful lifting and blue infinity as he banked to starboard, undercarriage up, and away over the receding ships.

Jack watched in admiration as each aircraft took to the air, trailing a throaty grumble as it climbed away from the convoy. The first task of the two leading Hurricanes was to chase away the reconnaissance plane, and preferably catch and shoot it down. How grateful he felt towards those diminutive fighters: a lightweight shield, but a shield nonetheless.

'Signal from *Vulture*, sir,' said Bunts. '"Have finished flying off fighters. Am resuming station."'

Midmorning, the powerful radar on HMS *Rhodesia* picked up the first incoming bombers and announced their approach to the convoy.

'Sound-off action stations, Number One, and hoist the red flag,' said Jack.

Alarm bells clanged and boots thudded their tattoo once more as sailors scrambled to their positions, loaders grabbed ammunition, and gunners climbed into their harnesses and seats. Jack watched Sub-lieutenant Fletcher and his team on the forecastle: layers, trainers and ammo carriers all primed for action. Nervous tension coursed through *Gannet.*

On *Vulture*, the tannoy squawked: 'D'ye hear there? Scramble Hurricanes! Scramble Hurricanes!' Once more, the carrier swung away from the convoy and into the wind, ploughing through the destroyer screen as fighters lifted off and climbed at full boost.

'Enemy aircraft, bearing green eight-oh, angle of sight two-oh!' called out Behardien from the starboard bridgewing.

The cruisers were the first to open fire with their radar-guided 5.25-inch guns. Again and again muzzles flashed, thunder cracked and smoke guttered from the barrels as black shell bursts pitted the northern sky.

'Ities, sir, looks like Sparrowhawks,' said Van Zyl, peering through his binoculars at the SM79 Savoia bombers. 'About twenty of the buggers.'

Jack surmised they were from one of the elite anti-shipping squadrons based in the Dodecanese. *Vulture*'s aircraft, accompanied by a handful of newly arrived Beaufighters from

Egypt, swept down on the Italians, trying to break up the attack before the enemy could release their torpedoes. But the first wave of Savoias had drawn the fighters to the north, and a second echelon approached from the southeast, diving out of the sun, then levelling off at wavetop height and spreading out line abreast, far apart to divide the anti-aircraft fire. The fleet destroyers turned, bringing to bear as many guns as possible and laying down a thunderous barrage. Shell bursts, splashes and smoke blurred the horizon and partially obscured the enemy aircraft. The convoy's main guns had found their rhythm, producing a wall of flak to put the pilots off, but although shells exploded ahead of and around the tiny targets, it appeared to have no effect. To the deep-throated booming of ships' horns, the merchantmen made a sharp turn to port, aiming their bows at the bombers in order to comb the torpedoes' tracks.

Jack watched the layers and trainers on *Gannet*'s 4-inch lining up their sights on one of the Savoias. As the bomber came into effective range, Jack lifted his loudhailer and bellowed, 'Commence firing!' The 4-inch banged out the first round as cordite ghosted over the bridge, momentarily engulfing Jack in its choking stench. His chest tightened: *once more, the fray*. The moment the recoil ejected the spent cartridge, loaders slammed home the next round to the cajoling of Sub-lieutenant Fletcher.

By now, Jack could make out the details of the nearest aircraft: a hump-shaped fuselage with spotty brown camouflage and three engines painted light grey. Each Savoia carried two torpedoes slung beneath its belly. Above the roaring of the guns, Jack heard the growl and whine of aero engines, the bombers weaving this way and that as though planing on a cushion of air above the wavetops.

'Shorter, blue barrage setting if you please, Number One,' Jack ordered, his voice pitched high with tension.

The 4-inch coughed again, joined by the jabber of the fo'c'sle's two Oerlikon cannons that looked like agitated lances attached to the chests of each gunner and swinging to the movement of his body. Jack followed the low arc of their fire, lit by streams of tracer spaced at intervals of one in every five shells. On came the bombers, the sky all about them pockmarked with flak. Put off by the intensity of fire, some aircraft dropped their torpedoes early, broke formation and sheered away, but a few courageous pilots pressed on into the maelstrom. Closer now, the blaring rattle of Oerlikons was joined by the chatter of Lewis guns and, with Jack's adjustment of *Gannet*'s course, the rhythmical tonking of the pom-pom, trained around to its full extent and its young handlers, Pickles and Booysen, yelling an unintelligible war cry as hot oil hissed and spat from their excited tool.

A pair of tin fish splashed in and knifed towards *City of Durban*, which went hard a-port and managed to dodge the threat. Dropping the last of their payloads, the Savoias banked away, wreathed in tracer. A final torpedo fizzed towards *Gannet*, Jack watching closely as the brightly polished arrow with a blue warhead passed within a cable's length. Due to the murderous barrage and deft handling by the merchant captains, all the projectiles missed their targets.

Jack's heart lifted as three Hurricanes, having returned from beating off the northern echelon, dropped from the clouds, ignoring the tracer, each one locking onto the tail of a retreating Savoia. There were clattering bursts as one bomber described a lazy somersault and crashed into the sea, another erupted in flames and pancaked in a welter of spray while the third escaped by climbing into cloud cover.

'That'll be lunch, gentlemen,' said Van Zyl, the Afrikaner imitating a British accent. 'Let us repair to the pavilion for beers and prandial chow.'

'You seem rather confident, Number One.'

'And a little siesta too, sah.'

'Dream on.'

As it so happened, the convoy *was* granted a reprieve, which allowed Porky and Hendricks to do the rounds with trays of corned-beef sandwiches and jorums of strong, milky, very sweet tea. Jack retired to his cabin and, since he'd not slept the previous night, allowed himself a short catnap, which did in fact entail a cat, with Fido stretching her curvaceous frame against his side and gentling kneading him with her paws. Within moments, he was adrift, Alana's body replacing Fido's … the jasmine fragrance of her hair, an arm across his chest, her soft breathing on his neck. His whole being ached for her, even in the dales of sleep.

'Action stations!' Sub-lieutenant Robinson's shout from above detonated inside his head. Wrenching himself upright beside a nonplussed Fido, he grabbed his helmet and scrambled for the ladder.

'Where away, Pilot?' Jack snapped as he reached the bridge.

'Aircraft bearing green five-oh, sir.'

Jack trained his binoculars on the faraway specs. Sea Hurricanes and Fulmars were trying to engage the enemy formation, but were being fended off by long-range, twin-engine Messerschmitt Bf 110s. Judging by the bulbous noses, the bombers were Heinkel He-111s, aircraft he knew well from 1940, both at Dunkirk and then England while recuperating from his wounds, the awful sound of their engines filling the London sky as he sought shelter in Underground stations.

The destroyers opened up and high-explosive shells began to burst around the Heinkels, but they pressed on, diving from 5,000 to 500 feet and fanning out. Brave pilots, thought Jack, as the bombers cleaved through torrents of tracer with suicidal indifference.

'Hard a-starboard,' ordered Jack as *Gannet* heeled over to take the nearest bomber on the nose. The merchantmen and escorts were doing the same, sirens and horns bleating as they made emergency turns to comb the torpedoes' tracks. The assault turned chaotic, the scene obscured by cordite smoke, shell bursts and splashes as the Heinkels powered through the convoy, their machine guns strafing the decks as they went.

One bomber tore out of the smoke between *Gannet* and the minesweeper. Pickles on the pom-pom, Lister on the port-side Breda, Malan on his Lewis and Jonas on his Oerlikon vented streams of tracer at the target. Rounds punched holes in the fuselage as the bomber staggered, then tongues of flame leapt from its port engine. It dipped a wing, clipped the water and cartwheeled away in a ball of fire and spray to the demented cheering of *Gannet*'s gunners.

Within seconds, all the surviving aircraft had banked away and were racing for home, but their torpedoes still arrowed towards the convoy. Lookouts scanned the sea for tracks and ships took the necessary avoiding action. Finally, Robinson looked up from his stopwatch and said, 'We're clear, Cap'n, all torpedoes will have passed through the convoy by now.'

'Another bloody miracle,' muttered Jack.

Meanwhile, some of the Sea Hurricanes had untangled themselves from the Messerschmitts and fell upon the retreating Heinkels.

'Going down, tallyho!' Douglas called into his R/T, carving his fighter into a power dive, his wingman following suit. The

Canadian switched the gun button to fire as he swept down on the bomber's quarter, closing until he had the wide-winged German squarely in his sights: six hundred yards … four hundred yards.

Now!

Pressing the button, the fighter quivered and jerked as Douglas raked the Heinkel's starboard engine and wing root with a long burst. The upper rear gunner reacted late, sending a line of tracer well wide, moments before the Perspex around him shattered in a hail of bullets. The bomber reared up, climbing steeply, its starboard engine disintegrating as it looped over onto its back and plummeted towards the sea.

'Got him, got the bandit!' Douglas shouted into the mic.

Almost out of ammunition, he dropped through the clouds and made for *Vulture*, flying low over the convoy, aware of the upturned faces and waving arms. He passed the stubby little *Gannet*, captained by his new chum, Jack Pembroke — strange fellow, terribly stiff and proper, troubled too, yet so likeable, and surely a lady's man with those film-star looks. How puny and insignificant the South African whale catcher looked, trundling along like a handmaid in the big boys' wake.

Douglas lowered the undercarriage with his right hand as he banked around the stern of the carrier. Aiming at the small, seesawing deck, he lined up the approach and lowered the flaps. Sweat beaded his forehead; his throat was sandpaper-dry — ever the old nerves. Low and slow. Bats, the deck-landing officer, stood on a catwalk at the aft end of the flight deck, waving his paddles to guide the fighter down. Lower, lower, starboard wing up a bit … steady as she goes.

The Hurricane crossed the quarterdeck turndown and smacked the deck with a squeal, skidding on the planking as the arrester wire grabbed hold and jerked the fighter to a halt.

Douglas slid open the canopy with trembling hands, blew the air from his cheeks and swallowed hard, then climbed out and dropped shakily to the deck as the handling party swarmed around, unhooking the fighter from the wire and wheeling it behind the crash barriers.

'Fantastic shooting, sir!' said an excited leading seaman, handing Douglas a tankard of lemonade which he downed in one go.

The final attack that day was the heaviest, comprising nearly a hundred bombers, mostly Italian Savoias and Cant Z1007 Alciones accompanied by German Ju-88s. They approached from astern after sunset out of the darkening eastern sky, which hampered the job of the gunners and presented the enemy with clearly silhouetted targets against the horizon's afterglow. The last fighter patrol of the day had just landed back on *Vulture* and was hastily scrambled once more.

The assault began with a high-level bombing attack from both quarters, while the torpedo bombers worked their way around to the south for a flanking approach. The skirmish was short and brutal, the bombers pressing home a single, massed strike. From the heart of the convoy came a deafening crack and flash of orange flame. Jack watched helplessly, his feet anchored to the deck, his heart thundering, as a column of water rose slowly up the side of MV *Hovden* and seemed to hang for endless seconds before torrenting down on the freighter. The Norwegian was surely done for.

CHAPTER 6

The torpedo had torn an enormous gash in *Hovden*'s number-one hold, blowing off the hatch and hurling tons of cargo skyward, which splashed into the sea around the nearby ships. The freighter slowed to a halt and began to settle, her foredeck a brutal picture of fallen derricks and contorted steel.

'Bunts, signal *Rhodesia*: "Permission to pick up survivors?"' instructed Jack, trying to keep his tone neutral.

After a short wait, the flashed response came: 'Permission granted.'

As *Gannet* closed with *Hovden*, the sea was already breaking across the freighter's foredeck and surging against her superstructure. There'd been no time to launch lifeboats and most survivors had already leapt into the sea. The freighter's ammunition cargo began to detonate, with tracer fizzing and erupting from one of the holds. Side netting and lines were prepared on *Gannet* as she slowed, then stopped to pick up the swimmers and a group who had scrambled aboard a Carley float.

'Number One, make sure the gunners keep their eyes peeled for aircraft, especially approaching from the east,' said Jack.

'Aye aye, Cap'n.'

'And give them permission to open fire without orders.'

Scalded and blackened Norwegians in oil-soaked clothes were helped aboard, some wounded and bloody, some vomiting up the diesel burning their internal organs. They were immediately wrapped in blankets stripped from messdeck bunks and led below. The badly wounded were ushered or carried to the wardroom, now transformed into a sickbay, where Porky administered makeshift first aid. Burn victims were liberally smeared with gentian violet, the more serious cases dosed with morphine to ease the pain and silence the screaming.

Throughout the night, a reconnaissance aircraft from Heraklion kept the convoy under observation. So too, an Allied Sunderland flying boat, which reported spotting the wakes of half a dozen E-boats seventy miles south of the convoy and heading in their direction. These boats of the Kriegsmarine's crack Third Flotilla based in Derna were later picked up on *Rhodesia*'s radar. Jack had come to know the *Schnellboot*'s reputation while serving in the English Channel as a junior minesweeping officer back in 1940. The E-boat was a formidable adversary — 115 feet long with three 1,630-hp Daimler-Benz engines, giving it a top speed of forty-eight knots. It carried a crew of twenty and was armed with four 21-inch torpedoes, one 37-mm gun aft, one 20-mm on the bows and a twin-mount amidships, plus various machine guns. Jack feared they would be in for a night of hit-and-run strikes, the low profile of a speeding *Schnellboot* presenting an almost impossible target in the dark.

At the order of Admiral Somerset, the MGB and both MTBs slipped their tow to take the small-boat fight to the enemy. Jack knew their captains would be heartily relieved to finally be off the leash and free to do their work, but he also worried that their presence might prevent the cruisers and destroyers from firing on their radar plots lest they hit one of their own tiny, fast-moving craft.

'Three bandits closing from the southeast: am engaging,' came a voice over the R/T from one of the fleet destroyers. Jack hoped that the outer ring would be able to deal with the

E-boats and prevent the enemy from creating enough confusion to slip through the screen. No doubt to that particular end, a flight of Heinkels arrived and began making intermittent bombing runs to sow chaos among the twitchy merchants. Jack watched through his binoculars as the MGB and MTBs closed up around a Polish destroyer, then raced off into the darkness to the southeast.

The ships in the outer screen fired occasional salvoes to drive the enemy off, but the elusive E-boats stayed in touch with the convoy, biding their time. Then the Heinkels began dropping flares, whose harsh light illuminated targets for bombing runs and perfectly silhouetted the convoy for the E-boats, which kept probing the destroyer screen, trying to find a chink in the armour between inconclusive skirmishes with the three Allied motorboats.

Jack peered apprehensively astern. Moody shapes lurked in the night's recesses, the distant thrumming of heavy diesels a stark counterpoint to the sound of Malan's off-key whistling on the bridgewing. A destroyer in the port screen must have picked up a target: one of her quadruple pom-poms banged into action and red tracer balls streamed across the wavetops. Jack heard the dull thud of hits to a hull, the sound snuffed out abruptly, while other rounds ricocheted off the water and arced high into the air. Now, there was the staccato stammer of automatic fire from many quarters as more tracer played back and forth across the sea like deadly tennis balls. By the look and sound of it, some E-boats had broken through the outer screen.

Jack could make out the shapes of the steel-helmeted crew down on the forecastle, their hands poised on the laying and training wheels, their eyes, like his, straining at the darkness, willing a glimpse of a target. His breath came in shallow pants, sweat trickling down his neck and along his spine.

Then they were all bathed in the brilliance of a star-shell bursting overhead.

'Alarm, green nine-oh!'

In an instant, the ghost took substantial form, morphing from mercurial vapour to salivating prow.

'*My fok*! Range 1,200 yards, aim for the waterline!' bellowed Fletcher, his toffy accent acquiring, in extremis, a South African flavour. *Gannet*'s lighter guns opened up as tracer laced the air in graceful loops.

'And … shoot!' shouted Fletcher. *Bang*! A blinding flash and jerking recoil. The HE round whistled into the night, its smoking shell case clattering to the deck. Through his binoculars, Jack saw a pillar of water just wide of the mark. Not bad. Another round rammed home, the breech clanking shut. Then the star-shell snuffed itself out and the target vanished. Smoke and bloody mirrors: Jack banged his fist on the rail.

The battle zone was crisscrossed with millrace wakes and lit by intermittent flashes as the small-boat gladiators dashed this way and that, in and out of searchlight beams in a helter-skelter stitched with sharp bursts of fire. All was deadly son et lumière confusion. The blast and jabber of heavy and light guns mingled with detonating bombs and towering geysers. There were staccato streaks to port and starboard, spectral vessels passing in torrents of spray. The enemy was sometimes so close that guard rails prevented the guns from depressing low enough to fire. Attacks were erratic and uncoordinated, keeping the convoy in a state of turmoil as fire from Bofors, Oerlikons and machine guns scythed between the ships.

Jack glimpsed another target. The sleek hunter with a pale-grey hull, dark upperworks and enclosed torpedo tubes tore past *Gannet* at over forty knots, high-winged bow waves peeling from an upright prow. A necklace of green tracer streamed towards the whaler on a flat trajectory. Jack felt the hot breath of supersonic rounds passing overhead, then a storm of clanging and ricocheting abaft the bridge, metal pieces ripped loose and men crouching for cover. Malan raked the enemy with his Lewis gun and a doll-like enemy gunner jerked dementedly before falling at his position. Pickles also got a brief bead on the intruder, his pom-pom barking into life. Tracer lanced towards the German, clawing at sea and air, some rounds biting the hull as the teenager bellowed at the top of his lungs. The E-boat swung away, grey clouds of artificial smoke pouring from dischargers on her stern as she beat a retreat.

Jack glimpsed another E-boat, briefly snared in a searchlight's ray, bearing down on them. Just a hundred yards off, it discharged one torpedo with a puff of compressed air. Ugly and phallic, the tin fish splashed in, its fins and propeller finding purchase as a bubbling path streaked towards *Gannet*, gathering speed as it came. Behardien let out an inarticulate howl. Helpless, Jack watched the torpedo track bear down on the whaler. Seconds from impact, there was no way they could turn in time. His ship was done for and there was nothing he could do, thought Jack, as the projectile reached *Gannet*'s flank. He went cold, squeezed his eyes shut and crouched down, bracing for the inevitable blast.

Nothing.

Stunned, he opened his eyes. Then it dawned on him: the torpedo's depth would have been set to sink a heavily laden freighter and had passed beneath the shallow-draught whaler.

There was no time to marvel at their salvation. In the glare of a star-shell, he spotted a skirmish between an MTB and an E-boat over to port. The MTB's two-pounder fired a steady stream of tracer that thudded into the E-boat, which presented her belly as she turned sharply. More shells ripped into the exposed hull in a storm of steel and high explosive. The wounded E-boat swung back to face the MTB and they raced towards each other, both craft burning from hits.

The E-boat swerved across the path of the MTB, the range closing as they spat fire at each other, their tracers intermingling as they banked away at the very last moment. Maimed, the MTB slewed to a halt with flaming fuel pouring like fiery blood from her wounds. Then came an almighty explosion as the British boat was torn apart, the detonation of her torpedoes adding to the carnage. The German limped off into the darkness.

In the mayhem, a lone E-boat approaching stealthily from the southwest had managed to penetrate the convoy's inner screen. The cruiser HMS *Heracles* made an Aldis-lamp challenge and a quick-thinking German signalman replied with the same letters, buying the enemy enough time to get within 400 yards of the cruiser. The icy beam of *Heracles*'s searchlight locked onto the E-boat just as her torpedo tubes coughed and the cruiser's lighter armaments opened up. *Heracles* went full ahead, swinging hard to starboard and firing both forward turrets as the E-boat described the tightest of turns, taking several hits from light armaments as she sped off into the night.

The first torpedo hit the cruiser on the starboard side abreast her aft funnel, sending up a towering sheet of flame. The second one struck aft, tearing away much of her stern and blowing her Y turret into the sea. Appalled, Jack watched as the remains of *Heracles*'s quarterdeck emerged from the smoke and flames to reveal a mass of mangled metal, a pillar of steam venting a tortured shriek. The cruiser slowed, making an erratic turn to starboard and listing exaggeratedly as she went. Realising his ship had been dealt a fatal blow, her captain ordered the men to abandon ship, instructing his pilot to throw the confidential books with their ciphers and codes overboard in a weighted bag and to smash the RDF panel with a stool. Amid the dark chaos and acrid fumes below, men groped along passages and up tilting companionways, trying to reach the upper deck.

Rhodesia instructed the nearest Hunt-class destroyer, a minesweeper and *Gannet* to pick up survivors. Fortunately, the E-boats appeared to have retired to the south, laying smoke screens to hide their exit, torpedoes apparently spent, their work done. Jack called for full speed to join the two other rescuers closing with the scene of disaster.

On board the sinking cruiser, there was no time to launch the motorboat or whalers, so Carley floats were being cut loose and tipped over the guardrail. The destroyer went alongside, banging against the hull and crumpling a guardrail, as men began to jump across the now narrowing, now widening, now seesawing gap. Thankfully the sea was calm and most jumpers made it safely across.

'Stop engine,' said Jack hoarsely. He could see into *Heracles*'s bridge and funnels as men slid down her tilting deck into the oily water. *Gannet*'s scrambling nets were lowered as she sidled closer and took the men off the nearest Carley, then lines and life rings were thrown as she began picking up the swimmers to calls of encouragement from the South African sailors. Booysen and Malan pulled off shirts and shoes and dived in, securing lines to the wounded so they could be hauled aboard. Retching and coughing sailors were led or carried to the overcrowded wardroom, where ammunition parties stripped off oil-soaked clothes and tenderly wrapped their oppos in blankets while Porky and Hendricks once again treated the men's injuries, applying bandages to wounds and splints to fractures.

Heracles sank slowly by the stern, the roaring of her fires silenced by waves that broke on and into her. The prow of the doomed ship reared up and pointed at the stars, hanging fifty feet in the air for a few moments before the cruiser began her final plunge, the water boiling and debris bursting to the surface. A young seaman stood in a puddle on the whaler's foredeck, weeping as he watched his ship disappear.

The sea all about was strewn with wreckage — planks, crates, rope, clothing, empty lifejackets — and lit by patches of preternatural fire burning on the surface. *Gannet*'s searchlight played across the remains of *Heracles*, every eye on the upper deck anxiously scanning for signs of life. A raft with automatic calcium flares raised hopes, but proved to be empty. There! No, just another corpse bobbing in its lifejacket.

Jack sent Van Zyl below to report on the situation. The confined, stuffy spaces were loud with the moaning and retching of the wounded, and reeked of oil, blood and vomit. A petty officer sat on the deck, coughing up the oil that was destroying his intestines, rocking back and forth, saying a name Van Zyl could not make out, perhaps 'Martha' or 'Mama'. Porky was trying to sew closed the gash on a killick's cheek that flapped open to reveal the bone — a rudimentary job, like the stuffed turkey he'd stitched for *Gannet*'s Christmas lunch. Hendricks worked on a burn victim's livid wounds with cotton wool and ointment, but the blistered, blackened skin kept coming away in lumps. The stoker had no hair or eyebrows left and parts of his face appeared to have melted. Eventually, to Van Zyl's relief, the lad passed out from the pain.

Up on the bridge, Jack knew that time was running out. The other two rescue ships had left the scene and the convoy was fast disappearing over the horizon. The occasional survivor was still being found, but *Gannet* could not linger. At this very moment, a periscope might be tracking their snail-like progress through the wreckage. A last downwind sweep, then they must return to the dubious safety of the convoy.

'Full ahead,' he said through gritted teeth, the words sounding to his mind like those of an executioner. *Gannet*'s pulse quickened as she drew away. Jack felt reluctant, guilty exhilaration to be moving swiftly through the water again, leaving behind a scene of pitiful flotsam, empty rafts and lifeless bodies floating upright in their Mae Wests ... a fresh harvest of images for his nightmares.

CHAPTER 7

On the morning of the third day, the convoy was due to pass through Bomb Alley, the narrowest point between North Africa and Crete. For the airmen of Fliegerführer Afrika and Fliegerkorps X, this was the moment they'd been waiting for, when the convoy was nearest their bases and Allied fighters from Egypt and Malta out of range. In anticipation, a large force of Ju-88s had been transferred to Derna in Cyrenaica, to press home the pincer attack.

'Just like Scylla and Charybdis, sir,' said Van Zyl, as a crimson sun rose astern of the convoy.

'Still thinking about your old Greek chum?' teased Jack.

'Aye, seems a lot like trying to sneak between a six-headed monster and a ship-swallowing whirlpool.'

'Shouldn't you be reading something lighter for all our sakes?'

'Lighter, sir?'

'Oh, I don't know. How about, "I wandered lonely as a cloud —"?'

Just then, alarm bells and klaxons echoed across the water from the aircraft carrier. *Gannet*'s sailors, eating a makeshift breakfast at their action stations, watched as fighters lifted off *Vulture*'s flight deck, the sun briefly igniting their wings as they banked away. Radar had picked up waves of incoming aircraft from both north and south and a yellow warning had been issued, repeated over every ship's tannoy, while yellow flags rose on signal halyards throughout the convoy. This was followed in short order by a red warning, which heralded the first arrivals, marching up the sky in serried ranks.

'Sending us in to bat again, sir,' said Van Zyl.

'Aye, Number One, with uneven bounce and rough patches at the Bells, Smells and Yells end.'

'Let's hope they opt for spin rather than their seamers.'

'Unlikely, I'm afraid.'

The initial attack was conducted by Italian Cant bombers, approaching in close formation at great height, barely perceptible specks in the growing heat haze. The Fleet Air Arm fighters were quickly among them and, soon after, the horizon to the northeast was pocked with shell bursts. One bomber was hit and reeled away from the formation, spiralling lazily down as the rest of the Cants advanced on the convoy.

The barrage grew fearsome and the Italian bombing proved inaccurate, molested as they were from all sides, but it was evident this was merely a foretaste of the main assault. Having drawn the Hurricanes high into the heavens, the ensuing attack was by waves of Savoia torpedo bombers coming in at wavetop height, but they too were unsuccessful, harassed by Fulmars and hammered by accurate gunfire before reaching effective range. A few Savoias struggled on, dropping their torpedoes haphazardly before retreating, leaving a number of their companions blazing on the surface of the sea.

'New bowler incoming, sir,' said Van Zyl. 'A quickie. Bit of a reputation.'

Jack panned his binoculars to the Messerschmitt Bf 109 fighters, painted in the leopard-spot desert camouflage of North Africa, escorting a large wing of Ju-88s. He fixed his lenses on the versatile twin-engine bombers with characteristic window-paned noses, each carrying a bombload of one-and-a-half tons. The formation began splitting into groups to attack from different angles and heights, thereby dividing the formidable firepower of 5.25-inch and 4-inch guns, Bofors, pom-poms, Oerlikons and parachute-and-cable rocket throwers.

While opposing fighter aircraft tangled high up in the blue, the bombers peeled out of formation and swooped down line astern to the high-pitched whining of their Jumo engines. The entire convoy erupted in barrage fire, a deafening thundercloud of shells exploding on set fuses overhead, creating a shrapnel curtain. On came the bombers, through bursting flak and streaming tracer. Now the staccato snapping of close-range weapons joined the deafening chorus. One German wobbled as an engine caught fire and began belching smoke, then it pitched into an ever-steeper dive as a wing tore free and the broken bird plunged into the sea.

Ships tacked this way and that, their helms hard over, trying to throw off the bomb aimers. Jack watched as doors in the belly of the closest Ju-88 swung open and black seeds came tumbling out, slow at first, then faster, falling in a parabola to the sound of a rising whistle. Water pillars rose from the sea astern of the French freighter, accompanied by loud detonations; another stick went in abeam of the Greek. Smoke and fumes from every quarter drew a murky veil across the scene, through which the sun's low rays struggled to penetrate.

Jack saw two Hurricanes extricate themselves from a high-altitude dogfight and follow the next wave of bombers into their dive. He spotted a cheetah on the cowling of the lead fighter, latching onto the tail of a Ju-88 as it pulled out of its run. Douglas opened up with a long, accurate burst that peppered the German, the rattle of machine guns clearly audible on *Gannet.* But the .303 rounds seemed to lack punch against the heavily armoured adversary. Mouth open, Jack watched as Douglas fired again and again, the Ju-88 taking brutal punishment with chunks coming away, but flying on regardless and escaping into a bank of cloud.

Everywhere Jack looked, in the heavens or upon the waters, high drama unfolded. His eyes were drawn to a Fulmar trailing smoke as it glided down to make a perfect pancake landing in the sea. Two figures climbed out the cockpit onto the wing, and it wasn't long before they were bobbing jauntily in a yellow dinghy beside their sinking plane, waiting for a destroyer to scoop them up.

Next, he focused his binoculars on *Vulture*, which appeared to have attracted a swarm of bees. Bombers dived at her from every angle, some chased by Sea Hurricanes and Fulmars following their quarries into the teeth of the carrier's gunfire. The enemy was concentrating its effort on *Vulture* in the full knowledge that neutralising her would eliminate the convoy's air cover. Each pilot chose a different height and bearing to divide and swamp the carrier's defences, powering through the dirty puffs as the guns of nearby ships joined in, followed at closer range by machine guns venting thin lines of tracer. Jack gasped as *Vulture* was obscured by a forest of splashes ... only to re-emerge, anointed from stem to stern, but unscathed.

The aerial assault was reaching a crescendo. *Gannet* shook from the concussion of her gunfire as sweating sailors rammed home round after round and explosions pitted the sky overhead. Cordite fumes shrouded the scene as four dozen ships hit back with every available weapon. Escorts zigzagged wildly, showering themselves in spray as bright tongues of flame lit the billowing gun smoke. Jack glanced back at *Vulture*: two sitting-duck aircraft were refuelling on deck with all that high-octane ready to ignite. It was nigh impossible to think clearly amid the bedlam, and he was thankful for the months of repeated drills he'd always insisted on that saw each man instinctively carrying out the motions of *Gannet*'s defence.

And now, at last, the sound of battle was diminishing as the bombers began returning to their bases. Jack heard a spluttering engine and turned to see a wounded Sea Hurricane wheeling in a wide arc, trailing smoke as it came in to land, wobbling and rapidly losing height. Nose up, scratching for air, it seemed certain the fighter would fail to reach the flight deck. Jack bit his lip, willing the pilot on. At the last instant, *Vulture*'s stern dipped into a trough, and the Hurricane smashed into the curved round-down of the overhang, collapsing its undercarriage and trailing sparks as it slithered across the deck and over the arrester wires, its propeller chopping at the planking, before ploughing into the island as men with fire-fighting equipment swarmed around it. The Hurricane burst into flames and was sprayed with foam, the pilot being dragged clear, his flying jacket smoking and forehead bleeding from a smack to the gunsight. The fire was quickly doused and the aircraft tipped over the side, splashing gracelessly in the carrier's wake.

The early afternoon once again offered a reprieve. The sweltering heat, however, provided an onslaught of its own, as though the sun's rays were bent on melting *Gannet*'s superstructure. Covered in sweat, their tin hats like ovens on their heads, gunners found what shade they could near their weapons. Every so often, they'd pour buckets of seawater over themselves, but relief was short-lived. The mess decks and wardroom, where the injured bravely bore their suffering, had become Turkish baths. During this lull in the fighting, Porky did his rounds with trays of bully-beef sandwiches, hard-boiled eggs, fannies of water and sweet tea served in enamel mugs. Sunburnt, exhausted and dehydrated, the crews remained at their posts throughout the afternoon, warily scanning the sky for attackers.

From the bridge, Jack surveyed his motley crew, dressed in all manner of attire, some wearing overalls tied at the waist, others half-naked in shorts, vests and gym tackies or sandals. Most wore helmets, but Sub-lieutenant Fletcher had somehow managed to acquire a Sherlock Holmesian deerstalker, which he wore with surprising panache.

'What would you be doing if you was back home, Pickles?' Booysen asked his oppo, lying sprawled on the deck beside their pom-pom.

'I joined at sixteen, so most of my mates are still in high school. A mid-afternoon in July, they're probably at rugby practice on a bone-hard, yellow-grass field in Benoni with Mister van Tonder — "Tonteldoos" we called him — bawling them out for not tackling properly. If I was there, my mom would be baking biscuits or crunchies for when I got home from practice. She really spoils me, given that I don't really have a proper dad and all. I miss home so much right now. What about you?'

'*Ja*. Probably a rainy winter's day in Cape Town. Dad will be downstairs tending the shop, Mammie and my two sisters upstairs.' Booysen paused, picturing the cluttered upstairs home above the District Six café in the heart of the city. 'Michelle and Fatima are probably just home from school and Mammie will be making them something to eat, maybe *vetkoek* or samosas. Ag, that *lekker* smell, man…' He tailed off and took a long drag on his Springbok cigarette.

'Seems helluva far away.' Pickles sighed.

'*Ja*, it really, really does.'

A yellow warning informed the convoy of another large formation of attackers. The subsequent red warning ushered in the umbrella barrage, which appeared to Jack as a continuous cloud of exploding shells haranguing the sky as Ju-88s and Heinkels poured down like feeding gannets, the air filled once more with the scream of engines, whine of bombs and thudding of gunfire.

Diving line astern out of the sun came the Sea Hurricanes, some of them pursued by Me-109s, weaving through the bombers' ranks, their guns chattering. A Heinkel peeled away with its port engine aflame; a Ju-88 flipped upside down to the mushrooming of parachutes. The Hurricanes passed through the enemy formation, swooped back up into the heavens and banked around for another run. One of them was caught at the top of its parabola, taking vicious cannon fire from an Me-109 until its engine exploded in a fiery shower.

Waves of bombers continued to arrive and the attacks grew chaotic, Jack losing count of their number, his brain numbed by the battle's smoke and thunder. Expending a vast amount of ammunition, the escorts did their best to parry each thrust, forcing most aircraft to drop their bombs early or from height, but the attacks were so frequent and so persistent that it seemed only a matter of time before someone was hit.

Jack watched three Ju-88s dive unscathed through a thicket of shell bursts, aiming at MV *Rangatira.* The cacophony rose a few notches as the short-range weapons joined the fray, pom-poms adding their percussive thumping. Falling upon the New Zealander, each plane released a five-bomb stick, so low they could hardly miss.

Multiple explosions rippled along the length of the ship. She staggered and heeled, then a tremendous detonation rent the air. The freighter erupted as 11,000 tons of fuel and munitions blew up with a single, deafening roar, instantly killing most of her crew and sending debris hundreds of feet into the air. The shockwave passed through the convoy like an invisible tsunami, knocking Jack to the deck. Razor-edged pieces of ship splashed hissing and boiling into the sea in a deadly meteor shower. Scrambling to his feet, Jack looked on, numb with horror, as red-hot debris rained down around *Gannet*, a steel plate five feet long clattering onto the quarterdeck. Smaller fragments continued to fall from the sky like Alexandrian ash long after *Rangatira* had disappeared.

Leaving a rescue ship to pick up a handful of survivors, the convoy pressed on into the west under a succession of attacks that continued throughout the day, the enemy using every available aircraft to claim as many victims as possible before nightfall. The sky remained filled with skirmishes as Me-109s fought to protect the incoming bombers: Cants arriving regularly to drop 160-kg bombs from a great height with little accuracy, Ju-88s making persistent diving attacks, and Heinkels and Savoias making torpedo strikes. The air was threaded with plunging, climbing, jinking aircraft, some on fire, some dropping bombs, some trying to elude fighters as tracer and flak stitched and pocked the sky. The sea reverberated with the thunder of gunfire, exploding ordinance and siren blasts from ships making emergency turns.

Gannet's weapons grew red hot and loaders cooled the sizzling barrels with buckets of seawater; gun positions were heaped with empty shell cases. Booysen's hands were bruised and bleeding from banging fresh clips, each weighing twenty pounds, into the pom-pom as Pickles kept up a brisk rate of fire. There was little respite between attack waves and every ship remained at action stations throughout the day. Jack wondered how his black gang were coping down below in their echoing, steel oven. The sound of gunfire and bombs were deafening in the engine room, as though its occupants were trapped inside a kettle drum during the orchestra's climax. And, being sightless, they never knew quite when or where the axe might fall.

Only darkness could bring relief, but the slow transition from day to night seemed to drag on interminably. Finally, the sun kissed the horizon and *Gannet* shone like an ingot. Bathed in golden light, the gunners were almost out on their feet; Hendricks and Porky were emotionally raw from dealing with the wounded; Potgieter sat dazed and punch-drunk from the concentration required to monitor his Asdic set, with Fido ensconced in the perceived safety of a cardboard box at his feet. The pilots on *Vulture* were practically asleep in their cockpits, parked on the flight deck waiting for the next raid.

Eventually, dusk brought respite, pilots stood down and sailors breathed more easily. *Gannet*'s first lieutenant glanced at Jack just as a tremor crossed his usually impassive face. To Van Zyl, his captain looked hard worn by his time in the Mediterranean. Jack's outward demeanour remained steely, but Van Zyl knew there was a powerful act of will going on to maintain the aura of command, and it was taking a toll.

'Do you think that's stumps, sir?'

'No, Number One, I don't. Unfortunately, with these bally umpires, while there's light — even if it's twilight — there's play.'

Sure enough, the last attack of the day arrived after sunset. A lucky hit from a Cant during an earlier raid had started a fire on board one of the fleet destroyers and, smelling blood, a flight of Ju-88s now concentrated on the smoking ship in the outer ring. Near misses shook the injured Tribal and concussions holed two fuel tanks, knocking a boiler off line and reducing her speed to nine knots. As she fell slowly astern, another trio of Ju-88s bored in. One bomb hit B turret — a flash, crack, billowing smoke — and Jack saw men running aft along the deck, some of them aflame. Both forward turrets looked as though a can opener had been at work on their armoured casings.

Another echelon of Ju-88s attacked head-on, scoring more hits on the crippled destroyer. A bomb exploded in the engine room, ripping through the contained space and mortally wounding the ship. She slewed to port, heeling over with a heavy list, the roar of escaping steam audible from *Gannet*'s bridge. The Tribal appeared out of control, her steerage gone, smoke and flames belching from ugly holes. Soon, she was down by the head and slowing to a halt, a few of her guns still firing defiantly. Then came a series of rumbling internal explosions, the upper bridge dislodging itself, the main topmast teetering for a moment before splashing into the sea. Men began casting off rafts and others jumped into the water even before the command to abandon ship.

Jack asked Bunts to signal *Rhodesia*: 'Permission to pick up survivors?'

The flashed response was immediate: 'Permission denied.'

Fortunately, before the destroyer slipped beneath the waves, a brave PO removed the primers from the depth charges so they would not detonate among the survivors when she sank. Sailors in the water and on the rafts were singing 'Roll out the Barrel' as two Hunts approached to pick them up and the convoy sailed on into the darkness.

Jack gave permission for his men to sleep at their action stations, and all about the decks figures lay slumped in duffel coats, using life jackets or their oppos' bodies as pillows. *Gannet* wallowed downwind in an uneven, following sea. Apart from the Asdic's monotonous pinging and the bow wave's wash, the whaler was quiet, her sailors speaking in hushed tones as if afraid to wake the enemy. Although the sky remained free of Axis reconnaissance, Jack had no way of knowing that the convoy was being tracked by very powerful radar, newly installed on an island to the southwest, and that their every movement was being relayed to enemy headquarters in Sicily and Taranto.

Gannet's captain was reluctant to go below and sat hunched in his high chair on the bridge. He found few comforts in the darkest hours, other than a cup of life-restoring kye and thoughts of Alana, made more sensual and hyperbolic by the circumstances. Her body was a shrine, beaming like a lighthouse in the fog of his dejection. How he longed to be wrecked, Odysseus-like, upon her shore. She was his Calypso, his salvation, even if it meant eternal enslavement to sensual pleasure. Perhaps especially if it did.

Deep in the first watch, Jack was roused by a rumbling from the deep. He was immediately on his feet, fully alert. The torpedo had struck a freighter in the port column, now lit by self-perpetuating detonations. She carved out of line and came to a halt abeam of *Gannet*: a broken, smoking thing. The merchant's demise was quick and silent, a rescuing minesweeper in attendance. Within minutes, she'd broken in two and sunk, taking many of the crew with her, leaving only flotsam and a spreading oil slick to mark her passing. The rest of the convoy pressed on, maintaining course and speed, like cars passing the scene of an accident. To Jack, it was another ghastly episode in the tortuous, protracted nightmare that was Operation Assegai.

Later, Sparks received a priority signal from C-in-C Ras el-Tin to Rear Admiral Somerset, his escort ships included in the address. With one hand pressing an earphone tightly to his ear and a stubby pencil in the other, he needed to make absolutely sure he got the message first time. Ships were under strict orders to maintain radio silence, so there could be no asking for a repetition. It was a short transmission in code, the priority rating lending urgency as he flipped through the codebook and transcribed the message on a flimsy. His jaw fell open as its import dawned on him. Bursting out of the wireless cabin, he dashed up the ladder to the bridge and handed the flimsy to Jack. His captain's face turned ashen as he muttered under his breath: 'Oh. My. God.'

CHAPTER 8

The signal read: 'Italian battlefleet has left Taranto, headed southeast.'

Jack would learn only later that an RAF photoreconnaissance aircraft from Malta had discovered one of Italy's modern Littorio-class battleships, accompanied by a heavy force of cruisers and destroyers, had left Taranto's Mar Grande. Plotting the enemy's position relative to the convoy's track and assuming a speed of twenty-five knots, the Italians could be in range within twelve hours.

Gannet's captain read the signal a second and a third time. Coming in the dead of night with Jack at his lowest ebb, the message cast a pall of despair. It seemed inevitable that Admiral Somerset's depleted cruiser squadron would be smashed by the Italians, who would then fall upon the smaller escorts and merchantmen, picking them off at their leisure. If the convoy turned tail and beat a retreat to Alexandria, the speedy Italians would certainly catch them and *Gannet* would die fighting, hammered to a pulp by the enemy's powerful guns. Jack remained hunched over in his bridge chair, trying to piece his way through the ramifications of the signal. Whichever way he looked at it, Operation Assegai was surely doomed.

Gannet steamed on towards Malta, her flared bows surfing the following swell, the wind from astern steadily building. In the early hours, there was a crackling sound from the ship's tannoy, then a squeak, followed by what sounded like a deep sigh.

'Good morning, Gannets. Your captain's voice is doubtless the last thing you want to hear at this ungodly hour. By now, the scuttlebutt will have informed you that the Italian battlefleet has put to sea. In order to reach us, the enemy will have to pass through a barrier of Royal Navy submarines. Our long-range bombers from Egypt and Malta will also conduct a dawn raid on the Italians. We are eagerly awaiting the results of those attacks. Upon them will depend our future movements, but we must be prepared to fight, and fight hard, this coming day. I do not expect anything significant to happen before dawn, so get as much rest as you can. That is all.'

Douglas emerged on the flight deck at first light to find handling parties swarming around the waiting Sea Hurricanes and Fulmars. He heard the blare of a bugle call cross the water as the nearest cruiser went to quarters, its skyward-pointing barrels ready for targets. *Vulture* came about and headed into the wind, preparing to fly off the first aircraft, her sheepdog destroyer turning with her like a faithful Ginger Rogers.

Striding across the flight deck, Douglas felt more nervous than usual, compounded by a building swell that tossed the flight deck about to an irregular beat. He climbed onto the wing and into the cockpit, strapped himself in and started the engine, awaiting permission to take off. Receiving a thumbs-up, he opened the throttle. With the green flag rotating faster, he fed in more power, then released the brakes and sped down the deck. At the moment of lift-off, *Vulture* dipped into a deeper trough. The bows fell like an axe, aiming his fighter at the water, and he found himself looking at sea, not sky. Cursing, Douglas pulled back on the stick and felt agonising weightlessness as the wheels came free. The fighter dropped sickeningly. For a few interminable seconds, the Canadian thought he was going to strike the water and be cleaved in two by *Vulture*'s prow. His undercarriage lightly clipped the crest of a swell before the propeller's grip dragged him aloft.

Nose up and rising through low, tufty clouds, he pointed his aircraft north, with instructions to search for any sign of the Italian fleet. Advance warning would give Admiral Somerset time to decide on the enemy's remaining strength after the bomber and submarine assaults, and whether to attack, disperse or turn back to Alexandria.

Cruising at 12,000 feet an hour later, Douglas had just emerged from a cloudbank when the sky ahead of him erupted in gigantic detonations of fire and smoke. For an instant, the Canadian thought he'd been hit, or his engine had exploded. Quickly glancing at the horizon, he spotted the cause: a sinister line of ships coming his way. He pulled back on the stick, climbed sharply and banked to throw off the gunners, then raised his binoculars to survey the enemy: by the look of it a battleship, six cruisers and a powerful destroyer escort heading south at full speed. Not one of the Italians appeared damaged. Allied submarines and bombers had made no impact whatsoever.

The battleship's turrets tracked his erratic progress. Although he was beyond the range of most of the anti-aircraft weapons, the bigger guns could easily reach him. Another salvo burst in the sky around him, flinging the Hurricane about like a ragdoll. Douglas had seen enough. He banked hard and dived away into the clouds. Switching on his transmitter to get a warning through on the R/T, he discovered his set was dead: the shell bursts must have shaken something loose.

Opening the throttle, he raced back to *Vulture* at the Hurricane's best speed. After landing on, he thrust himself from the cockpit, leapt to the deck and sprinted for the island.

Within moments he was on the bridge, making his report between gasps. Admiral Somerset was immediately informed and a few minutes later, interception and battle plans were being finalised. With twelve hours of daylight remaining, there was no way of evading the enemy until nightfall. They would have to fight.

Meanwhile, a yellow warning saw *Vulture*'s pilots scrambling to meet a wave of incoming bombers. Douglas hastened back to his partially refuelled Hurricane and prepared to take off as Albacores were being raised to the deck and readied for a torpedo attack on the Italian heavies.

Douglas was soon airborne once more, climbing steeply to gain as much altitude as possible before the arrival of the bombers and their consorts. With the ships growing smaller behind him, his eyes keenly scanned the northern sky for bandits. Just then, a desperate call came through on the R/T from the carrier: 'Alarm, alarm! Torpedoes running to starboard!'

On *Gannet*'s bridge, Jack watched as the flat top heeled hard over in an emergency turn, clawing round to face the danger. But it was too late. Three torpedoes struck *Vulture* in quick succession, raising columns of water that stood three times the height of her topmast. Every stoker in boiler room A was instantly killed, along with all the greasers in the starboard engine room. The carrier took on an immediate list as thousands of tons of seawater poured through gaping holes, dragging her to a standstill. The pilot of a Fulmar that was about to take off tried to accelerate but fought in vain to compensate for the growing tilt, and his aircraft slid off the deck into the sea. At least he and his crewman had a better chance of surviving than many others on the stricken *Vulture*, thought Jack.

Black smoke and steam billowed out of open hatchways as terrifying screams echoed across the water from those trapped below. More aircraft rolled like toys off the flight deck and splashed into the water. Soon, the carrier lay at forty degrees and there appeared to be no chance of saving her. Sailors began to abandon ship, some leaping from the flight deck too late, only to be smashed on the rising torpedo blister, leaving trails of blood. Others slid down the flight deck to leeward and jumped or fell into the sea, while destroyers raced back and forth, dropping depth charges in a frenzy of revenge-seeking but with no apparent result.

Jack looked on, aghast and impotent, his body trembling. This could not be happening: *Vulture* was their mothership, their protection, their shield. How on earth had a U-boat managed to evade both destroyer screens? There were already hundreds of men in the water by the time HMS *Vulture* tipped with tired grace onto her side, the terrible sound of rending metal and exploding bulkheads reaching across the water to *Gannet*. Then, with a deep sigh, the carrier turned turtle, exposing her red bottom and big bronze screws. A few diminutive figures had walked upright round the bilge keel as she turned and now stood like survivors on a desert island. They would not have long to live. Jack stifled an agonised gasp as *Vulture* slipped from the scene in a welter of geysers and filthy whirlpools that sucked more sailors to their deaths.

The convoy's air shield was no more.

Three destroyers with scrambling nets down and lowered boats lay stationary among the grey life rafts and bobbing survivors. Two Fleets continued to drop depth charges way over to starboard, hunting in vain for the U-boat. Jack glanced aloft and saw a pair of circling Hurricanes, one of them with a winged cheetah on the cowling. Then the fighters turned west and climbed for the clouds, no doubt making a bid to reach Malta. Jack took a rough guess at the range of a Sea Hurricane, assuming its tanks were full at the time of take-off. With an aching heart, he realised their chances of reaching the island were impossibly slim.

Douglas and his Australian wingman climbed higher. Feeling stunned by anguish and despair, the Canadian glanced back at the vanishing convoy, already just a cluster of specks on the eastern horizon. The two pilots' judgement was clouded by the shock of *Vulture*'s loss, and they weren't paying attention to the sky above them. Suddenly, an Me-110 arrowed out of the sun, nose-guns flaring. The Australian's reactions were too slow, and rounds peppered his engine and cockpit before the two Hurricanes jinked hard, tipping into steep dives to be swallowed by cloud. Emerging from the cotton wool, they were lucky to be free of their pursuer, for they could not afford to waste any fuel on dogfighting.

'I've been hit, Grayson,' gasped the Australian over the radio. 'Losing … a lot of blood … going to have to —'

'Hang on, Arlo. Keep your nose up; watch the horizon,' urged Douglas, edging closer to view the damage: large holes in the fuselage and a heavy fuel leak. 'Okay, you'll have to turn back. Ditch next to a destroyer and you'll be rescued in a jiffy.'

'Not sure if … if…'

'Keep talking to me, Arlo.'

'Been hit in the chest, the arm … can't manage the throttle. Oh, God, it hurts like hell…'

'You must turn back and ditch, Arlo.'

'Didn't see…'

'That's an order, dammit!'

'Didn't see him…'

'Please, Arlo, you'll make it, I promise.'

'Tell Sarah how … how much…'

The Hurricane's nose dropped sharply, its pilot having blacked out, and the aircraft spiralled down towards the sea like a leaf. Fighting the tears, Douglas circled to watch it crash with an almighty splash, then swung his aircraft back on course. Aiming west-northwest, he climbed slowly to 12,000 feet and flew at 150 mph, the best height and speed to conserve fuel. The weather was hazy, but a strengthening tailwind helped his progress. Any small advantage might save his life.

Douglas felt the sun through the Perspex, hot on his burn-scarred left cheek, inducing a mood of soporific resignation. He kept checking the fuel gauge, dismayed at its rapid descent towards the red. Perhaps this was his last flight; best try to savour these final moments aloft. His mind drifted back to his early days learning to fly in a Tiger Moth above the forests of Ontario, then his graduation to the sturdy and faithful Harvard. He glanced to starboard, beyond the red and blue roundel at the tip of his wing: somewhere beyond the horizon lay Sicily, from whence the trouble would come, if come it would.

All too soon, his fuel gauge reached the red. It appeared his luck had run out. As he lifted his gaze, Douglas noticed a fluffy stack of cumulus rising out of the heat haze ahead: that was good, or at least potentially good. He'd been told clouds often built up over Malta during the day, but by now his fuel was down to thirty gallons and still no sight of land. So close and yet … he was going to have to ditch.

But hang on! There, beyond the milky blur of his prop, could it possibly be the pale shape of an island? *The* island. A wave of overwhelming relief coursed through him. Descending slowly, a pair of isles — Malta and her smaller cousin, Gozo — gathered definition, revealing themselves as exquisite yellow disks set in a carpet of deep cobalt. He saw a cliff-lined shore, waves breaking on rocks and scrawling white calligraphy in the water; behind them, fields crosshatched by stone walls formed a patchwork quilt in shades of tan. Beautiful. Just beautiful.

'Luqa Tower, this is Hurricane Delta Foxtrot inbound from HMS *Vulture*. Permission to land, over?'

'*Vulture*? Good grief…' A crackling silence. 'All right, Delta Foxtrot, Luqa is under attack, so you'll need to orbit offshore south of the airfield until it's safe to approach. Over.'

'Luqa Tower, negative. Repeat, negative. My fuel is at bingo level, over.'

'Delta Foxtrot, the runway is being bombed.'

'I'll take my chances.'

Douglas was flying on fumes, his engine starved of fuel and beginning to cough. His body was wet with sweat; his head ached from concentration and thirst. Lower now, he was skating over an olive grove, the ground rising fast to meet him. Ahead, the airfield looked like a lunar landscape, pitted with craters and large bites out of the runway. As he threaded the needle, a dry-stone wall loomed before him. He raised his aircraft's nose a little… It would be touch and go.

At the very last moment, Douglas lowered his undercarriage. The wheels locked into place with a thump just as a Macchi C202 Folgore swept in behind him, filling his mirror as tracer rounds streaked over his canopy. With no time to retract the landing gear, he jammed his Hurricane into a tight skidding turn at almost stalling speed. The Italian overshot and climbed away, wreathed in tracer from Luqa's gunners. With his engine loudly spluttering from lack of fuel, Douglas pushed the stick forward and bounced down onto the strip, raising clouds of white dust.

Relief coursed through him like antivenom to his terror as a shirtless erk in khaki shorts ran towards the Hurricane, waving his arms. Douglas slowed his aircraft and the man climbed onto the wing, directing him off the runway towards a protective 'sangar' fashioned from sandbags and four-gallon petrol cans filled with earth and wired together. To his left, a Bofors opened fire with its four-beat tattoo, lending urgency to his progress across the bumpy field. Douglas pulled into the blast pen just as his engine died. Pushing back the canopy, he let out a very deep, very long sigh.

'Welcome to RAF Luqa, sir!' said the smiling Cockney erk.

'Thank you, but I'm afraid I don't have a reservation.'

'Not to worry, Guv, we'll find you a table. Champagne?'

'Yes, please.'

'A lady companion?'

'Yes, please.'

Douglas climbed stiffly out of the cockpit and jumped to the ground. His legs trembled, his body was soaked in sweat, his eyes stung and his throat raged with thirst. Taking a moment to get his bearings and digest what had just transpired, the Canadian felt profoundly disorientated: he'd lost his ship, his home, his friends, and arrived out of the blue on a strange island with only the clothes on his back. He was, most definitely, not in Kansas anymore.

Unclipping the straps, Douglas handed his parachute to the corporal, then removed his leather helmet and flight gauntlets. Squaring his shoulders, he filled his lungs with a long, deep draught. The air smelt of baked earth and dust, smoke and sea. It was also hellishly hot and Luqa shimmered in a distorting haze. Debris was strewn everywhere, along with several charred aircraft, including the large carcass of a Wellington bomber. With the burnt-out trucks and shattered buildings, it was as though he'd landed in the heart of Dante's Inferno. Glancing back at his Hurricane, he saw that riggers, fitters and armourers were already at work, preparing it for combat.

'Malta is desperately short of aircraft, sir,' said the corporal by way of explanation. 'Your bird might need to be airborne again within the hour, and not necessarily with you as pilot. We have a sort of hot bunking system, what with Jerry and the Wops bombing us round the clock.'

'And I have no say in this?'

'No, sir.' The corporal smiled toothily. 'Do you perhaps know how long you'll be visiting us?'

'I haven't the foggiest.'

CHAPTER 9

More details about the Italian battlefleet reached the convoy via Alexandria and, by late morning, Jack knew for certain they were facing a force of three heavy 8-inch cruisers, probably Trento and Bolzano class, three light 6-inch cruisers and about a dozen destroyers. Sailing in their midst, and wearing the flag of Rear Admiral Albani, was a fearsome Littorio-class battleship. Displacing more than 40,000 tons, she was powerful and fast, with a top speed of 30 knots and a complement of nearly 2,000 men. She carried three aircraft and was armed with nine 15-inch guns and twelve 6-inch guns, as well as a vast array of anti-aircraft weapons. Her broadside outweighed the combined firepower of Somerset's entire fleet. By all naval logic, the Italians should annihilate the convoy.

Gannet's tannoy hummed and Jack blow-tested the mic. 'This is your captain speaking. I want to bring you into my confidence about what I know of developments since last I addressed you. Our bombers — torpedo Wellingtons and Beauforts from Malta, and Liberators from Egypt — have been harassing the Italians, but apparently not enough to deter them. Interception is expected this afternoon. Our convoy has lost some fine ships, including HMS *Vulture*, which provided our umbrella, but we are protected by a powerful cruiser force under the command of a great admiral. Much will be expected from all of us today.' There was a long pause, then a rough clearing of his throat. 'I have no doubt whatsoever that HMSAS *Southern Gannet* and her loyal servants are up to the task at hand … and that she will bravely take the fight to the enemy, come what may. Thank you, that is all.'

By mid-afternoon, and with no sign of the battlefleet, Jack was beginning to hope against hope that either Allied bombers had managed to detain them or that darkness might indeed come to their rescue, given that the Italians were unlikely to take on radar-controlled British gunnery at night.

'Smoke, sir, green seven-oh!' cried Behardien.

No such luck, then. Despairingly, Jack raised his binoculars. Sure enough, the faintest of whisps leaked from the northern horizon, moving left and trying to head off the convoy.

'Sound action stations, Number One.'

With *Gannet*'s bells clanging in his ears, Jack watched as the British cruisers did the same, large red warning flags jerking to the yardarms and tin-hatted ratings swarming like termites to their guns. Weighing up the convoy's options, Jack reckoned the south-easterly wind from astern might well offer favourable conditions for laying a smokescreen. It appeared to be just the right strength to waft smoke towards the enemy and hide the convoy's manoeuvres. Admiral Somerset would certainly need every shred of advantage that could be gained in the coming hours.

'Flagship signalling,' said Bunts, pointing at HMS *Rhodesia*'s yardarm. 'I for India, sir.'

Jack opened his docket and flipped through the typewritten orders until he came to 'I'. When the signal was lowered, denoting the executive, the cruiser squadron, accompanied by the main body of fleet destroyers, would turn northwest, increase speed and advance towards the Italians, while the merchantmen and smaller escorts would turn southwest, with *Gannet* riding lone shotgun astern of them. The admiral would thereby be placing his strike force between the Italians and the convoy, and no doubt try to head off the enemy to the northwest. In confirmation, a signal was flashed by lamp from

Rhodesia to convoy commodore, repeated to all ships: 'Convoy will alter 55 degrees to port on the executive and steer 220 degrees until further orders.'

'Thank you, Bunts, acknowledge,' said Jack.

The line of cruisers made a formidable sight as they bore away, fo'c'sles flaring white as they gathered speed and aimed their prows at the Italian foe. Battle ensigns jerked aloft, the massive flags presenting a brave sight on the foremast of each cruiser. *Nelsonic, even,* thought Jack, a lump forming in his throat. But unlike Trafalgar, the cruisers would be severely hamstrung, needing at all times to keep themselves between the convoy and the Italians who were sailing at full steam, trying to work their way around the head of the convoy to outflank the British and bar the merchants' path to Malta.

If only Admiral Somerset could hold them off until sunset … but nightfall was many hours away and the Italian heavyweights had plenty of time to carve through the cruiser squadron and fall upon the flock. Jack thought again of the odds: a 14-knot convoy versus a 30-knot battleship, 6-inch versus 15-inch guns. *Like a hot knife through butter.* He pictured a diorama of the Mediterranean and its adjacent landmasses, rendered in swathes of black and red — all of it balanced on the fulcrum of this patch of sea, and this pregnant moment.

'Permission to hoist battle ensign, sir?' Signalman Gilbert cut into his thoughts.

'Aye, Bunts, of course, good thinking,' replied Jack. 'Might as well be dressed in our Number Ones for the dance.'

The signalman pulled the largest ensign from its locker, clattered down the bridge ladder and ran aft to the boat deck, where he clipped the flag to the halyard and, hand over hand, raised it to the mizzenmast gaff. The flag broke open in a burst of white emblazoned with the red cross of St George. Jack's heart lifted at the sight of the ensign streaming out stiffly.

As always in times of need, Coxswain February took the wheel: eyes on the compass and gnarled, intelligent hands easing the spokes this way and that, ever so gently, anticipating *Gannet*'s quirks and vagaries in the awkward following sea.

'Enemy battleship in sight, sir,' announced Behardien, a tremor in his voice.

The lookout's words passed like an electric shock around the bridge. Jack tried to focus his binoculars on the biggest of the dots as it rose out of the horizon's haze. He realised that what he'd taken for a small ship was merely an upper fire-control position. Beneath it, lifting from the murky distortion came a bridge, then a second bridge, funnels, and finally, three massive turrets. A grotesque behemoth — as fast and powerful as anything the Royal Navy possessed, and more formidable than any other ship in the Mediterranean.

'She's definitely Littorio class,' said Van Zyl.

'And the three ahead of her, Number One?'

'Heavy cruisers. They've certainly brought their first eleven. Some decent batters there.'

'Aye, especially the portly chap.'

The cruiser squadron had worked up to full speed, sailing line astern, with Admiral Somerset on *Rhodesia* calling the shots as the opposing forces converged. In a parallel line abeam and to port of the cruisers rode the sleek Tribal destroyers. As Jack looked on in admiration, he could not help but feel that, one way or another, history was to be made this day. If the enemy broke through… Jack pictured the shooting gallery at the Oxford fair on St Giles': *a teddy bear for every Itie captain*, he thought ruefully.

The leading Italian turned slightly to starboard, exposing the entire length of her flank, and thus her broadside. *Yes, upon such days are empires made. Or lost.* The other ships followed suit, forming line of battle and preparing to open fire. Jack ran the calculations in his head: the battleship would be in range at any moment, but the Royal Navy cruisers needed to get a whole lot closer before their 6-inch guns could come into play.

There was a ripple of flashes on the horizon as the battleship fired.

Jack's binoculars tracked back to the British line at the very instant nine gargantuan geysers rose from the sea a few cables short of the leading cruiser. The faint yellow colour of the falling water meant high explosive. The British responded by turning directly towards the Italians, trying to close the range as quickly as possible — just as *Hood* had done to *Bismarck* the previous year, with catastrophic results. Another salvo of 15-inch shells: this time six of them short, but three of them over. The battleship had found the range.

Soon after, the three leading Italian cruisers glittered as their heavy weapons opened up. That would be the enemy's 8-inch guns, but still the British could not respond. Twenty seconds later, a cluster of white steeples rose from the sea, all of them short, but not by much. The Italians were warming to their task against a silent, impotent foe.

Closer still, the sea was repeatedly sown with waterspouts and curtains of falling spray. Jack stared in awe at the battleship, flying the colours of Admiral Albani, her enormous gunnery control tower and those monstrous 15-inch guns clearly visible now. An iron fortress. His lenses tracked back to the British squadron just as a string of flags broke out on Rhodesia's signal halyard. He knew their gist, even before Bunts read off the message.

Having been stationed at the Cape, Jack had grown to loathe the south-easterly gales that could make life in Simonstown a trial. But at this moment, the strengthening southeaster might prove a godsend. Originating in the Sahara and carrying dust clouds far across the Mediterranean basin, the desert khamsin had built itself into a heavy sirocco. Admiral Somerset had cannily placed his squadron so that this wind, of exactly the right strength, blew from his cruisers to a point just ahead of the racing Italians.

'Signal from flagship to squadron: "Make smoke",' said Bunts.

'I knew it!' Jack exclaimed, slapping the rail with excitement. He pictured the petty-officer stokers deep in the bowels of each ship, adjusting their valves to allow too much oil into the furnaces and not enough air for full combustion. Almost immediately, black smoke began to belch from the aft funnels of all six cruisers and streamed briskly downwind. The sooty fog rolled out upon the waters in Biblical fashion, shielding the flock from evil eyes. To get at the merchantmen, the Italians had three options: try to pierce the smokescreen, work their way around its thinning western end, or go the long way round, beating upwind to the east and attempting to get behind the convoy.

Attacking through the smokescreen would result in a chaotic melee at close range, with torpedoes a lethal threat. Somerset was gambling that the Italian admiral would not want to risk his battleship in such a venture, nor would he fancy a long upwind beat into the strengthening southeaster, allowing the convoy to get ever closer to Malta as the day drained away. He surmised that his adversary would keep his force together and try to work his way around the smokescreen to leeward.

But the British cruisers were nimble and Somerset could play a canny game of cat and mouse to keep the enemy guessing. To this end, each cruiser was ordered to dart through the smoke at erratic intervals, fire a few salvos, and then retreat behind the screen before the Italians could find the range and smite them with their one-ton shells. A single 15-inch projectile, properly landed, could sink a cruiser. Although spotter planes had been launched by the enemy, their shooting over the smokescreen had, thus far, been inaccurate.

Jack watched the last cruiser in line, HMS *Apollo*, veer to starboard and plunge into the widening bank of smoke. Two minutes later he heard the thunder of her broadside and marvelled, once again, at all the calculations that went into sending eight 6-inch shells high into the upper atmosphere, from a ship moving at thirty knots, to come down on or as close as possible to, a ship eight miles away, also moving at thirty knots. Again and again, he heard *Apollo* firing at a rate of one salvo every ten seconds, then silence. Had she been hit or disabled? Jack waited another two agonising minutes before she burst back through the smoke, went hard a-starboard in cascades of spray and resumed her station.

Although shielded by the cruisers, the merchantmen were being constantly harassed by long-range bombers — Ju-88s, Heinkels and Savoias — from Sicily. Lacking the anti-aircraft punch of the larger escorts, the convoy had to fend for itself. A handful of twin-engine Beaufighters from Malta arrived on the scene, but were operating at the limit of their range and their numbers were too few to have much effect. The enemy mostly attacked downwind from the port quarter, diving from 8,000 feet and releasing their bombs at 2,000 feet. The convoy was having to expend an enormous amount of ammunition parrying these attacks, so much so that Jack began to worry that a lack of ammunition might prove critical on the final lap to Malta, just as it had for Operation Vigorous.

Gannet had fallen back quite some distance, having diverted to pick up the crew of a downed Beaufighter. As they approached the sinking aircraft, Jack heard a bloodcurdling scream from the aft lookout: 'Enemy cruiser, bearing green one-six-oh!'

Jack spun around and froze in horror as the big Italian burst through the smokescreen. The sight before him was a gross impossibility, unnatural even, counter to the order of things. Against such odds, there was not a shred of hope for *Gannet.*

CHAPTER 10

Racing up from astern, the Italian cruiser was almost upon them, a stampeding bull venting fumes and menace. Her huge turrets trained around, the barrels foreshortening as they settled on *Gannet*. Then her main guns flared, billowing clouds of smoke. Was it his imagination, or did Jack glimpse four dots streaking across the dark blue of the sky? He counted off the seconds, heard the wheezing of shells passing overhead before towers of yellow water rose from the sea 200 yards beyond the whaler. The aimers would be shortening the range for the next salvo.

'It's *Glowworm* all over again,' said a rattled Van Zyl, referring to the loss of the small destroyer pulverised by the cruiser *Admiral Hipper* off the coast of Norway. 'We won't even put a dent in that brute.' He read the agonising indecision etched on Jack's face, then, a moment later, a perceptible clenching of his captain's jaw.

'We're damn well going to try, Number One. Hard a-starboard!' bellowed Jack, his voice seared with emotion.

'Sir?' Van Zyl gasped, not quite believing the order as February spun the wheel and *Gannet* heeled hard over, turning to face the foe.

'We've got to buy time for the convoy, Number One.'

The whaler steadied on the new heading, her bows aimed straight at the Italian, just as another salvo erupted ahead of her.

'Twenty degrees to port,' said Jack into the voicepipe, steering towards the splashes to throw off the enemy's aim. It was in such extreme moments that Jack sensed he was most wholly a part of *Gannet*, when his instinctive reactions and her movements were in concert. He was the head, she the body, and the distinguishing line between the two unclear. He must delay the Italian, draw her fire onto himself, give the merchants a chance to widen the gap and the cavalry a chance to arrive — if arrive they would, for they had seemingly vanished downwind in the confusion of smoke, haze and spray.

The next instant, Jack felt a hollow sucking in the pit of his stomach, accompanied by a loud tearing sound. The shell detonated just off *Gannet*'s prow, whiting out his vision with a wall of water. He felt utterly helpless as his ship was lifted and shaken, splinters whining overhead and clattering into the superstructure like grapeshot. Tons of Mediterranean brine rained down. On Jack's tongue, the water tasted more of cordite than salt.

'Good Lord,' he murmured, then, collecting himself, 'Come thirty degrees to starboard, Cox'n.'

Straight at him, no mucking about, but keep to the erratic zigzag.

'Thirty to starboard, sir,' came February's laconic reply.

At full speed and leaning into her turns, *Gannet* laid a smokescreen from both her funnel and the canisters mounted on her quarterdeck in the hope of shielding the merchantmen for as long as possible. In so doing, she increased her own isolation. Looking astern, Jack could see no sign of any cavalry, no friendly vessel, caught as he was in this lonely joust with a seemingly invincible foe.

The range was rapidly closing, so too its inevitable outcome. *Gannet*'s bows rose high, her wake streamed out wide, her spinning screw sent a shuddering vibration throughout the ship. Chief McEwan was holding nothing back. On the fo'c'sle, the 4-inch crew aimed their modest weapon at the enemy cruiser. The somewhat eccentric Sub-lieutenant Thomas

Fletcher had struggled through the mathematics of his gunnery course at HMS *King Alfred*, that bleak officer-training establishment in Hove. He'd received a grounding that prepared him for the basics of firing a 4-inch gun, a grounding that had been refined in recent months on the Tobruk convoys, moulding Fletcher and his men into a well-oiled unit. Those months of practice sat most precisely on this moment, as the giant Italian bore down on them and Fletcher instructed AB Palmer to set his sights on the enemy bridge. If they could not hope to sink the cruiser, they might at least poke her in the eye.

Jack looked down at his foredeck warriors on their seesawing bandstand: the statue-like ammunition carriers waiting with shells in their arms, the loaders inserting a round, the breech banging shut, the range being set and the layer aiming his sights at the rapidly growing target.

'Shoot!' cried Fletcher.

The 4-inch answered crisply: a tongue of flame, sharp recoil, the belching of cordite and an empty shell case clanging to the deck.

Jack watched for a waterspout — to the left and long. Sub-lieutenant Fletcher was red-faced and bawling: 'Load HE, me hearties! Right five, down 300…'

Another quartet of fountains bracketed *Gannet*. The next salvo must surely have them.

'Shoot!' barked Fletcher.

Clunk, nothing.

'Misfire, sir!' cried Palmer.

'Oh Jesus, Mary, Mother of God!' Fletcher cursed. From gunnery school, he remembered the drill was to wait half an hour before opening the breech. He knew this only too well as he yanked open the breech and grabbed the gleaming brass shell.

'Sir, are you sure?' said an appalled Palmer.

'Perfectly,' said Fletcher through gritted teeth, struggling to keep a proper grip on the slick, verdigris-stained cylinder. Then, with the misfire held clumsily against his stomach, the sub-lieutenant tottered under its weight across the lurching deck, and balanced the shell for an instant on the rail, before heaving it overboard. There was a short silence, then the misfire exploded, sending a torrent cascading over the deck.

The gun crew had already slotted a new round into the breech. Fletcher took the briefest moment to collect himself from the near-death interlude, then bellowed: 'Resume firing, yer bastids… Shoot!'

Palmer allowed for *Gannet*'s pitch and roll, then came a loud bang, followed by the whine of the round on its short odyssey. This time, a tiny prick of red and a plume of smoke on the Italian bridge.

'By Jove, a hit! Sir, sir, a palpable hit!' shouted Fletcher, looking back at Jack with a demonic grin.

'Bravo, Mister Fletcher!' called Jack.

The smoke from the enemy bridge thickened, the cruiser veering hard to port as if trying to shake off a momentary blinding. It took a while — more precious minutes won — before she regained composure and turned back towards *Gannet*, visibly increasing speed, her two forward turrets locking onto their target. Clearly now, the game was up.

Suddenly *Apollo* tore at full speed through the smokescreen on *Gannet*'s port quarter, followed by *Demeter*, their prows throwing tall bow waves as they sliced through the swell, the loud thrumming of their fans and turbines reaching Jack like orchestral music across the narrowing gap. The smoke they'd inhaled while passing through the screen gushed from ventilators, giving them the appearance of avenging dragons. Admiral Somerset must have anticipated that some of the Italian squadron might turn east to work around the rear of the convoy, and had ordered two units to double back after a sortie through the smokescreen.

Both cruisers opened fire at the same time, their first salvos bracketing the enemy. The Italian quickly shifted its aim away from the whaler and returned fire, scoring a lucky hit on *Apollo*. Jack saw the starboard pom-pom sponson erupt in a shower of flame and metal, the limbs and torsos of its crew hurled into the air. But their sacrifice had saved *Apollo* from a more serious, perhaps fatal, wound had the shell exploded deep inside her. The British cruiser wore a gaping hole and was aflame amidships, but she pressed on as fire-fighting parties swarmed about her decks. The Italian, in turn, received two hits and began belching smoke. She had had enough and turned tail, making rapidly for the smokescreen.

'Check, check, check!' Jack called through his loudhailer as the gong sounded and the 4-inch fell silent. Fletcher's crew straightened from their labour, coated in sweat, their cordite-blackened faces stunned by the short, sharp engagement. Silence rang almost as loudly in their ears as the deafening shots of moments earlier. Wordlessly, the gun crew went about clearing the forecastle, tossing empty cartridge cases over the side like the remains of gutted fish.

The afternoon wore itself long, the sun ebbing towards the horizon and the window of opportunity closing for the Italians. The British cruiser squadron, now back to its full complement with the return of *Apollo* and *Demeter*, had drawn steadily closer to the enemy, darting in and out of their advancing smokescreen. Hits and near misses had damaged ships on both sides but none proved decisive. Still, the Italians tried to work their way around the western edge of the smokescreen and right now, with the battle apparently reaching some sort of culmination, it seemed as though the enemy's fastest destroyers, out ahead of the heavy units, may have created an opening. They'd reached the end of the smoke line and turned south, threatening the merchantmen. So this, then, was the Italians' chance.

Jack knew that Somerset needed to change the dimensions of the battle and the admiral now opted for a daring roll of the dice, sending his own destroyers through the smokescreen and urging them to get as close to the battleship as possible before firing their torpedoes. For some minutes his Tribals — thinner-skinned and more vulnerable than the cruisers — would be exposed to withering fire from the whole Italian battle line, but Somerset hoped the torpedoes would force the enemy to turn away, buying him more valuable time as the Italians ran out of options and daylight. Seven fleet destroyers, four torpedoes each: a single volley of twenty-eight tin fish launched at the same moment. It was worth a go.

Jack watched the destroyers turn north and increase speed, their sterns set deep, their battle ensigns taut and quivering as they were swallowed by the roiling smog. He knew instinctively this was the battle's climax. It was not long before disaster struck as the first Tribal was hit by a 15-inch shell, which obliterated the destroyer in an enormous fireball. Somerset needed an immediate rethink. He had to divide the Italians' fire with a bold attack through the smoke by all six cruisers. The screen was by now so close to the enemy that even twelve-pounder guns were within range, and the cruisers' rapid fire might blind and confuse the enemy for long enough to give his destroyers a chance.

Jack watched with a sense of foreboding as the line of cruisers turned and was swallowed by the smoke. Two minutes later, he heard the rolling thunder of their guns and tried to picture what was happening: the cruisers blazing away at the Italian line and the destroyers converging on the enemy at an acute angle, their torpedo tubes trained to starboard, their crews awaiting the order to fire. The roaring of the guns reached a crescendo as hundreds of shells ripped past each other in mid-air, then plunged into the sea around the antagonists in a hailstorm of splashes. Feeling the weight of the moment, Jack found it maddening that he could not see.

Ahead of *Gannet*, a destroyer limped back through the screen with a gaping hole in her quarterdeck, both X and Y gun turrets missing. Jack imagined the five remaining destroyers tearing on undeterred, like a pack of wild dogs on the hunt, with 8- and 15-inch shells falling about them, their 4.7-inch peashooters useless against the Italian armour. Meanwhile, out of sight, the destroyers released their torpedoes as one, sending twenty arrows at a depth of twenty feet towards the Italian battle line.

Taking no chances, Albani immediately turned his ships away, presenting their narrow sterns to the incoming torpedoes. The projectiles slowly caught up with the racing Italians and passed between them without scoring a single hit, but by now the range had widened considerably, the sun had further westered and the wind gathered strength. The Italian attack was faltering and their destroyers, so close to reaching the merchantmen, had lost the support of their heavy units and were being engaged by the British destroyers. Albani had seen all he needed to. The infernal Royal Navy had held him at bay just long enough for his window to close. He did not return his battlefleet to the fray and withdrew to the north, hastening back to Taranto. The British squadron retired once more behind its screen and the misshapen orange sphere settled on the western horizon, flared momentarily as though taking a direct hit and then melted away. The convoy resumed its direct course for Malta, the air attacks thinning with the fading light until the sky was clear once more. Somehow, they had survived another day.

Jack looked aft to where Bunts was hauling down the battle ensign, now embellished with crisply edged brown holes. Exhausted men sank to the deck beside their guns, pulling off helmets, mopping brows and gulping mugs of water and lemon juice, their faces and bare torsos blotched grey with cordite dust and streaked with sweat.

After nightfall, their job done and with ammunition running low, the cruisers and fleet destroyers turned back to Alexandria. Although Jack knew this had always been the plan, watching the dark shapes swing away and head east was nevertheless a low point. Under Admiral Somerset's instructions, the convoy now dispersed, each of the surviving freighters proceeding at her best speed with the Hunts, one damaged Tribal and the smaller escorts loosely shepherding them to Malta, or at least trying to get them within range of close fighter support by morning. Those ships that had not reached Malta by dawn were to regroup in convoy formation and fight their way through to Grand Harbour.

'We're in a spot of bother, Captain,' said Robinson, appearing on the bridge after having studied the charts.

'How so, Pilot?' asked Jack.

'This afternoon's mucking about has driven us so far south that at our current speed there's little chance we'll make Malta by first light.'

'I see, thank you, Pilot,' said Jack, glancing across at SS *Callisto*, their charge for the night. 'We'll have to shove the Greek a little harder then.'

'The morning promises to be lively, sir,' said Van Zyl.

'Lively as Hades, with Stuka parades to boot.'

'Your favourite, sir.'

'Aye, Number One.' Ever since losing his ship at Dunkirk, Jack had a particular loathing for the German dive bomber.

With the wind and swell directly from astern, *Gannet* was pitching and yawing uncomfortably, smoke from her funnel adding to the discomposure of those on the bridge. Hendricks made a welcome appearance with a plate of corned-beef sandwiches for the famished officers.

'I thought corned dog was for lunch,' said Fletcher, prodding the stale bread.

'Affirmative, sir, that it is,' said the beaming steward. 'And for breakfast, and tea, and supper.'

Fletcher sighed theatrically and Jack stifled his laughter. A few minutes later, Hendricks returned with bowls of peach slices in syrup. 'Compliments of Porky, hearing of your distress and all, sir,' said the steward. 'They're from the Cape, Wellington to be precise.'

'Jolly good show, nectar of the gods,' said Fletcher, grabbing a bowl. 'Life is once again worth living.'

The sky was a black velvet cloak sprinkled with glitter. *Gannet* zigzagged ahead of her consort, probing the depths with the sonic pulse of her Asdic. An exhausted Jack would not leave the bridge, drinking endless cups of strong coffee and thick, dark kye. He did, however, allow himself to doze in his upright chair. Alana was suddenly there, striding ahead of him up the side of a dune, light-footed in the yellow sand, just out of arm's reach. She turned and smiled, beckoning to him. He looked back to where *Gannet* lay tethered to the bank of the Nile, sailors floating and cavorting in the brown water. Jack quickened his step, but his lover drew further away. He tried to break into a run, but the heavy sand sucked at his feet.

'Alana!' he called out. She didn't look back.

'Alana, please, stop!' he yelled, jerking himself awake and looking around the bridge. Had the lookouts heard him? They continued to scan their quadrants, seemingly undisturbed.

Later that night, enemy aircraft arrived and began dropping flares in an attempt to illuminate targets for unseen bombers whose droning could be heard above the wispy clouds. Back and forth they flew, toying with the sailors' nerves. Then suddenly, a lone Ju-88 swept in at mast height, pouncing on *Callisto*. The Greek went hard a-port as three 500-pounders tumbled from the aircraft's belly before either ship could fire a shot. Two bombs exploded adjacent and one hit amidships, lifting the freighter out of the water as shrapnel peppered the hull. Shuddering from the blows, the Greek slowed to a halt and began taking water.

Jack brought *Gannet* alongside to assess the damage. *Callisto*'s smoking decks looked like a breaker's yard, with her cargo on fire and lifeboats dangling at odd angles. The crew had already begun to spray water into the burning holds, starting with the area closest to the ammunition locker, but the hoses had been riddled with shell splinters and the water came in dribbles and starts. While some sailors tried to mend the leaks, others turned to buckets, forming a chain and tipping water onto the flames below. One team managed to work its way to the ammunition locker and began tossing red-hot shells over the side, suffering terrible burns in the process. At any moment, *Callisto* could go up.

The two near misses had disabled the main engine and dynamos as well as fracturing the steam pipes. In the bowels of the freighter, stokers were trying to dam the steadily rising water and get the pumps going. The third engineer dived beneath the filthy water to unclog a bilge suction and then managed to raise enough steam to work one of the pumps. But it still looked to be a losing battle.

The crew were poised to abandon ship when the Athenian captain had a change of heart. For some minutes, *Callisto* appeared not to have sunk much lower and it seemed possible there might be a chance to get her to Malta. The ship's carpenter took soundings and found that apart from number two hold and the engine room leaks, the rest of the ship was intact.

Jack aimed his loudhailer at the merchant's bridge. 'A tow, perhaps?'

'Yes, *parakaló*, very kind of you, Captain!' came the reply.

Towing would not be easy, but *Callisto* was fortunately the smallest of the convoy's freighters, for *Gannet* was diminutive herself. Jack wondered absently whether ninety hours without proper sleep had impaired his judgement; whether the wiring of his brain had not, perhaps, sustained water damage, for this decision might well have signed both ships' death warrants. Two vessels shackled together and moving at turtle pace would present the most attractive of targets when daylight came.

A heaving line was tossed to *Callisto* and a six-inch manila rope fed through the whaler's stern leads and across the gap. Jack could see little of the operation from the bridge, entrusting the operation to Van Zyl and the bosun. Once the Greeks had fastened the line to their anchor cable, Jack edged *Gannet* ahead at dead slow, making sure he did not foul the tow around his screw. The hawser rose from the sea and went bar taut, shedding spray. *Gannet* stopped dead. Jack ordered more revolutions. The freighter gave a reluctant lurch and began inching forward. Although her engine room was, by now, eight feet under water, at least she could still be steered. To avoid any sudden jerk that might part the tow, Jack and Chief McEwan increased speed by only a few revolutions at a time, until they were wallowing along at four-and-a-half knots in a quartering swell that threatened at any moment to sever the line.

Jack didn't leave the bridge for the rest of the night, keeping a close eye on *Callisto*, rolling uncomfortably about their stern in the dark. He was painfully aware that Malta would still be a distant goal at dawn. Meanwhile his dirty and unshaven gun crews lay beside their weapons all through the pitch darkness of the graveyard watch and towards the dread arrival of first light.

Somewhere in the early hours, Sparks clattered up the ladder to the bridge bearing a flimsy from C-in-C Ras el-Tin. Jack shook himself into full wakefulness, crouched down and switched on a torch, shading it with his hand as he read the signal. More distressing news. The other Malta convoy, Operation Fortress, had been ambushed in the Sicilian Narrows after their main escorts had retired to Gibraltar. Caught by a squadron of Italian cruisers out of Palermo, the lightly protected freighters had been all but decimated and a handful of survivors had turned back in a desperate bid to reach Gibraltar. The few remaining merchantmen of Operation Assegai were now Malta's only hope. Jack scrunched the flimsy into a ball and dropped it to the deck.

The tethered pair made slow progress through the night, increasing revolutions to a respectable six knots, but dawn was about to find them still a very long way from their destination.

The darkness began to ease as the stars slowly dissolved and the sea took on a dull grey cast. Jack's nerves, like block and tackle, registered the heavier strain of the coming day. He wished that some hefty counterweight could be attached to the sun to retard its upward passage. But no, *Callisto*'s outline took firmer shape, then the first colours — pale washes of peach — began to bleed into the eastern sky. With the light came a Cant Z506 Airone floatplane, materialising above the northern horizon and no doubt already homing its charges onto the scattered prey. Spread out over thirty miles, the merchantmen — all of them damaged and forced to reduce speed — had failed to regroup and made perfect individual targets. Jack hoped with all his heart that the RAF would for once put in an early showing.

The sun burst upon the scene, confident and brash in the haze, and with it came Hendricks bearing smoking mugs of coffee. Some men slumped at their posts, staring glassy-eyed at the sky; others continued to doze on the deck. To compound their fatigue, the humidity after the previous day's sirocco left everyone feeling drained and limp. February clung to the spokes of his wheel for support, knowing he might collapse in a disreputable heap if he let go. Jack rolled his shoulders and took a sip of coffee, trying to blink away the sleep that groped hungrily in the shadows of his consciousness.

Just then, keen-eyed Behardien let out a high-pitched yelp: 'Land ho!'

Jack snatched his binoculars … and there, sure enough, upon the vaporous, north-western horizon, sat an uneven grey smudge.

'The VC for that man,' said Jack, eliciting a broad grin from the Bokaap lad.

But the euphoria lasted only a matter of minutes before Malan sang out: 'Enemy aircraft bearing green one-oh, high! Heavy formation.'

Van Zyl lifted his binoculars and, his voice taut with trepidation, said, 'Stukas, sir.'

CHAPTER 11

Jack took a deep breath, closed his eyes for a few seconds, then opened them wide and said hoarsely, 'Sound action stations and hoist red warning flag, Number One.'

The sky ahead of them swarmed with pestilential dots. Eighteen Ju-87s — three flights of six aircraft each — approached from the northwest, accompanied by Me-109 fighters in characteristic four-finger *Schwarm* formation. By the look of it, they'd be concentrating on the most prized target, *Lexington*, lying far ahead of *Gannet* and over to starboard. The tanker's two escorting Hunt destroyers opened fire, joined by her own anti-aircraft guns, filling the sky with brown puffballs.

Jack watched, his body beginning to tremble, his breath coming in shallow pants, as the batlike Stukas peeled off one by one in near-vertical dives. The hollow thudding of gunfire mingled with the tormented screaming of the bombers' Jumo engines. Death merchants, Valkyries. The leading aircraft began to stream black smoke, juddered drunkenly, then blew up in a comet of flames.

Jack banged the rail with his fist and hissed, 'Yes!' His mouth was sandpaper-dry, his heart thudding wildly. His mind was filled with fevered memories of Dunkirk, of howling Stukas and his beloved *Havoc* torn apart in fiery detonations. The images were urgent and visceral, clouding his judgement.

The next gull-winged vixen fell upon the tanker in a murderous dive, steeper and steeper. How could it possibly miss such a big, ponderous target? Three oblong shapes dislodged themselves from the Stuka's belly just before it swooped back into the heavens. The bombs detonated and

Lexington vanished. Jack watched in dread as curtains of falling seawater mixed with high explosive subsided and the tanker slowly emerged, first her prow, then her bridge, followed by the funnel and aft superstructure. Somehow, the bombs had missed.

'Hurricanes!' yelled Malan, pointing to the west as the fighters streaked in.

'And Spitfires above them!' exclaimed Van Zyl.

'About bloody time,' muttered Jack.

The attackers were quickly among the bombers and their escorts, breaking up the formations, two Stukas soon tumbling from the sky in flames. Everywhere Jack looked, aircraft were banking, climbing and diving to the chatter of machine guns and thud of cannons. He watched a Hurricane close to within 200 yards of a diving bomber and open fire. Bright flashes danced across the fuselage and engine. Smoke poured from the Stuka, which failed to pull out, and hit the sea in an eruption of spray. As the Hurricane carved over *Gannet* on her wing tips, Jack noticed the naval camouflage and caught a glimpse of a winged cheetah on the cowling.

'Well, I'll be damned,' he murmured in joyful amazement. 'So, you made it through after all. Well done, you old dog.'

Much higher up, another enemy formation had arrived without being intercepted, the black-painted Italian Stukas — nicknamed woodpeckers — tipping into their attack. Red and white tracer stitched the sky around the leader, tearing off pieces as it came down, before scoring a direct hit.

The next Stuka in line dived from almost directly overhead, through the smoke and haze, its approach too swift and vertical, too hard upon its leader, for the guns to respond properly. Lexington's captain spotted the danger, and frothing turbulence at the tanker's stern confirmed that she was at full speed with the wheel hard over. The 1,000-pound bomb, held in a cradle beneath the aircraft, wobbled free and plummeted towards her. Jack held his breath.

The bomb struck the stern with a terrific detonation, the aft gunners hurled high into the air by the blast. The next Stuka landed another hit, the bomb passing through the boat deck and exploding on the boiler tops. Clouds of white powder from the asbestos lagging choked the engineers who scrambled to escape the boiler room. Flames quickly spread through the hull as *Lexington* slewed to a halt and began to settle. Jack saw tiny figures all about her decks and catwalks fighting the blaze with hoses and chemical extinguishers. Gouts of fire spat from holes in the deck; flaming kerosene bubbled up from broken tanks and poured down her flanks like lava. The Stukas kept coming as bombs rained down around *Lexington*, and still her Bofors and Oerlikons fired while sailors fought the growing conflagration. Jack admired their bravery, but knew the ship was almost certainly doomed.

The tanker's lifeboats had turned into blazing faggots and the sea around her glowed with flaming aviation spirit as men began to jump overboard, aiming for patches of water that were not on fire. The two Hunt destroyers moved in to pick up survivors while still trying to fend off diving Stukas. Approaching the apocalyptic scene, Jack gagged at the stench of roasting flesh, burning oil and smoking ship. The terrified screams of sailors in the water rose above the crackle of advancing flames that turned their heads to devilish kindling, alight upon the sea's placid surface. By now, a pillar of black smoke stood 4,000 feet above the sinking ship, the heat of the fire radiating across the water. *Gannet* and *Callisto* pressed steadily on, leaving the Hunts to their gruesome task.

The island was much closer now and Jack could make out individual buildings, but the Stukas were hungry for more victims, widely scattered as they were across the approaches to Grand Harbour. A newly arrived formation picked on the towing pair for their attention. By now, both ships were dangerously low on ammunition and Jack ordered guns to be fired only at point-blank range and at incoming, not retreating, aircraft.

He looked skyward and watched the line of Italian Stukas tipping into their dives from 10,000 feet, aiming at *Gannet*, their throttles wide open, falling at nearly 400 miles per hour, their wings straining almost to snapping point. The 'Jericho trumpet' sirens that had terrorised so many victims in previous years had been removed to save weight, but such vertical attacks were no less panic-inducing. The screaming in Jack's head was part Stuka, part terror, part hate, and he needed every ounce of willpower to fight his instinct to cower under the onslaught.

Staring the enemy down, Jack tried to judge the bomber's angle of dive and trajectory. With *Callisto* in tow, he had no way of manoeuvring. His head was filled with the quick-fire thudding of pom-poms, the clatter of Lewis guns, and the high-pitched rattle of Oerlikons and Bredas, answered now by the Stuka's machine-guns. The enemy was upon him, a raptor with outstretched wings, an egg uncoupled from its belly, falling and falling. Nowhere to hide.

The aircraft carved out of its dive with a deafening roar and hurtled skyward as the 1,000-pound bomb hit the water on the whaler's port quarter. The sea stood up, forming an instantaneous mountain. *Gannet* shuddered from the blow as shockwaves and white-hot splinters tore into her side and stern. For the crew aft, it felt as though they'd sustained a mortal hit as tons of water deluged the upper deck. *Gannet* groped through the maelstrom, water gushing from her scuppers. But the Stuka had also suffered damage from the whaler's concentrated fire. Smoke billowed from its engine as it limped away, low to the water. Its undercarriage struck a swell and the aircraft bounced, then pancaked in a torrent of spray to ragged cheering from the South African gunners.

Down in the engine room, Chief McEwan was increasingly alarmed by the repeated concussions beating on the ship's flanks, and the torment being heaped upon his beloved engine. He harboured a fatalistic certainty that a bomb would eventually land in their midst. Another deafening crash, and all the lights were snuffed out. McEwan bellowed for a torch as he groped for the master switches that had been thrown out by the violence of the blast.

'Och, I'll need to have a wee word with the old man about this level of abuse,' he muttered under his breath.

Jack stared aloft at the next sky assassin, his mind casting this way and that for a hold on the disintegrating moment. The Stuka was almost upon them, ravenous, diving through a curtain of flak and tracer. *Gannet* lay at the epicentre of this frenzy — this screaming of aero engines and barking of guns, all clawing at Jack's tattered wits. The bomb dislodged itself, aiming straight for his head. This time, his luck had surely found its cul-de-sac.

A sheet of blinding light and a great sucking of air. The eggshell world cracked open, and blackness enveloped him.

Wooden duckboards, a boot, stickiness. Alana and his mother together in a field of green, *Havoc*'s upright stern, her propellers chewing air, unto the ages of ages, world without end. A church bell chiming across a meadow. *Roll up, roll up, come and see…* Jack lifted his groggy head; he was bleeding from somewhere. He sat up slowly, his mind groping for purchase. Captain, Mediterranean, *Gannet.*

Ears ringing, he stood up gingerly and surveyed the damage. The men on the bridge had all been skittled but appeared largely unhurt. The ship's forward end was intact, but a chunk had been taken out of the port side just abaft the funnel. The Breda hung at a drunken angle from the boat deck and its gunner, AB Lister from Port Elizabeth, had been decapitated. His body was draped over the rail, blood pouring from the stump of his neck and leaving a trail down the ship's side.

Steel plates were bent and twisted into improbable shapes; the ship's boat was splintered to braai wood and the smashed Carley float equally useless. Amid the carnage, Pickles remained at his post, tears streaming down his cheeks and blood trickling from wounds in his back as he scanned the sky, ready to parry the next attack. Flames licked the boat deck around him and smoke billowed away on the wind.

'Get extinguishers and hoses onto those bloody flames, *right now*!' croaked Jack.

Chief McEwan reported from below that the steering gear was undamaged and the engine, although stopped, was still serviceable despite steam leaking from a number of joints and the peppered hull spouting myriad leaks, which were being filled with wooden plugs. The largest hole had been stuffed with collision mats, tarpaulin and timber, but water still seeped in. The pumps were managing to hold the water level in the engine room at ten inches below the boiler fires.

'Thank you, Chief. I'm going to jettison paravanes and depth charges to lighten the ship.'

'That will help, sir. And any other extraneous materiel, like some of the lazier louts.'

'Good idea, Chief.'

With *Gannet*'s power much reduced and the pumps only just keeping her afloat, Jack would have to let go of the tow. Fortunately, the Hurricanes had chased away the Stukas, so they might be granted a reprieve.

'Damage report, quick as you can, Number One,' said Jack while Porky bandaged the wound on his captain's head.

Van Zyl hurried from the bridge and made a turn around the ship. There were three dead — AB Lister and two rescued sailors who'd been recovering from their injuries in the PO's mess — and four wounded, including Pickles, who'd got nasty splinters in his back. The large hole in the ship's side was edged with jagged knives of steel and the PO's accommodation had been reduced to a smouldering wreck. The paint on its bulkheads had burst into flame; so too had the bunks, table and benches. The contents of the lockers — clothing, letters, books, precious photographs — had all been incinerated. Van Zyl climbed down into the bosun's store and magazine, which he found to be watertight. The engine room flooding remained a concern, but for the moment the pumps were handling the inflow. The first lieutenant reported his findings to Jack.

Still tethered to one another, *Gannet* and *Callisto* lay dead in the water. Jack was pondering his next move when Behardien solved the problem for him.

'Vessels approaching, sir, fine on the port bow.'

The paddle-wheel naval tug *Hardy*, with the king's harbour master at the con, came splashing out of Grand Harbour to take over the tow. There were none of the usual exchanges of banter and pleasantries between ships, lending the impression that, after two years of siege, Malta was a serious place focused purely on survival.

'*Hardy* looks rather old and shagged out,' said Van Zyl.

'Don't be rude, Number One, but yes, not in her first flush.'

'I was rather hoping for a yacht with Maltese Calypsos draped about her deck.'

'Dream on. You should stop reading that racy Greek stuff.'

Interrupting their banter, the bosun shouted, 'All gone aft, sir!' as he knocked the slip off the tow.

Jack ordered, 'Slow ahead, midships.'

With *Callisto* and the tug sailing astern of them, and the freighter *Kimberley Castle* ahead, the procession was joined by the Malta-based HMS *Rye*, a Bangor-class minesweeper, to lead them up the swept channel. All ships except *Gannet* streamed paravanes and stuck to the centre of the channel, flanked by a minefield to starboard and the Xgħajra shore to port, with little room for manoeuvring if the bombers returned. Down in the engine room, McEwan and his exhausted stokers toiled on, sweating it out in the gloomy space with water rising about their legs, the overheating engine befouling the air and venting clouds of hissing steam.

Up on the bridge, Jack allowed himself a moment to admire the view. Here at last was brave, beleaguered Malta, pale khaki in colour and giving off waves of heat that distorted its contours. He'd read so much about this fabled island that looked, from this vantage point, on this fine summer's morning, just as it must have done to Napoleon and Nelson. On the headland before him stood the bomb-battered defences of Fort Ricasoli and, just across the harbour mouth, the white-gold ramparts of St Elmo, the star-shaped fort that had borne the brunt of the Turkish attack in the Great Siege of 1565. And behind it, the city of Valletta, a masterpiece of sixteenth-century architecture — 'built by gentlemen, for gentlemen'. Jack wondered how much of it remained standing after two years of Axis bombing.

'Fair isle of the lotus eaters,' he murmured.

'Not really, sir,' Van Zyl cut in. 'That would suggest lotus fruit and, by the sound of it, the Maltese are starving.'

'Just my luck to have a Classics know-it-all as Number One.'

The ragtag remnants of Operation Assegai began rounding the breakwater and sailing through the opened boom gate into Grand Harbour. Jack looked down at his men, stripped to the waist, greasy with oil and sweat, tin hats pushed back, their guns still pointing skyward. But on all their young faces, aside from the exhaustion, was something that looked very much like quiet pride. Spitfires wheeled in sweeping figures of eight overhead, their throaty growl lifting Jack's spirits. He took a deep breath: Malta smelt of dust, smoke and desiccation.

Often described as the most beautiful port in the world, Grand Harbour opened like a vast theatre set. Crossing this hallowed patch of water, age-old home to Britain's Mediterranean fleet, was like entering the pages of history. Sloping limestone bastions, built by the Knights of St John, towered on either side. Beyond them stood domes and spires, all in pale shades of cream and sandy yellow. But on closer examination, Jack saw that this was also a shattered place: many buildings lay in ruins, and the harbour basin was dotted with half-sunken hulks and burnt-out ships, some showing only masts and funnels above the water; other wrecks lay beached in Rinella Creek.

To starboard, the Lower Barracca terrace garden and adjacent bastions were crammed with thousands of cheering islanders. Men doffed their hats, women in black hoods and cloaks twirled white handkerchiefs and wept, and young boys excitedly waved the Union Jack, Stars and Stripes and red and white Maltese flag. Citizens thronged every vantage point, lining ramparts and wharves, standing on roofs or climbing the hillocks of rubble that had once been their homes.

A Royal Marine band on the Lower Barracca struck up spirited renditions of 'Rule, Britannia' and 'God Save the King' as the survivors of the convoy sailed by. The night before had been especially brutal, with two merchantmen destroyed by aerial bombardment and one by submarine on the final approach to Malta. Only three battered and charred merchantmen out of ten had made it, and no tanker. Two were low in the water, the pumps barely keeping them afloat; a big hole in *Kimberley* Castle's bows allowed spectators to see right through her. But these surviving merchantmen carried a combined load of 19,000 tons of general cargo and 4,500 tons of military stores, extending the island's target date by a further eight weeks — on very short rations. No one knew better than the Maltese how great had been the sacrifice of these valiant sailors and how precious their cargo. They cheered and cheered until they grew hoarse, and then they cheered some more.

To the onlookers, *Gannet* presented a battered sight, her upper works riddled with shrapnel wounds, her plates blackened and an ugly gash in her side. The ship's company lined the rails as she slowly crossed the calm blue waters, making her way through the inlet. The whaler saluted the flag of the island's second great fortress and Royal Navy headquarters, HMS *St Angelo*, lying to port. Behind it, the three ancient cities of Vittoriosa, Cospicua and Senglea had been pulverised into rubble, but still the massive bastions of Fort St Angelo, hewn in the sixteenth century and rising in tiers from the water's edge, stood defiant — a last symbol of British power in the Mediterranean.

Next, to starboard, came the Upper Barracca Gardens adorned with classical arches, and directly below it, the Saluting Battery with its cannons, from where the island's governor,

Lord Gort, looked down from his lofty vantage point. The crowd grew silent as a lone bugler sounded the 'Still', its haunting call echoing around the basin. Jack felt the heft of the moment welling in his throat. So many ships and men lost for one small victory. These three pockmarked, bullet-holed freighters, with their blistered paintwork and cratered decks, were the pathetic remnant of Operation Assegai, but Jack also knew another convoy would be mustered. And another. And another. That was the promise of these ships.

Gannet passed the narrow Dockyard Creek to port, followed by the fortified peninsula of Senglea, known for its ancient watchtowers carved with eyes and ears to denote their vigilance, but now mostly reduced to mounds of stone. Next came French Creek, where *Kimberley Castle* — reeking of oil and burnt paint and with some of her superstructure still smouldering — was tying up at Parlatorio Wharf. A fire engine on the dock had begun to douse the smoking vessel, while a fire float sidled up to spray her from the other side. Stretcher-bearers and walking wounded filed ashore, where a row of camouflaged ambulances stood waiting. Meanwhile, stevedores and dockyard workers were already swarming about the freighter.

The South African whaler sailed further into the narrowing harbour towards Marsa, crammed with tugs and lighters, many of them wrecked or half sunk, the adjacent warehouses reduced to ruins. Jack looked astern and saw a listing *Callisto* come alongside a pontoon connected to the shore by rows of moored lighters and barges to create makeshift gangways.

Gannet was ordered to secure deep inside the creek at Boat House Wharf. While some of the Hunts also moored in Grand Harbour, most escorts were directed to the adjacent Marsamuscetto Harbour on the northern side of the Valletta peninsula. They were due for hasty refuelling and rearming from the island's meagre store to be ready to set sail for Alexandria after dark that evening. Fortunately, this time they would be able to proceed at maximum speed and think only of their own defence. Given her damage, there would be no such opportunity for *Gannet.*

The whaler ghosted up to the wharf, barely creasing a bow wave. A heaving line arced through the air, then the headrope was hauled ashore and dockyard workers secured it to a bollard, followed by the stern rope and springs until, at last, the welcoming squeak of motor-tyre fenders. As soon as the gangplank was rigged, stretcher-bearers hastened aboard to take off the wounded and a mobile dockside pump coughed into life to empty out the waterlogged engine room.

Van Zyl gave the crossed-hands signal to wrap up the mooring lines, Bunts carefully folded and stowed away his signal flags and Jack called into the brass-bell mouth of the voicepipe: 'Ring off main engine, Chief.'

'Such a charmer, Cap'n, thought you'd never ask,' came the gravelly voice of McEwan.

Stillness and silence at last. So numbed were the crew — and somewhat doolally with fatigue and shock at what they'd endured — that some of them sank to the deck and fell sound asleep. Jack looked around at the haggard, dirty, unshaven faces of the men on the bridge and said, 'Well, gentlemen, against all the odds, it appears as though we might just have made it.'

CHAPTER 12

Given the threat of imminent air attack, there was feverish activity on and about the three merchantmen. Meanwhile, some of the wounded were transported to Bighi, the naval hospital overlooking Grand Harbour, while the rest were sent to the larger, 90th British General Hospital at Imtarfa, set on a ridge in the centre of the island near the ancient citadel of Mdina.

Later that morning, the tannoy crackled into life and everyone on *Gannet* stopped what they were doing. 'This is your captain speaking.' The exhaustion in Jack's voice was palpable. 'I just wanted to take a moment to commend you all on your actions over the past few days. We have been through hellfire and made it safely to Malta, thanks to your courage and resilience. The damage to our ship has been extensive, so we will not be returning to Alexandria with the rest of the escorts. For the time being, this island will be our home. As soon as I have more information, I will convey it to you. I'm sure you are all very keen on a run ashore, but let me remind you that this is a devout Catholic island. Although I know you want to let off some steam, you are all members of the Seaward Defence Force and, as such, you are South African ambassadors. Conduct yourselves accordingly, but do also have some fun. Thank you again, brave Gannets.'

'Let off some steam, hey!' said Booysen.

'I hear The Gut is where all the action is,' said Pickles.

'Even the old man thinks we deserve some fun.'

'Aye, best not let him down then.'

Unloading would take a number of days, but there was to be no repeat of previous convoys, when sluggish discharging had seen ships bombed and sunk at their moorings while still laden with provisions. This time, Maltese stevedores and soldiers of the Cheshire Regiment had been waiting at the berths, and unloading by human chain had begun at pace. Valletta was a port that also employed lighters for unloading, more so with most of the wharves and cranes damaged by bombs, and ships were already discharging some of their cargo into lighters which ferried them the short distance to shore, a cumbersome process offering good targets for enemy aircraft.

It was to be a round-the-clock operation that saw the goods moved speedily to storage dumps and bomb-proof caves around the island, a Maltese policeman travelling in each lorry to prevent theft. Roads adjacent to the harbour had been cleared, animal-drawn traffic prohibited and special routes demarcated with coloured arrows by day and hooded lamps by night.

The enemy had made its own preparations and bombers were soon picked up on the island's radar, approaching from Sicily like vultures homing in on a kill. A bugle call sounded from Fort St Angelo, air-raid sirens wailed across the city and a red warning flag jerked up the mast atop army headquarters at Auberge de Castille, the highest point in Valletta, repeated on towers throughout the city. Sparks tuned his wireless set to Malta's fighter-direction wavelength and broadcast the unfolding action over the intercom so the crew could follow the dogfighting.

Everywhere Jack looked, people were streaming towards the city's various shelters — bunkers cut from the limestone, the old railway tunnel or the many catacombs and caves beneath the bastions. In recent months, the residents of Malta had been reduced to a troglodyte existence, spending up to twenty hours below ground on a bad day. Those who risked remaining in their homes at night slept fitfully, ever alert for the wail of sirens, the dreaded drone of aero engines.

Jack watched from *Gannet*'s bridge as some dockworkers scurried into nearby rock tunnels, while others took a chance and slipped behind the steel plates stacked beside a workshop. From every vantage point, gun barrels were aimed at the sky. Even the heavy artillery of the forts — useless against high-level aircraft — were raised to disrupt bombers at the bottom of their dives. Grand Harbour was also lined with chemical dischargers that began to pump out fumes to shroud the port with a foul-smelling smokescreen and hopefully compel the enemy to bomb blind.

Jack tracked the rows of oncoming foe. The first wave comprised high-flying Fiat BR20 Cicogna bombers, silvery specks against the blue, the ack-ack following their progress with staccato cracks and cotton-wool bursts. He saw an Italian take a direct hit from one of the 3.7-inch coastal guns and explode in a glittering shower that rained down on the sea.

The bombing of the first wave was wildly inaccurate, but the second was German and comprised shallow-diving Ju-88s, followed by steep-diving Stukas. High above them were flights of protecting fighters: Me-109s accompanied by Fiat G50 Freccias and Macchi C202 Folgores. A desperately small number of Spitfires and Hurricanes rose to confront the massed enemy ranks.

The city's barrage released a thunderous cone of steel directly above Grand Harbour, denser than anything Jack had ever witnessed, so loud and terrible it cowed the senses. The basin was transformed into a cauldron of fire and smoke. *Gannet*'s gunners joined in with the other ships, the clamour echoing around the limestone bastions until the ancient city shuddered as shrapnel splinters, nose caps and spent bullets clattered down upon the roofs like hail.

A line of Ju-88s dived through the box barrage, their engines howling. Bombs fell and the city shook to their brutal handling as flocks of pigeons took to the air, their grey wings beating a panicked tattoo. All around was the terrible crumping of detonations, shockwaves passing through the streets with hurricane breath, and the rumble of falling masonry.

Jack ducked as a bomb fell close to *Gannet*, turning turquoise water into an upthrust tower of muck and spume. Another bomb hit the base of a crane, which toppled onto the wharf with a reverberating crash. One Stuka dropped a stick of five bombs so lightly fused they exploded on the surface of the water, riddling everything in the vicinity with shrapnel and turning a moored launch into a colander.

By now, Allied fighters had got among the incoming bombers, disrupting their runs. Through the drifting fumes and smoke, Jack watched a Hurricane follow a Stuka in its headlong plunge, flak exploding about the pair, tracer pouring past them. The fighter caught up with the bomber just as it released its payload and hosed the fuselage with accurate fire. The German wobbled, lifting its nose over the ramparts of Fort St Elmo, then flipped onto its back and dived into the sea to wild cheering from the bastions' gunners.

During a brief lull in the bombing, Sparks appeared on the bridge with a flimsy. 'Signal, sir.'

Jack read the slip of paper: *Welcome to Malta. Lieutenant Pembroke to report 1400, Naval HQ, St Angelo. NOIC.*

Gannet's captain went below for a hasty wash while Hendricks gave his best tropical uniform an iron and his shoes a lick of Blanco white. Jack lathered his face with a brush and began to shave. Then he stopped, razor in mid-stroke, and stared, incredulous at his reflection in the mirror. His face looked much older, haggard and darkly tanned with rough, four-day-old stubble, bloodshot eyes edged with crow's feet and lashes crisped with salt, chapped lips, a peeling nose and the Dunkirk scar on his temple almost purple. When he'd finished shaving, he unpeeled the bandage from his head and inspected the wound: thankfully, it looked like a quick healer.

Having changed into a clean white shirt and shorts, with white shoes and stockings, Jack donned his cap and climbed the gangplank. Stepping ashore, he tested his leg, feeling a tweak as the old wound made itself known.

'Sir, sir, down here!' came a thickly accented Maltese voice from below the rim of the dock. 'Dghaisa for St Angelo, three shillings?'

Jack peered over the edge and saw a graceful red rowing boat, almost like a Venetian gondola, with a high stem and sternpost.

'Water taxi, Kaptan,' said a man with a straw hat standing amidships and beckoning to him.

'What about the bombing?'

'The enemy, he is having his lunch, maybe a leetle siesta too — no bombing for a while.'

'I see. Well then, yes, thank you. I only have piastres and South African pounds.'

'*Mela*, any money, I take.'

'Jolly good.' Jack climbed down a flight of stone stairs to a small pontoon, stepped aboard and took a seat at the stern. The man cast off and, with his back to Jack, began rowing across the harbour, plying the oars from a standing position, his muscular arms dipping the blades to an easy rhythm.

'A rough passage, Kaptan?' he said, glancing over his shoulder.

'Yes, we did get knocked about a bit.'

He stopped rowing and turned to look at Jack. 'In our hearts, we are very grateful. All of us.'

'Thank you.'

The oarsman picked up his stroke again.

'Why do you stand and push your oars instead of sitting and pulling like we do?'

'Ah, sir, as you can see, we have lots of traffic in Grand Harbour. Better to have your eyes facing front, no?'

'Aye, good point.'

Passing Senglea, Jack was able to take a closer look at the damage. Almost every building had been hit, some reduced to a single wall or box balcony standing over a pile of limestone debris. As they glided past the devastation, the oarsman began to sing a Puccini aria that filled Jack with emotions he could not rightly place.

The man was still crooning '*O mio babbino caro*' as they turned into Dockyard Creek and came alongside. Jack nodded his thanks and stepped ashore on a stone landing beneath the towering battlements of Fort St Angelo.

'Lieutenant Pembroke, HMSAS *Southern Gannet*?' enquired a portly leading seaman from the top of the steps.

'Aye, Killick, that's me.'

'This way please, sah.'

Jack was led past a sandbagged entrance, up a stone ramp and through a forbidding portcullis. The fortress had been Grand Master De la Valette's headquarters during the Great Siege and Jack keenly felt the history of the place as they proceeded down flights of stairs, past an underground bunker and along a passage cut from limestone, intermittently lit by lightbulbs trailing loops of wire.

'Carved by the Knights of St John and safe from the bombing, sah,' said the wheezing killick.

They came to a steel door and the leading seaman knocked, then ushered Jack into an office. A bald, red-faced and heavy-jowled officer sat behind a desk piled with dockets.

'Ah, Pembroke, you're late,' said Commodore Huffington-Smythe, raising a pair of bushy eyebrows. 'Grab a perch.'

'Thank you, sir.'

Through narrowed eyes, the commodore took a moment to size up the lieutenant with the wavy gold stripes of the RNVR — hostilities-only 'amateurs' — on his shoulders: a poorly ironed uniform and patchy shave. The young man before him looked properly fagged out and seemed to be holding his body as if carrying a wound. He had a drawn face with a stiff jaw and a livid scar on his temple, but the ladies would like that. Yes, probably handsome, in a clichéd sort of way. The son of a British admiral on a South African ship: it was certainly something out of the ordinary. He was prepared to let the lieutenant's slovenly appearance pass … this time.

'You'll be reporting to me while you're in Malta. I believe *Southern Gannet* was mauled on the way in.'

'Yes, sir. Considerable bomb damage and taking on water. She needs urgent repairs.'

'I see. Drydocking?'

'Affirmative, sir.'

'Very well, I will make the necessaries. We can billet your men at the naval barracks while she's on the hard, but you'll have to leave some shipkeepers on board. You and your officers can be accommodated here at St Angelo.'

'Thank you, sir.'

After a brief discussion about repairs and harbour procedures, the commodore said abruptly, 'Right, then, I have to get back to the war. The killick will show you to your quarters.'

'I'd like to remain onboard with my men until we drydock, sir,' said Jack.

'Very well, carry on.'

The leading seaman led him back up towards the light, pointing out aspects of the fort as they went. To Jack, St Angelo felt a bit like a stone battleship with its moat, artillery, cisterns, food stores, chapel and messes. The pair emerged onto a terrace atop one of the battlements, then passed through a doorway and down a corridor. Jack's cabin looked like a cell, simple and monastic with limewash walls and a small, barred window overlooking Grand Harbour. There was a narrow single bed and a desk: it was all he required.

'Before I leave you, let me show you the wardroom, sah,' said the killick.

Later, gin and tonic in hand, Jack sat reading the latest *Times of Malta* in a comfy leather chair beside a grand fireplace that he could hardly imagine ever being required. Van Zyl had everything in hand on *Gannet* and Jack felt he deserved some quiet time to himself and then, perhaps, a siesta. He'd only just glanced at the headlines when a familiar figure appeared in the wardroom doorway, angelically silhouetted by the limestone's reflected light.

'There you are, Jack old sock! Thought I might find you hiding out up here.'

'Grayson Douglas, our very own Houdini! How glad I am to see you. Would you like a G and T?'

'Is water wet? Yes, please.'

Once they'd settled in adjacent armchairs, the two officers told their respective tales of reaching Malta.

'I'm based at Takali Airfield in the middle of the island and the tempo of fighting is simply incredible,' said Douglas. 'Makes the Battle of Britain look like a slow five-day game with plenty of rain delays. We have to scramble many times a day and we're never short of targets, to put it mildly. Although things are bally tough, morale is sky-high. The flying here is also quite different, with the heat doing astonishing things to the air. You might suddenly hit extreme turbulence just as you're coming in to land and your bird gets tossed all over the shop.'

'How are you faring against enemy fighters?' Jack asked.

'Well, Sea Hurricane IBs like mine are no match for the latest 109s or Macchi Folgores. Ours are 1930s aircraft up against the most advanced Axis technology. Some of their fighters are a hundred miles an hour faster than mine. I really, really need to get myself a Spitfire.'

'Any chance?'

'Not while my Hurribird is still in decent nick.'

'And how do you rate their bombers?'

'The Italians not so much, but the Germans are first eleven. I've got bags of respect for the Ju-88: rugged, well armoured, fast, and it carries a heavy load. Malta's RDF can detect them while they're forming up over Sicily, and Fighter Control usually scrambles us in good time. We try to gain height early, Hurricanes at 15,000 feet and the Spitfires above us at 25,000 feet. It's our job to mix it with the bombers, while the Spits fend off enemy fighters. My section flies almost line abreast, each pilot watching the others' tails.'

'A bit like a Luftwaffe *Schwarm* formation?'

'Yeah, similar. If we can scratch together enough planes, there'll be three flights: red, white and blue. It's really important to have speed and height when we hit the bombers. I've had to learn bloody fast. Dogfighting here is so different to Britain or what I got used to on banana boats. The conditions are unique, our numbers so few and the enemy so damn plentiful. We are *always* outnumbered. But our brand-new AOC, Air Vice Marshal Park, is a real go-getter —'

'*The* Keith Park, of Battle of Britain fame?'

'The very one, just transferred to Malta. He wants us to be much more aggressive, intercept the enemy long before they reach the island, force them to jettison their bombs or at least break up the formations. We attack head-on and get in a few squirts as we pass through them. In a flash, the bombers' boyfriends dive down on us, Spits on their tails, and it becomes a twisting, turning frenzy. You quickly lose your wingman in the melee as you keep trying to take a pot at the bombers, constantly looking over your shoulder for 109s and Macchis. All too soon, you run out of popcorn and corkscrew away, down to the deck and back to the drome, refuel, rearm and get ready for another round.'

'Rather you than me. Your nerves must be shot.'

'I suppose they are, a bit. The ack-ack over Grand Harbour is just stupendous and the gunners usually do a good job of recognising friend from foe, but not always. Sometimes we follow the bombers into the barrage — strictly illegal, of course, bursts of flak all around us — but not nearly as scary as having a 109 on your tail.'

'The whole show seems like history repeating itself: Malta's gladiators facing impossible odds,' said Jack. 'Do you know much about the Great Siege? Fascinating stuff.'

'Not a lot, but there are definite similarities, as every josie from toddler to granny will tell you. Just like the Knights of St John, who hailed from all over Europe, the RAF has pilots from all over Europe and the Commonwealth.'

'A small, courageous band against a murderous horde?'

'You get the picture. It certainly makes good copy in the newspapers.'

Their conversation was interrupted when a steward turned up the volume on the Rediffusion and a hush settled over the handful of officers in the wardroom. It was the sombre voice of Lord Gort: 'As most of you know, a convoy arrived this morning, bringing much needed sustenance to our island. Through the mercy of Providence and the courage of our seafarers, this fair isle has been given succour in its hour of need. The people of Malta and its garrison have endured great privation with fortitude and an abiding faith in the justice of our cause. We shall not waver in our resolve to see this through to the end … to victory.

'Although these merchantmen offer us some reprieve, it is with a heavy heart that I must tell you that most of the ships did not get through and that we will have to tighten our belts even more, for there is no telling when another convoy can be arranged. But let us remember that the most glorious sieges in history have always meant hardship, and without hardship there would be little glory. We have received some 20,000 tons of stores from the ships that have arrived. It is a help, but a very small part of what we had hoped for. I cannot tell you the new Target Date, for we do not want the enemy to know this, but I can tell you that the convoy has bought us more time, until another convoy can fight its way through.

'Our island goes forward, determined to justify his Majesty's continued confidence in the fortitude of the people of Malta to resist all attacks by the enemy and to never betray the great trust of being the Empire's sentinel in the Mediterranean, a bulwark of Christianity since the days of St Paul. Let us remember that on Valletta's famed Mount Sceberras stands an image of Christ the King, surrounded on all sides by bomb craters and demolished buildings. It remains unscathed after the most intense and prolonged air bombardment in the history of the world. Trusting in Him, and guided by Him, we shall surely pass out of the darkness and into the light. I thank you and may God bless you all.'

'And if the next convoy fails…' muttered Jack.

'Lord Gort believes in taking the islanders into his confidence.'

'Risky but admirable, I suppose.'

'It all boils down to flour and fuel,' said Douglas. 'Having lost the tanker, things are going to get a lot worse before they get better. Like all sieges in history, it might be decided by bread.'

Air-raid sirens began to wail across the city and the two officers stepped out onto the terrace.

'They're gathering for the afternoon session,' said Douglas. 'Have a gander at the flag signals on St Angelo's mast: white means fighters, red means bombers. Work generally carries on until it's red, otherwise everyone would be constantly trekking back and forth to the shelters. In Grand Harbour, they usually take cover only if the dockyard hooter sounds.'

The pair remained on the terrace as the raid developed. The canisters on the wharves began to pump out thick grey fumes that drifted up to them, bearing a pungent, sunflower smell.

'Those chaps working the smokescreen are from your neck of the woods — the Basuto Pioneer Regiment.'

'They're a long, long way from home.'

'Like all of us.'

'Do you miss Canada?'

'I do, especially my wife, Sally.'

The low rumble of aero engines was punctuated by the faraway thumping of coastal ack-ack. Jack and Douglas watched as a paltry few Spitfires and Hurricanes rose to meet the oncoming ranks. Now the Royal Marine gunners of St Angelo opened up, adding their Bofors' metal to the box barrage filling the air above Grand Harbour.

'It's mesmerising!' shouted Jack, fingers in his ears. 'Like Hell's orchestra.'

'I know, but there's an old Maltese saying: "Whoever spits at the sky, it comes back in his face." So we'd best get below decks, unless you want another headwound.'

There were two more raids that afternoon, but at sunset the guns fell silent and Jack took a dghaisa back to *Gannet*. He loved the first night in port after a long voyage: water breathing against the ship's side, the creaking of mooring lines and all the familiar shipboard sounds of dynamos humming, Morse bleating, gramophones tinnily playing and, given *Gannet*'s injuries, the ever-present throbbing of the pumps. How he hoped the enemy would grant them a night-time reprieve.

Echoing across the water came the clanging and shouting of the stevedores, going about their round-the-clock unloading. Jack lay on top of his cot, reading a book about the Great Siege, a whisky in one hand and Fido recumbent against his flank, quietly licking a paw. He'd considered donning his striped pyjamas but knew it was tempting fate and would doubtless precipitate an immediate raid. Only barely conscious of the words on the page, he was thinking about the mask of competence and resolve he was compelled to wear, as much for himself as for his men. How he wished he could sometimes let it fall and surrender to the feelings he had to keep battened down. How he longed to slip into Alana's understanding arms and forget, forget, forget.

It was not long before the sirens began their mournful keening. Jack gently replaced himself with a pillow so as not to inconvenience Fido and made his way to the bridge.

'All guns closed up, hoses run out and sand buckets filled,' said Van Zyl.

'Very good, Number One. Hard hats on, then.'

The harbour gunners were at their stations, watching and waiting, barrels probing the sky like pikes. Jack watched the searchlights coming on, their cold white beams raking the night, followed by the first firework patter of flak, then the first tracer, like fireflies rising in single file, reaching up to the heavens, then the crump of bombs falling to the north on Sliema and Marsamuscetto Harbour.

'"The isle is full of noises … a thousand twangling instruments,"' Jack recited.

'The Bard, sir?' asked Van Zyl.

'Aye, *The Tempest*.'

'I thought so. We did it in Standard Nine.'

Grand Harbour's deafening defence filled every corner of the night, taken up by the ships, the noise echoing back and forth between the ramparts. A parachute mine drifted to earth like a ghostly interloper. Red tracer reached up, groping for the drum-shaped object, as small-calibre guns joined in. It landed in the middle of Valletta to an almighty explosion that flattened a city block and sent a huge fireball roiling into the sky.

A searchlight snagged one of the bombers, then another blue-white blade locked onto the target, then another, forming a great cone of light. Bofors barked and tracer rose in red streams, but the aircraft jinked and dived back into darkness, leaving the beams to grope at empty sky. Another silvery bomber was snared and winged, one of its engines flaring orange as it flipped onto its back and careened like a shooting star towards the sea. There were joyful cries from the gunners, taken up by cheers from unseen figures in doorways, some bravely emerging onto roofs, the sound of their delight lifting the hair on Jack's arms.

It was a brief attack and the 'raiders passed' siren soon rang out, followed by a hollow silence that settled over the harbour. Jack returned to his cabin, opened his desk drawer and took out the White Horse: another dose of golden liquid to calm his jangling nerves. He slid a Cavalla from its tin, lit up with trembling fingers and took a long drag. After five days without proper sleep, he knew that, despite his galloping mind, at least this night, bombers willing and with the whisky's benediction, he would sleep the sleep of the dead.

CHAPTER 13

Next morning, preparations were made for drydocking and an oil barge came alongside, sending hoses across to pump out *Gannet*'s fuel. Meanwhile, the crew set about ensuring everything movable was stowed and locked away or moved ashore for safekeeping. They knew from past experience, both in Simonstown and Alexandria, that where dockyard mateys were involved, just about any item could grow legs.

Later, a Malta pilot boarded the whaler to guide her into Number One Dock and make sure she was sitting properly on the blocks as the water was pumped out. Jack, Van Zyl and the Chief climbed down a steel ladder into the damp pit to examine *Gannet*'s wounds, which amounted to some nasty gashes under the bunkers and a number of splits in the plating.

'Blimey,' said the Chief, 'it's a wonder the old girl isn't resting on the bed o' the Med.'

'A wonder indeed,' said Jack. 'I'm afraid we might be stuck in Malta for quite a bit longer.'

'Bright lights, fine dining, golden beaches, pretty girls,' muttered Van Zyl.

'Dream on, Number One.'

A posse of engineers arrived and corroborated the sailors' initial assessment. Patching was needed below the waterline and, given the number of blows it had received from near misses, the keel would have to be strengthened. Due to the frequency of air raids, which severely hampered dockyard work, *Gannet* could expect a lengthy spell in drydock.

Apart from a couple of watchkeepers, the crew relocated to the RN barracks. Her officers moved to HMS *St Angelo*, their cabins close to Jack's on a top tier of the fortress, which made for an arduous trek down to the bunkers during air raids, especially in the early hours of the morning. Once settled into their new accommodations, the men of *Gannet* looked forward to substantial liberty and the opportunity to sample the somewhat meagre delights of Valletta. That evening, clad in their best shore-going rig, they headed through an ornate city gate and up a steep street into the heart of the old town, accosted at every turn by islanders who wanted to shake their hands and mobbed by exuberant children shouting, 'Convoy! Convoy!'

Jack remained at St Angelo to catch up on paperwork while his three officers made their way to Marich's for eggnogs, before proceeding to an exclusive club that served a wide selection of Pimm's, each of which had to be sampled, or so insisted Fletcher, and he was paying. Next, they headed to the Union Club on Kingsway for a late-night snack before indulging in horse and cart races, tearing around Valletta to the consternation of the long-suffering, but handsomely remunerated drivers.

Dressed smartly in their fore-and-aft rig, *Gannet*'s three petty officers — February, Combrink and Cummins — went ashore in search of a decent restaurant. They asked a local man, who looked at them curiously, explaining that just about every restaurant was closed due to rationing. When he saw the POs' disappointment, he took pity and invited them to his family's bomb shelter, carved from the rock below Floriana. The South Africans joined the group for a simple meal by lamplight. When leaving, February asked to borrow a pillowcase, which he promised to return the following day at the same time and place they'd met. The man duly returned the next evening and was handed a pillowcase containing a large gammon of bacon, liberated from Porky's stash.

Every sailor in the convoy had received complimentary tickets to the Manoel Theatre and local cinemas, but on their first sortie into town, most of them headed directly to Strait Street, also known as The Gut — a long, narrow lane hemmed by tall buildings that appeared to lean inwards, closing out the sky. Notorious for haunts such as Captain Caruana's Bar, Maxim's, Cinderella and Auntie's, The Gut's raucous nightlife was tolerated by the authorities, but stood in the starkest contrast to the strict Catholicism of the rest of the island. It was on this street that the Knights of Malta had once fought their duels, and fighting was still popular but of a more chaotic, gunwales-under ilk.

Whenever a convoy was in port, The Gut's cafés, bars and bordellos were crammed to bursting, and although most escort ships had already set sail and many establishments had suffered bomb damage, the lane was nonetheless heaving with custom. In its clubs and dens just about anything was tolerated: red-lipped, fake-bosomed men in dresses, boys of ill repute, girls demanding a sherry the moment a sailor entered, and then a whole lot more than sherry.

Women sat on steps and in entrances, beckoning to passersby. Young boys called from doorways: 'Come in Royal Navy, big eats! We love you Navy, good cheap drink. Nice girls make love to you.' A pod of Gannets found a tavern that wasn't too crowded, although it did reek of stale alcohol and cigarette funk, its low ceiling stained black from the candles. They sat at trestle tables, singing old favourites such as 'Sarie Marais' and 'It's a Long Way to Tipperary' to the background noise of vomiting and brawls in the lane.

To relieve the strain of recent days, every Gannet knew the best medication was alcohol, and lots of it. Given that Malta's breweries had stopped production, a bottle of Cisk cost an eyewatering ten shillings, so beer was supplemented by the cheaper Amtout, a rough red wine known variously as 'jungle juice', 'screech' and the 'red infuriator'. The more they drank, the more they thawed and the jagged edges slowly wore themselves smooth. They were in the bosom of their shipmates and could, for a little while, forget. And if nothing else, The Gut was a place of forgetting.

Some Gannets drank until they were legless; others acquired female companions who sat on their laps, laughed at their jokes and helped them spend their money. A few became animated and tetchy, while others grew docile and glassy-eyed. Many sailors found they were unable to hold a glass or bottle without trembling, and downed the contents quickly instead. In one way or another, all of them were suffering from the aftershock of the convoy, as though experiencing the calm after a violent hurricane, and were trying to find ways of stopping the terrible moving pictures in their heads.

'Get your grubby paws off me tits!' came an indignant yelp, followed by the sound of breaking glass. The situation grew uncomfortable when Greek sailors off *Callisto* began throwing chairs at a group of taunting Maltese gunners. At the shrill sound of military police whistles, the Gannets exited by way of the windows, mere seconds before the Red Caps burst into the bar, wielding their batons.

Strait Street was also known for its jazz — local musicians having learnt to emulate the songs of popular records brought from the United States — and the South Africans next went looking for a nightclub. They came to a doorway that oozed melodic strains and stepped inside to find a scantily clad cabaret singer draped from a microphone stand while a drummer teased the skin of his instrument with wire brushes, joined every now and then by a warbling saxophonist in an ill-fitting suit. The singer's makeup ran messily in the heat as she wailed and crooned, twirling a feather boa about her not inconsiderable frame while stroking the microphone with bejewelled fingers. A handful of couples, propping each other up more than dancing, manoeuvred their way around a sailor who had passed out on the tiny dancefloor.

As the evening drew to a close, most South Africans headed back to the barracks, while a few joined the queue outside a knocking shop. Business was brisk in the dimly lit rooms, and the Gannets who partook were encouraged to be quick about their business. 'No need to take off yer shoes, luv, nor yer trousers.' A lined face with smudged lipstick, putty thighs, a bushy triangle and a quick set of gyrations barely registered through thick Durex. A shuddering release, then a hasty buttoning up and the cry, 'Next one!' in a throaty bellow that sounded uncannily like the bosun.

In the morning, Van Zyl was called to retrieve three Gannets from the rattle. Bruised and reeking of alcohol and vomit, the trio made a pitiful sight as they were led back to the barracks by a longsuffering Number One, where they were added to a growing list of captain's defaulters: drunk and fighting, drunk and disorderly, drunk and malicious damage to property, drunk and indecent, or just common-or-garden drunk. A room was found in St Angelo for the proceedings, with each charge loudly intoned by February: 'Palmer, Able Seaman. Drunk and urinating in a telephone booth, upon himself and other personages.'

'Anything to say for yourself, AB?' asked Jack.

'No, sir. I don't have an exact and proper recollection of the incident. Not one I would readily put my name to, so to speak, sir.'

And so it went. Fortunately, there was nothing serious for Jack to worry about; just the usual haymaking after a bad run at sea.

After parting ways with his fellow officers the previous evening, Sub-lieutenant Fletcher had also indulged in a heavy night on the town. It had involved a spot of gambling, a lot more drinking, and some customary womanising at an establishment that catered for the well-heeled gent, especially those with alternative tastes, for Fletcher was *Gannet*'s Casanova with a prodigious appetite for the fairer sex. His exploits in Alexandria and Beirut had been the talk of the wardroom, and Jack always marvelled at how many scented and lipstick-embossed letters his rakish gunnery officer received.

Fortunately, Fletcher had the next day at liberty and woke very late in his St Angelo cabin with a pile-driving headache. After lunch, he took a dghaisa to Valletta for a stroll along Quarry Wharf to try to clear his head. Ambling along the esplanade, admiring the harbour view, he noticed a young Maltese woman in a black, knee-length dress and wide-brimmed straw hat approaching from the opposite direction. Drawing closer, he saw that she was a creature of unique loveliness, the like of which he'd never encountered before. Although such happenstance was an almost daily occurrence, this time he felt a strange, lightheaded queasiness that was more than just his hangover and more than much of what he'd ever felt before. As she drew level, he became convinced that the apparition before him was an incomparable paragon of beauty.

The young woman had also noticed the tall, blond officer with the dancing eyes and sensual mouth — a handsome young man in tropical whites that were perhaps not ironed too well, but that did not matter. It was fortuitous that she was wearing her prettiest work dress, one that showed off her figure to the best advantage.

As luck would further have it, a gust of wind plucked the sunhat from her head, perhaps marginally helped by the tilting of it, and sent it fluttering to the water below. Fletcher knew destiny when he saw it and, without a word or further thought, yanked off his cap, shoes and stockings, and dived in to mild protestations from the young woman.

Hat retrieved, he climbed a set of stone steps and re-emerged on the esplanade, where he stood before her, hat in hand, as though lifted godlike from the sea. A little bit oily and smelly was that sea, being the middle of a working harbour, but that too did not matter.

'Your hat,' he said in a voice betraying an uncharacteristic quaver.

'It is, *grazzi*.'

'I think it's a bit buggered.'

'I'm sorry?'

'No, no, apologies… I mean sopping. Damaged. Holed below the waterline.'

'Sorry?'

'Gosh, tongue-tied. Most irregular. I … I…'

'So unnecessary of you. It's an old hat, but thank you ever so much.'

'My pleasure,' he said, unable to take his eyes off her face. He thrust out a wet hand. 'Tom Fletcher, how do you do?'

'How do you do?' she replied with an enigmatic smile. 'My name is Martina and you are a sub-lieutenant, RNVR, off one of the escorts, probably HMSAS *Southern Gannet.*'

'Oh, golly, you know your stuff.' He sounded a little crestfallen.

Martina Zammit was nineteen years old, olive-complexioned with a delicate frame and full breasts, a petite chin, large brown eyes and a full, sensuous mouth that naturally curled up at the corners to match her witty sense of humour.

'In my work, I come into contact with lots of officers.'

'What work is it that you do?'

'I would have to shoot you.'

'Oh, my word.' He laughed cautiously.

'And now, I need to return to work. Goodbye, Tom.'

Somewhat taken aback, he watched her turn and start climbing a flight of limestone steps towards the Saluting Battery.

'Martina, please, wait a moment, if you will?' He took a few paces forward, then stopped. 'May I see you again?'

'Why? We have only just met and you know nothing about me, other than that I would be prepared, at the drop of a hat, to shoot you.'

'The drop of a hat. Oh, I say, that's jolly good.'

She looked deep into Fletcher's eyes but said nothing.

'I … I…' What the Dickens had come over him? He was supposed to be a smooth, debonair man about town. This was preposterous. 'I… Gosh, you are just so overwhelmingly lovely! It would mean…'

'Yes?'

'It would mean —'

‘All right, Tom, if you insist.’ Her smile was irresistible.

‘Smashing! How do I find you?’

‘My family is in the telephone book. Rodney Zammit is my father’s name, and we live in Sliema. But you’d better not call the house. I doubt my parents would approve of us meeting. Better to ring me at War HQ.’

‘Oh, I say, in the ramparts?’

‘Yes, that’s where I work, in the bunkers beneath the Upper Barracca.’

‘Good grief.’

‘Now, Tom, I must hurry back. I only get a very short break for lunch. Thank you for rescuing my *Titanic* hat.’

CHAPTER 14

Sandflies and mosquitoes plagued Jack intermittently throughout the night, accompanied by their larger Axis companions that sent him down to St Angelo's bunkers for a few uncomfortable hours. At sunrise, the drone of mosquitoes mercifully died away and he fell into a deep sleep. Harbour noises eventually woke him and he climbed stiffly out of bed, drawing open the blackout curtains. Laid out below was the sweep of Grand Harbour and, just across the narrow tract of water, the bastions of Valletta gilded by benevolent early light. The vista always lifted his spirits, no matter the severity of the night's raids or his recurring nightmares.

Gazing at the limestone battlements, Jack thought of how, among other things, they spoke of millennia of death, untold billions of crustaceans having perished to form this living rock, tinted with Sahara sand carried by the sirocco across the Mediterranean. Its pale-yellow colour gave the ramparts a warmth akin to the Cotswold sandstone he knew and loved from Oxford. But his appreciative eye also took in the bold fortress architecture with its scarps and counterscarps, embrasures and parapets, encircling the harbour like an amphitheatre. So different to the low-slung port of Alexandria, where perimeter walls and gates excluded prying eyes. Here, everything was on show, each arriving ship subject to an audience and the possibility of fanfare.

Directly opposite, high on Valletta's summit, stood Auberge de Castille — headquarters of the British Army in Malta. Over to the left lay the shattered dockyard with its broken buildings and warehouses; to the right was the Lower Barracca and Fort

St Elmo. His gaze also took in the bustle of port life: picket boats with glinting brasswork puttering across the creek; a red-and-green Gozo boat loaded with fruit and vegetables for the hungry city chugging around the breakwater; colourful dghaisas everywhere playing taxi, the erect bodies of their oarsmen moving rhythmically to the splash and heave of their blades.

A steward arrived with coffee and Jack took a seat at his desk, which offered a partial view of the harbour. Avoiding the mound of paperwork, he mused instead on the dramatic episodes of the Great Siege, trying to match events to the locations within the ambit of his view. To protect the harbour, the knights had strung a heavy boom that could be raised or lowered across the mouth of Dockyard Creek. Forged in Venice, the hefty chain was more than 200 yards long. At the beginning of the siege, the knights' galleys took shelter in the creek and a thousand slaves employed a huge capstan to raise the chain to the surface and secure it to pontoons and rafts, creating a floating wall that the Turkish ships could not penetrate. *Just like today's dome of iron formed by the anti-aircraft barrage*, thought Jack.

Anticipating the Ottoman siege, the island's defences had been reinforced, its granaries and water cisterns filled, livestock brought in, fields stripped bare of crops and the wells poisoned. Nearly four centuries later, although the beleaguered island faced a different aggressor, there was some comfort in the knowledge that the Maltese had walked this path before — as had the British.

After breakfast in the wardroom, Jack went to inspect the progress on *Gannet*. Walking past the bustling wharves, he noticed the exhaustion on the faces of the dockyard workers and stevedores who moved about lethargically, scant rations having reduced them to automatons as they went about the unloading and repair work. When he got to the drydock, Jack peered into the long, tiered pit, his ship looking like a toy resting ever so precariously on high heels. He descended a ladder to watch Maltese workmen removing a piece of his beloved home with acetylene cutters amid fountains of sparks. After receiving an update from a foreman in filthy overalls, he climbed out of the hole and hailed a dghaisa, intent on having a few hours to himself while visiting Valletta's sights.

Stepping ashore at the foot of Capuchin Bastion, he took the stairs to the old town and wandered the bomb-ravaged streets, guidebook in hand. A few horse-drawn *karozzins* still offered a taxi service, but the animals showed their ribs and the drivers looked equally worn. Here was the famed city described by Sir Walter Scott as 'quite like a dream' — now mostly in ruins. He came to the remains of the Royal Opera House, once considered the finest building in Valletta, now utterly wrecked with only a few columns and arches left standing. Jack shook his head and walked on.

He passed a row of pots and saucepans lined up on the pavement outside a Victory Kitchen, each container representing a local avoiding the heat but keeping a place in the food queue. A chalkboard announced today's rations: a bowl of *minestra* vegetable soup cost 3d or *kawlata* meat soup cost 6d. Jack had heard that salt was currently in such short supply that Victory meals were being boiled in seawater.

Heading deeper into the city, he encountered off-duty Gannets, who saluted and greeted him with a smile. They too were exploring Valletta, visiting the few shops, bars and cinemas still open, but mostly ending up at Command Hall, formerly the Knights' hospital, where servicemen could play table tennis, billiards or practise their aim in the .22 shooting gallery.

Jack wandered streets that — despite the piles of rubble and limestone blocks, the emboldened rats and mangy, skin-and-bones dogs — still exuded a certain grace. He loved the austere façades with their colourful wooden window boxes, and marvelled at the grand architecture of the knights' buildings, roughly contemporary with the colleges he knew so well from Oxford, and somewhat reminiscent of them.

As it was high summer, encampments had mushroomed around the entrances to both private and public air-raid shelters, along with ad hoc washing lines strung with tattered clothing. Barefoot children played in the street and women prepared meagre meals over makeshift stoves on the pavements. Families, priests and Maltese soldiers sat around on chairs and benches, passing the time of day and moving with the shade as it progressed from one side of the road to the other.

Yes, the island was bomb ravaged, its inhabitants battered and bruised, but there remained a magical quality to this place. It was there in the Renaissance buildings and limestone fortifications, the sparkling blue water framed at the end of every street; and it was there in the quiet, steadfast spirit of the Maltese and the garrison's doughty Tommies.

Jack came to the damaged St John's Co-Cathedral and stepped through the doorway into a dark interior shimmering with gold leaf. He was greeted by a black-robed priest, who offered to accompany him as he explored the cavernous space. Walking down an aisle, their feet treading on the gravestones of knights embedded in the floor, the priest directed Jack's gaze to the image of a skeleton blowing a trumpet while seated on a clock: 'This is the final resting place of Don Gaspar de Figuera. The inscription says: *Venit hora eius. Veniet et tua.*'

'The Catholics don't exactly do subtlety,' muttered Jack.

'Pardon, Lieutenant?'

'Nothing, Father. "His hour has come, and yours will come."'

'You know your Latin.'

'Not really, but I had a public-school education.'

'Ah-ha, very good.'

Donning his sunglasses as he stepped out of the cathedral into the blinding sunlight, something made Jack look up. High up in the atmosphere, a black speck trailed a thin white line. The dot grew larger, accompanied by an unearthly howling. Closer now, he saw that it was a Macchi C200 Saetta pitched slightly over the vertical in a terminal velocity dive. An object, perhaps the pilot, detached itself from the fuselage. Closer still, the fighter appeared to be aiming straight at Jack, but he remained rooted to the spot as the high-pitched screaming filled his head. He began to tremble. His vision clouded, then filled itself with a diving Stuka, his breath coming in short pants, *Havoc* heeling hard over at full speed … no chance of escape.

The Macchi struck the earth a few streets away with a reverberating crack, the ensuing explosion scaring the pigeons into panicked flight. The Italian pilot, unable to properly deploy his fouled parachute, twisted and writhed as he fell, and went in after his fighter. From the streets and lanes in every direction came the sound of cheering, then the clatter of running feet as people flocked to the crash site. Jack had seen more than enough carnage and turned in the opposite direction, heading for the tip of Valletta's peninsula. Needing sustenance, he stopped at a hole-in-the-wall café.

'Sorry, *sinjur*, very little on the menu,' said the bearded proprietor.

'Not to worry, just something light.'

'Much better after the next convoy!'

'Let's hope. What *have* you got?'

'Only *pastizzi*.'

'All right, whatever that is, I'll take it.'

The man handed over a flaky, oblong pastry filled with ricotta cheese and, eating as he walked, Jack thought it both filling and delicious. Reaching the end of Kingsway, he came to Fort St Elmo, site of the fiercest battle of the Great Siege. He found a bench and, trying to picture the unfolding scene of 377 years before, opened his guidebook and began reading.

Suleiman the Magnificent, Sultan of Turkey, Conqueror of Eastern Europe, Possessor of Men's Necks and Allah's Deputy on Earth, had come within a hair's breadth of subduing Malta, thereby laying open France and Spain to his men-of-war. At the time, the ramparts of Christendom were an imaginary vertical line through the middle of the Mediterranean. All that stood in the sultan's way was Malta's small warrior band, the Knights Hospitaller of St John of Jerusalem, lying at the sea's fulcrum.

Jack read once again how Suleiman had arrived in the offing with a Turkish battle squadron of 180 ships and nearly 40,000 men, including cavalry horses, massed artillery and 1,500 cut-throat pirates from Tripoli. Opposing him was a fighting elite of 641 knights backed by 6,000 troops of uneven quality, including European volunteers, slaves and Maltese civilians.

The Turkish plan was first to subdue St Elmo, which protected the harbour entrance, then proceed to the island's other strongholds. The little fort was well defended with gun emplacements and slits designed for enfilade and crossfire, but a week of bombardment by three dozen Turkish cannons reduced much of St Elmo to rubble. De la Valette, Grand Master of Malta, ordered that the wounded be evacuated each night and the defenders be resupplied from across the harbour. Over the ensuing days, the Turks made repeated assaults on St Elmo's shattered walls. Inside the fort, the slaves and hired galley oarsmen fought and died as bravely as the knights.

Suleiman's men finally overran St Elmo — killing all 1,500 defenders, but sparing nine of the knights — and raised their banners over the ruins. Although the Turks had succeeded in capturing the fort, allowing their fleet to enter the harbour, the siege had cost them 6,000 men. The captured knights were decapitated, their heads impaled on pikes for display on St Elmo's shattered battlements. The headless bodies, chests slashed with the mark of the cross, were tied to wooden crucifixes and floated across the harbour to Fort St Angelo, Suleiman's next target. In retaliation, De la Valette decapitated his own Turkish prisoners, loaded the heads into cannons and fired them back across the water into the enemy encampment.

Sitting on the bench, Jack was imagining St Elmo's sixteenth-century defences while perusing its modern six-pounders and Bofors, its searchlight embrasure and concrete fire-control towers. Here was history repeating its practised dance steps. First Suleiman, then Napoleon, had been defeated; now Hitler and Mussolini must be put to the sword.

The sun stood high and the limestone walls baked under the onslaught. Jack was feeling the heat and decided to take a slow amble through the city and catch a dghaisa back to St Angelo. He hadn't got very far before the air-raid sirens began their bawling and people flooded into the street, hastening for the shelters. The opening salvos of the anti-aircraft guns and growl of unsynchronised aero engines arrived at almost the same instant. A man called out to him, 'This way, *Logutenent*, down here, quickly!'

Jack scampered through a sandbagged entrance, around a baffle wall and down a flight of steps cut into the limestone. Passing an alcove with a statuette of the Madonna lit by an oil lamp, he emerged into a chamber smelling of chalk. Bare electric bulbs hung from a low ceiling in a space that was already filled with townsfolk who'd come bearing stools, fold-out chairs, rolled-up bedding, gas masks and baskets of food. The unique humid smell took him straight back to London in the autumn of 1940 when, while awaiting transfer to the Cape, he'd spent many nights sheltering from the Luftwaffe in crowded Underground stations.

A second chamber was furnished with three-tiered wooden bunks and it appeared that some people, no doubt having lost their homes, were living down here. The bomb-shelter complex gave the impression of a termite mound with side tunnels leading to alcoves for ablutions, a dressing station, makeshift surgery and maternity bay. Jack noticed a group of workers busy enlarging one of the chambers, chipping away with pickaxes, jemmies and iron hammers. Malta's Third Neolithic Age, he mused.

An elderly woman wearing a traditional faldetta headdress offered him a seat beside her on a bench, which he gratefully accepted. A mother with a baby plugged to her breast reclined on a mattress at their feet. Jack felt he was in the presence of Malta's heroes, a citizenry that had been pitchforked into a long and terrible siege, innocents in a struggle not of their making. Enemy bases lay less than a hundred miles away, bringing the weight of Axis airpower down upon their heads. For two years, they'd endured almost daily bombardment, suffered starvation and disease, seen their houses and churches destroyed and been forced to make new homes below ground. And still there was no end in sight.

Little boys kept running up and down the stairs to the mouth of the shelter to report excitedly on the progress of the raid. As the crump of bombs drew nearer, babies began to wail, then shriek. The assembled broke into prayer: 'Hail Mary, full of grace...' From his limited Latin, Jack knew they were butchering the classical tongue, but the low, heartfelt incantation was nonetheless deeply moving.

Just then, there was a thunderous crash. Jack hunched down, locking his hands over his head as the walls shook, lightbulbs flickered and dust clouds billowed through the confined spaces. Another loud bang and the lights went out. An ARP warden with a torch appeared at the top of the stairs and called for calm as people began lighting the candle stubs, most of them carried in their pockets, as well as homemade lanterns made from jars containing pieces of string splashed with paraffin. It grew ever stuffier as the flames consumed the oxygen, the Flit insect repellent employed against mosquitoes only adding to the foul atmosphere.

Hours passed. The enemy was no doubt making another concerted effort to destroy the three remaining merchantmen at their berths. Each time it seemed the raid was over, more waves of bombers arrived. The shelter's denizens whiled away their time playing games or telling stories, some of them in English, probably for Jack's benefit, such as the age-old yarn about the bride of Mosta kidnapped on her wedding day and spirited away by Muslim pirates; or the white lady-ghost of Verdala who still terrorised sentries at the governor's palace. There were tales about Malta's latter-day knights, such as 'Screwball' Beurling with his legendary dogfighting skills, or the bomb disposal teams risking their lives each day, or the valiant submariners, such as Lieutenant Commander Wanklyn, who sank twenty-two enemy ships before his boat, *Upholder*, was lost with all hands three months previously.

The day wore on. Condensation dripped from the ceiling and ran down the walls; the air grew increasingly fetid — a combination of body odour, unwashed feet, urine, faeces, babies' vomit and garlic. Jack was made painfully aware that soap had also become a rationed commodity. Buckets were employed for ablutions with strips of the *Times of Malta* used as toilet paper. There were times when Jack wanted to hold a handkerchief over his nose and mouth but thought it would look disrespectful.

Another attack was developing, the howl of diving aircraft and the whistle of bombs reaching them in muffled form below ground. A tremendous explosion shook the chamber as a hot gust of acrid smoke and dust blasted through the space, snuffing out the candles and eliciting cries of panic. Jack knew a bomb had struck the building overhead and listened in anguish to the collapsing masonry as an avalanche of rubble tumbled down the steps, blocking their exit. One hysterical mother hugged a baby to her breast, screaming incoherently.

Jack heard the scratching of matches as lamps were relit. In the flickering, dust-heavy light, terrified faces were turned aloft, fearful that the bunker might at any moment collapse and bury them alive.

'Don't worry, people, the escape exit is undamaged!' called out the ARP warden. 'And the raid is over: listen!'

As a siren sounded the 'all clear', Jack followed a group up a narrow flight of stairs in the second chamber, emerging into a world of light, smoke and fire. His fellow evacuees were white from head to foot as though bags of flour had been emptied over them. Dazed, disorientated and coughing to clear the dust, Jack took in the devastation. The road was strewn with blocks of stone, roof beams, shattered glass and bits of furniture; the air reeked with the stench of a burst sewer.

Some islanders had been caught before they'd reached the shelter. Jack laid his hand on the chest of an old man without apparent scars, but found no sign of life. He must have succumbed to the blast. A priest bent over a woman whose abdomen was crushed under a large slab of limestone: he anointed her, offering sacramental absolution with the sign of the cross on her forehead. Her wild, terrified gaze immediately softened; he held the woman's hand until her shallow breathing ceased. Ambulance crews and Civil Defence volunteers with stretchers arrived to remove the wounded.

Walking towards the harbour in a daze, Jack came to a small *pjazza* where a row of corpses covered with blankets awaited transfer to the Floriana morgue. He passed the remains of a donkey, its stomach ruptured and parts of its carcass scattered all about. The roadway looked and smelt like a butchery. Jack knew that the animal's remains would soon disappear, the meat too precious to go to waste.

Everywhere he went, there were firemen, medics and rescue workers toiling to free the trapped and put out fires. Citizens joined in, scratching with bare hands in the wreckage in search of those who might still be alive. A warden raised a whistle to his lips to call for silence so they could listen for any sign of life … nothing. Jack saw an ARP warden trying to console a little girl in rags standing beside a ruined house, screaming for her mother. He thought of his own mother's bombed-out home in South Kensington, that horrifying mountain of rubble on Onslow Square. He forced his mind back to the present: he must not let his thoughts venture down that road.

Reaching the esplanade, he found that Grand Harbour had taken another heavy pounding. Their Greek friend, *Callisto*, had been hit again, a Stuka's bomb having threaded her funnel and exploded in the engine room, causing terrific damage. A tug and two fire-floats were alongside, hosing her with foam and water, but the flames were getting closer to an as-yet unloaded compartment of ammunition. It was also apparent that *Callisto* had begun to sink, and Jack watched as she was towed across the harbour like a vast, floating pyre, to be beached in Rinella Creek where some of her stores and coal might still be salvaged and the ammunition retrieved by divers.

Arriving back at St Angelo, Jack was told to report to the commodore immediately. There was no time to change out of his dust-and-sweat-stained uniform.

'Pembroke, I'd like to have a word with you about personal discipline,' said Commodore Huffington-Smythe from behind his enormous desk.

'Sir?' Jack felt as if he was back in the headmaster's office at Winchester.

'It has been brought to my attention that your South African sailors imagine uniform to be optional. I want to see no more of those gym vests, colourful scarves and strange hats.'

'It's just that —'

'*Henceforth*, you will ensure that your men are neatly turned out in number fives without the trimmings at all times. And, Lieutenant, I don't care who your father is: I expect *you* to set a better example by appearing neat and smart while in port. Am I understood?'

'Sir, if you —'

'*Am I understood?*'

'Affirmative, sir.' Jack flushed with hot embarrassment.

Back in the wardroom, he conveyed the gist of the commodore's harangue to Van Zyl, who was similarly indignant.

'After everything our Gannets have been through! Let Huffington-What-Not do a convoy run from Alex and see whether he still considers a purple cravat or a fleck of marmalade on a collar to be a life-and-death matter.'

'Easy there, Number One — he is the NOIC. But let it be put on record that I, for one, think your purple cravat is smashing.'

'But, sir, it's not about the cravat!'

'Of course not, but let's do what we can to make things more pusser and try to stay out of the commodore's eyeline.'

CHAPTER 15

The sun rose from the Mediterranean into a scrambled-egg sky. Douglas was flying at 15,000 feet in a four-finger formation, cruising almost line abreast so the pilots could watch out for one other. His Sea Hurricane with its maritime-blue camouflage stood out from its companions in their drab khaki-and-brown livery. Spitfires soared high above them — tiny, elliptical-winged crucifixes catching the early light. The moment an attack commenced, they would split into pairs, which often became singles in the ensuing chaos.

Douglas soon spotted the large enemy formation that had already been picked up and tracked on radar, and the Hurricanes began to climb in a left-hand sweep to get above them. The bombers dipped into a sixty-degree dive towards Takali Airfield and the Canadian chose his target, a mustard-coloured Ju-88, the black crosses on its wings clearly visible. Douglas followed the bomber down into the flak, cutting the corner as it pulled out and catching up over Mosta.

Closing to 200 yards, he squeezed the button and fired a long burst from the starboard quarter, his Hurricane juddering from the recoil as rounds crept along the bomber's wing and stitched the aluminium siding, but still the rugged aircraft flew on. Douglas fired again. His fifteen seconds of ammunition was almost spent when he saw the starboard engine begin to stream white glycol vapour. Twisting and turning, the German dived into scrappy cloud, finding cover then losing it, then finding it again. The Canadian stuck with him, firing the occasional short burst when he got the chance. Now dead astern, a good burst drained the last of his ammo. Nothing.

Then there was a sudden flaring of the wounded engine, black smoke, and the bomber going into a death spiral towards the sea. One parachute blossomed, followed by another.

'Got him! Nailed the bugger!' Douglas shouted into the R/T, unable to contain his excitement. He was immediately reprimanded by Group Captain Woodhall, the senior controller, for breaking with radio protocol.

He glanced up to see Spitfires in a fierce engagement with the Me-109 cover, the sky above him a writhing spaghetti of white trails. Suddenly, a bandit appeared in his mirror, orange flashes and hot tracer balls tearing past the cockpit. He jinked and flipped his plane over, peripherally aware of Malta dialling through the quadrants, now above him, now below him. He dived into a thicket of cloud and emerged out the other side having shaken off the enemy. Sucking in deep draughts of air, the adrenalin coursing through him, he descended to the deck and made for Takali.

Once *Gannet*'s repairs were finally completed, she was moved to Dockyard Creek, likely to be her berth for some time — at least until she could join a return convoy to Alexandria. Her NCOs and ratings reverted to shipboard messing, while the officers remained in their shore accommodation and Jack went aboard each day to oversee final snags and repainting. When he got to his cabin one morning, he found Fido entertaining a friend. She lay curled up on his cot beside an emaciated black Maltese of uncertain pedigree — one of the scruffy urchins that frequented the wharves of Grand Harbour. Hendricks appeared in the doorway.

'Ah, yes, Cap'n, apologies. I've been meaning to bring this matter to your attention.'

'Yes…?'

'As you can see, Fido has acquired a chum. You might be thinking NQOC, so to speak — in cat terms, that is — but the little ragamuffin was awfully hungry and so Fido took him in, doing her bit for the war effort, seeing as how Malta has been so mishandled by the Ities and the Hun and all, sir.'

'So, we approve of this friendship, do we, Hendricks?'

'Yessir, in my humble opinion, we do.'

'Very well, let's leave them be, shall we?'

'I think that would be very gracious of you, sir.'

The city cats were indeed in a sorry state, mad with hunger, many having been abandoned by families that had moved to the countryside to escape the bombing. The felines had taken to stealing anything they could lay their claws on, and dockyard guards were known to take pot shots at the scavengers. Although no one in their right mind could mistake the slow, portly South African marmalade for a scrawny, fleet-footed Maltese, Fido nevertheless had to watch her step when venturing ashore.

Late morning, with work on *Gannet* being ably overseen by Van Zyl, Jack decided to cadge a ride to Takali Airfield to visit Douglas. The RAF driver collected him in a khaki-coloured Bedford lorry patterned with dark lines to create the illusion of stone walling, its mudguard adorned with an eight-pointed blue-and-yellow Maltese star. They headed west along a road lined with pine trees and prickly pears. As they neared the airfield, situated on the bed of a dried-up lake, Jack noticed that almost every building in the vicinity was either destroyed or damaged. Over to the right, he spotted caves set into low hills, which housed the aircraft workshops.

Jack was dropped at a Nissen hut beside a bomb-cratered airfield resembling a lunarscape and fringed with scruffy palm trees. Dozens of men — soldiers of the Manchester Regiment, assisted by Maltese civilians — were busy filling in the many holes using picks, shovels and an ancient steamroller. It looked to be a full-time job. He also noticed red flags fluttering beside some of the craters, denoting unexploded bombs or the nasty anti-personnel mines known as crackerjacks. Armed and fuelled Hurricanes and Spitfires waited in front of their blast pens, ready to get airborne at a moment's notice.

Jack made his way to the dispersal area, comprising a hut and a few bell tents with their flaps tied back. The centrepiece was a large table crammed with telephones connected to fighter control at War HQ. The moment the powerful radar atop Dingli Cliffs picked up a plot of incoming aircraft, the RAF controller in Valletta would call up Takali and order a scramble for interception. Duty pilots with yellow Mae West lifejackets around their necks waited to be called, some sprawled in comfy chairs or snoozing on canvas stretchers, others reading magazines or drinking mugs of tea. A handful sat around a card table fashioned from the wrecked wing of a plane. To Jack, they seemed a disparate bunch, unshaven, with long hair and motley attire — a bit like a troop of dandy, underfed brigands. He spotted Douglas, dressed in long khaki shorts and stockings, a creased khaki shirt and a battered cap, sitting in a deckchair reading a paperback.

The Canadian glanced up. 'Jack, me hearty, welcome to the home of 249 Squadron!' he exclaimed, springing to his feet and shaking hands. 'Nice of the navy to pay us a visit.' Despite his broad grin, Douglas's face was grey with exhaustion, his eyes red-rimmed; a nerve twitched in his cheek.

'You look chin-strapped,' said Jack.

'I am a tad. We've been flying almost back-to-back sorties for the last few days. Smiling Albert's boys have been concentrating on Takali. Sometimes there are so many craters on the runway, we can't take off. On a bad day, the airfield gets plastered with as many bombs as the Coventry blitz.'

'Good grief, that seems barely credible.'

'God's honest.'

'Do you have today off?'

'Not really, but my bird got shot up this morning, and the erks are busy with repairs.'

'A big job?'

'No, just a few scratches, but our fighters are taking a hammering, and compounding the problem is the bally dust. It gets kicked up by the slipstream and sucked into the engine. Even our Vokes filters don't entirely solve the issue. Spare parts are also a constant headache. Our riggers and fitters cannibalise damaged aircraft, but the attrition is astounding.'

'I'm told the dockyard chaps are helping to fashion items such as propellers,' said Jack.

'So they are. I have to say, my erks are ruddy amazing, the unsung heroes of the Malta show, often working through the night to get us airborne again the next morning. And they go out of their way for us pilots. For instance, it gets so hot in the cockpit when we're at the ready, twiddling our thumbs, waiting to take off. So, our riggers have made cardboard canopies to place over the Perspex to keep us cool. Between you and me, it doesn't really work but hats off to the lads for their ingenuity.'

Jack heard the throaty grumble of a Merlin engine, and they turned to watch a Spitfire coming in to land and taxi to a three-sided blast pen topped with camouflage netting where the ground crew waited. Post-flight checks were conducted while a fuel line was hastily passed from a bowser to the wing and armourers checked the guns and reloaded the magazines.

'A squadron on standby must be off the ground within two minutes,' Douglas explained, 'a squadron at immediate readiness within three minutes and a squadron at readiness within five. Come, let me introduce you to some of the gang — all of them veterans of France, North Africa, the Battle of Britain, you name it. There's no rank distinction here, with officers and NCOs mingling freely and, as you can see, uniforms are a hodgepodge.'

'Our NOIC needs to take a leaf out of 249's book,' grumbled Jack.

'If something needs doing, everyone pitches in — no standing on ceremony or rank here — and there's a marvellous esprit de corps. But the pressure is just stupendous and the lads are undernourished, often coming down with ailments such scurvy, typhoid or the dreaded dog.'

'What's that?'

'Malta dog is probably caused by gigglegogs in the water, a bit like gyppy tummy, and it comes with hallucinations, fever, stomach cramps, black drizzle, the works.'

'Sounds dreadful.'

'Trust me, you don't want to catch the dog.'

'I shan't imbibe another drop of the local haitch-two-oh.'

'By the way, that's our energetic squadron leader, Laddie Lucas, just stepping into the tent. He was a sports writer for the *Sunday Express* in the olden days — just got himself awarded a DFC.'

'Looks like a mixed bag of nationalities among your pilots.'

'We've got Kiwis, Aussies, Poles, Free French, Springboks, Rhodesians and a Yank or two. They're an unruly lot, but I couldn't have asked for a better bunch. Oh, and that's George 'Buzz' Beurling sitting over there, all on his lonesome. He's our number-one ace — a Canuck like me and still only a flight sergeant.' Jack glanced over at the blond pilot with the sallow complexion and piercing blue eyes, wearing shorts that appeared far too big for him, a shirt with stains down the front and socks around his ankles. He was jotting something in a small black notebook.

'Is he the one they call "Screwball"?' asked Jack.

'The very one. He's a maverick, headstrong as hell, highly strung and a teetotaller. Not too big on authority either, but boy can he fly! Brilliant eyesight, agile in the air, an uncanny sixth sense and courage in spades. Buzz can take down a Messerschmitt at eight hundred yards with a deflection shot — just masterful. He's already bagged ten bandits this month.'

Another Spitfire came in to land, this one with a stuttering engine and an undercarriage that appeared faulty. The fighter wobbled in the air and Jack noticed the tip of one wing had sheared off. A silence fell over the dispersal as pilots stood up, every pair of eyes tracking the damaged bird. Slowing now, the Spitfire lined up for a belly landing.

'Easy, boy. Easy,' said Douglas through gritted teeth.

The fighter kissed the dirt, bounced once, then sat down hard with a crunch, followed by the shrieking of metal as it skidded along the runway, propeller blades bent like paperclips, until it came to rest, enveloped in clouds of dust. With an ambulance and fire tender already on their way, ground staff sprinted towards the aircraft, but the pilot stood up in his cockpit, jumped down onto the wing, waved and gave a theatrical bow.

'Lucky bastard,' hissed Douglas, visibly shaken.

Later, the two officers strolled over to the NAAFI tent for a bite to eat. 'Our transport has recently been shot up, so we have to walk the two miles from our digs in Mdina to Takali. As you can imagine, we usually stay at the airfield all day rather than traipse back up the hill for lunch.'

As they neared the tent, a rocket flare soared into the sky and a red flag jerked up a nearby mast.

'Trouble?' asked Jack.

'Yes, imminent attack,' said Douglas. All around them, men were hastening for cover. 'Rather spoils lunch, I'm afraid.'

Out of the blue, a pair of Me-109s with yellow noses tore towards them at fifty feet, their machine guns stammering. The pair threw themselves to the ground, hands clasped over their heads as the fighters thundered past.

'Run!' yelled Douglas. They jumped up and sprinted across open ground towards a slit trench just as a line of Ju-88s swooped in, vapour streaming from their wingtips, and began to strafe the airfield. One nose gunner spotted the two darting figures and took aim. Jack ran faster, gasping, desperate, his old leg wound screaming in protest. Bullets kicked up a line of dust spurts towards them as they dived for the trench, swallowing mouthfuls of sand, with gravel and stones showering them.

The air crackled with small-arms fire, accompanied by the coughing of Bofors and the jabber of a nearby twin Browning. One bomber passed directly over their trench, the roar of its twin Jumo V-12 engines filling Jack's head, the pop of a Lee-Enfield rifle offering a futile riposte from the soldier beside him. Next came the whistle of bombs and earth-tremor detonations, followed hard upon by volcanoes of dirt. Jack cowered, head in his arms, mouth open in anticipation of the pressure differentials following the blast. One bomb struck fifty feet away, lifting him off the ground and sucking the air from his lungs.

Another echelon of Ju-88s lunged at Takali, dropping their load on the northern dispersal. A Hurricane and its bowser burst into flames, sending a column of acrid black smoke climbing into the blue. The fighter's ammunition caught fire and bullets fizzed across the airfield, keeping everyone's heads down. Then its undercarriage collapsed like a big log fire, the carcass enveloped in ugly orange flames.

'That's another Hurricane spitchered,' said Douglas bitterly.

'Spitchered?' Jack's voice was a hoarse whisper.

'Local dialect. It means "of no further use" ... buggered.'

The raid was soon over and the two officers climbed groggily out of the trench, their bodies twitching and ears ringing. Dusting themselves off, they surveyed the carnage: one aircraft destroyed and two damaged, while a direct hit on a slit trench had left a gaping crater but no corpses, only a few body parts, chunks of flesh and bloody rags scattered about.

Firmly crossing his arms to still his shaking hands, Jack asked, 'Is this always how you welcome guests to Takali?'

'Pretty much, yes.'

Fletcher stood waiting for Martina under a stone arch beside the tunnel-like entrance to War HQ, guarded by a soldier with a rifle. At 1301, she emerged into the light, donning her sunglasses and straw hat. They kissed on both cheeks, then climbed the steps to the Upper Barracca and proceeded along Kingsway to the Union Club.

'What does that graffiti mean?' asked Fletcher, pointing to the words *Ħobż, mhux George Cross* daubed in red on a ruined building.

'Bread, not the medal,' said Martina.

'I don't understand.'

'The Maltese are grateful that your king —'

'*Our* king.'

'*Our* king ... awarded us the George Cross for gallantry, but what we really want is an end to starvation. The daily bread ration is four ounces per woman or child. Bread is our staple.

For us, it is life. A sack of flour costs forty pounds on the black market.'

'But that's bloody extortionate!'

'It is.'

They entered the club and were ushered to a table in the Snakepit, a long room that served as a mixed bar, beneath a large picture of Churchill emblazoned with the words: 'Hold Fast and We Win.' Lunch was a shared plate of chips and lemonade, the conversation turning once more to food.

'I know a woman who traded her gold wedding ring for eggs,' said Martina. 'There is no olive oil or sugar. Snails became suddenly popular; now they are all eaten up. Even *soppa ta l'armla* — widow's vegetable soup, the poorest meal for peasants — has become a luxury. With so few herds left, goat's cheese is like gold dust. We have no milk without goats. Tinned milk is only for children or the sick. Even wealthy islanders, sometimes my own family, have begun to visit the Victory Kitchens for their meals, if you can call a piece of shoat gristle floating in grey water a meal.'

'What's shoat?'

'A mix between a sheep and a goat, but sometimes I think it's dog or cat.'

'We'd better not let our ship's cat, Fido, wander too far from *Gannet*.'

'People are using rope or rubber from old car tyres to replace the soles of their shoes. You can't buy any new clothing, so we patch and darn and mend. I had to use the curtains from a spare bedroom to make a dress. I look like a wreck most of the time.'

'Nonsense, you always look ravishing.'

'You are mistaken, but very kind. For Maltese women, parachute silk has become a most cherished item. You cannot buy a safety pin for love nor money. I mean, really: a safety pin! As for lipstick or makeup… Some of my friends have taken to grinding rice very fine to make face powder.'

'Goodness me, the lengths —'

'Our cigarette ration is two packets a week. You will see a hundred people queuing overnight outside a tobacco shop. Some have even started using the dried leaves of figs and lemons as a substitute. As for alcohol, there are men who keep a daily watch on the chimney of the Cisk brewery to see when beer production restarts. They have the dedication of Romans awaiting Vatican smoke to signal a new pope.'

'The Maltese are remarkably resourceful, and strong. You've had to withstand sieges throughout your history —'

'You make it sound romantic, Tom. It is not. We have no choice and we live so much of the time in fear. Great world powers are throwing everything at our tiny island, starving us, machine-gunning women and children in the street, driving us underground. Many old people are giving up … just fading away. Also, some of the babies and the weak. Children cry themselves to sleep with hunger. Sometimes, it is all too much.'

'Do you hate them?' He reached out and placed his hand on top of hers. She did not draw it away.

'I don't know. I suppose so, but I think of them more as a kind of storm, a powerful tempest that we must endure until the sun comes out again.'

'Do you feel proud?'

'Of my people, yes. Especially my little brother, Luca. He's only eighteen; he's just finished school and is manning an anti-aircraft gun next to War HQ.'

'What exactly do you do in that underground warren of yours?'

'I'm a plotter at Fighter Control. Unlike England, where WAAFs do the work, they use civilian girls here. It's Malta's nerve centre.'

'Sounds like a dark, secretive labyrinth.'

'I suppose it is, in a way.'

Martina went on to describe her workplace as a network of tunnels and chambers, carved from the limestone deep within the bastions, housing the headquarters of all three services. It contained offices, dormitories, chartrooms and cubicles for wireless operators and Typex decoders. The RAF Ops Room had a large map of the central Mediterranean overlaid by a grid mounted on a plotting table and overseen by controllers in a gallery above. Reports of incoming aircraft received from radar and observation posts were fed to the plotters, who marked the raiders in red and the friendlies in black. Listening through headphones, they would trace the progress of each enemy 'plot'. Controllers were in direct radio communication with RAF pilots and could vector them into the best position for interception.

'So far this year, we've had only one day without a raid. It all gets rather depressing: so many incoming bombers and so few defending fighters. Sometimes none at all. We even make fake plots to try to fool the enemy, hoping Axis controllers listening in will hear Malta exchanging messages with non-existent fighters and divert their bombers.'

'Does it work?'

'Possibly. Lately, I've been doing the night shift and every time the sirens begin to wail, my stomach tightens as I watch the enemy come marching across the table. I think of all the thousands of people being woken, suddenly alert and terrified, gathering their children and their pets and their pillows, and heading for the shelters. It makes me so sad — I feel a kind of weakness in my limbs.'

'The nightly Via Dolorosa.'

'Yes, I suppose so. Then the curtain goes up, everything starts moving fast and there's no more time to mope. Our night fighters are vectored in, the reports start arriving from the anti-aircraft guns: Spinola battery opening fire, followed by Tigné. All we hear is muffled thudding. Then a call from the searchlight table: "Aircraft illuminated over Grand Harbour". A radio crackles into life on the loudspeakers: "Got him, got him!" from one of our boys. "His starboard engine on fire, going down in flames!" There'll be a brief outbreak of applause, then it's back to work. Every night the same.' Her voice and face were animated, but Tom could see the ache beneath the surface.

'They're lucky to have you.'

'Oh, I'm just a tiny, insignificant cog.'

'A very beautiful cog.'

She blushed and looked down at his hand still resting on hers.

'I would like to take you out one evening — something nice, like a dance,' he said.

'There are hardly any decent places left, and my parents are rather strict.'

'Perhaps the pictures?'

'I'm not sure. You'd have to meet my parents first. Mama is very devout.'

'And are you religious?'

'I go to church. Do you?'

'Actually, I was brought up Catholic, but my parents are mostly lapsed and I'm entirely lapsed.'

'I'm not certain where exactly I stand.'

'Do you believe in saints and miracles and that sort of thing?'

'No. Yes. I don't know. We had a miracle three months ago during a service at Mosta Cathedral.'

'Really?' He tried not to sound sceptical.

'A German bomb crashed through the dome during Mass, bounced off the wall and landed among the congregants, but did not explode.'

'And you think that's a miracle, not just a dud bomb?'

'My mother says it is a miracle.'

'Then it's a miracle.' He smiled.

'Good boy, you're learning fast.' She leant across the table and kissed him lightly on the cheek, then wiped away the lipstick with her thumb.

CHAPTER 16

A white sun stands high in the sky and Alana, in a flowing cream sundress, climbs the dune ahead of Jack. She disappears over the lip and he breaks into a run, fearing he might lose her. Up the dune, soft sand is filling his shoes, sucking at his legs, heavier and heavier. Straining now, desperate, he reaches the crest to find undulating dunes stretching to infinity. By now, Alana is much further away, striding ahead, her feet barely touching the ground. The heat is oppressive, his body coated in sweat. He calls out but she doesn't look back. He tries to scream, but the only sound produced is a soft cry of despair.

'Alana!'

Jack shook himself awake with her name dying on his lips, overwhelmed by a sense of loss. The twisted sheets were damp with sweat. Befuddled and feverish, he gulped water directly from the jug on his bedside table, then lay back and, before long, slipped once more into fitful sleep, his nostrils filled with the smell of vomit from the bucket that the fort steward assigned to him had placed next to the bed.

Jack was suffering from a bad dose of Malta dog, the hours passing in a blur of fever, nausea, diarrhoea, migraines and stomach cramps. All food tasted like fat and he was barely able to keep anything down. After a few days of the dog, he'd lost almost a stone. Sandflies and mosquitoes plagued him mercilessly, stabbing his flesh through the pyjamas or sheets to leave him cursing with rage. Twice each day, his steward sprayed the room with Flit to deter the insect *Schwärme*, but they soon regrouped to attack once more.

For air raids not directly targeting Grand Harbour, Jack took his chances and remained in bed. He lay thinking of the many thousands of islanders in their shelters listening to the drone of bombers, the gunners at their posts, the priests in their churches, the sailors on bridge watch: every ear tuned, like his, to the sound of aero engines. Were they Wellingtons or Junkers, Messerschmitts or Spitfires, Stukas or Swordfish? Sometimes a lone intruder would fly around in circles at night, tormenting those below who were waiting for the axe to fall. Finally, they'd hear the growl of quickening engines as the enemy swooped down, followed by the thud and detonation of its payload. During heavier raids, or those directed at Grand Harbour, Jack would drag himself down to St Angelo's bunkers. When he was in a particularly bad way, his steward would help him down the stone steps and sit beside him as he lay on a bench, alternately sweating and shivering, a bucket close at hand.

Another night, another nightmare: Jack is on the bridge staring down at black water. Alana swims towards him, *Havoc*'s grey hull standing up like a titanic tooth behind her, the propellers still slowly turning. He waves both his arms above his head, but she doesn't see him. The bulky lifejacket is hindering her progress through the water. The destroyer begins to sink, sucking her backwards into its vortex. She spots him now and her face lights up as a great whirlpool opens behind her, a Charybdis-like monster slowly swallowing the sea. Tears streaming down his cheeks, Jack yells with all his might, but no sound passes his lips. He climbs onto the rail and dives into icy water. The current takes hold, dragging him towards the swirling black hole. Like two riders on a merry-go-round, he and Alana lie on opposite sides of a maelstrom of death. His teeth chatter, his body shakes, as he slides into the sea's ugly maw. Twisting and turning, Alana is impossibly out of reach…

Gasping for air, Jack wrenched open his eyes to find the bedclothes and duffel coat wrapped tightly around him like a serpent, his icy body shivering with fever. Knocking over the jug of water with a crash of shattering glass, he scrabbled about for the switch to his bedside lamp.

After a few days, Jack began to show improvement. One morning, the steward arrived with a breakfast tray, drew open the curtains and said brightly, 'Adam and Eve on a raft for you, sir.' He handed Jack a plate with two fried eggs on a piece of toast.

'Thank you, AB,' he replied, sitting up in bed.

'That's more like it, sir. You've some colour back in yer face.'

'I think I'm on the mend.'

'Question is, sir, can you fart without danger?'

'Frankly, I'm not yet sure.'

'Best to test yer wind in a safe space, sir, and not wearing sparkling whites. You don't want to end up with a Japanese sunset in yer kecks.'

'Aye, point taken.'

After consuming his tea and toast, Jack climbed gingerly out of bed, took a seat at his desk and gazed out the window, still too weak to do anything profitable, but happy to take in the handsome view. As he perused the scene, the narrow stretch of water below him began to fill with the unmistakeable shape of HMS *Welshman*, the courageous blockade runner, and what a glorious sight she made. The minelaying cruiser had evidently accomplished another one of her lighting dashes from Gibraltar carrying vital stores. She was an odd-looking ship sporting three funnels, the middle one fatter, with her main guns bunched far forward and far aft. Jack knew her powerful turbine engines were capable of pushing her along at an astounding forty knots and could maintain such speed for long periods.

Welshman slid towards a specially cleared berth in French Creek where lighters, lorries and army teams waited to conduct a speedy unloading. They would be joined by all manner of civilians — schoolchildren, businessmen in suits, priests and dghaisa oarsmen — forming human chains to hasten the transfer of goods. Jack found out later that *Welshman* had made it to Malta by hugging the North African coast disguised as a Vichy French destroyer of the Léopard class and, somewhat disconcertingly, had been escorted some of the way by Ju-88s. Her cargo of essential fuel, foodstuffs, replacement Spitfire engines and ammunition would help push out the target date a little longer. Unloading and refuelling were due to be completed by nightfall, when she would set off on her return dash to Gibraltar.

But Jack knew the enemy would soon get wind of her presence. Sure enough, minutes later sirens began to wail as the smoke machines belched their grey-green miasma. Jack shrugged on his paisley dressing gown and made for the bunker.

One of the benefits of *Welshman*'s visit was the many sacks of mail she brought in her belly. Stuck as they were on a pimple of land in an Axis-controlled sea, contact with the outside world was precious, especially for garrison soldiers so far from Blighty. For *Gannet*'s ratings, these letters, doled out by February from a sack like Father Christmas, brought tidings of home and loved ones, an emotional lifeline extending the length of the African continent.

From his devoted young mother back home in Benoni, Pickles received another parcel of Nestlé chocolate, boiled sweets, biltong and fruitcake, which he generously shared with his oppos. February's thick envelope was filled with drawings of Kalk Bay Harbour by both his children, Shamilla and Taliep. The mail sack also bore the regular packages from SAWAS, containing everything from tinned ham and sporting equipment to 'glory bags' filled with goodies courtesy of Ouma Smuts's Gifts and Comforts Fund.

Van Zyl received three letters from his Jewish girlfriend, Sylvia, an Austrian refugee studying fine art at the University of Cape Town. The black-and-white photo of her, taken at the Sea Point Pavilion in the spring of 1941, took pride of place above his bunk. She was seldom far from his thoughts and inhabited his dreams, a beacon of hope for a future world without war. He wrote passionate replies to her letters, filled with the poems and watercolours he'd managed to produce during snatches of free time. Van Zyl also received a short letter from his mother, penned in her rounded cursive, that betrayed the pain of a family torn apart by war. Stellenbosch was enduring a heavy winter filled with gales and her garden was suffering; his father was his usual grumpy self. She offered little news of his two older brothers, who occupied opposite ends of the political spectrum: the elder languishing in a POW camp near Rome, his middle brother still on the run from police due to criminal activities on behalf of pro-Nazi Afrikaners.

Jack lay in bed with his own stash of mail, some administrative, some personal, and one containing back issues of *Punch* for the wardroom. A letter from his father brought him up to speed on the political and military situation in the Union, Japanese advances in the Indian Ocean and the progress of the invasion of Vichy-controlled Madagascar, a combined operation between the Royal Navy and the South African Air Force and army. That theatre of the war appeared to have degenerated into attritional jungle warfare, not unlike Burma. There was news, too, of his younger brother Harry, who was still on wearying Atlantic-convoy duty, lately routed far to the north in summer waters with twenty-four hours of daylight.

A letter from his former girlfriend, Clara Marais, still managed to quicken his heart, but mostly with pangs of residual regret. Her words were kind and concerned for his safety, and she wrote at some length about her studies and her work with SAWAS. There was, of course, no mention of Henry, the pilot who he suspected had taken his place. As ever, Clara revealed almost nothing about her feelings, and certainly not in relation to him.

From Alana, by contrast, he received a slim, precious-beyond-measure envelope with a 'passed by censor' stamp on the front. Oh, how this sheet of thin blue paper held the key to his heart. Filled with passion and longing, it was a life-ring cast from Alexandria, sailing out across the Mediterranean to snare him. He wrote back immediately.

My beloved Alana,

I miss you more than I imagined possible: every hour of every day. How I ache to see you, to wrap you in my arms once again. To treasure you.

The convoy to Malta was a difficult one and we lost many good ships and many good men. I held you in my thoughts each waking minute, even during battle, as though you were a lighthouse in a storm-ravaged sea. You were the only beacon of sanity I could find in a demented world of fire and devastation.

We are stationed on the island for the present and I do not know when we will be returning to Alex, but it is my ardent hope that it will be soon. Malta is the most remarkable place: pulverised by the enemy on a daily basis, but the spirit of the islanders remains unbreakable. I have made a new friend, Grayson Douglas, a fighter pilot with a terribly scarred face from burns suffered when he was shot down. He has a beautiful young wife back in Canada, so we are able to compare notes on our longing and console one another about our lot. We both feel a bit like lovesick castaways on a beleaguered isle.

Oh, how I long for you, Alana — your nut-brown skin, your sensual exquisiteness — and how I miss our long, rambling conversations about love, life and the world. Each night I drift off to sleep in your embrace, enveloping you tightly in my arms. Your burning kisses, your fragrant scent, your lips as soft as satin … sometimes it quite overwhelms me, as though you were some powerful opiate. You are my sun and moon, my stars, the very air I breathe.

After all this brutal madness is over, I want to be with you, always. My darling, let us make it so. Please write again soon.

Your devoted amante,

Jack

An uncharacteristically nervous Fletcher boarded the Marsamuscetto ferry to cross the harbour to Sliema, a suburb on the northern headland opposite Valletta. The rust-bucket was an old coal-fired affair, painted black with a funnel amidships and the helm in the bows, where a white-capped skipper sat on a high chair at the wheel. Fletcher found a bench seat amid a group of sturdy women, some wearing hooded faldetta headdresses, their menfolk in striped flannel trousers and waistcoats. Most were either barefoot or wore rough sandals made from canvas and rope. Opposite him sat a priest in brown and white robes and a flat round hat, accompanied by a pair of nuns all in black with starched white coifs. A busker struck up a jaunty tune on his violin, an upturned hat on the deck before him. The engine coughed into life as the pistons, visible to passengers, began their up-and-down jig.

'*Ħoll il-ħbula!*' cried the skipper between teeth that clenched a pipe. A dock hand cast off and the ferry went astern, turned and chugged slowly across the harbour's millpond water. Fletcher gazed over to port at Manoel Island plugging Lazzaretto Creek, which was home to the Tenth Submarine Flotilla. The base had been vacated earlier in the year due to incessant bombing, but now one sleek, dark boat was back at the moorings, most likely HMS *Unbroken* — and what a brave captain she possessed. In truth, Fletcher knew she'd have to spend considerable time submerged while in port, resting on the bottom to avoid raids that focused on the creek whenever a submarine docked, but at least the island had an offensive naval element, albeit a small one, that could strike once more at Rommel's supply lines.

Stepping ashore in Sliema, he soon found the three-storey limestone villa on the waterfront close to the ferry stop. It had a columned portico with a big doorknocker in the shape of a dolphin and an ornate shoe-scraper on the top step. The shuttered windows had brown paper stuck to them in the shape of an X to prevent the glass from shattering. Fletcher paused before the tall front door, the beat of his pulse having upped its revolutions at the prospect of meeting Martina's parents.

Lifting the brass dolphin, he gently knocked. A few moments later, a servant opened the door and welcomed him into a hallway with terrazzo floor tiling and a wide marble staircase, then led him through to a reception room. Martina jumped up from the sofa and took his hand, ushering him forward and introducing him to her stylishly dressed parents and brother, Luca, who wore the uniform of the Royal Malta Artillery. At that moment, Fletcher felt that he'd much rather be on the forecastle facing down an Italian cruiser.

'*Omm, Missier*, this is Tom,' said Martina.

'Very pleased to meet you, Mr and Mrs Zammit,' said the young lieutenant.

With pleasantries cursorily concluded, Mr Zammit began an interrogation Fletcher thought worthy of the Gestapo. Where had he grown up, who were his family, what school, university, political views, war record, proposed career? Fletcher thought it prudent not to mention his desire to one day tread the boards of the West End. The subtext of the questioning was obvious: what were his intentions with their only daughter? It was clear that Mr Zammit would defend Martina's honour by any means possible, even, perhaps, to the extent of hiring a swarthy Maltese assassin. The interrogation showed little sign of abating as they moved through to the dining room, and Fletcher had no idea whether he was passing, failing or was about to be rusticated.

A servant arrived with bowls of thin soup made from turnip stalks, accompanied by a circular loaf of Maltese bread whose centre was scooped out and filled with tomatoes and garlic drizzled with precious olive oil.

'A very simple meal, Tom, but you surely understand,' said Mrs Zammit.

'It looks delicious, thank you.'

'We have forgotten what butter tastes like,' she added. 'The best imitation is lard, which we get from any meat fat we can lay our hands on. Feeding a household is a daily trial.'

'It must be, Mrs Zam—'

'Just look at this off-colour bread! It has no crunch. It's criminal how they add maize and potatoes to make the flour go further. Adolf and Benito have so much to answer for: everything is rationed these days, even water. We receive eight gallons a day, which might sound like a lot to a sailor, but one flush of the toilet swallows two gallons!'

'Next thing, they'll start rationing the air we breathe,' grumbled Mr Zammit. 'You see, Tom, rationing is cumulative. When coal stocks start running low, the power stations can't operate and the electricity supply becomes intermittent. So we switch to kerosene for heating and lighting. When kerosene runs low and starts getting heavily rationed, we switch to candles and wood, but now those are in short supply. And so it goes: shortage begets shortage, week after week, month after month. I'm not sure how much more we can tighten our belts.'

The servant entered with a small dish of *kapunata* — a salty, sweet-and-sour vegetable salad — served with slices of prickly pear.

'My brother has been dying to meet you,' said Martina, trying to lighten the atmosphere. The lad smiled and blushed. 'Luca, tell Tom what you do.'

'Martina, please.' His voice sounded younger than his eighteen years.

'Oh, go on.'

'Well, all right then… When I finished school, I went straight into basic training. Lots of drilling on the parade ground, route marches, dismantling a rifle while blindfolded and, oh boy, the dusting of everything! But how do you get rid of dust on Malta? It's just impossible.'

'Luca also had to learn to wash and iron his own clothes,' Mrs Zammit interrupted. 'He's always had servants to do *that* for him.'

'*And* blanco my webbing *and* polish the brass of my buttons and badges,' said Luca.

'Puts hairs on your chest, young man,' said Fletcher, trying to sound avuncular.

'Next came lots of artillery practice, firing time-shrapnel out to sea, that sort of thing. When training finished, I was posted to the 7th Light Anti-Aircraft Brigade. There are six of us on a Bofors — a wonderful gun, fires two 40-mm explosive shells every second, but of course you know all that. I'm a loader, feeding clips into the hopper, back and forth, sweating like a dog. Our station is the Saluting Battery and we practically live at our position, grabbing sleep next to the gun, a sandbag for a pillow.'

'Gosh, that must be a very lively spot,' said Fletcher.

'Very. Our gun barrels get worn out so fast. Sometimes we're ordered to ration our ammo. Until recently, we were only allowed fifteen rounds a day. *So* frustrating. Some locals even thought we were too afraid to fire. There is much strain and much emotion everywhere, but at least the ammo situation is a bit better now, thanks to your convoy.'

After the meal, Martina walked arm-in-arm with Fletcher back along the Sliema waterfront, ever more slowly to prolong their time together. Nearing the ferry stop, he spontaneously pulled her into a doorway and kissed her passionately on the lips.

'No one must see us,' she gasped, coming up for air. 'It's broad daylight and I'm a good Catholic girl.'

'After dark then?'

'Still a good girl.' She tittered.

'I'm falling in love with you, Martina. I've lived a feral life, all over the place in so many ways. The women I have… But this is what I want. You are what I want.'

'You're a sailor, Tom. You will set sail again. All Maltese girls know this about the British. It has always been so.'

'Is that why your father was sizing up which weapon to use on me?'

'Yes.'

Mid-morning found Grayson Douglas once again cruising in formation at 15,000 feet, heading north to intercept bombers that had been picked up on radar. It was not long before one of the pilots reported a mass of dots on the horizon. At that moment, Douglas happened to glance down and see a line of Stukas sneaking in at low level towards Valletta.

'Bandits directly below, am attacking, tally-ho!' he called into the R/T, tipping his wing and carving into a steep dive, following the enemy through the barrage as flak explosions began to rock his Hurricane. Having lost his wingman in the dive, Douglas caught up with the trailing Ju-87 just as it released its bombs and pulled up over Grand Harbour. He'd been warned that the problem with attacking a Stuka was overshooting the much slower bomber, so he eased back on the throttle, approaching from directly astern and opening up at 150 yards with a four-second burst that sent red fireballs at, over and into the ungainly aircraft. Everything juddered and shook as bits started coming off the German, then the glass canopy tore free and tumbled through the air. Banking away, Douglas saw the gunner slumped over, his arm out the side and what was left of his face a bloody mess. The pilot managed to struggle free and bail out — a burst of white as he took to the silk — and the Canadian watched the Stuka hit the sea in a slow-motion eruption of white water. Douglas well knew the pilot's adage — 'Remember, the Hun comes out of the sun' — but he'd momentarily lost focus…

'Behind you, Dougie!' a voice boomed in his ears. He shot a glance at his mirror only to find it filled with an Me-109 spitting fire. The Canadian tried a desperate jink and dive as bullets and cannon rounds tore into his fuselage with a heavy thudding. He cowered behind the seat's protective armour-plating as his instrument panel shattered into fragments and the cockpit was peppered with metal.

There was a searing pain in his right shoulder and a loud clanking from the propeller. He looked to starboard and saw a splintered aileron madly flapping as it tried to tear itself loose. Flames licked and spat around his legs; choking fumes filled the cockpit. With his Hurricane plummeting headlong towards the sea, he had only seconds to bail out. Fighting the pain in his shoulder, he reached up to open the canopy … only to find it jammed. Panic clawed at his throat. He *must* get out. The fighter turned lazily upside down, dust from the footwells enveloping him, the control column limp in his hands as the blue eternity of the sea rose up to claim him.

CHAPTER 17

One final effort … and the controls miraculously responded, offering some purchase. Douglas righted his crippled aircraft, trying to quell the panic, coughing as smoke continued to fill the cockpit. *For Christ's sake, remember the drill!* Wave crests and troughs filled his vision.

Another Herculean effort, straining at the canopy handle… Suddenly, it thrust backwards. A gale of inrushing air. Desperately fumbling, he yanked off his mask, undid the radio and oxygen cords, and pressed the Sutton safety-harness release as flames lapped at his gloved hands. Flipping the Hurricane over onto its back, he pushed forward on the stick and dropped from his seat. He felt the wind-rush of freefall, his stupid fingers grappling to find the rip cord. At a thousand feet, he was still struggling as he plummeted towards the water. At last, he tugged the cord and felt a sharp jerk at 800 feet as the chute opened like a big umbrella, but not properly; he was still falling way too fast. Flailing desperation, thrashing silk… Out the corner of his eye, the broken Hurricane smacked the sea with an almighty splash. Between his feet, the Mediterranean's white horses were rearing up to meet him.

He struck the water hard and went under.

Bubbles, gasps, salty swallowings. He burst to the surface, wind filling the chute and dragging his bruised body over and through the swells. He gulped more water … until he managed to rip himself free of the harness and watched the parachute billow downwind like an amphibian jellyfish. Exhausted and in agony, he bobbed for a while in his Mae West, before gathering the strength to unclip the little yellow dinghy from his parachute harness and inflate it by turning the cap on the CO2 bottle. His legs singed, and bleeding from multiple light shrapnel wounds to his torso, he painfully pulled himself aboard using the two looped handles. Meanwhile, having sent a mayday, his wingman circled overhead, ready to fend off any molestation while they waited for the rescue launch. Every airman knew the stories of enemy fighters shooting up Allied parachutes and dinghies.

Eventually, high-speed launch *HSL107* of the Air-Sea Rescue Service based in Kalafrana came racing towards the downed pilot, her powerful Napier engines growling rowdily, her flared bows dancing across the waves and sending up tall arcs of spray. She slowed, banked steeply and came alongside the bobbing dinghy while her .303 Lewis guns — mounted in a pair of bulbous, aircraft-style turrets — busily quartered the sky. Douglas was hauled aboard and helped below to be wrapped in blankets and given a shot of stiff Navy rum. Somehow, he'd lived to fly and fight another day.

An Australian nurse wearing a white headscarf and an apron with a red cross led Jack between the rows of bedridden men, some with awful burn wounds, some without limbs, the reek of charred skin and antiseptic filling the ward. They climbed the stairs to an officers' section with polished linoleum floors and a line of iron beds overlooking Imtarfa Hospital garden. Beyond it, a plain stretched towards Valletta and the Three Cities, shimmering in the distance. Most patients were bomb casualties, some on crutches, others sitting in cane chairs, one with blood dripping from a bottle down a tube into his arm. The ward was light and breezy, the atmosphere surprisingly cheerful. Douglas was propped up with pillows, reading the newspaper, his arm in a sling and bandages on his legs.

'Jack, the old seadog, what a swell surprise!' he exclaimed.

'Good to see you looking so chipper. How are you shaping up?' Jack asked.

'Fine, just fine, all the better for seeing you. A few bits of shrapnel removed, nothing serious. I'll be flying again in a few days.'

'Best not to rush it.'

'I can't stand being cooped up in here, watching the dogfights from my crib.'

'At least you've got a grandstand view.'

'Yes, but during the heavy raids, patients get sent, or wheeled, down to the rock shelters. We've got sixty-foot red crosses painted on the roof, but the bastards still bomb us. Lieutenant Ellis, wounded and in his dressing gown, had to defuse an unexploded thousand-pounder in the courtyard. I really need to get the hell out of this place.' Douglas lit a 'V for Victory' cigarette and offered one to Jack.

'No thanks, you'd better hang onto your ration.'

'These V fags taste like dried horse shit, probably more straw than tobacco, but one has to make do.'

'Give up smoking?'

'Not on your nelly. It's one of the few pleasures I have left.'

'A nice bunch of fellow patients, it seems.'

'Smashing. Although Kingsley over there is a tad bomb-happy: disappears under his bed at the merest drone of an engine, whimpering like a baby, poor chap. And good old Freddie, Yank pilot in the corner bed, copped a bad one, followed a Stuka into the barrage and next thing he remembers, he's hors de cockpit, falling headfirst towards Sliema, wondering what the hell happened to his Spit. He got his chute open and descended through the flak, bombs falling past him, but broke his neck on landing.'

'Prospects of recovery?' asked Jack.

'Not good. And in the bed opposite me, snoring like a freight train, is Tenente Mario Bonfatti, pilot of a Macchi Folgore. Claims to have shot down a Blenheim and three Hurricanes, but got bounced by a Spit a few days ago.'

'A bit odd having the enemy in your midst,' said Jack, taking a closer look at the handsome, deeply tanned Italian.

'Not at all. Seems like a decent chap. They've had to remove his left arm below the shoulder. Cannon shell. Not a lot of English, but we make ourselves understood. He's from Milan, a good family, but he doesn't care much for Sicily — says it's a backwater and the girls all have moustaches. Not a fan of Musso either, or so he leads us to believe. He still thinks his lot will win — says Malta will be invaded before the autumn and then *he* will be offering *me* cigarettes. Not so, Mario?' he said, raising his voice.

'*Sì*, Grayson,' said the Italian, waking groggily and giving a broad smile. He was introduced to Jack and a halting conversation ensued. It was stilted but amiable, and soon turned to the perennial subject of rationing.

'I am told you no have *dentifricio* — um, toothpaste — on Malta,' said Bonfatti. 'I am sure we can arrange for an Alcione to drop some on one of its bombing runs. Or maybe I go fetch for you? Ha ha.'

With Porky's connivance, Fletcher had plundered *Gannet*'s diminishing supplies and arrived one evening at the Sliema villa with a wooden crate containing tins of sardines, bully-beef and Boland peaches, as well as flour, boiled sweets and bars of Cadbury's ration chocolate. The four Zammits were gathered once more in the sitting room and Martina bounced up when he entered, smiling radiantly.

'Oh, this is just wonderful, Tom, thank you,' said Mrs Zammit, having warmed to the young lieutenant. 'And sardines, how nice. We never get fish these days, what with the enemy pestering our boats.'

'Of course, fishing at night with a flare or a lamp attracts more Luftwaffe than flying fish or squid,' said Martina's father.

'And tinned milk too!' exclaimed Mrs Zammit, unpacking the box. 'You certainly know the way to a lady's heart.'

A supper of egg noodles in the shape of seashells was served, accompanied by a bottle of Gozo wine — honey-coloured and smoky on the palate — a treat for the bearer of gifts. Conversation flowed more freely than on his last visit and Fletcher felt that he was, perhaps, beginning to find acceptance in the tightknit fold.

'Due to the bombing, many residents have left Sliema to stay with relatives out of town, but we're not budging,' said Mr Zammit between mouthfuls. 'I'm not going to abandon my house to thieves or looters; better to take our chances with the Luftwaffe.'

'And when the bombing gets very heavy?' asked Fletcher.

'Regrettably, Sliema doesn't have caves and tunnels like Valletta, but we do have a large shelter just off the Strand. Fortunately, Sliema is not really a target, although bombs aimed at Manoel Island and Fort Tigné often go astray.'

'Mostly we take cover beneath the stairs and pray to Our Lady,' said Mrs Zammit. 'She has saved Malta before and she will save us again.'

Luca was excited to chat to a fellow military man: 'Sometimes, at the bottom of their dives, the Stukas fly below our Bofors' lowest elevation. Last Saturday, we nailed one with a burst of four shells, two just ahead and two bracketing him.

He went into this ginormous smoking corkscrew before crashing into a bastion, with debris splashing into the harbour.'

'Your gun position is certainly in the thick of it,' said Tom.

'You bet. Yesterday, an Me-109 attacked the Saluting Battery and we all had to dive for cover. Our sandbags were peppered with holes, but fortunately no one was hurt.'

After supper, they returned to the sitting room, now stuffy due to the thick blackout curtains the servant had drawn. Martina turned on the Rediffusion set, connected by landline to homes throughout the island and broadcasting on two settings, A and B, offering English and Maltese. For Fletcher's benefit, Martina switched to A for the BBC news bulletin, followed by classical music. Halfway through a violin concerto, the announcer's voice cut in: 'Air raid warning! *Tahbit mill-ajru*!'

'Oh well, there goes Sibelius,' said Mr Zammit, sighing. 'Only a small, nuisance raid by the sound of it. Let us repair to the stairs.'

Martina and Luca doublechecked the blackout curtains, lest an air-raid warden find the slightest chink, while Mrs Zammit lit the kerosene lamp beneath the staircase where, in anticipation, the servants had placed five upright chairs in a circle. First came the purring, twin-engine sound of Beaufighter night-fighters heading north to intercept the intruders, then the heavier droning of bomber engines and the subsequent thudding of the guns to set the windows rattling as bombs began to fall on Valletta, their crumping reverberation echoing across the contained waters of Marsamuscetto.

There was a sharp whistling and a loud explosion as a stray bomb struck close by. The walls shook as plaster came free in chunks and clouds of dust billowed through the house, followed by an uneasy silence. Martina's father dragged a mattress over the five cowering figures and her mother began an earnest prayer to Our Lady of the Sacred Heart, imploring that the Zammit home and family be spared. In the background, Fletcher could faintly hear the orders being bellowed by gunners on Manoel Island, followed by the four-beat thudding of a Bofors' tattoo.

Eventually, the raiders-passed siren wailed across Sliema and residents emerged onto the street to take stock of the damage. Later still, Martina and Fletcher walked hand in hand back along the esplanade to the ferry stop, where they sat on a bench in a tight and passionate embrace, made more urgent by the earlier attack, waiting for the boat from Valletta to come chugging across the still waters of Marsamuscetto.

Fletcher dined at the Zammit home whenever his duties allowed, his continued raiding of *Gannet*'s store making him a welcome guest. The next Saturday, after a family supper, the young couple went dancing at the Sliema Club, Martina dressed in a shelter outfit with her dancing dress packed in a basket for changing in the cloakroom at the club. Entering the hall, Fletcher noticed a number of submariners from the adjacent base and Martina pointed out the beautiful 'Death Sisters' among them. Every pilot who'd dated these Maltese siblings had either been shot down or suffered an unpleasant fate, so only non-fliers were prepared to risk dancing with them.

For Martina and Fletcher, it was both a thrill and a joyful release to twirl around the floor to a waltz or palais glide, but the evening slipped by all too quickly. The band stopped playing at 2300 sharp, after which time the worst raids usually occurred, and the couple wandered slowly back to the Zammit home, taking a lengthy detour along the esplanade, past the Z-shaped shelters and ferry stop.

The next Wednesday they both had liberty. Martina suggested they borrow her uncle's boat and spend the day on the tiny island of Comino, halfway between Malta and Gozo. The couple set off early, taking the blue bus from Valletta, through the suburbs of Hamrun and Birkirkara, past Mosta Cathedral with its massive (holed) dome, the road zigzagging through arid countryside and crossing the Victoria Lines, a scarp fortified by the British in the nineteenth century to deter invasion. The farmland was partitioned by low stone walls and dotted with farmhouses and small white churches with single bell-cotes. Passing a red watchtower, the bus descended to Marfa Bay on Malta's northern peninsula and dropped them off at a small inlet bobbing with fishing vessels.

'That's my uncle's *firilla*,' said Martina, pointing to a double-ended boat painted red, green and blue, moored to a buoy just off the jetty. The strange craft had a tall, upright prow and sternpost, a long white bowsprit and a stubby mast.

'It looks a bit like an overgrown dghaisa,' said Fletcher.

'I suppose it is, more or less.'

'How do we get to it?'

'We swim. Leave the bags: we'll pick them up on the way.'

They stripped off, Fletcher trying not to stare at her petite, shapely figure, the black one-piece leaving little to the imagination. Martina dived into luminous green water, surfaced and floated on her back like an otter. 'Come on, slowcoach!'

Fletcher performed an ungainly bellyflop and they swam breaststroke to the *firilla*, pulling themselves aboard. Martina sorted out the rigging while he fitted the oars, released the mooring line and rowed them over to the jetty, where she jumped ashore to collect the bags and picnic basket.

'*Ejja*, let's go!' she said, stepping down onto a thwart and taking the tiller. Fletcher rowed them out to the wind, shipped the oars and helped raise the heavy, quadrilateral sail. Martina steered and worked the vangs while Fletcher took charge of the tiny jib attached to the bowsprit.

'Such a strange sail configuration,' he said. 'I think it's what they call a sprit rig.'

'A *tarkija* in Maltese.'

'And why do you have an eye painted on each bow?'

'Those are the eyes of Osiris to see us safely over the water. It's a custom that goes back to the Romans. Don't you have them on *Gannet*?' she asked mischievously.

'I'll have a word with my captain, but he's quite proper, likes things pusser, so I don't think he'd agree.'

'Pembroke sounds like a stick-in-the-mud.'

'Um, not really. An Oxford man like me, bit of a loner, a troubled soul, weight of the world on his shoulders and all, but I wouldn't want to go to sea with any other. He's just the man you need when the balloon goes up.'

'They say he's rather good-looking.'

'Who's they?'

'Oh, just the girls at HQ.'

'I've never really thought about it, but yes, I suppose in a stern sort of way.'

'Not nearly as handsome as you, dear Tom.'

'Nor as charming, irresistible and debonair?'

'Something like that.'

They sailed towards the sparsely populated isle lying a mile offshore, the grey cliffs of Gozo rising in the distance behind it. Playing the fluky breeze, Martina aimed for Lantern Point crowned with the square tower of Santa Marija, dating from the fifteenth century. After a few minutes of diminishing breeze, she tacked, opting for a long beat to the northeast in search of more wind.

'That's very odd,' said Fletcher.

'What is?'

'Look there, those planes should most definitely *not* be flying together. Three Spitfires and what looks like an enemy bomber.'

'Why on earth aren't they shooting it down?'

'I haven't a clue.'

As the aircraft drew nearer, Martina identified the Italian as a Cant Z506 Airone — an ungainly, three-engine floatplane often used for sea rescue. It lumbered overhead, the Spitfires remaining above and astern as it flew lower and lower, past St Paul's Bay, then touched down in a series of splashes and motored towards the shore with the fighters circling overhead.

'Would you believe it? I think the RAF just captured an Itie,' said Fletcher. 'The Brylcreem boys earning their keep for once.'

Martina tacked back towards the barren isle, sailing close to the limestone cliffs of Lantern Point and aiming the *firilla* at a channel separating Camino from the islet of Cominotto. With hardly a breath of wind for propulsion, she skilfully negotiated a narrow passage between rocky outcrops and sailed into an enchanting lagoon, gliding over transparent, cyan water. Fletcher dropped the sail and, at Martina's command, lobbed the anchor over the side. The *firilla* came to a halt in the chest-deep water of a sandy isthmus. There was not another boat in sight, nor any sign of humans on either shore.

'This is paradise,' he said.

'Yes, it is.'

'The colour of this water is —'

'I know, isn't it just?'

Martina stood up and executed a shallow dive. Not trusting the depth, Fletcher lowered himself over the side into the warmest seawater he'd ever encountered. She swam closer, her face inches from his, water glittering on her long lashes, wet hair snaking across her shoulders, full lips dark as plums. He pulled her to his chest and they kissed, lips immediately parting, her arms wrapping around his neck, her legs around his waist. Suspended, they remained locked in a long and silent embrace.

Later, they waded ashore with the picnic basket and spread their towels in a sandy, limestone-walled cove not much bigger than a bedroom.

'You'd better put on your hat and maybe a shirt too,' she said. 'Your English skin does not enjoy this weather.'

'Aye, another scorcher. There's no respite from the heat.'

'In Maltese we say, "*Xemx taqli l-bajd*" — a sun that fries eggs.'

'My skin certainly feels toasted.'

Martina unpacked the basket. Porky had contributed sandwiches, Mrs Zammit lemonade, figs and small, crisp pears. Away to the southeast, they could see puffs of flak accompanied by the hollow thudding of coastal guns, followed by the distant rumble of exploding bombs. Condensation trails stitched the sky with the vaporous threads of dogfighting.

'Grand Harbour is getting pasted again,' said Fletcher.

'It seems like another world.'

'An eternity away.'

Martina lay back and gazed up at his enchanting face, haloed by the sun and an unruly blond cowlick, the vague hint of freckles on his nose and cheeks, now darkened by his sunburn. They kissed again, their lips tasting and exploring. Her heart was enraptured, but so too was her body, which was saying all manner of things it should not. She was grappling with the idea of how this aching desire she felt for her lover's body could, through the simple act of marriage, become acceptable, even sanctioned by God. For now, here, it was sin incarnate. Only through holy union … but what of her entire being burning to be one with his at this very moment? Her kisses grew hungrier. She must remember the rules and the guardrails, despite the tempest raging inside her. Using all her willpower, she gently extricated herself from his embrace, stood up and playfully ran into the limpid water.

The afternoon wore on, windless and sweltering. They swam repeatedly in the lagoon, then lay in each other's arms on the sand, cradled by the limestone walls of the cove, shielded from the rest of the world and from prying eyes. Their amorous play grew increasingly dangerous. He pressed himself against her, his hands on her breasts, gliding over her bronzed body, pulling back her costume, his fingers venturing between her thighs. His urgency matched her own, but no, this could not happen. Not here, not now. Martina tenderly pushed his hand away.

They returned to the water and floated together in a close embrace. The afternoon had burnt itself to an amber hue, the limestone glowing like honey, the water reflecting the colourful paintwork of their *firilla.*

'Look at how scarlet the sun has turned,' he said.

'Just magical, and yet everything out there is turmoil.'

'But here, with you … it's perfect.'

'I never want to go back.'

There was a long silence as they stared into each other's eyes.

'Martina, darling, there's … there's something I would very much like to ask of you.'

'What is it?' she whispered, noting the seriousness in his voice.

Another long pause, filled with the shrill pulsing of distant cicadas.

'My love … will you … will you marry me?' he whispered.

'What did you say?' she exclaimed, her eyes wide.

'Marry me. Will you?'

'Have you lost your mind? It's the sun's doing. Englishmen—'

'Marry me.'

'Tom?' Her eyes began to well.

'Yes?'

'Tom!'

'Yes.'

'*Iva, mela*! Yes, yes, of course I will.'

CHAPTER 18

Douglas strode across the cratered field towards his new aircraft with its khaki and mustard camouflage. He ran an appreciative eye over its gleaming three-bladed propeller with the big mouth of a Vokes tropical filter beneath it to limit the intake of dust and sand. He also noted with delight that his erks had painted a winged cheetah on the cowling. The Spitfire Mark V was indeed a thing of beauty: an all-metal fuselage and supercharged Rolls Royce Merlin engine delivering almost 1,500 horsepower. It had a narrower undercarriage and less range than his Sea Hurricane, but in every other respect, it was a big step up.

In addition to four Browning .303 machine guns, there were two Hispano 20-mm cannons, extending like spears from the leading edge of its wings, which would give him a whole lot more punch. He'd asked his armourer to adjust the guns to converge at 250 yards, a good range to swamp the enemy with a deluge of rounds.

Fortunately, the Canadian had done a Hurricane to Spitfire conversion course back at Number Eight Flying Training School, RAF Montrose, so the switch should be a smooth one. Besides, given recent losses, Malta needed every pilot and aircraft it could get into the air. He must just remember how to deal with the notorious blind spot behind the nose on take-off, as well as the Merlin's powerful torque that had a nasty habit of swinging the bird off its line.

Douglas had been granted a short, early-morning practice flight south of the island to reacquaint himself. He climbed into the narrow cockpit — a tight fit for his big frame —

positioning the parachute in the bucket seat to form a cushion. He connected the oxygen tube to his mask, plugged the R/T jack into the instrument panel and checked the fuel gauges. The rigger and flight mechanic had already rolled the trolley accumulator into place and were slotting the lead into the engine mounting under the wing. The fitter gave a thumbs up and Douglas opened the throttle lever a fraction — mixture to rich — then switched on the engine. There was a throaty cough, followed by a gratifying roar as flames spat from the exhaust stubs. A voice from Takali tower crackled in his ears, giving him clearance.

Douglas rolled out of the blast pen, kicking up clouds of dust. He kept the canopy hood open for a few more moments of relatively cool air as he taxied to the end of the runway, turned and came to a halt. It was somewhat intimidating to be back behind the controls of a Spit and he was apprehensive, the wound in his shoulder pulsing with added urgency. Pulling the hood closed, he began accelerating, hardly able to see the runway over the nose, already feeling the sensitivity of the controls and the fighter's tendency to veer. Wheels drilled over gravel, followed by a few bounces, then the aircraft took off easily, the controls more responsive as the Spitfire gathered airspeed. Lifting away from Takali, he pumped the handle to retract the undercarriage. Higher now, relishing the unbelievable rate of climb, light and free and fast, he felt the heady exhilaration once more, his bird responding to the barest touch of rudder or elevator.

It was a short flight, just enough to start getting comfortable in a Spit once again. Back on the ground, Douglas hardly had time for a cup of tea and a glance at the newspaper headlines before being scrambled.

'Green Leader, sixty-plus bandits, twelve miles north-northwest, angels twenty,' said the voice in the R/T as he climbed away from the airfield. Angels twenty meant 20,000 feet. The squadron of Takali Spitfires climbed to 25,000 feet, trying to get above the intruders. Douglas was the first to catch sight of a cluster of dots approaching at the same height: the enemy fighter cover of at least forty Me-109s and Macchi Folgores. Turning tail would be fatal, so the Spitfires headed straight towards the enemy, Douglas experiencing an injection of adrenalin and terror in equal measure. The opposing fighters streaked towards each other at a combined speed of more than 600 knots, neither side giving way.

'Our cup runneth over with targets, lads,' crackled the voice of the squadron leader. 'Tally-ho!'

The Spitfires opened fire just before ploughing through the enemy ranks in a streaky blur, then carved sharply to port and starboard in pairs. Within moments, the skirmish turned into a twisting melee, bandits everywhere, the sky a chaotic tangle of diving, weaving, climbing aircraft. Douglas banked hard, attaching himself to the tail of a Folgore, and pressed the firing button. A storm of .303 rounds juddered from his wings, the slower bop-bop-bop of his cannons offering a baritone accompaniment. How different this felt to a Sea Hurricane. A cluster of explosions tore pieces off the enemy fighter, before it jinked away and was lost.

A yellow-nosed Me-109 locked onto his tail, spurting fire. Douglas pulled back on the stick, the centrifugal force pressing him down hard in his bucket seat. Limbs and controls grew heavy as G forces exacted their toll. Flirting with blackout, he eased off, flipped over and dived, but the wretched German clung on like a limpet, firing another burst. Tracer tore over his canopy.

Douglas tried an old trick, pulling back on his throttle and kicking hard right rudder, almost bringing the Spitfire to a halt and forcing the 109 to overtake him. Then hard left rudder and throttle jammed forward to regain speed, with the enemy now presenting itself as a target. He pressed the firing button and scored a few hits as the German went into a steep climb. Eyes, hands and feet working together, he clung to the Messerschmitt's tail, squeezing off short bursts each time he got the chance.

Closer now, every detail of the 109 stood out — the twin radiator, retracted wheels, dark crosses on the underside of blue wings. He waited a few seconds until the enemy's wingtips filled his gunsight, then pressed the button again, firing an accurate, four-second burst. Chunks of fuselage ripped free as oil and glycol from the German's cooling system vented a white stream. Douglas eased out to one side and watched as more pieces broke away. The enemy pilot turned a leather-helmeted face in his direction. Then the 109's fuel tank blew up and the fighter flipped over, plunging towards the sea in a death spiral. The Canadian stayed on its tail, nearing the vertical, Mediterranean blue rushing towards them: he needed to see this kill concluded. The Messerschmitt hit the water with a towering splash and Douglas pulled up as gently as possible, almost blacking out in the process.

Jack caught a dghaisa across the harbour to the esplanade, then walked uphill to the Floriana terminus at Portes des Bombes city gate. The bus — a bulbous-shaped wheezer with all its windows missing — stood waiting at the stop. Somewhat disconcertingly, locals crossed themselves as they climbed aboard, as though embarking on a dangerous voyage. Jack noted with surprise that the passengers included a nanny-goat and three rowdy chickens. The interior was richly decorated with patterns in bold colours and, balanced on the dashboard, a silver vase with artificial flowers beside an image of the Virgin Mary. They set off with a loud grinding of gears and clouds of exhaust fumes, the driver weaving his way around potholes, craters and the remains of bombed-out buildings.

Given Malta's severe fuel shortage, the bus went only as far as the Takali turnoff and Jack had to walk the last stretch to Mdina in the blazing, midday heat. He paused to let a Spitfire riddled with bullet holes taxi across the road on its way to a pen, then continued through an orange orchard and up the hill towards Mdina's battlements. Crossing a moat, he entered the citadel through a monumental gate topped with an intricately carved escutcheon.

Inside the walls, the cool, silent alleys were lined with grand medieval façades. Jack had to press himself against a wall as a horse-drawn *karozzin* passed by, the sound of metal-shod hooves and steel-rimmed wheels echoing off the flagstones. Everywhere he looked were petite palaces and ornate churches, domes and pilasters, all rendered in yellowing Maltese limestone. Here was peace and timelessness, an ancient precinct untouched by bombs, standing in the starkest contrast to Valletta and the Three Cities. Jack found his way to Palazzo Xara, passed through a courtyard fragrant with flowers and entered a lobby with tall ceilings and paintings of nobles in gold frames. At that moment, Douglas appeared through a mahogany door.

'Rather posh digs you've got,' said Jack.

'Certainly beats dear old *Vulture*. It's the palace of Baron Chapelle, requisitioned by the RAF for the duration.'

Douglas led Jack up a broad staircase to a long, wide terrace built into Mdina's ramparts. Jack's gaze swept from Mosta's dome and RAF Takali to the hazy spires of Valletta and south to RAF Luqa.

'What a sumptuous view: a window on the world,' said Jack. 'And the twin Lewis guns?'

'Oh, they're for taking potshots at Jerry if he flies too close. Spices things up a bit when the lads are bored.'

'You must spend a lot of time up here.'

'We do. Legendary drinking and lots of pranks too, pilots letting off steam after a hard day at the office. We stay up late on these balmy evenings, talking, singing, reminiscing about home ... like a family. It helps.'

The Canadian ushered Jack to a table. A steward brought beers, followed by plates of Maconochie meat-and-veg stew with Number Nine 'dog' biscuits.

'You'll find the M and V tastes a bit odd. Our chef — although that's perhaps too grandiose a term for the urchin from Whitechapel — uses Merlin engine oil to heat the food. It gives it a funny flavour.'

'Mmm, tastes sooty.'

'You get used to it, especially if you're starving ... and we're always bloody well starving. I sometimes feel I could eat a cow between two bread vans. The food situation leaves us all feeling rather weak and crotchety at times. My dreams and fantasies used to involve my beautiful wife, giving the ferret a run, that sort of thing; now they're filled with T-bone steaks and chocolate eclairs.'

'Surely pilots get better nosh than the rest of us.'

'Marginally better, but it wouldn't be right and Lord Gort says military personnel and islanders must get the same rations. Damn right too.'

'My cook, Porky, tells me the going rate for rats is one shilling, mice are ninepence and sparrows five shillings a pair.'

'Decent prices, those. Our chef also gets supplementary rats, trapped by a local farmer whose little terrier is an excellent ratter. The chap pitches up at the mess every now and then with what look like small chicken breasts. Fried with garlic and onions, the lads love 'em.'

'No, thank you.'

'Last week we had a proper treat. Our cook sold two parachutes riddled with bullet holes to Maria Ferugia, who runs the local lacemaking shop, and then put the cash to good use. He knows a gharry man in Floriana who had an old horse no longer able to pull his carriage. Money changed hands; the horse was led to an out-of-the-way spot and knocked on the head. An RAF van and trailer collected the carcass to be butchered. Needless to say, we ate damn well for a few days.'

A pilot with long blond hair and a high forehead appeared on the terrace, eclectically dressed in an army battledress blouse, baggy grey trousers, a white silk scarf and desert boots.

'That's Flight Lieutenant Adrian Warburton, DSO and DFC. He's our whizz photo-reconnaissance guy — a bit of a loner and eccentric as hell, but boy, what an airman.'

'I've heard his name mentioned.'

'Warby is absolutely fearless. To get his photos, he'll happily fly through an enemy harbour, at mast height, in daylight, under murderous crossfire. Let me introduce you.'

Douglas waved the pilot over.

'Come join us, Warby. Meet Jack Pembroke, captain of HMSAS *Southern Gannet*, the plucky little whaler left behind after Assegai.'

The two officers shook hands and Warburton took a seat. A horse's neck and ice was delivered moments later by the steward.

'I believe you're both Oxford chaps,' said Douglas.

‘Oh, jolly good, which college?’ asked Jack.

‘Not university, just school — St Edward’s,’ said Warburton.

‘And what do you fly?’ asked Jack.

‘Until recently, Martin Marylands, but currently long-range Spitfires.’

‘They’re high-altitude jobs, painted blue, beautiful creatures,’ cut in Douglas.

‘We have Marylands in South Africa too, mostly for coastal patrol,’ said Jack. ‘You fly reconnaissance, don’t you?’

‘Yes. I do a regular snoop of Taranto to keep tabs on what the Regia Marina is up to —’

‘He’s very modest,’ Douglas interrupted. ‘Warby did the groundwork for the Swordfish attack that crippled the Itie fleet back in 1940, *and* he gave us early warning about the enemy setting sail during Assegai.’

‘Much obliged for that,’ said Jack.

‘Don’t mention it. All in a day’s work.’

‘Warby also guided the Wimpies and Beauforts into attacks on the battlefleet on its way to intercept Assegai.’

‘How exactly do you do it?’ asked Jack.

‘Well, I shadow the Ities and our bomber boys pick up the rooster in my Maryland from about fifty miles away, which guides them in. I think we got a torpedo hit on one of the cruisers returning to Taranto, but the spotting conditions were ghastly, so it’s only a probable.’

‘Show Jack your wristband.’

‘Really, Douglas!’

‘Oh, go on.’

Warburton reluctantly held out his hand.

‘He won’t tell you, but I will,’ said Douglas. ‘Warby got into a dustup with an Airone floatplane and three Italian fighters. A bullet struck his instrument panel, penetrated his harness and hit him in the chest. With an engine on fire, he still managed to bag the floatplane and one of the fighters. Then, cool as a cucumber, he extracted the bullet with his fingers, and that's it mounted on his wristband.'

'Astonishing,' said Jack.

'Douglas is such a nob,' said Warburton, blushing.

'Anything of note happening in Taranto at the minute?' asked Jack.

'Not really. But lately I've been buzzing a little island in the Pelagie Group on which Jerry has installed a powerful RDF.'

'I heard it was tracking us during Assegai,' said Jack.

'Yes, it seems to be posing a serious threat to shipping.'

'Oh, hello,' said Douglas, pointing to Takali, where four Spitfires were climbing steeply from the strip, followed soon after by another three, their Merlins roaring to gain altitude. The officers stood up and walked to the balustrade.

'Stukas,' said Warburton. Jack's eyesight was good, but it took him a few moments to notice the specs.

'Lots of fighters above 'em,' Warburton added. 'The Spits will have their hands full. They might try to get in underneath the Stukas and hit 'em on their way down.'

'As you can imagine, we spend a lot of time on this terrace, analysing tactics,' said Douglas. 'Anything for a slight edge. The game never stops evolving.'

'Just like gladiators,' Jack said.

'More like jousters,' said Warburton.

Soon, dogfighting vapour trails began to weave ethereal webs against the blue, and the straggling line of Stukas tipped into their dives from almost overhead Takali. One of them tailed a Spitfire, its Hispano cannons clearly audible, echoing across the valley. Tentacles of crimson tracer reached up from the airfield, accompanied by the four-beat thump of Bofors. The aircraft dropped through the barrage, one Stuka taking fire, then exploding, but the rest coming on regardless. At the bottom of each run, three bombs came loose and arrowed into the airfield, sending up mushrooms of dust as the gull-winged aircraft described an astonishingly tight pull-out and climbed back to the safety of altitude.

'We should really be wearing tin hats,' said Douglas. 'The other day Bob Sergeant was hit by a stray bullet here on the terrace — clipped his lower lip and jaw. He's fine, but it was an abject lesson that there's a war on out there beyond our palazzo.'

The aerial skirmish reached a crescendo as the aerodrome disappeared behind towers of dust and smoke, the thud of the bombs reverberating from the valley. A Spitfire was alight in its pen; a Hurricane, caught out in the open while taxiing, had been destroyed; a Stuka crashed into a vineyard with a livid splash of orange, two parachutes following it down. One Spitfire, clipped by friendly flak, began trailing smoke and went into a left-hand spiral dive that grew ever steeper. At the last moment a parachute appeared, blossoming in the smoke, to much clapping and cheering from the terrace. To Jack, it felt a bit like a much deadlier version of the Brasenose cricket pavilion beside the Isis. The entertainment was over in a matter of minutes and the officers returned to their tables for postprandial coffee.

After lunch, Douglas fetched his bicycle, Warburton lent Jack his own and the pair set off in a south-westerly direction towards Għar Lapsi through a parched land roasting in the mid-afternoon heat. Jack noticed that, as in Britain, signposts and milestones had been removed or defaced to confuse any would-be invader. The countryside was webbed with drystone walls and solid limestone farmhouses with pumpkins ripening on their roofs, the fields dotted with olive, carob, lemon and fig trees. A group of young boys spotted the wings on Douglas's uniform and chanted, 'Speetfire, Speetfire!'

'You're rather popular,' said Jack, riding abreast of his friend.

'Nothing personal. Anyone who looks vaguely like a pilot gets the full treatment by the kids.'

They wended their way down to the coast on narrow roads lined with Cape sorrel plants imported from South Africa, which were now a ubiquitous weed. The pair passed wayside shrines, each with a small statue of a patron saint, and the odd cyclist or horse-drawn cart. An army truck overtook them, throwing up clouds of limestone dust and covering them in powder that melted with their perspiration to leave white streaks on their skin. They paused beside a pond so that Jack could look at the assembled waterfowl, and he was pleased to spot a greenshank and a black-winged stilt to add to his Malta list.

Condensation trails high above them spoke of more dogfights, but they felt quite safe — that is until they heard the loud grumble of a fighter. Both cyclists slammed on their brakes with a spray of gravel and dived into a ditch as an Me-109 roared overhead, heading for Luqa aerodrome. Dusting themselves off, they made a few jokes at each other's expense, then continued cycling.

The duo arrived at the crest of a cliff, the sparkling Mediterranean stretching to the southwest and the rocky islet of Filfla, used for target practice by the RAF, lying a couple of miles offshore. They chatted to a sentry, who led them past a machine-gun pillbox and through a gap in the barbed wire. The two officers picked their way down a path, the air filled with the plaintive calling of yellow-legged gulls floating on the updraught of the cliffs, until they came to a pretty cove of emerald water. There was a slipway and a few fishing boats pulled up on the rocks. They changed into bathing trunks — Douglas had brought a pair for Jack — and reclined on towels laid out on a smooth slab of limestone in the shade of an overhang. Conversation turned to their immediate future.

'Do you think Malta will be invaded?' asked Jack.

'I don't know. There's plenty of talk. The powers that be still think it's possible, hence more barbed wire and landmines, more coastal gun emplacements and anti-tank defences, more pillboxes at every landing point.'

'What about gliders, like the Germans used on Crete?'

'Not likely. Thank God for Malta's farmers: all those stone walls around their fields should deter, or at least limit, that kind of attack and paratroopers couldn't do it alone. Come on, let's have a dip.'

They climbed over the rocks, entered the lukewarm water and swam out to a channel where the sea sucked back and forth, tossing them about like corks. After a while, they slithered onto a ledge and lay basking.

'Did you hear about the Italian floatplane captured by some of our chaps?' asked Douglas.

'My gunnery officer mentioned he'd seen it landing, but didn't know the details.'

'Stranger than fiction, old boy.' Douglas went on to recount the story of the Bristol Beaufort of 217 Squadron, piloted by Edward Strever of the South African Air Force. After torpedoing an Italian freighter off the Greek coast, the bomber had been badly hit by flak and was forced to ditch. The pilot and all four crew members survived the crash and were subsequently rescued and taken to a nearby Italian base. Next day, the crew were put on a Cant Airone, bound for Taranto and internment, but during the flight, the prisoners overpowered their guard and took over the floatplane, diverting it to Malta. Although attacked by Spitfires and suffering a number of cannon hits, they managed to make it known to the fighters that they were surrendering.

'Astonishing,' said Jack. 'And you say the pilot was South African?'

'Yes, never shy of a spot of skulduggery, those Springboks.'

'Don't I know it. Aren't you happy they're on our side?'

'Sometimes I'm not so sure.' They both chuckled.

After a long silence, Douglas said, 'You know, things are so fast-paced around here that one hardly gets the chance to think about what we're *really* doing.'

'Which is probably a good thing.'

'Probably. But I can't help feeling that we're actually conducting trophy hunts up there above the clouds. We're preying on other men — men just like ourselves — in these deadly one-on-one duels. It's quite grotesque. And with an audience of islanders watching below, it's as though we're in this vast, aerial colosseum.'

'Dogfighting does make war incredibly personal,' said Jack. 'Sometimes I take a step back and wonder what the hell all this is about. The Mediterranean has been a cauldron of war for thousands of years, often with the same adversaries rehashing the same battles again and again down the centuries.'

'But Hitler and Mussolini are different,' countered Douglas. 'Fascism is different. It has to be destroyed.'

'Yes, I suppose so. That's certainly what I thought back in thirty-nine. But then again, that's exactly what Malta's knights would have said about the Turks. War solves nothing. Somehow, man has got to find another way of living on this planet of ours.'

'Can a leopard change its spots?'

Both men grew silent. The light of the westering sun bloodied the cliffs as the temperature mellowed to a pleasant balminess.

'Idyllic,' said Jack. 'Such peace.'

'Peace. A strange word. We've had so many losses recently. Kesselring has reinforced Fliegerkorps II with two bomber *Gruppen* and a fighter *Gruppe* of Me-109Gs packed with aces and led by Hauptmann Heinz Bär, he of 113 kills. Nearly fifty per cent of our fighters have been destroyed in the air or on the ground so far this month. Good pilots lost, good friends, although newly made, but made in the forge of battle. Suddenly they're not there in the mess and they leave this terrible hole, their laughter and their joshing gone. But there's no time to grieve; we can't afford to grieve. It would be too … much.'

'I know how you feel. After Dunkirk. After Tobruk.'

Douglas took a deep breath. 'I think a lot about death, you know. Despite my burns, I've been lucky. But when it happens, if it happens, how will I take my leave? Bleeding to death from bullet wounds as my bird drifts to earth? Unable to bail out and burnt to a crisp? Instant annihilation in a detonation of flak? Crashing into the sea and drowning?'

'You mustn't be so morbid, Douglas. You need to try to stay positive.'

'One gets morbid, Jack. You should know. You've also been through the mill.'

'Aye, I suppose so.'

CHAPTER 19

Jack got back to Fort St Angelo after dark and received a message to report without delay to the NOIC. He hastily pulled on a clean shirt, combed his hair and hurried to Huffington-Smythe's office. Jack knocked on the door and a booming voice told him to enter. The commodore was in earnest conversation with an intelligence officer and the room was rank with cigarette smoke.

'Pembroke, late again!' barked the anchor-faced commodore. 'Sit down.'

Something was wrong: Jack's heart began to pound.

'Lieutenant, you are in very, very deep trouble.'

'Sir?' Jack's voice was hoarse. Where on earth was the axe going to fall this time? 'My ship?'

'No. Regrettably, it's a sordid matter of the heart. I'll hand over to Major Trahern.'

The ginger-haired giant with a neatly rectangular moustache and cold eyes sat forward, elbows on the table, his gaze boring into Jack. 'We understand that you have been conducting an affair with a Spanish national, a certain Mrs Alana Vilar, of Alexandria.'

'Sir, I don't see how —'

'We've been informed by Intelligence that Mrs Vilar has been arrested for spying.'

'But —'

'Once her interrogation is concluded, she will be tried for high treason and, in all likelihood, sentenced to death.'

'That's … that's … impossible,' whispered Jack, the blood draining from his face. The pain in his chest was like a knife blade. He needed air. 'I … I… There is no way —'

'You do, of course, realise the calamitous position this places you in, Lieutenant? You see, Mrs Vilar's father is a good friend of the shipping magnate Baron de Sacrelirio,' explained Major Trahern, 'who is a good friend of Admiral Canaris, head of the Abwehr. Mrs Vilar's husband is —'

'Alana's husband was killed by the fascists in the Civil War,' muttered Jack.

'Wrong, Lieutenant. Her husband is alive and well and living in Madrid. He is an ardent fascist, providing intelligence to the German secret service via De Sacrelirio.'

'That's just not possible,' whispered Jack, his body beginning to tremble.

'Because Mrs Vilar told you so?' Trahern said sarcastically. 'Please, Lieutenant, you have been played by the oldest trick in the book. We need to know exactly what you have divulged in your pillow talk.'

'Nothing, sir, nothing at all.'

Huffington-Smythe brought his open hand down on the table with a loud smack that made Jack flinch. 'Come off it, Pembroke!' he bellowed. 'None of us was born yesterday. Think, damn it!'

Trahern continued, 'We know that De Sacrelirio has been passing on highly sensitive information, particularly shipping movements, to the Nazis. We can't move a rowing boat anywhere in the Med without Berlin knowing about it. What the hell have you told that conniving harlot?'

'I can't think of anything significant, sir. I was always very careful. We just spoke vaguely —'

'Come on, Pembroke!' roared the commodore.

'Vaguely about —'

'I am running out of patience.' The major's voice had grown soft, almost conversational. 'Let me help you understand the gravity of your predicament. Mrs Vilar's father was discovered to have business dealings with suspicious individuals in Alexandria, Cairo and Palestine, which got our intelligence boys interested in him. Surveillance revealed that he was meeting a group of pro-German officers from the Egyptian army, in particular a worrisome individual named Gamal Abdel Nasser and his pal, Anwar Al-Sadat. Our intelligence chaps have been keeping close tabs on that lot — as nasty a bunch of backstabbing turncoats as you're likely to find. They'd welcome Rommel with roses and champagne if he ever reached Alex.'

'But, Major, I don't see how this relates to me.'

'Then your eyes need to be opened, Lieutenant. Spies have been gathering intelligence on the Royal Navy: convoys, cargos, shipping movements. Mrs Vilar was one of those spies and *you* were the perfect oracle.'

The grilling was thorough and deeply disturbing, Jack's mind anxiously tacking back and forth over the previous months as he sought its painful recalibration. The major forced him to review everything he'd told Alana that could have been compromising. Jack's tone became wooden as, with complete candour, he recounted every detail he could remember of their conversations about anything to do with the war. After three hours of cross-examination, the two officers seemed satisfied enough with his answers and dismissed him. Major Trahern would return in the morning to continue the interrogation and take a full written statement.

His legs barely able to carry him, Jack slowly climbed the stairs to his bastion room in a state of shock, his mind in uproar, his heart filled with the kind of grief he'd not known since the death of his mother. He had not eaten supper, but felt no hunger, only a yearning for a return to the world of just a few hours earlier. Jack lay down on his bed and stared blankly at the ceiling, letting the ache course through him. Was everything he'd experienced with Alana an illusionist's trick? It seemed he had placed her on a pedestal of delusion and lies. Was their union, her love, merely a thing of smoke and mirrors: a chimera? He wondered whether she had felt anything at all for him or simply used him as a tool — a willing one at that. Did any part of the woman of his waking dreams even exist? Resentment and loathing were sure to come, but for now he was still in a state of turmoil and disbelief.

He opened his desk drawer, pulled out the White Horse and took a long swig straight from the bottle. Anger had begun to boil inside him as he pieced together the jigsaw of their relationship. Alana had been so intoxicatingly enigmatic, but he saw now that she had only told him enough about herself to keep him from asking more. Probing her past had offered mostly closed doors, so he had stuck to the present. The present had been fine with him, but he now realised her secrecy had only added to the allure and heightened his enthralment. She had duped him with consummate ease. He punched the wall with the side of his fist. *Fool that he had been*!

And what *had* he told Alana? The whisky helped dislodge fragments of conversation. Yes, she'd always demanded to know when he was leaving and returning, where the convoy was going, how dangerous it might be. He'd viewed her questioning through the lens of concern for his safety. On that last night of passion at the Hotel Cecil, what exactly had he let slip? How many lives might he have endangered? How soaked in blood were his hands? He let out a sound that was half sob, half groan. Sleep, he must find the sanctuary of sleep, and please God let soft oblivion keep the nightmares at bay. He tilted the bottle and finished its remains with a few long slugs.

Douglas had been strapped into his seat for an hour, waiting to take off. It was another scorching, windless day, the metal in the cockpit so hot it burnt his skin when touched. At last, the hooter sounded from Takali's control tower and a flare looped into the air.

'Scramble, scramble, scramble!' came the voice through the R/T.

Douglas pulled out the photograph of Sally, put it to his lips, and returned it to his breast pocket. Taxiing to the end of the runway, he swung his aircraft around and opened the throttle, dust clouds billowing from his wheels as he rumbled down the strip, lifted off and climbed away at a steep angle.

'Green Leader, airborne,' he said into the mic.

Four Spitfires rose rapidly to 20,000 feet, where they soon encountered incoming enemy fighters. A Macchi Folgore was flying a parallel course, but had a bit of height on Douglas, who went straight into the attack. The skirmish developed into a series of rolling scissor turns, his Spitfire managing to cut the corners and granting him a 45-degree deflection shot from 350 yards. The Italian steepened his climb and turned hard, condensation trails streaming from his wingtips. Douglas clung on and fired a longer burst from 100 yards. The Folgore tried a side slip to port, but was too late. Rounds punctured his engine and the mortally wounded Italian spun out of control. Glancing down, Douglas noticed a flight of Stukas making for Grand Harbour and was about to tip over into a dive…

He felt body blows to his aircraft as cannon shells punctured the fuselage. In his mirror was an Me-109, huge and flashing fire, the acrid smell of incendiaries filling his nostrils. The Merlin engine exploded, venting flames and gouts of black smoke as large chunks tore free. He knew immediately his Spitfire was done for. Fighting the panic, he dragged open the canopy, flipped the aircraft onto its back as Grand Harbour twisted beneath him, and dropped into the blue, grappling for and then yanking the ripcord.

Far below, Jack was on *Gannet*'s bridge, staring skyward at the swirling dogfights. As usual, Sparks had his R/T tuned to the fighter pilots' channel and broadcast its chatter on the ship's intercom. Over the preceding minutes, strained and breathless voices had echoed through the messdecks, fuelling Jack's apprehension.

'Four o'clock low!'

'I can't see 'em, you lead.'

'A flock of Stukas.' Jack thought he recognised the Canadian accent.

'Bigger flock of 109s above.'

'Tally-ho.'

'Jesus, Green Leader, watch out, *behind you*!'

Then, quite distinctly: 'I've bought it! I'm bailing out!'

It was definitely Douglas's voice. Jack's gaze tracked the broken Spitfire, engulfed in flames, spiralling down towards the harbour. Higher up, and to his profound relief, he spotted the snapping open of a parachute.

Then, seemingly from nowhere, a yellow-nosed Me-109 tore in and fired a burst, its tracer narrowly missing the defenceless pilot. Jack bellowed, 'No, you bastard!' as the German made a close pass, banked hard and returned, opening fire at the dangling pilot and puncturing the silk canopy, then collapsing it with the Messerschmitt's slipstream. Jack watched in horror as the limp pilot plummeted to the sea beneath the shredded remains of his chute, falling faster and faster until the body of his friend struck the water off St Elmo point with a silent splash.

Overcome with emotion, Jack's whole body trembled uncontrollably and, fighting back the tears, he climbed unsteadily down the ladder to his cabin.

CHAPTER 20

'Urgent message from NOIC, sir,' said Sparks, appearing in the doorway. 'You are requested to report to War HQ immediately.'

Feeling utterly distraught from what he'd witnessed earlier in the day, Jack hastened ashore. He hailed a dghaisa and sat in the stern, watching the bastions of St Angelo glide by, his grief-stricken mind barely holding itself together. Had more information come to light about Alana's betrayal, or perhaps his own guilt? Could this be the end of his naval career, the career he had not sought but that had found and embraced him?

His Dunkirk leg wound throbbed as he climbed the stone steps to the Upper Barracca and arrived at a side entrance in the bastion, where he showed his pass to the sentry. Inside, he was met by a petty officer who led him down the many flights of stairs, the air growing cooler as they proceeded deeper into the bowels of War HQ, then along a passage carved by the knights and enlarged by the British, past alcoves loud with the tinkle and clatter of telephones, typewriters and teleprinters, until they came to a dimly lit room thick with the fug of cigarettes. Officers sat in canvas-backed chairs around a table covered in charts and aerial photographs. Could this be some form of court martial? An ashen-faced Jack came to attention and saluted stiffly, his throat dry, sweat beading his face.

'Ah, Pembroke, took your time,' said Huffington-Smythe. 'Sit.'

Surely this was too disparate a group — a Met officer accompanied by RAF, navy, army and intelligence officers —

for any kind of court, and the two RN lieutenants he knew to be the captains of the MGB and remaining MTB from Operation Assegai. *Gannet*'s captain was briefly introduced to the men, who had obviously been gathered for some time, the ashtray full and shirts darkened with sweat stains, except for Huffington-Smythe in his spotless whites. 'I believe you know Flight Lieutenant Warburton,' said the commodore. The pilot winked at Jack and nodded reassuringly.

'Yes, sir, he kindly lent me his bicycle.'

'Not exactly relevant, Pembroke. Shall we proceed?'

Jack flushed and looked down at his hands.

'Warburton has once again been putting his PRU Spitfire to good use,' said Huffington-Smythe. 'He's flown a number of photo recces and isolated what we think to be the culprit.' The commodore leant across the chart and stabbed his finger at a tiny, oval-shaped isle. 'As you're all aware, there are five Italian islands to the south of Malta — each one a greater or lesser thorn in our side. To the southwest lie Linosa, Lampedusa, Lampione and Pantelleria — which Mussolini insists on calling the Italian Gibraltar. To the southeast is Isola del Sacramento, a small volcanic island that has become particularly bothersome of late. It appears the Germans have installed a powerful RDF that gives them an all-seeing eye in the Gulf of Sirte able to pick up any shipping bound for Malta.'

'Any vessel traversing the central Med, sir,' said Jack.

'Thank you, Pembroke.' The commodore raised an eyebrow. 'Major Shankland is an expert on RDF and can give us the details of our target.'

'Certainly, sir,' said the short, ruby-faced officer. 'Those strange transmissions around the 560-megahertz frequency, picked up by the Assegai convoy, focused our attention. We believe the RDF is similar to, but larger than, the kind of

Würzburg installations recently set up along the coast of occupied France. After analysing Flight Lieutenant Warburton's photographs, we became convinced.'

'Plonked near the edge of a cliff, at first I thought it was a goat pen,' said Warburton with an impish smile.

'We asked for another recce,' said Major Shankland. 'Lower this time —'

'Plenty of flak, like bally Guy Fawkes,' Warburton interrupted.

Jack's anxiety had been replaced by growing curiosity. Why on earth had he been included in this meeting?

'The flight lieutenant bagged some excellent pictures — low and oblique — that left us in no doubt about what we were looking at,' said the major, laying out a handful of black-and-white photographs on the table. 'As you can see, the antenna is a parabolic dish with a diameter of about twenty-five feet, and its electronic paraphernalia appears to be housed in a small shed at the base of the aerial. A nearby farmhouse probably accommodates the technicians and guards —'

'And doubtless a few *ragazze* for a spot of leg over,' murmured Warburton.

'The RDF is an almost impossible nut to crack,' said the commodore. 'We think the thing can be retracted into a concrete bunker using some sort of hydraulic device. A medium-level Wellington raid proved ineffective, the flak too heavy and the target too small. So too, an attempted low-level attack by Beauforts, which suffered losses we cannot sustain. In short, when the wretched thing is snug in its bunker, wrapped in a thick layer of concrete, it's nigh impossible to hit with the resources at our disposal.'

There was a long, pregnant silence, before Huffington-Smythe cleared his throat and said, 'And so, gentlemen, this is where Lieutenant Pembroke comes into the picture.'

Jack sat up, eyes wide, as though he'd been slapped in the face. 'Sir?' he said, aghast.

'After lengthy consultation with the RAF and the army, it has been decided that this is a job for the Andrew,' said the commodore.

'But surely, sir, if they have such powerful RDF, no ship could approach without being identified and attacked,' said Jack.

'Unless, Pembroke, they thought it was one of their own.'

'I don't understand, sir.'

'Every few weeks, during a dark-moon phase, a large Italian trawler is sent from Sicily to resupply the island. It takes an indirect route far to the east of Malta to avoid our patrols, rounding a rock 160 nautical miles southeast of Syracuse and 50 miles north of Sacramento, arriving at about midnight. The rock is where you will lie in wait for the enemy.'

The commodore went on to explain the naval component of the plan. The MTB and MGB, the latter recently fitted with radar, would accompany *Gannet* and lay a trap for the trawler. After the Italian had been eliminated, the South African whaler would continue on her own, disguised as the trawler, and enter Sacramento's only port bearing commandos who would conduct a lightning strike on the radar facility. The plan was only made possible by a spy in Sicily who had ascertained the departure date and time of the next shipment from Syracuse, and the code used for entering Sacramento's harbour. If either of these intelligence nuggets were inaccurate, the raid would fail.

'It just so happens that HMSAS *Southern Gannet* looks uncannily like the Itie trawler,' said the commodore. 'No offence to your good ship, Pembroke.'

'None taken, sir.'

'Some minor adjustments will be needed to *Gannet*'s profile, and a new paint job, but from a distance in the dark, no-one should spot the difference.'

The commodore handed over to Captain Campbell of the SBS to provide details of the commando element of the attack. The captain was tall, lean and very tanned, with a bushy moustache and square face — an eccentric of aristocratic stock who'd spent the pre-war years big-game hunting in East Africa.

'Isola del Sacramento is strongly fortified with defences sited to cover all lines of approach, so deception is key,' said Campbell, his voice sharp, his words clipped with barely any trace of a Scottish accent. 'The island has concrete gun emplacements and pillboxes at strategic points with mutually supporting fire and surrounded by barbed wire. There are extensive minefields at every location a landing might be affected, hence the need for a stealthy attack through the tiny port. Our target is the RDF, but we will also need to neutralise any naval vessels present, as well as a small fort overlooking the harbour.'

'How small?' asked one of the officers.

'Oh, just an overgrown watchtower from Napoleonic times, but it could make our lives difficult. The garrison is billeted in a village a few miles inland. Once we've kicked the hornets' nest, the clock will be ticking. The Italians will be able to deploy a considerable force against us, so there'll be no time to bugger about smelling the roses.'

'Any tanks, sir?' asked Jack.

'Armoured cars, we think. The raid will consist of three landing parties. One will take out the fort and then hold the main road, the second will head up a narrow cliff path to destroy the RDF, and the third will cripple the defences to the north. There are a pair of 9-inch guns situated inland that are well defended and too complicated to tangle with, but nearer the port there are 4-inch guns, searchlights and lighter ack-ack emplacements that we'll knock on the head.'

'Won't the 9-inch guns make mincemeat of *Gannet* as she tries to escape after the raid?' Jack asked.

'At night, the big guns are guided by the RDF, so once that's been eliminated you should have a good chance to get away under the cover of darkness,' said the commodore. 'To that end, taking out the searchlights will help your cause.'

Campbell continued: 'Lieutenant Jenkins and I will lead the attack on the RDF. We think it has about eight to ten German operators — two on duty, two on watch in the lookout post and a handful of guards in an adjacent bunker. The lookout post has a machine gun and telephone with a direct line to the island-defence reporting centre, which controls the gun batteries. We must assume that the radar will be retracted into its bunker as soon as the shooting starts.'

'So, your chaps will have to winkle it out,' said the commodore.

'Precisely, sir. I need to stress again that time will be of the absolute essence. This has to be a blitz raid, hitting hard with a small, lightly armed force before the enemy can properly react. We are allowing just two and a half hours ashore. Then it will be Lieutenant Pembroke's task to get us out of there. Whatever happens, we must leave the island by 0200. Axis aircraft will be hunting for us at first light, so we'll need the remaining hours of darkness to make good our escape.'

'And hopefully get within range of Malta's long-range fighters,' said Warburton.

'What if we haven't retrieved all three landing parties by 0200?' asked Jack.

'There will be no heroics, Pembroke,' said Campbell gruffly. 'You leave without us.'

Back on *Gannet*, Jack tried to set his guilt and his grief aside and was all determination and industry. He'd been offered a lifeline, even if it displayed all the hallmarks of a fatal one — the chance to make amends for the damage his indiscretions may have caused, the opportunity to hit back at the enemy. His three officers immediately noticed the change in their grim-faced captain as he briefed them on the coming operation and set the crew to work preparing for sea and painting the hull black to match the Italian trawler. The sailors were given no details, but everyone knew something critical was afoot and the scuttlebutt hummed with rumour and speculation.

'What do you think, Pickles?' asked Booysen as they sorted belts of pom-pom shells in the ammunition store.

'Must be a big one. I've never seen so much extra ammo coming aboard.'

'And I've never seen the old man so preoccupied.'

'*Ja*, he looks really, really angry. Best stay out of his way.'

Jack oversaw a day of feverish activity, taking over tasks that would normally have been ably handled by his officers. That evening he retired early to his cabin and hardly touched the steak and kidney pie served by Hendricks, opting instead for the whisky bottle. His mind tracked back and forth between his two losses. Obsessively, he tried to rehash every encounter he could remember with Alana, every conversation, running them over and over in his mind. For instance, their romantic felucca trip down the Nile: what exactly had he told her late that night, under the stars? And she'd always had questions after each Tobruk convoy. And that last night at the Hotel Cecil: yes, he was certain now that he'd divulged nothing other than the obvious, or what every other spy in Alex would have already surmised. He *had* always been careful about classified information, but the doubts continued to gnaw and gnaw.

What of dear, brave, steadfast Douglas? Jack could not get the picture out of his head of his friend's body, twisting and turning as it fell through the sky. One of their last conversations had been about death, Douglas musing about his fate with Jack trying to reassure him. 'Trophy hunting' was the term Douglas had used. Jack felt utter disgust, infused with an overwhelming sadness and loss. Tossing and turning in his narrow cot, he longed for a drugged, dreamless sleep: the sleep of the dead.

Next morning, a water barge came alongside to top up the whaler's tanks, then an oiling lighter, followed by lorries bearing stores. Under the direction of PO Combrink, yet more ammo boxes streamed aboard and the crew lugged them down to the already overflowing ammunition store beneath the ratings' accommodation. Every weapon on board received a careful cleaning, and extra splinter-proof matting was fitted around the superstructure.

Jack was in his cabin, nursing a hangover and trying to focus on his paperwork when there came a knock at the door. It was Sub-lieutenant Fletcher.

'May I have a private word in your ear, please, Cap'n?'

Jack noticed the earnest look in the young man's eyes. 'Of course, Sub. Pull up a bollard.'

Fletcher closed the door and took a seat. 'I realise you perhaps think of me as something of a rake...'

Jack smiled but made no comment.

'As do some of the other ... well ... most of the other chaps.'

'Fairer-sex imbroglios, Tom?' asked Jack, cutting to the chase. 'Someone up the duff?'

'Oh no, sir, not at all, nothing like that — quite the contrary. The young lady I have been seeing, Martina Zammit, she's just ... lovely. Really rather smashing on all fronts.'

'I see. So, something a bit more serious than your previous dalliances?'

'Oh gosh, sir, I've put all that behind me. The wild oats of youth and all. Martina is ... well, she's ... I suppose, what I've been waiting for. The other, er, liaisons, were, in a sense, treading water, so to speak.'

'Energetically.'

Fletcher blushed. 'Thing is, we would very much like to get married. Soon.'

'Goodness, Tom, getting hitched! You surely don't want to rush into something like matrimony. Especially with a war on. We're only on Malta for a short spell, and what with the coming operation —'

'I am aware of all that, sir.'

'You know the old saying about marriage: "Admirals must, captains should, commanders may, lieutenants mustn't."'

'Aye, sir, but both of us are dead set.'

'Dead set?'

'Dead set.'

'I see.' Jack leant back in his chair and regarded the young gunnery officer in silence for a moment. 'And you are, of course, aware that Maltese girls have a good motive to wed

British servicemen, as it guarantees a marriage allowance and, if you have children, a family allowance.'

'Martina is from a wealthy family, sir, so that's not a factor.'

'Quite — just thought I had to mention it. I don't want to sound like a stick-in-the-mud, but it's also my duty to inform you that from peacetime experience we know these unions seldom last. After a year or two in servicemen's married quarters back in grey, wet Blighty, the girls usually want to return home to their families. And as you well know, divorce is almost impossible for Maltese Catholics.'

'I know, sir.'

'At least you're Catholic, I suppose.'

'Lapsed, but yes, it helps. Us going on this cloak-and-dagger operation has brought things to a head. We would like to get married as soon as we return, if we return, and before *Gannet* gets sent somewhere else.'

'I understand, and you want my blessing?'

'Actually, a bit more than that.'

'How so?'

'I would very much like you to be my best man.'

'Oh, I say, Tom. Gosh, it would be the greatest honour.'

'Thank you very much, sir!' Fletcher beamed.

'Gives us both a damn fine reason to make it back to Malta in one piece, does it not?'

Later that very afternoon, the couple visited the Archbishop's Curia to make a statement under oath that there were no canonical impediments to their union and they were in a free state to marry. No mention was made of the sub-lieutenant's carpet-tomcat past and it seemed that, with Mr Zammit's agreement, a wedding could be arranged as soon as Martina's and Fletcher's duties allowed.

*

It was their last evening in port and although liberty had not been granted, Jack allowed his most junior officer to go ashore and say goodbye to his fiancée. Fletcher climbed the steps to the Upper Barracca and found Martina, looking gorgeous in a pale-blue summer dress, waiting for him on a bench. The bastions glowed pink in the evening light and the harbour lay spread out at their feet like a romantic stage set, *Gannet* snug against the Birgu wharf opposite.

'I'm not allowed to tell you, but we'll be leaving tomorrow.'

'Oh no, surely not back to Alexandria?' Martina's voice betrayed her alarm.

'No.'

'I thought not. I would have heard as much on the HQ grapevine.'

'It's all extremely hush-hush.'

'I see. It must be serious.'

'It is. A short operation.'

'So, we have only this.'

'Yes.' They kissed and Fletcher could taste tears leaking into their mouths.

'You haven't asked where I'm going.'

'I have not. It is not my place.'

They kissed again, more ardently. Dusk was falling and the surface of the harbour had turned to mercury, stained by the reflections of the embracing ramparts. Valletta appeared to be sinking into gloom, an echo of the darkening sky, awaiting the first air raid of the night. House shutters clapped shut; silence fell over the bomb-ravaged streets. From a nearby building came the faintest tinkling of a piano as someone practised their scales.

'On Malta we have a proverb: "*Fahhar il-bahar il ibqa' fug l-art*,"' said Martina. 'It means, "Praise the sea, but remain on dry land."'

'Not exactly compatible with the life of a sailor.'

They held each other closer, not speaking, not wanting to let go.

'If you find yourself in grave danger —'

'I will keep you in my thoughts, always.'

'Yes. But also, you must lift your heart and mind to God, recommending your soul to His divine mercy. And I will pray to the compassionate Virgin for your safe return.'

Far below them, *Gannet* was at last ready for sea. The men had finished supper and a handful relaxed on the boat deck, enjoying the balmy evening and the last of the light. Below decks, some lay on their narrow bunks reading well-thumbed issues of *Reader's Digest* and a week-old *Daily Telegraph* that was doing the rounds, while Cole Porter warbled from a gramophone, relayed by Sparks on the intercom. Many sailors were writing their last letters home; others sat around the hinged mess-deck table playing games of Crown and Anchor, Liar's Dice and Uckers.

Van Zyl reclined on his bunk, tinkering with his poems, romantic invocations of the grace of a seagull in flight, the ever-changing blues of the Mediterranean, and an attempted 'Ode on an Egyptian Urn' that fell disappointingly short of the original. He had tried but given up on composing poems of battle, of the gore and horror he had witnessed, finding that his verses lay dead on the page, as lifeless as the body bags he'd seen tipped into the deep.

Jack was at his desk with a tumbler of whisky close at hand, his mind very far away, his heart heavy with grief for his friend and the betrayal by his lover. Yes, the coming operation perhaps offered an opportunity to redeem himself in the eyes of the navy, as well as the chance to exact some form of 'revenge'. That might help with the dark fire burning in his heart. A part of him felt wildly reckless, willing to risk everything or die in an act of self-immolation. It was only his love for his men, and for *Gannet*, that tempered his melancholic ruminations.

A blank sheet of paper lay before him. He was vaguely aware that Sparks had switched to the BBC Overseas news broadcast which told of bombing raids on the Ruhr Valley and London, a convoy attacked by the Luftwaffe in the Western Approaches, and renewed fighting on the El Alamein Line. The bulletin was followed by *Forces Favourites*, which made for pleasanter listening as the voices of Bing Crosby, Dinah Shaw and Jane Froman filled the mess decks.

Jack took another sip of whisky, picked up his fountain pen and began to write:

Dearest Father,

By the time this letter reaches you, I might have sacrificed my life, along with many others, for the ideals by which we have fought this war. The task at hand has the potential to be a one-way trip. We will be inserting ourselves into the very jaws of the foe. If our mission is successful, we will have blinded the enemy's eyes in the central Mediterranean, an action that could make the passage of Allied ships safer, and hopefully pave the way for the retaking of these waters.

If the worst comes to pass, I would like you to write a letter to Clara, and let her know what has happened, and that I have kept her in my thoughts and in my heart all this time.

I have led a very full life and I am grateful to you and Mama for all you have done for me: our marvellous childhood, the privilege of being sent to Winchester and Oxford, our happy holidays on the French Riviera. After

Dunkirk and Mama's passing, you were a steadfast rock for me, and your presence and help in Simonstown of immeasurable value.

We have just finished supper and Grand Harbour is glittering with starlight. There has been no air raid so far today and all appears deceptively peaceful. The men are in good spirits, despite the grave task at hand, of which they are imprecisely aware. I could not ask for a finer crew. They would go to the ends of the earth for me, and I for them.

It seems ever so strange to be penning this letter to you. Our heightened existence here in Malta feels so far removed from Simonstown and Alexandria. I often think of your lovely villa among the boulders, the milkwood trees and that enchanting crescent beach below the house. I picture you and Imogen sitting on the veranda at sunset, watching the changing colours of False Bay and listening to the guinea fowl clucking in the foliage. How I long to return once more to that faraway Eden.

Well, Father, I will sign off now. If this is my last epistle to you, please do not be too sad, and tell Imogen and Harry to be strong and keep their chins up. You have been a great inspiration to me, both as an officer and as a father. I hope that in the coming hours my actions, and those of my valiant Gannets, will make some small contribution to achieving ultimate victory, and to peace.

Please give my fondest love to everyone.

Your devoted son,

Jack

CHAPTER 21

Next morning, *Gannet* bustled with industry as the crew made ready for sea and the raiding party of forty commandos in battledress filed down the gangplank, burdened with heavy kit. Soon the mess decks were crammed with quiet, dangerous-looking men who'd be hot-bunking with the South African sailors. Major Campbell would share with Jack, while the commando lieutenant joined *Gannet*'s three officers in their cabin and the two sergeants were accommodated in the NCO's mess aft. The crew helped the new arrivals find homes for boxes of grenades and ammunition, cases of mortar bombs, detonators, fuses and explosives. From their accents, it appeared that Scotsmen and Irishmen predominated, which was typical of any volunteer raiding force from the United Kingdom.

Jack greeted Campbell at the brow — a firm handshake, cold eyes — and ushered the major to his cabin, where he poured two stiff gins. The pair sat discussing the operation and contingency arrangements if plans went awry. Campbell also filled Jack in on the background to the raid, describing how his men had undergone intensive training at Anderson Manor in Dorset during the winter, then transferred to Egypt for advanced instruction at Kabrit on the Great Bitter Lake, before being delivered to Malta the previous week by Sunderland flying boat.

For the raid, most commandos had been issued with the new Sten submachine gun, favoured for its high rate of fire, making it particularly effective in close combat at night. Revolvers and Lee-Enfield rifles would also be carried, as well as Mills bombs and 2-inch mortars. Each of the three landing parties included a marksman equipped with a Canadian Ross rifle.

'I think I'd better put my chaps out of their misery and let them in on the gen,' said Jack. 'I'd like to have them fall in on the foredeck, along with your commandos, if that's all right with you, sir.'

'Indeed, good idea. We're all in this one together. My boys know the specifics of the target but not our precise destination.'

A few minutes later, the men were mustered under the blazing sun in a semi-circle around Jack. He wanted the briefing to be informal, not an address to subordinates standing in ranks. Before him were the dependable hands of *Gannet* and the many new faces of the commandos: some eager, some fearful, some dispassionate.

'I'll get straight to it, gents. As you will have gleaned from the scuttlebutt and from our new friends, this is a very special, very important mission. The risks are not inconsiderable.' Jack could sense the tension, like a held breath. 'We are to attack and destroy a powerful RDF installation on Sacramento, the easternmost island of the Pelagie group.'

There were murmurs of surprise and some groans of concern. Jack went on to give a bare outline of the approach, attack and extrication from the island. The men remained silent, some perhaps awed by the prospect of what lay in store. Campbell took over from Jack and filled in more details about the mission and its various targets so that everyone was in the picture.

Jack brought the assembly to a close, saying, 'And so, it is our job as Gannets to land our commando friends on the island, and then to bring each and every one of them safely back to Malta. I don't need to ask you to do your best or to give your all. I know enough about this fine ship and its men to feel certain that you are more than up to the task. We depart at noon. Are there any questions?'

There was silence, an atmosphere heavy with unease having settled over the foredeck. Then the high-pitched voice of Pickles piped up from the back: 'Beg pardon, sir, but me and the lads were wondering: will there be any chance of shore leave on Sacramento?'

The tension was broken as sailors and commandos burst out laughing.

'If at all possible, yes!' shouted Jack. 'Thank you, and God speed. Carry on.'

At 1155, Thomas arrived on the bridge and announced, 'Signal to proceed when ready, sir.'

'Thank you, Sparks.'

A minute later, Van Zyl said, 'Special sea-duty men closed up, sir.'

'Very good.'

'Main engine rung on, sir.'

'Very good. Let go aft.' Lines were released and sailors on the quarterdeck pulled in the greasy coils of wire.

'All gone aft, sir.'

'Very good. Let go for'ard, but hold onto the headspring.'

A neatly turned-out sailor stood in the bows, ready to lower the jack as soon as they got underway.

'Slow ahead.'

Gannet's propeller threshed the turquoise water into milk as the whaler went forward, straining against the spring until her stern swung away from the wharf.

'Stop engine, let go headspring, slow astern.'

The whaler throbbed quietly as she backed into the basin, turned to aim her bows at the tip of the St Elmo breakwater, and stopped her engine. Jack took a moment to glance around him. To starboard, lay the angular ramparts of St Angelo and to port, the Saluting Battery and Upper Barracca. He felt this to be a most auspicious leave-taking: *Farewell to this throne of knights, this scepter'd isle, this fortress built by Nature for herself against infection and the hand of war.*

'Slow ahead.'

This happy breed of Maltese men, this little world, this precious stone set in the silver sea.

Jack had the strange, counterintuitive sensation of a substantial weight being lifted from his shoulders. There were no more land-mired decisions to be made. He would do his best to close the door on thoughts of Alana Vilar and Grayson Douglas until his return to Malta. His ship slowly gathered way, creasing a wake across the basin. Fletcher was up on the fo'c'sle, a row of sailors mustered beside him. Jack followed the line of his sub-lieutenant's gaze to a handful of scruffy, cheering boys on the Lower Barracca. Beside them stood a young woman in a black dress, waving her scarf. Fletcher's eyes did not leave her petite frame, as though the passage of his gaze were chain-linked, until *Gannet* had threaded the black buoys of the boom gate and turned southeast. Reaching open water, the whaler began to move with an easier gait.

A motor launch approached at speed from astern to lead them down the swept channel, followed by the MTB and MGB, emerging from Marsamuscetto Harbour. Growling with the contained power of their leashed engines, the two sleek craft passed *Gannet* to port and took up station line ahead.

Jack lifted his binoculars to take a closer look at the whaler's two consorts. The MGB was a Fairmile D, or Dog Boat — 115 feet long with a hard-chine hull. He knew Fairmiles well, having witnessed their construction at Quay Four boatyard in

Cape Town's Victoria dock. For such small craft, motor gunboats offered tremendous firepower, which included a pom-pom in a turret on the fo'c'sle, two twin Vickers .5 turrets, a 20-mm Oerlikon above the engine room, a twin .303 on each bridgewing and a six-pounder mounted aft. They were powered by four 1,500-hp Packard supercharged petrol engines, giving a maximum speed of 30 knots but, most importantly, this particular Dog Boat had been fitted with radar to help locate the Italian supply vessel.

The motor torpedo boat was less well armed but faster than the MGB, which might prove vital if chasing trawlers was the order of the night. She was a 70-foot Vosper with a planing hull, driven by three Packard V-12 marine engines, and capable of almost 40 knots. The MTB carried a pair of 21-inch torpedoes, an Oerlikon and twin .5-inch machine guns mounted in a circular bin behind the bridge.

Jack glanced back at Valetta, the outline of its spires and bastions already growing indistinct in the heat haze. He sensed the tension mounting once more on *Gannet* as the land receded and the threat of the enemy seemed to rise imperceptibly like a miasma from the deep. Did the crew share his foreboding, this heaviness in the pit of his stomach?

Just then, most irregularly and without orders, Sparks switched on the tannoy. He'd picked up a Maltese broadcast of 'Pennsylvania 6-500' and decided off his own bat to transmit the Glen Miller song at full volume throughout the ship. Suddenly there were smiles on every deck, the music lifting the spirits of the sailors and commandos as they joined in for the catchy refrain. *Gannet* went back to war trailing a jaunty swing tune that eddied across the water to the motorboats, its brassy notes twirling in their wake.

'Defaulters book for Sparks, sir?' asked Van Zyl.

'Aye, with a recommendation for keelhauling.'

'Damn good, though, isn't it?'

'Just the ticket. He read the mood perfectly: conjured an antidote from the airwaves. Let the song finish, then a quiet word in his ear.'

The voyage to the southeast progressed without incident, Spitfires taking it in turns to fly lazy circuits high above them. Some commandos lounged on deck; others remained in the mess cleaning and oiling weapons, sharpening daggers, greasing detonators and sorting the wires, fuses and packets of explosive. The sea was viscous, the going easy. There was a stillness on board *Gannet*, most men lost in contemplation, as though sensing they were bound for some sort of reckoning.

Jack sat hunched in his high chair, staring at the horizon, the lookouts on either side of him raking the sea and sky with their binoculars. Some commandos were seasick, despite the calm water, the smell of vomit wafting up to the bridge. He let his thoughts pick their way through the raid's various acts and possible pitfalls, of which there were plenty, given the number of moving parts. How would he react to a radical change of plan … or to disaster? The Asdic maintained its insistent pinging as the afternoon wore itself into mellowness, Jack eventually allowing his mind to drift into an almost soporific state.

At sunset, PO Cummins presided over darkening ship. On this night, of all nights, not even a sliver of light could be shown. With *Gannet* blacked out and the dusk's last colours draining to the west, the mood onboard sank even lower. Jack found himself gripped by anguish for what lay in store, compounded by Alana's betrayal and the cowardly slaying of Douglas. Out there in the dark wastes of the Mediterranean basin, his aching heart could find no harbour.

The three vessels reached the rocky outcrop marked Scoglio Panettone on the chart and formed a picket line two miles apart. The radar set was housed in the MGB's tiny wireless cabin and its Welsh operator sat on the edge of his chair, intently watching the screen. The radar's aerials, mounted above deck, were directional and worked by hand from the cabin below. The little screen presented two lines at right angles, the horizontal one spiky with flickering green fingers. If the aerials were pointed in the right direction when a target came within range, a green blip would appear above the line, its space from the vertical indicating the distance.

Minutes crawled by as the three vessels lay doggo, awaiting their prey. On *Gannet*'s bridge, Jack was lost in thought, his eyes probing the darkness to the northwest and glancing down every now and then at his watch: they were running out of time. If the trawler arrived late, and it appeared the commandos would be unable to complete their task by 0200, they'd have to abort the mission for fear of being caught near the island at sunrise. It was going to be very, very tight.

Hardly a moment later, two sets of powerful marine engines thundered into life and a shaded Aldis lamp flashed the good tidings from the Dog Boat: 'Target bearing three-one-five, am attacking.'

'Full ahead! Steer twenty degrees to port,' Jack called into the voicepipe.

'Twenty to port it is, sir,' came the dependable growl of February.

The three vessels raced towards a target that only the radar eye could see, the MTB and MGB soon far ahead of *Gannet*, following at her best seventeen knots. It wasn't long before the horizon began to dance with fire as the two boats opened their account, taking the Italian completely by surprise. Red tracer from the MTB's Oerlikon streamed on a low trajectory, hammering away with a steady thudding, joined soon after by her .5-inch machine guns. The MGB opened up with a six-pounder, pom-pom and a second Oerlikon. To prevent an SOS signal being sent, the Italian's radio cabin was the initial target and was quickly reduced to a smoking wreck. The enemy offered belated and desultory return fire, probably from a Breda, but the trawler was punched and battered, venting lurid explosions, its superstructure dancing with flames.

Gannet arrived on the scene, slowing as she drew nearer the Italian, lying dead in the water and already reduced to a smoking hulk, while the MGB dragged survivors from the waves. Jack noted the trawler's profile — about 130 feet long with a gun mounted on a high fo'c'sle — and was struck by the similarities to his own ship. She had a longer foredeck than *Gannet*, a black hull and no mizzen mast, but bows-on she was almost identical. He ordered Bunts to signal the other vessels to stand clear as he intended to finish her off. The whaler increased speed and closed with the listing trawler. Jack called into the voicepipe: 'Pass the Itie to starboard, Cox'n, close as you like.'

'To starboard, close as I like,' said February with a broad grin.

'Quarterdeck stand by, two depth charges, shallowest setting.'

'Standing by, Cap'n.'

As they steamed past the stricken trawler, Jack gave the order and PO Combrink bellowed, 'Fire one!', pulling the green lever for the starboard rack, and the first depth charge rattled down its track and off the stern. 'Fire two!' The red lever and another splash. A few moments of pulsing quiet then a pair of titanic geysers grew around the trawler in loud, white detonations, tearing her to pieces as *Gannet* shuddered and bucked to the blows. When the cascade subsided, Jack saw that the explosions had broken the Italian's back and her remains were fast disappearing.

According to the plan, the motorboats would remain to the west of Scoglio Panettone and *Gannet* was to proceed alone to the island. The trawler had been late and they'd lost precious time: the period ashore would need to be almost halved if they were to leave by 0200. Heading south at full speed, commandos and crew prepared for the coming attack. PO Combrink distributed all the armoury's Lanchester submachine guns and Lee-Enfield rifles to sailors not already manning a gun. The commando medical orderly, who would remain on *Gannet* during the raid and attend to any wounded brought aboard, set up shop in the wardroom, laying out surgical instruments, bandages and syrettes of morphia on fresh muslins.

In the mess deck, men in brown battledress were blackening their faces with boot polish and making final checks to their weapons, ammunition pouches and explosives. They wore felt-soled boots for stealth, their headgear a mix of green berets and helmets. While Sub-lieutenant Robinson took the bridge watch, *Gannet*'s officers joined the two commando officers and two sergeants in the dimly lit wardroom for a final briefing around a map of Sacramento. The deck swayed gently and the baritone pulse of *Gannet*'s racing engine, punctuated by the Asdic's occasional ping, seemed to heighten the drama of the gathering.

'Having lost time neutralising the trawler, everything is going to need to happen at the double,' said Major Campbell. 'We will now have only one and a half hours ashore. Once the party led by Lieutenant Jenkins and myself has destroyed the RDF, I will fire a green flare to signal a general withdrawal. If he has not already done so, Sergeant O'Connor will extract his party from the gun emplacements and return to the ship along the north shore. Sergeant Murphy will wait exactly ten minutes before withdrawing his party holding the main road at the top of the pass. Those ten minutes will allow my RDF party to link up with him, if feasible, and retreat together down the road. If we have not reached Murphy in time, it will mean my party has decided, for whatever reason, to return to the port via the cliff path.'

'What if you suffer severe losses early in the attack, before the RDF is eliminated, sir?' asked Fletcher.

'In an extreme situation, it might be necessary to ask Lieutenant Pembroke if he would be so kind as to lend us some sailors.' Campbell offered a wry smile, and the men gave a few uneasy chuckles.

'Certainly, Major, as long as I have enough men to fight and sail *Gannet*,' said Jack.

'Let's hope it doesn't come to that. Unless there are any more questions … best of luck to all of you.'

The light was switched off and the officers filed out of the wardroom. On the upper deck, all eyes strained at the darkness ahead.

'How long to go?' asked Campbell, appearing at Jack's shoulder.

'About half an hour, give or take.'

'I loathe the waiting. One just wants to fire the bloody starter pistol.' The major's accent had grown more Scottish, perhaps betraying his anxiety.

Gannet pressed on southward, the tension on board mounting with each passing mile, each passing minute. Despite his best efforts to concentrate on the task at hand, Jack's mind was adrift. He kept thinking of the night he'd met Alana at the Auberge Bleue, an apparition with dark olive skin and sensuous lips, the silky, black dress that showed off her curves, its low cut revealing perfect breasts. During their first waltz, they'd twirled across the floor and he'd been entranced, one hand in hers, the other on the small of her back. He remembered her playful eyes and unexpected wit. Despite the dastardly revelations, every part of his being longed to hold her, to inhale her heady scent.

'Land ho!' sang out Malan. 'Fine on the starboard bow.'

Jack lifted his binoculars. 'Yes, good eyes, AB! I can just make out the broken cone of the volcano.'

'At last, thank you, Pembroke,' said Campbell. 'You got us here with a minimum of fuss.'

'Aye, but there might be a lot more fuss on the way back.'

'Nothing you can't handle, I'm sure.'

Gannet was aimed at the eastern tip of the dark smudge as she closed with the island, her men at action stations.

'One mile to go,' said Robinson.

'Half ahead,' said Jack into the voicepipe, trying to control the shortness of his breathing. The engine's dull throb chimed with his heart's industry, dragging blood through the thin corridors of his frame. He could taste the bitterness of his own fear.

As instructed, almost everyone on the upper deck had hidden himself, save for a few sailors lounging about in scruffy attire, trying to look like Italian trawlermen. Fletcher's crew were concealed behind ready-use lockers and gunwales on the forecastle. At Jack's command, Bunts pointed a shaded signal lamp at the harbour mouth and flashed the code in deliberately inexpert fashion.

There was no reply.

'Again, Gilbert,' Jack said softly.

Still no response.

'Damn and blast,' hissed Jack. 'Keep sending the signal.'

The staccato slapping of the lamp's shutters sounded like thunderclaps to the men on the bridge.

'Five cables to go,' intoned Robinson.

'Slow ahead,' said Jack into the voicepipe.

Gannet crept towards the breakwater and those watching began to make out the buildings surrounding the little fishing port.

'The code might have changed,' muttered Jack.

'Unlikely,' said the major. 'Our Italian agent has never let us down.'

'Perhaps they smell a rat? If they illuminate *Gannet* with a searchlight, the game will be up.'

Bunts continued to blink his Aldis lamp, repeating the code but eliciting neither acknowledgement nor challenge.

'Five hundred yards,' breathed Robinson.

'Starboard ten, Cox'n,' said Jack hoarsely.

'Ten o' starboard, sir.'

'Dead slow.'

Jack listened to the sibilant sloshing of water down their flanks; he smelt the tangy seaweed. Could they be sailing into a trap? Were Italian guns on the cliffs and in the port already trained on *Gannet*, waiting only for the command to open fire at point-blank range? And if this were, indeed, an ambush, the likelihood of escape was diminishing by the minute. Jack could make out waterfront houses clustered around the harbour, terraces on the hillside with vines and olive trees, a concrete pillbox on the breakwater and above the blacked-out village, a boxlike fort overlooking a road that zigzagged up the side of a steep incline to Sacramento's interior.

'Captain, sir, a reply!' gasped Bunts, as Morse flickered from a lamp at the end of the harbour wall. 'The code is correct.'

'Thank God,' said Jack under his breath, turning to inform Campbell, but the major had vanished.

As *Gannet* made her final approach, the commandos remained out of sight, the gunners in hiding near their weapons. Able Seaman Levy, who could speak passable Italian, stood in the bows clad in a white vest and fisherman's trousers. Jack had removed his cap and donned a brown coat, while the rest of the bridge party crouched below the rail.

'*Buonasera, come state?*' called the lamp man from the wall.

'*Stiamo bene, grazie!*' cried Levy.

Forty yards to go. Jack spotted a handful of men winching open the boom gate.

'*Un viaggio tranquillo?*'

Twenty yards. The boom gate was open. Jack found that he was holding his breath.

'*Sì, molto tranquillo.*'

Gannet chugged through the narrow entrance, Jack waving at the boom party, his heart's artillery thundering in his ears. A quick scan of the little harbour revealed, to starboard, a row of fishing boats tied up along a wharf, nets and floats piled on their decks, more colourful wooden craft tethered to buoys ahead and, over to port, a couple of naval craft.

'*Dov'è Luigi?*' asked the lamp man.

Who the hell was Luigi?

'*È malato,*' called out Levy. Good lad, thinking on his feet, but how long could he keep this up? Jack's trembling hand rested on the alarm button.

'*Hai un nuovo albero?*' asked the Italian, pointing at *Gannet*'s mizzen mast.

'*Sì.*'

Then, at last, a bloodcurdling scream: '*Allarme*! *Allarme*!'

'Open fire!' bellowed Jack, pressing the button as bells clanged dementedly throughout his ship, setting free the dogs of battle.

CHAPTER 22

Nesting the worn butt against his shoulder, Behardien was the first to open fire, his Lewis gun rending the silence with demented clatter. Machine-gun rounds tore the lamp man to shreds as *Gannet* swung to starboard, aiming for a spot on the wharf between a mahogany motorboat and a trawler. Jack glanced across at the MAS boat — a motor torpedo vessel capable of forty-five knots — moored to the opposite wharf and a small, lightly armed patrol boat astern of it. Figures were pouring like ants from hatchways on both craft, making for their guns.

Looking to starboard, Jack noted the concrete pillbox and an artillery piece mounted near the end of the breakwater. Targets, targets everywhere. He saw men sprinting along the wall towards the gun, a Semovente da 90/53 cannon by the look of it, a lethal weapon similar to the German 88mm. A heavy-calibre machine gun stuttered into life from the pillbox and Jack ducked instinctively as tracer streaked low over *Gannet.* A minor adjustment, followed by the whine and thud of rounds striking the hull. The whaler's starboard guns — Johnson on the Breda and Levy on his Oerlikon, joined by Pickles on his pom-pom — opened fire, inundating the pillbox with lead, smoke and powdered concrete. Meanwhile, Behardien tried to pick off the gunners making for their cannon.

'Mr Fletcher, those two boats at nine o'clock, now!' Jack bellowed through his loudhailer.

'Aye aye, Cap'n!' called the sub-lieutenant, his layer and trainer already setting the 4-inch sights on the MAS boat. 'Aim for the waterline, amidships. Deflection zero.'

'Trainer on.'

'Layer on.'

'Fire!'

The 4-inch jerked back on its mounting, the bang echoing off the buildings and the low, embracing cliffs. The shell struck the MAS boat near the bows, tearing open a jagged gash. Meanwhile, the lighter armaments on *Gannet*'s port side vented a hail of fire, red tracer sowing the harbour basin with splashes, punching holes in the two boats, or ricocheting off the wharf and into or over the flat-roofed houses, the night torn asunder by bright flashes, billowing smoke and the cacophony of gunfire.

Fletcher barked orders and the 4-inch cracked again and again. His five-man crew worked in limber unison, shells coming up from the ammunition store in a steady stream to be handed to the loader. Then the breech slammed shut, there was a loud crash and the empty shell case clanked to the deck in a huff of fumes. 'Yes, me hearties, just what the doctor ordered, in spades! And again…' *Bang*!

Another semi-armour-piercing round struck home, bursting through the MAS boat's thin skin and exploding inside her. The Italian began to burn more fiercely, emitting showers of sparks, the flames thrusting up and out of the cockpit, licking their way onto the wharf and flickering on the façades. The little patrol vessel was also riddled with holes and sat heavily in the water, afloat only due to the awkward embrace of bar-taut mooring lines. *Gannet* approached the wharf and Rademeyer climbed onto the rail, ready to leap ashore and secure the headrope. The commandos were gathered on the foredeck and quarterdeck, poised to disembark as soon as *Gannet* came alongside.

Just then, the Semovente cannon fired with a loud boom. Jack spun round as the shell streaked over the boat deck and detonated on the hillside behind the village. Somehow, a few wounded Italians had made it to their beast of a weapon, which now posed a grave danger to the mission.

'Mister Fletcher, get that bloody cannon!' yelled Jack.

Wheels spun and the 4-inch traversed smartly. The Italian fired again: a blinding flash and deafening explosion as *Gannet* quivered, the blast knocking Jack to the deck. Momentarily stunned, he dragged himself upright using the binnacle for support and looked down at the foredeck. He heard screaming, moaning, cries for help. The shell had landed in the midst of the commandos, splinters scything through them to wound and kill indiscriminately. Jack's mind was in turmoil as he surveyed the carnage. He saw bodies torn, limbs severed, a commando on his knees, clawing at his gaping throat as blood gushed down his chest.

'Fletcher, do it!' he yelled hoarsely.

The 4-inch barked a riposte, its shell striking the cannon with an almighty crack and tossing the Italians like ragdolls from their weapon. Trying to regain his composure, Jack appraised the situation: the pillbox was still firing the occasional Breda burst and his machine-gunners were replying, but once *Gannet* was alongside, the large trawler would partly shield her, so the pillbox was of less immediate concern.

Major Campbell, who'd been on the quarterdeck at the time of the hit, appeared on the bridge and, breathing heavily, said, 'Five dead, four wounded, but the mission continues, each party with reduced numbers. Unfortunately, Lieutenant Jenkins has lost a leg and Sergeant O'Connor has been killed. Can you spare two senior men, one to act as my second in the RDF party and one to join the attack on the fort?'

'Certainly, Major.'

'Please sir, may I?' asked Van Zyl.

'No, Jannie, I need you in case —'

'Please, Captain!'

Rademeyer made a leap from the starboard bow, moments before *Gannet*'s fenders smack-kissed the wharf, squealing in protest.

'Oh, dammit — all right, Number One, go with the major. And let's send Firebrand Fletcher to lead the fort party. Your black working dress is fine, but both of you need to change your shoes and blacken your faces. Combrink will issue you with Lanchesters and extra ammo. At the double!'

'Aye aye, sir!' said a beaming Van Zyl as he darted from the bridge.

Commandos streamed onto the wharf, some jumping ashore, those with heavy packs waiting for the hastily rigged gangplank. One group immediately made its way towards the pillbox using fire and movement, and the cover of dockside crates and nets. With the port-side Oerlikon maintaining heavy fire to distract and blind the Italian gunners, the pillbox was quickly neutralised with hand grenades through the gun slit. By now, the tiny fort on the hill had woken up and was harassing the whaler with inaccurate machine-gun fire from long range. It would be the first task of Fletcher's party, whose experienced corporal would direct the attack.

Black-faced and armed, Van Zyl and Fletcher joined the commandos on the wharf, having acquired suitable footwear and ammunition pouches from among the wounded. With hardly a word exchanged, the three groups set off in different directions. Sergeant Murphy's party headed north towards the headland to assault its guns and searchlights. Major Campbell and Van Zyl led their men down a lane between whitewashed houses and onto a narrow path that led up a steep incline west of the harbour. Fletcher and Corporal Doherty's group jogged past the church and up the main street, then snaked southwest out of town towards the fort, perched on a knoll halfway up the slope and commanding the only road that led to Sacramento's upland interior.

Fletcher's party soon drew machine-gun fire from the square-shaped fort and took cover behind a dry-stone wall. The sub-lieutenant let Doherty do the talking: an attack from three sides, get in close and use the mortar. Fletcher peeped over the top of the wall to get a closer look at the squat tower built from black lava rock in the last century. Arcs of yellow tracer — probably a Breda M37 — spat from a wide embrasure facing the road: rifle fire from the parapet above. He ducked at the crack of rounds whipping past his head and thudding into the soil behind him.

During a burst of return fire from the commandos, Fletcher and the party's marksman broke cover and ran at a crouch up the slope to the right, weaving between pine trees, their footfall soft on the needled earth. Finding a good vantage point, the pair dropped to the ground behind a fallen tree trunk. Taking a moment to assess his bearings, the marksman worked the stiff bolt action of his Canadian Ross rifle and took aim at the embrasure. There was a long pause, then a loud whack and a distant scream from inside the tower. Another pair of commandos far over to the left had set up their mortar behind a shepherd's hut and began methodically pummelling the fort with 2-inch rounds. All the while, well-aimed bursts from a Bren gun helped to keep enemy heads down on the parapet.

The Italian fire began to falter, the commandos using short dashes to work their way closer to the tower. A shrill blast on Doherty's whistle and two grenades exploded against the heavy wooden door. Bellowing inarticulately, the commandos charged the entrance, a sweating and gasping Fletcher at their heels. A fly kick from Doherty and the damaged door gave way. Within seconds, the men were inside, bursts of Sten gun fire lighting the darkened confines to desperate shouts of '*Mi arrendo*! *Mi arrendo*!'

Meanwhile, Sergeant Murphy's headland party was experiencing mixed fortunes. They'd managed to destroy two large searchlights near the shoreline and had begun attacking the gun emplacements. Using Bangalore torpedoes to penetrate an outer ring of barbed wire, they engaged a battery from three sides with accurate fire, first taking out the pickets, then working their way close enough to lob grenades and eliminate the gun crew. A corporal rushed forward to swaddle the cannon with high-explosive sausages and Cordtex fuses. Then he pulled the igniter pins and ran for cover, followed by an almighty blast.

But the second gun emplacement was proving more difficult. Entrenched soldiers were putting up stiff resistance and the commandos couldn't get close enough to spike the guns. Then Sergeant Murphy was shot in the hand, the bullet passing through his palm into his arm. After injecting a syrette of morphine, he was still able to fire, but the skirmish had turned into a stalemate, with both attackers and defenders holding their ground.

In the interim, Major Campbell had been leading the third party up the cliff track with Van Zyl at the rear. They ascended past cultivated terraces, the shaggy leaves of banana trees at times embowering a steep footpath whose flagstones released the day's residual heat. The night was moonless and intensely dark. Sweating profusely, Van Zyl inhaled air that was herb-scented and tanged with the sea's saltiness. Sten guns slung across their midriffs, the commandos scanned the slopes on either hand as they climbed. The lance corporal ahead of Van Zyl looked like a tortoise, his rucksack bulging with plastic-explosive sausages.

Lagging behind and out of breath, the sub-lieutenant heard a crunching sound over to the left and immediately crouched down, his heart thumping. Aiming his Lanchester at a low-boughed fig tree, he tightened his finger on the trigger. Was that a shape moving among the leaves…? Then he became aware of a soft, munching sound. It was a goat. Feeling a wave of relief, Van Zyl came upright, eliciting a snort and clatter of hooves.

Nearing the top of the path, the lance corporal held up a hand and Van Zyl halted. The commandos crouched down. The shrill song of crickets filled Van Zyl's head as he strained his eyes, glimpsing a hint of movement above them on the lip of the cliff — perhaps a sentry at the head of the path. At a hand signal from Campbell, one man quietly put down his pack and Sten gun, drew a Fairbairn-Sykes fighting knife and crept forward, vanishing round a bend in the path. Van Zyl fixed his gaze on the rim of the cliff, but saw nothing more.

After a few fretful minutes, the commando reappeared and they pressed on. Van Zyl brushed against a prickly pear and felt its hairy spines sticking to the back of his hand. The peaceful clinking of a goat's bell echoed from the plateau above, a peace they were about to shatter.

The commandos topped out into open country, stepping over the sentry's body splayed in the path, his neck opened almost from ear to ear. They halted so that Campbell could get his bearings. From behind and below them came the popping sound of small-arms fire in the valley, punctuated by the occasional crump of grenade or mortar. The party headed inland along a narrow lane with fields demarcated by dry-stone walls on either side. Up ahead in the distance, Van Zyl could vaguely make out an odd, angular structure that became clearer as they drew nearer. Surely, it must be the radar. For some inexplicable reason, the upright dish had not been retracted into its bunker and was still aimed at the sea.

They came to open ground that rose towards the crest of a hill. Approaching the installation at a crouch, they were stopped by a belt of barbed wire, probably kept low to avoid electrical interference with the radar. The commandos lay flat while one of their number worked his wire cutters, making a hole through which they slinked in single file. At the harsh rattle of a Spandau machine gun, everyone fell flat as rounds split the air above their heads. Without needing orders, the men leopard-crawled away to the left and right, seeking cover. Van Zyl stuck close to the boots of Campbell, making for an outcrop of lava rock. He heard the staccato jabber of return fire, punctuated by the occasional crack of a rifle and agitated German voices.

'We need to get closer,' said Campbell in a stage whisper. 'There's a trench and a lookout post, possibly some more wire.'

Taking a furtive peek over the rim of the rock, Van Zyl could just make out a gully close to the enemy position. He vaguely registered the fragrance of the aniseed their bodies had just crushed.

'Georgie boy, cover us with that Bren of yours!' Campbell called sotto voce into the darkness.

'Yessir!'

'Forward on the count of ten, Van Zyl, in your head: ten, nine, eight…'

Van Zyl mouthed the remaining countdown, his palms sweating, his mouth dry, muscles bunched in anticipation.

'Now!' hissed Campbell, as the Bren gun stuttered into life. Up and sprinting, feet barely kissing earth, rounds coughing up soil, whipping past his head, the major's dark shape beside him … then a headlong dive into the gully. Breathing heavily, the two officers, now covered in dust, grinned wildly at each other.

Over the ensuing minutes, the commandos worked their way forward. When all his men were in position, the major called out, 'Ready, lads?'

Affirmatives from the darkness.

'I have a lousy throwing arm,' said Campbell. 'You any good at cricket, sailor?'

'First eleven for my *koshuis* back in Stellenbosch, sir.'

'Good,' said the major, handing him a grenade. 'Drop this Scotch egg in Jerry's trench. Last wicket on day five and you're throwing from third man to the bowler's end.'

The Mills bomb felt like a small pineapple, cold to the touch. Van Zyl pulled out the pin and, keeping the lever depressed, stole a quick glance over the gully's lip: the trench was a line of disturbed soil and behind it, the contraption sat on a rotating platform, its dish far bigger than he'd expected.

Steeling himself … *now*. Up into a crouch, the trench swimming ahead. Drawing his arm far back, he threw with all his might, the tiny orb travelling on a high arc into the night. He ducked back down. *Crack*! An orgy of flashes and bangs as more grenades looped in from all quarters, accompanied by screams of agony. Campbell's whistle emitted a cicada-like scream.

'Charge, lads! Kill the bustids!'

Breaking cover, the commandos sprinted forward. Van Zyl was on the heels of Campbell, expecting bullets to rupture his flesh at any moment. Oh God, if he must die, let it be quick. To his left, a commando faltered, grabbing his chest and going down on both knees.

'Come on, Daffyd, for Christ's sake!' His oppo lifted him with one hand and kept him moving. A few more steps and the man called Daffyd collapsed in a heap, the life gone out of him.

Now the commandos were into the trench, using Sten guns and revolvers to good effect. Van Zyl jumped in after the major, giving a squirt from his Lanchester at a fleeing figure. There were maddened yells from the machine-gun nest, then an explosion. Another Mills bomb was dropped through a grill into an underground bunker, followed by a muffled blast and gusts of smoke. Then all was abruptly quiet, as though someone had lifted the needle from a gramophone.

Commandos took up positions to form a perimeter defence, while Campbell, Van Zyl and the demolition expert, Lance Corporal Gallagher, approached the contraption, which protruded from the empty cavity of its bunker, the steel trapdoors wide open. Van Zyl scrutinised the huge parabolic aerial mounted on a chassis and the large box — containing its transmitter, local oscillator and mixer — attached to the rear. A smaller box housed the IF amplifier and pulse generator, Van Zyl noticing that each item of equipment was branded with a Telefunken label. An adjacent cabin accommodated the set's display gear and operator's seat. The radar's personnel must have been among the dead.

While the lance corporal prepared the demolition charges, bullets began pinging off the dish and punching the sandbags around the emplacement. Soldiers and off-duty radar operators from the nearby farmhouse had evidently organised themselves into an attack party. For the moment, bursts of Bren and Sten gunfire, and the occasional crack of a Lee-Enfield, were keeping the enemy at bay, but the demolition party needed to be quick about it.

Then, a soft thud. Van Zyl turned sharply, his eyes widening, and gasped, 'Oh no! No!'

CHAPTER 23

Lance Corporal Gallagher sank to the ground with a bullet through his eye socket. Horrified, Van Zyl leant over the body and checked for a pulse. Nothing. Now what? Looking up, he saw headlights coming from the west: garrison reinforcements were on their way. It would be up to Fletcher's party holding the main road to delay them for as long as possible. But first, the problem of the radar. He looked at his watch — 0134 — twenty-six minutes until *Gannet* was due to sail.

'Shouldn't be too difficult, although it's been a while since I fiddled with these thingamajigs,' muttered Campbell as he stepped onto the mounting and continued attaching Gallagher's sausage-shaped packets of gelignite to the radar. Bullets fizzed and pinged about the dish, but the major did not so much as flinch. Explosives in place, Campbell then linked the fuses and, bent double, walked backwards, carefully making his way down a narrow path, uncoiling the fuse as he went, with Van Zyl following at a crouch. Reaching the remains of a dry-stone wall, Campbell screwed the wire to a small battery-operated switch produced from a rucksack.

'Everyone, take cover!' he shouted as commandos scattered from the radar, the Germans using the opportunity to advance over open ground. Van Zyl and Campbell fell flat as bullets peppered the wall.

'Fire in the hole!' bellowed the major as he twisted the switch. A flash, an enormous explosion and a blast of hot air swept over them, followed by a storm of gravel and stones chattering down. Van Zyl waited a few moments before taking a quick glance over the wall to see the burning wreckage of the radar. Campbell pulled out his Very pistol, inserted a cartridge into the barrel, and aimed it at the stars. He pulled the trigger to a shower of sparks and a few seconds later, there was an eye-searing brightness overhead, throwing the landscape into sharp chiaroscuro. The green, pear-shaped lantern wobbled slowly down the sky, signalling the general withdrawal.

'Will we head for the road, sir?' asked Van Zyl, just as a burst of Schmeisser fire pulverised the prickly pear beside them, producing a pungent vegetable smell.

'Yes, we've got ten minutes to reach Fletcher and withdraw together. It's our best chance.'

During a brief pause in the shooting, Campbell called into the darkness: 'Fire and movement, lads! Cover each other's arses, just like at good ol' Anderson Manor. South to the main road, on the count of ten. Ten, nine, eight…'

It was a well-executed, fighting retreat. Their pursuers were mostly guards, not experienced infantry soldiers, so the commandos were able to keep them at arm's length without too much difficulty. According to the plan, Fletcher would be holding the high point of the road before it began winding down to the port. Campbell aimed his party at a spot just to the east of Fletcher's probable position.

Nearing the road, and taking his cue from the others, Van Zyl sprinted across an open field and reached a dilapidated barn. Taking cover, he heard the grumble of engines in low gear and peered around the wall to see a line of trucks coming slowly uphill from the west. A Bren gun opened fire, tearing into the cab and shattering the windscreen. There was a squealing of brakes as more guns opened up, puncturing the canopy and raking the soldiers within. Survivors tipped out the back of the lorry and dived for the ditch. The second truck was right behind and swerved hard, burst through a wooden barrier, slid down the slope and toppled over, crushing some troops, while others leapt free. A third truck stopped further back to disgorge soldiers, who quickly fanned out.

Campbell's party broke cover in small groups, sprinting forward to take up positions behind the commandos defending the road, and prepared for a leapfrog retreat. Van Zyl dived into a ditch and leopard-crawled forward until he came to the boots of Fletcher.

'*Goeie môre*,' said Van Zyl. 'You're up early.'

'Coffee and rusks?'

'Waiting for us on *Gannet*. Any casualties?'

'One killed, one walking wounded. We sent him back to the ship.'

Another truck arrived and more Italian troops debussed, spreading out on either side of the road, their rifle and machine-gun fire growing heavier and more accurate as they sought to outflank the commandos.

'Getting rather hot around here,' muttered Fletcher.

'*Gannet* sails in fifteen. Thanks for waiting for us.'

'Don't mention it, old sock. But now we need to scarper.'

'What's that sound?'

'What sound?'

'Listen … that!'

'It's not a truck.'

'Something heavier.'

'Oh, Jesus.'

The boxy shape of an Autoblindo 41 armoured car rounded the bend and came growling uphill towards them. Behind it was another lorry, which stopped as more helmeted figures leapt from the tailgate, then another armoured car, and another. At the shrill trilling of Campbell's whistle, the commandos began to pull back. Van Zyl and Fletcher made a dash, using a wall for cover, until they came to a roadside cottage behind which the major and a few commandos had taken position. It stood on the crest of a rise where the road narrowed between dry-stone walls before descending to the port far below. Van Zyl could see *Gannet* snug against the wharf, awaiting her passengers, and he felt a stab of longing to be back on board: she seemed a million miles away.

'We can't outrun that armoured car,' said Campbell. 'We'll have to swat the bloody skellum.'

'How?' asked Van Zyl.

'Mills bomb. The front tyres of an AB 41 are vulnerable.'

'But what about the other armoured cars?'

'If we knock out the first one right here, where the road narrows, it'll block their path and might buy us enough time.'

The car's 20-mm Breda opened up to loud cracking sounds as holes were punched in the cottage and the façade began to collapse. Van Zyl snatched a quick look around the wall. The khaki-coloured AB 41 was much nearer, a group of soldiers advancing in a huddle behind it. Campbell handed him a grenade.

'Same again, sailor. Test match this time.'

'Now, sir?'

'No, let him get closer.'

They waited a little longer, then the major shouted, 'Covering fire!'

As small arms erupted, Van Zyl stepped out into the roadway, bent his back, took aim, and hurled with all his might, then jumped back behind the wall. The grenade arced through the air and struck the car, bouncing off its frontal armour and exploding harmlessly.

'May I have a go, sir?' asked Fletcher.

'It's my last bomb, Sub. Make it count.'

Fletcher felt the weight of the grenade in his hand, took a deep breath and withdrew the pin. As covering fire burst from either side, he stepped out from behind the cottage and aimed low, bouncing the grenade along the road. It skipped twice before hitting the rim of a mudguard, which deflected it downwards before exploding. The tyre disintegrated and the AB 41 slewed sideways into a wall.

Fletcher stepped back jerkily, like a marionette, and sat down hard beside Van Zyl, crying out in pain.

'What is it, Tom?'

'I think … I've been … Jannie.'

'Where?'

'In … in my leg.'

Van Zyl reached down and felt the wetness of blood pulsing from a hole in Fletcher's right thigh. He ran his hand further down the leg and found another wound in the calf.

'Llywelyn, get yerself over here!' shouted the major.

A young lance corporal skidded down the slope in a cloud of dust and gravel. 'Sah?'

'You're handy with bullet wounds. Attend to Sub-lieutenant Fletcher — no time to lose.'

'Yessah!'

Llywelyn set to work, jabbing a morphine syrette into the undamaged leg. He asked Van Zyl to apply pressure to the larger wound to stop the bleeding, while he dug in his pack for iodine and dressings to plug both holes. Meanwhile, enemy soldiers tried to work their way around the commandos on the slopes above and below the road. Although they were being held back by accurate fire, the commandos were running low on ammunition and *Gannet* was minutes away from departure.

'Leave me,' croaked Fletcher.

'Don't be stupid, Tom.' Van Zyl's voice was desperate. 'Two of us can carry you. After a Maltese diet, you're light as a feather.'

'It's no use, Jannie. Lugging me … you'll have bugger-all chance of reaching the old girl.'

'Tom —'

'Please … please … just —'

More 20-mm Breda rounds punctured the cottage and part of the roof collapsed in a shower of timber and terracotta.

'We have to pull out, right now!' barked Campbell.

'Leave me with a Bren and a few Mills bombs,' said Fletcher. 'I'll give the bastards a bloody nose.'

'Just surrender when they get close, damn it.'

'Buy you … some time.'

Four grenades and a Bren were produced, along with a few extra .303 magazines.

'All right then, laddies, a fast, fighting retreat, leapfrogging down to the port,' Campbell called out. 'The Ities will keep probing to see if we've scarpered. Sub-lieutenant Fletcher has kindly offered to give us a head start. We have nine minutes to get ourselves on board the Dover ferry. It'll be touch and go. On my whistle.'

'Goodbye, Jannie,' said Fletcher.

'Goodbye, Tom. It's been the greatest pleasure … an honour.'

'Tell the captain that I, I…'

'Of course, Tom.'

'And Martina … tell her that I wasn't afraid … there was no pain … that I love her more than anything … anything on God's earth.'

A whistle ripped the air with its icy call.

'Aye, Tom, I will. Give 'em hell.' Van Zyl choked back the tears as he turned to go.

'Run, Jannie, run,' whispered Fletcher, cocking the Bren and rolling onto his stomach. He dragged himself to the corner of the wall, leaving a trail of blood but feeling little pain. Resting the gun on its bipod, he aimed carefully at the nearest figures, who were confidently advancing up the road. His world had emptied itself into this moment and yes, he was not afraid. The young sub-lieutenant closed his left eye and sat the luminous foresight neatly in the 'V' of the backsight.

'I love you, Martina,' he whispered, then inhaled deeply, letting the air leak slowly from his nostrils before gently squeezing the trigger.

CHAPTER 24

Jack stood on *Gannet*'s bridge, scanning the high ground where the road began its descent to the port. The little harbour was surprisingly quiet, save for the crackle of flames from their lightning attack. The air smelt of fishing nets, seaweed and smoke. Round-bellied boats sat in the still water attached to buoys like tethered horses; others softly nudged the wharf with their fenders.

Then Jack saw the sharp flash and pop of grenades at the top of the pass and heard the faraway stutter of machine guns, echoing off the cliffs. He glanced at the luminous hands of his wristwatch: it was almost time. Commandos from the northern headland also started retreating along a coastal track, firing as they came, keeping the Italian infantry away from the village to give Campbell and Fletcher's parties a chance to fall back to the port.

Then silence, abruptly, at the head of the pass: the position must have been overrun. Italian soldiers now began advancing down the road in pursuit of the commandos, their numbers swollen by the arrival of more lorries. The first of Campbell's group reached the village and set up a perimeter defence among the houses to cover the stragglers. Apart from Fletcher, they'd left one commando dead and one mortally wounded on the pass; two walking wounded were being helped down the last stretch under fire, but their progress was painfully slow.

Lifting his binoculars, Jack scanned the scene: he could just make out that the garrison soldiers coming down the hill had reached the fort and were fanning out among the pine trees along the southern ridge overlooking the harbour; the infantry to the north were doing the same along the cliff line. *Gannet* lay in the midst of a cauldron and would soon be taking small-arms fire from three sides. He looked at his watch: 0156.

'Come on, damn it,' he hissed.

The first Italians reached the western edge of the village, which erupted to the jabber of submachine guns and the electric flash-banging of grenades. Jack glimpsed helmeted figures advancing through the streets in short dashes, outlined by flames. Sparks danced off cobbles and puffs of whitewash spat from peppered walls.

Exhausted commandos came running along the wharf and began to board *Gannet* while one group remained in the village to hold back the enemy tide with bursts of Sten gun fire. The two wounded men were helped towards the ship, one having passed out and needing to be carried by a pair of burly commandos. Just then, there was a distant cough and whistling sound, followed by a blossoming splash near the harbour mouth.

'Mortars, sir,' said Robinson. 'They're zeroing in.'

'Aye, Pilot, we need to get the hell out of here.'

'What about Van Zyl and Fletcher, sir?'

'We'll give them a few more minutes.'

'It's 0201, sir.'

'I know, goddammit!'

Jack's eye was drawn back to the pass, where he spotted movement. Adjusting his focus, he was alarmed to see the boxy shape of an armoured car coming down the hill. The second AB 41 had managed to push the damaged vehicle out of the way and was now leading the charge, rapidly overtaking some of the infantry and bearing down on the commando rear-guard still holding one corner of the village.

'Armoured car on the pass!' shouted Jack through the loudhailer. 'Open fire!'

Gannet's guns erupted in staccato hammering, but the car was an elusive target in the dark, partly shielded by a dry-stone wall running parallel to the road and by pine and olive trees that grew thicker near the town. The car disappeared among the houses and *Gannet*'s weapons fell silent. As for the infantry, there was no way the South African gunners could discern friend from foe among the darting figures.

Whoosh! Another mortar round, splinters clattering against the hull and a water column rising in the middle of the basin. A machine gun opened up from the flat roof of one of the waterfront villas. February ducked as a row of splinter holes stitched the wheelhouse bulkhead inches above his head, shattering the glass. The ship's weapons replied noisily, smashing into the villa, shredding its entire façade as the roof caved in and with it went the machine gunner.

At that moment, fiery orange tongues stabbed from an alley as 20-mm rounds tore over *Gannet*. The dark shape of the armoured car passed from right to left between the cottages and the whaler's guns replied, their discordant voices haranguing the night, offset by the brassy clatter of shell cases hitting the deck. But the AB 41 had vanished among the houses, and now another armoured car was descending the pass.

The last of the commandos had begun their withdrawal, firing bursts as they retreated using the cover of doorways and walls. Now that almost all of their number had reached the wharf, *Gannet*'s weapons could shoot at will, sweeping the approaches with blistering fire as tracer laced the village, reducing buildings to rubble in a riot of smoke, sparks and dust. The gunners were joined by volleys of small-arms fire from the whaler's decks, but still the Italian soldiers advanced from all quarters, rifle and automatic rounds clanging against the hull.

Jack looked around at *Gannet*'s shouting, cursing defenders, their faces lit by flaring snatches. There was Pickles, the overweight teenager from Benoni, splattered with hot oil from the noisy and inaccurate pom-pom he had grown to love. He plied his trade faithfully, working in synchronicity with his loader — young Booysen from the backstreets of District Six — squeezing the trigger and sending streams of tracer towards the houses, shops and tavern, the measured thud-thud-thud of his pom-pom accompanied by the loud rattle of Bredas and Oerlikons.

For the retreating commandos, the last stretch along the wharf was completely exposed and they had to run the gauntlet from the cover of a warehouse. One group only got halfway before a mortar round exploded among them, its blast tearing one man apart and blowing another into the water. Jack saw a commando drag himself to his feet and continue without an arm, the side of his battledress soaked in blood. Another sat staring at the remains of his leg and the protruding stump of bone. Men raced from *Gannet* and dragged him, screaming, the last forty yards to the gangway.

The few remaining commandos sprinted from the warehouse, singly or in pairs. Sporadic fire from an Italian machine gun in a doorway played around and among them. The pom-pom opened up, punching holes in the building until a wall collapsed, silencing the gunner, but bullets still poured from almost every direction as Italian infantry flooded the town, closing in on *Gannet*.

'More wounded coming aboard, sir,' said Robinson at Jack's shoulder. 'Porky and the medic have got their hands full in the wardroom.'

'Very well.'

Hot metal streaked past Jack's cheek, followed immediately by the sharp clink of a round hitting the ventilator behind him. Probably a sniper. The armoured car turned into a lane and grumbled towards the wharf, spitting machine-gun tracer at them. Shells from its 20-mm struck the water beside the quarterdeck and the concrete wharf, then traversed left and punched holes in the stern. *Gannet*'s return fire groped for the AB 41, then found it, venting a vortex of dancing shells upon its armour. There was a fiery explosion as the turret erupted like a champagne cork, but the car's hull kept on coming until it reached the wharf and plunged into the water with an extravagant splash.

Another stiletto-snouted AB 41 came nosing down a lane, its muzzle flaring as shells penetrated *Gannet* somewhere low and for'ard. The 4-inch replied smartly with a direct hit. The armoured car halted and took flame as figures leapt from the doomed vehicle.

'Fine shooting, PO Combrink!' shouted Jack.

Just then, Campbell appeared on the bridge looking dishevelled and bleeding from his cheek.

'Welcome back, Major,' said Jack. 'Are you all right?'

'Just a scratch.'

'Successful, sir?'

'Yes. RDF destroyed, last of the lads coming aboard, quite a few injured.'

'And my two officers?' asked Jack.

'Fletcher was badly wounded on the pass. He didn't want to hold us up, asked to be left behind with a Bren. Damn fine chap, brave too. I don't know about your Number One. He was right behind me, but we got separated.'

'I'll wait a little longer. Van Zyl has a habit of being late.' He leant out from the bridgewing and called through his loudhailer: 'Make ready to cast off!'

Right then, Jack's nuanced ear caught a familiar cadence amid the din of battle, but for a moment he couldn't quite place the sound. Tobruk, perhaps? Clinking. Like the grinding of metal teeth. To his horror, he realised it must be a tank. In the eerie light of the fires and flashes, he glimpsed a menacing shape lumbering down the hill.

'Combrink!' he yelled. 'Tank, up on the pass!'

Closer now, the thing looked like a monstrous beetle — by its profile, probably a Carro Armato M 14/41. The 15-ton Italian squealed to a halt and fired, its 47-mm shell passing clean through *Gannet*'s funnel and exploding on the wharf.

'Shoot!' Combrink bellowed. The 4-inch jolted back on its recoil, followed by a puff of dust above the road, the breech opening and a shell case ejected, belching acrid smoke. 'Over, down one! Again!'

Gannet sounded the long, baritone note of her horn, its echo booming back and forth across the harbour and reverberating off the cliffs. The badly wounded commandos left behind on the hillside knew there was now no hope: they could surrender as soon as *Gannet* cleared the breakwater. Three commandos came rushing from between the houses, bullets fizzing about them as they made a final dash for the gangplank. Jack would wait for them, but where the hell was Van Zyl?

Crunch! A shell penetrated the hull below his feet.

'After those three lads, I don't think we'll be getting any more,' said Campbell, an edge to his voice.

'Aye … all right,' Jack said, desperately scanning the wharf for any sign of his Number One. 'Let go stern ropes, but hold onto the headspring. Slow ahead.'

The three stragglers were close now, running for their lives, the whaler's stern easing away from the wharf. The gangplank scraped across the concrete, still only just touching land when the gasping trio were helped aboard. A shell struck a bollard on the wharf, sending splinters in all directions, some of them finding their mark.

'Stop engine. Let go headspring.'

Another blast on the ship's horn as a wounded Rademeyer released the rope from the bollard and made a running jump, grabbing the gunwale and being dragged aboard by Hendricks and Palmer. A 47-mm round sliced through *Gannet*'s thin skin and out the other side without exploding.

'Half astern.'

Jack was abandoning Fletcher and Van Zyl, his left and his right hand. Rage and bitterness welled inside him as *Gannet* turned and aimed her bows at the harbour mouth. The gunfire reached a crescendo as bullets clattered like hail against the hull and superstructure. Jack made a last scan of the harbour and thought he glimpsed two hunched figures coming down an alley: could it possibly be?

Gannet's captain could not have had any way of knowing that Fletcher had not remained on the pass. Van Zyl had covered less than a hundred yards after leaving the wounded sub-lieutenant before misgivings turned him back.

'You again!' hissed Fletcher. 'What the hell?'

'Can't get rid of me,' said a heavily breathing Van Zyl as he crawled up beside him.

Grimacing, Fletcher squeezed the trigger and fired another burst. 'Like gum to a shoe.'

'Look, Tom, I've been giving it a good deal of thought.'

'Thirty seconds of thought.'

'Something like that.' Out of the corner of his eye, Van Zyl caught sight of figures higher up the slope to the left, working their way around behind them.

'If we duck off the road, down to the right into that thicket of prickly pears, and lie doggo for a bit —'

'You seem to have forgotten my leg is spitchered.'

'You'll lean on me.'

'Jannie —'

'That's a bloody order.'

Fletcher gasped as Van Zyl stabbed another morphine syrette into his good leg.

'We'll never make it.'

'Come on, let's go,' said Van Zyl, hurling a Mills bomb as Fletcher emptied the magazine, aiming low and letting bullets ricochet off the road beneath the crashed car where infantry had taken cover. Using the cottage and wall as cover, Van Zyl dragged Fletcher upright and, half carrying him, staggered thirty yards back down the road and through a wooden gate. The pair dived headlong into a thicket of cactus, oblivious to the spines pricking their skin.

'Let the first wave pass,' whispered Van Zyl. 'They're more interested in getting to the harbour than finishing off stragglers.'

'Then what?' Fletcher murmured through clenched teeth.

'We edge north along the slope till we reach the cliff path.'

'Rough going?'

'Affirmative.'

'How far?'

'About three hundred yards. After that, I know the path. It's in a gorge with lots of cover.'

'Slow, though.'

'Aye, but we might still make it if *Gannet* is delayed.'

CHAPTER 25

The whaler let out another mournful blast.

'Full ahead!' ordered Jack as the threshing screw churned up sandy water and *Gannet* gathered speed towards the end of the breakwater. The Italian tank emerged from a lane, rolled onto the opposite wharf and stopped, taking careful aim at *Gannet.* Jack glanced quickly astern and saw two figures materialise from the smoke. He thought he could hear shouting and stepped towards the bridgewing for a closer look, just as the tank fired.

Bang!

Jack ducked as a 47-mm shell rent the air above the bridge. The next moment, *Gannet* sailed through the harbour mouth and her captain called into the voicepipe: 'Hard a-port!'

The whaler heeled steeply, cutting behind the breakwater and using the wall to shield herself from further harassment by the tank, which would have to drive around the harbour to get another shot.

'Everything you've got, Chief, and then some,' said Jack into the voicepipe. 'Open up those precious valves of yours.'

'I might need to have a word with your superiors in the Admiralty,' grumbled McEwan as the ship responded with an increased juddering of her decks. They were still taking small-arms fire from various quarters, but this dwindled as *Gannet* drew away from the land.

Adrenalin still coursing through him, Jack looked back at Sacramento, feeling relief infused with profound guilt. He'd abandoned Fletcher and Van Zyl on the shores of that pestilential island. Perhaps those two figures… He should have waited just a little bit longer. The tank could have been dealt with, the soldiers held at bay. Jack had a clear picture of the first time he'd met Jannie Van Zyl, reporting late for duty in Simonstown and blaming beach sand on the railway tracks for delaying his train. It had been an inauspicious start for the young Afrikaner who'd become his most trusted Gannet, and friend. If only he'd waited a few more minutes…

A searchlight on the northern headland snapped into life, its icy beam probing the darkness, growing in strength, playing across the wavetops like a malevolent tentacle. It quickly found its target and steadied, locking on, snaring *Gannet* in a blinding wash of preternatural light.

'Erratic zigzags, Cox'n, just like Tobruk.'

'Aye, Cap'n, erratic zigzagging it is,' growled February up the pipe.

A star-shell burst high above them, bathing the sea with eerie light, followed by the booming of a gun on the headland, its 4-inch round whining through its tall parabola to explode over to port. With the radar out of action, the coastal battery was firing by sight.

'Make smoke!' Jack called into both the engine room and quarterdeck voicepipes.

Almost immediately, black clouds belched from the funnel, inundating the boat deck with choking fumes. Standing at the stern rail, Bosun Cummins opened the smoke-canister valves with gloved hands and thin jets of acid began to squirt from their nozzles, turning to a white smoke cloud that further helped mask their retreat. A column of white water rose from the sea over to starboard. Jack ordered the dropping of occasional calcium flares to simulate hits and confuse the Italians as the whaler weaved her way clear of the island and waterspouts continued to grow from the sea around her.

Boom! An Italian 4-inch shell found its mark with a flash and deafening crack just behind the bridge. The scalding blast flung Jack to the deck as *Gannet* staggered under the impact. The shell had sliced the funnel in two and exploded in the waist, sending white-hot splinters in all directions. One decapitated commando cartwheeled into the water; another staggered aft, an eye blown from its socket and hanging down his cheek.

Jack lay on the deck, smothered in silence, his world turned to cotton wool, his head aching and his throat stinging from the acrid smoke. For a few moments, he remained stunned, his vision blurry — then came the hot breath of fire and the stench of fumes. Rousing himself, he touched his ear, his fingers coming away bloody. Leaning on his hands, trying to claw himself upright, he sank back to the deck.

'Behardien, Malan, are you all right?' he croaked.

'Aye, sir,' said the dazed lookout, sitting up slowly.

'Malan ... Malan!' rasped Jack. The sailor lay slumped beneath the Lewis gun, his back peppered with holes.

'I think he might have bought it, sir.'

As *Gannet* swung to port, Malan rolled over, blood pouring from his mouth. Robinson and Porky arrived on the bridge, the sub-lieutenant tending to his captain, the cook to Malan. Bending over the bloodied sailor, Porky immediately shook his head and let out a husky sigh.

'Get that fire out,' gasped Jack, sitting upright.

'The lads are already on it, sir,' said Robinson. 'No, don't try to stand; you've taken a nasty blow to the head. I'll rustle up some men and get you to your cabin.'

'Stuff and nonsense, Pilot. Just make me comfortable here.'

Robinson half lifted Jack and carefully propped him against the aft bulkhead. Porky took two flags from the signal locker and draped them over Malan's body, then disappeared down the ladder, returning in a flash with pillows, a blanket and water. Having made his captain comfortable, Porky wound bandages around Jack's head and ear.

'Robinson, you're the only functioning officer left,' said Jack hoarsely. 'The watch is yours. Get us back to Malta in one piece.'

'Aye aye, Captain, I'll do my best.'

Jack noticed smoke leaking from one of the voicepipes and said, 'Check … check on the engine room.' Then he passed out and slumped to the deck.

'Chief?' Robinson called down the pipe. There was no answer. 'Chief McEwan!'

'Who's that?' came a groggy voice.

'Sub-lieutenant Robinson at the con. How are things?'

'Och, a spot o' bother doon here, but we've got the extinguishers going,' he said, followed by a bout of violent coughing.

'Manageable?'

'Aye, I think so, for now at least.'

'Very well.'

For the moment, the searchlight had lost them in the murk of their own making. The fires were mostly doused, the hull intact and *Gannet*'s engine still in working order. Maybe, just maybe, they were going to get away.

'Enemy vessel approaching from astern!' came the bosun's voice through the quarterdeck voicepipe.

'Bearing?' asked Robinson testily, his ear bent to the brass funnel.

'Don't rightly know, sir. Can't see nothing in all the smoke, but I can hear an engine. Something fast.'

'MAS boat?'

'Negative, sir, something lighter.'

'Open fire as soon as we have visual.'

Fletcher had hung heavily off Van Zyl's shoulder as they struggled painstakingly down the cliff path and took shelter behind a derelict house on the waterfront. Here they paused, gathering their strength and waiting for the right moment to make a final dash along the wharf. Somehow, miraculously, *Gannet* was still there, spitting fire across the basin. Just a hundred yards to salvation.

The whaler sounded her horn just as the two lieutenants broke cover, Fletcher crying out in pain as Van Zyl forced him into a hobbling trot. But to their anguished dismay, they saw the last mooring line snake aboard and a figure leap for the gunwale.

'No, no, stop!' yelled Van Zyl. '*Gannet*, ahoy, wait for us!'

The whaler's departure drew all the enemy's attention and fire, allowing the pair to reach the vacated spot on the wharf, still calling out and waving. It was no use. A crestfallen Van Zyl cast about for another solution. Caught in the open with nowhere to run, surrender appeared the only option. He glanced down and saw a motorboat tethered to the wall, dancing agitatedly from the disturbance of *Gannet*'s wake. It was a sleek, twenty-foot vessel, doubtless the plaything of someone wealthy, perhaps marooned on Sacramento by the tide of war. Fashioned from mahogany, the craft looked nimble and fast.

'Hurry, Tom, into the boat. It's our only chance.'

Van Zyl supported Fletcher down a flight of slippery steps and helped lift his damaged leg over the gunwale. With a shove and a heave, they were aboard, a grimacing Fletcher collapsing on a leather bench seat at the stern while Van Zyl tried to work out how to get the engine started. A bullet sucked past his head and buried itself in the concrete with a *tonk*. Someone had spotted the escapees.

He scrabbled around frantically until he found a short piece of wire, which he used to link the red cable on the starter to the male push-on lug. A hasty jury rig and the engine was hotwired, roaring into wakefulness and venting a cloud of smoke. He quickly released the mooring lines and pushed hard off the wall to the cracking sound of bullets penetrating mahogany. Ducking low behind the steering wheel, he opened the throttle and aimed for the harbour mouth. The windscreen shattered and the stern was peppered with rounds as the water all about them sprouted splashes. A darting zigzag to throw off the aim, then through the bullnose and a sharp carve to port behind the breakwater. Full throttle now, the distance rapidly widening and Italian fire beginning to dwindle. Van Zyl was whooping at the top of his lungs as they sped into the night at thirty knots.

On *Gannet*'s bridge, Sub-lieutenant Robinson stared aft, trying to spot the chasing vessel amid the billowing smoke. Both he and the bosun caught a glimpse of the spectral pursuer at the same instant.

'Open fire!' cried Cummins.

Pickles was the first to react, red fireflies spitting from his pom-pom as he poured a stream of tracer on a low trajectory at the enemy. Straining to see the result, Robinson noticed a white cloth waving agitatedly from the trailing craft.

'Check, check, check! Cease firing!' he shouted into the loudhailer and sounded the gong.

The pom-pom stopped abruptly, the last round ricocheting off a wave and looping over the speedboat.

'What's going on, Pilot?' croaked Jack from his prone position.

'Picking up passengers, sir.'

'Two of 'em?'

'Aye, sir.'

'Gannets?'

'By the look of it.'

'Sand on the tracks?'

'Probably. The old Snoektown excuse.' Both men smiled broadly, only their teeth visible in the darkness.

'Thank God.' Too moved to say anything more, Jack felt his throat constrict and tears beginning to well.

Following a direct, north-westerly course back to Malta, *Gannet* made good progress through the remaining hours of darkness. The PO's mess accommodated the less seriously injured, who sat or lay in complete darkness as shrapnel had torn large holes in the bulkheads that would betray any show of light. They were wrapped in blankets, an enamel mug of neaters passing from lip to lip.

The gravely wounded were housed in a dimly lit wardroom that reeked of smoke, ether, iodine and blood, its deck littered with soiled bandages. Porky, Hendricks and the medical orderly busied themselves providing first aid as best they could. The commando who'd survived the mortar explosion was in a bad way, the remains of his leg a mess of livid meat. Porky cut away his trousers and removed what was left of the boot, along with the foot, which required a razor blade to sever the slender thread still connecting it to the leg. Trying to stifle his nausea, the cook injected morphia, wrapped the stump in a towel and bound it, then moved on to the next patient, who needed pliers to extract a wedge of shrapnel two inches long from his skull.

Despite the two bullet wounds to his leg, Fletcher wasn't in any immediate danger and was made comfortable in his own bunk. Porky had assured the young lieutenant that his crown jewels were unscathed, 'what with the forthcoming nuptials and all.' Far more serious was Major Campbell, who'd been in the captain's cabin when the 4-inch round had hit and a large piece of shrapnel had punched a hole in his chest. He lay in Jack's cot, drifting in and out of consciousness amid the wreckage of the cabin. The boyish medic plugged gauze bandages into the gaping wound, but his efforts barely staunched the bleeding. Porky joined him to offer assistance, tearing open another field dressing and stuffing it into the wound. And still the major bled.

On the bridge, Jack was feeling stronger and had been helped into his upright chair, where he sat askew, as though nursing a back injury. Hendricks arrived with mugs of kye — thick, dark pusser's cocoa — laced with rum. Jack lifted it to his lips, the hot nectar seeming to offer a shard of light in the unrelenting blackness of the middle watch.

Porky appeared at his shoulder and said solemnly, 'Beg pardon, Cap'n, just to tell you, sir, that … that Major Campbell has not made it.'

Jack's gaze remained fixed on the western horizon, the darkest corner of a firmament whose eastern rim had begun to pale, as if an answer lay somewhere out there in the invisible stitching between sea and sky. He sighed deeply.

'Thank you, Porky. I know you did your best.'

'Aaah, sir, the poor man just bled and bled and bled. And … and…'

'I understand.'

Porky stood beside his captain for a long time, neither of them speaking. Then he said, 'Do you think we'll ever see Snoekie again, sir?'

'I'm sure of it, Porky.'

The eastern sky grew steadily lighter, slowly acquiring a soft pink blush, the sea's surface seemingly shot through with silver. From the thin shroud of mist ahead came the thrumming of engines.

'Action stations!' ordered Van Zyl, alarm bells clanging throughout the ship. Most gunners had been dozing beside their weapons, so the journey to full readiness was a short one. Tired eyes probed the gauzy haze that grew brighter with each moment in anticipation of the sun's appearance and, perhaps, fiery battle once more.

'They're ours!' yelped Levy, the Jewish lad from Sea Point who'd replaced Malan as bridge lookout.

Jack straightened in his chair and watched as the two grey forms took a more substantial shape, bow waves flaring as they streaked towards the battle-scarred whaler, their hulls rising on the easy swell, then sitting down lightly in the troughs with a mushy kissing sound. Every Gannet and commando on the upper deck was cheering as the two motorboats carved about, reduced speed to the whaler's stately sixteen knots and took up station on either beam.

'What happened to your funnel?' came a shout from the MGB captain.

'What about it?' replied Van Zyl through the loudhailer.

'It's not there.'

'Oh, we hadn't noticed. Must've got spitchered in the kerfuffle.'

'Looks like a shark also took a bite out of your side.'

'You're full of compliments so early in the day.'

'We aim to please. But seriously, Gannet, very well done!'

The MTB came alongside and took off the most gravely wounded, then opened her throttle and raced ahead. She would reach Malta many hours before *Gannet.* The MGB took up station ahead of the whaler and the pair continued northwest, the sun lifting out of the sea astern of them and bathing the vessels in red light.

Gannet sailed into the brightening day, her dead laid out on the foredeck and covered with blankets. Dirty and exhausted commandos began to emerge from below and sat basking on the upper deck, sipping mugs of coffee. All eyes nervously scanned the sky. Their audacious mission had kicked the hornets' nest, and Axis aircraft would doubtless be out hunting for them from bases in Sicily and Tripolitania.

Sure enough…

'Enemy aircraft, bearing green two-oh, angle of sight four-oh!' cried Behardien.

'Action stations!'

The whaler's guns were already swinging towards the threat, commandos reaching for their weapons to join the fray. Jack wearily lifted his binoculars, eyes watering as he tried to make out the precise nature of the threat.

'Belay that — they're friendlies,' he called.

'In that case, I think we're almost home and dry, sir,' said Robinson.

'You may well be right, Pilot, but best not count our chickens just yet.'

'Gannets, sir,' said Robinson.

'I beg your pardon?'

'A little joke: don't count your gannets before they —'

'Ah, yes, very good, Pilot.'

Four Beaufighters roared towards them, catching the early light, the leader rocking its wings in salute, the men on both vessels cheering and waving in gratitude and relief. The stocky aircraft began to circle, forming a protective umbrella, replaced later that morning by Spitfires. Their passage had not been troubled by enemy aircraft and, as Malta's yellow-grey shape hove into view, it did indeed seem as though their luck would hold all the way to Grand Harbour.

Jack felt a surge of affection for the doughty island, wobbling uncertainly in the haze. There she still sat, all on her own in splendid isolation, a thorn in the enemy's side, bleeding Rommel's supply lines and hampering his preparations for the ultimate desert battle to come. Hitler had dispatched his best Luftwaffe units from France and Russia to bomb the island into oblivion. And still she stood, defiant in her own rubble. After every raid, out came the brooms and dustpans, no matter how severe the destruction. She was unyielding and unbowed.

Jack thought, too, of the thousands of families taking shelter in the island's dugouts and tunnels, the elderly living out their last years in caverns below ground, mothers giving birth in musty darkness, school lessons conducted in slit trenches, sermons held in the roofless ruins of churches. The Maltese had outlasted Phoenician, Roman and Arab invaders and overlords centuries before they had faced the Turks and then the French. Jack was certain they would survive the enemy once again, clinging to their Promethean rock. Until the Axis stranglehold had been broken, the slender lifeline of the occasional hard-fought convoy, 'magic-carpet' submarines or greyhound deliveries by the likes of *Welshman* would have to suffice. The Maltese were indeed people of the rock, steeled by the golden example of their knights and by a chivalric code stretching down the centuries, by a toughness born of the limestone upon which and in which they dwelt. So long as the Maltese held out, the tide would turn. It had to turn. And despite the numbing fatigue, Jack felt pride that *Gannet* had done her tiny bit to help the island survive.

The two vessels parted ways off St Elmo, the MGB making for Marsamuscetto and the whaler entering Grand Harbour. The stub of *Gannet*'s circumcised funnel leaked smoke from dozens of splinter holes, while the wound in her side sported jagged edges and a view into the PO's mess. There were no cheering crowds to meet them. The lower Barracca was empty, save for an elderly woman walking her fluffy white Maltese. A Bofors gunner on the terrace of the saluting battery waved enthusiastically, but no one else paid the bedraggled whaler much heed. *Gannet* dipped her ensign to acknowledge HMS *St Angelo*, then took a lazy turn to port and ghosted at dead slow to her berth in Dockyard Creek.

On the wharf stood a lorry and three ambulances painted in the island's characteristic stonework camouflage. Mooring lines arced ashore, took the strain and were secured. As soon as the gangplank was fitted, hospital orderlies bearing stretchers hurried aboard.

'Ring off main engine.' Jack's voice was thick with fatigue. Stepping to the bridgewing, he took stock of his battered, punctured and peppered ship, his dog-tired sailors and the surviving, bloodied commandos. How on earth had they done it? He looked at the stub of the funnel: Chief McEwan would hold him personally accountable for its amputation. Only good whisky would mollify him. Jack very much looked forward to that whisky.

'Ship secured,' said Van Zyl, swaying on his feet like a drunkard.

'And there goes Mr Fletcher on a stretcher,' said Jack. 'You did very well, Jannie, bringing our bridegroom back safe and almost sound. Very well indeed.'

'Thank you, sir.'

'I feel utterly mortified about having abandoned you.'

'You did the right thing, saving *Gannet*. And our taxi was more luxurious than the old girl. Pity we had to sink her, given all those holes.'

'Aye, she would have made a very glamorous ship's boat.'

A black staff car pulled up ostentatiously beside the whaler. Jack watched Huffington-Smythe get out and cleave through a throng of orderlies and dockworkers. The commodore paused to offer a winning smile and shake the hand of a commando on a stretcher, then crossed the brow to the trill of a bosun's pipe.

'Welcome aboard HMSAS *Southern Gannet*, sir,' said Jack, saluting wearily. 'Sorry about the shambles.'

'Not at all, Pembroke, and welcome back to you and your men. How did it go?'

'RDF destroyed, sir.'

'So I've been told. Arrows all round! Wretchedly sorry to hear about Major Campbell, but a fine showing nonetheless.' The commodore beamed. 'I knew you were up to the task, Pembroke. Splendid. Simply splendid. You've done your father proud.'

'The men did magnificently, sir.'

'They did indeed. Your butcher's bill?'

'One Gannet was killed — AB Malan — and a handful of men were wounded. The commandos lost half their number: some killed, some wounded, we presume a few captured.'

'And your ship?'

'We took a few direct hits and near misses, plenty of small-arms fire. Lots of holes, but she'll live.'

'Good, nothing the dockyard chaps can't patch up in a jiffy. Oh, and I'm recommending you for a bar to go with that DSO of yours.'

'But, sir, my men, especially my Number One and Sub-lieutenant Fletch—'

'Yes, yes, on your shoulders, though. Send me a list of recommended decorations and a motivation for each.'

'Thank—'

'I'll be off then, Pembroke — tea with the governor.'

Jack saluted the commodore's back, neither anger, incredulity nor gratitude gaining the upper hand among his vying emotions. He looked down at the wharf, where hands were already dragging shore powerlines aboard and dockyard workers were arriving with welding gear and pieces of steel plate.

Leaving the bridge, he poked his head into the wardroom to find Hendricks clearing away the soiled bandages and trying to make things shipshape. The scuttles were wide open to release the smell of blood and the anguished ghosts. Jack's own cabin, when he reached it, was pierced with holes that let in soft sunlight. He sat down hard on his cot and collapsed onto his back without taking off his shoes. Fido climbed onto Jack's chest, her engine puttering throatily. Having made herself comfortable, forepaws tucked beneath her, she closed her eyes. But Jack had beaten her to it and was already dead to the world and snoring softly.

CHAPTER 26

At the appointed hour, a staff car disgorged *Gannet*'s officers at the Sanctuary of Our Lady of the Sacred Heart in Sliema. The elegant neoclassical façade of yellow limestone was still crowned by two imposing belfries, but the rest of the church had suffered bomb damage. The officers were dressed in their Number Ones, shoes a dazzling white and swords polished. They helped the groom, his gimpy leg solidly bandaged, ascend the stairs with the aid of crutches and enter through the tall doors. Although the interior was ornately decorated with gilded sculptures, chandeliers and frescoes depicting scenes from the life of the Virgin Mary, parts of the nave were reduced to rubble, letting in the sunlight. To best man Jack, the damage seemed strangely appropriate to the nuptials.

A *karozzin* pulled by a white horse, hired by Mr Zammit to bear his daughter on her wedding day, arrived in the narrow street outside, trailing a small crowd of onlookers. Jack stood beside Fletcher at the altar, his mind gliding back over the fateful events that had brought them to this moment: their perilous passage from Egypt, the extraordinary resistance of the Maltese, the painful loss of Grayson Douglas and *Gannet*'s daring raid on Sacramento. He thought of the terrible toll it had exacted. He pictured Alana… Just then, the opening fanfare of the wedding march boomed from the organ as the bride and her father made their way slowly down the aisle. Martina looked exquisite in a dress of delicate ivory lace, with long sleeves and a veil.

'Are you nervous?' whispered Jack.

'Aye, worse than going into action,' said Fletcher, now standing without the crutches, and slightly unsteady on his pins. 'A bit seasick too.'

'You'll be just fine, Tom. You've got every Gannet behind you. Keep your eyes on the horizon and breathe deeply.'

A priest in white robes with an embroidered gold cross on his chest greeted the congregation and called for God's blessing. The service followed the customary rituals and refrains, punctuated by the soft thudding of faraway bombs. At the culmination of the ceremony, the priest intoned: 'Thomas Fabian Bartholomew Fletcher, do you take Martina Helena Zammit to be your wife? Do you promise to be faithful to her in good times and in bad, in sickness and in health, to love her and to honour her all the days of your life?'

Jack was only vaguely aware of Fletcher's quavering voice saying, 'I do,' his thoughts having drifted back once more to Alana, his lover, his betrayer. His heart still ached, but since the raid something had shifted inside him. He thought he had found a way to put Alana behind him, or at least confine her to a dark corner of his mind where she could do less harm. His head and heart had both been battered; perhaps a degree of battle-hardening had taken place. Certainly, he was learning acceptance. He would put to sea once more, take *Gannet* back into the fray, and continue to fight until whatever conclusion fate had in store...

'In the sight of God and these witnesses,' said the priest, cutting into Jack's reverie, 'I now pronounce you husband and wife. You may kiss!'

Fletcher carefully lifted Martina's veil, stared for a moment into her deep almond eyes and kissed her gently on the lips. As the congregation burst into applause, Jack gazed fondly at the smitten young sub-lieutenant beside him. Like Tom, he would find love again; of that, at least, he felt sure. As the bride and groom proceeded to the signing of the register, the church echoed with the final hymn: 'The Lord's my Shepherd, I'll not want'.

Jack, Van Zyl and Robinson stood on the steps with a number of other officers, their drawn swords held aloft to form an archway for the couple to pass beneath. The carriage was waiting to convey the bride and groom to the reception, the horse richly adorned with white feathers. Confetti fluttered down on the smiling couple as Luca Zammit, smart in his best Royal Malta Artillery uniform, helped his freshly minted brother-in-law up and onto the *karozzin*'s bench seat.

'She's jolly well-fed,' muttered Van Zyl.

'How very rude,' said Jack.

'Not the bride, the horse.'

'What exactly are you suggesting, Number One?'

'She looks delicious.'

'Don't be uncouth, Number One, but I take your point. They must keep her under lock and key, chaperoned whenever she steps out.'

'Aye, tragic.'

The guests followed the carriage downhill to a reception at the Zammit's waterfront home. Despite the island's strict rationing, Martina's parents had pulled every possible string to provide a feast worthy of their only daughter. The buffet boasted veal loaves and baked *timpana* — pasta in rich meat sauce encased in shortcrust pastry. Mrs Zammit had begged, borrowed and hoarded flour, sugar and eggs for a tiered wedding cake. From a farmer friend, Mr Zammit had managed to acquire a twenty-gallon barrel of wine made from the sweet muscat grapes of Mdina. A small brass band provided musical accompaniment, interspersed with speeches, Jack paying fulsome tribute to the courage and loyalty of his young gunnery officer and making only a passing reference to Fletcher's philandering past, to much laughter.

In the late afternoon, Martina descended the marble stairs wearing a knee-length, navy-blue going-away dress, a white hat and gloves. She was greeted with loud applause from the guests. The wedding party gathered on the pavement, along with the booming and wheezing band, as a chauffeur helped the couple into the back seat of a Humber cabriolet — a special favour extracted by Jack from the top brass at *St Angelo*, with the commodore's tacit blessing. Mr and Mrs Fletcher would be driven to the northern tip of the island to catch the ferry to Gozo for a short honeymoon in the romantic citadel of Victoria. Being an agricultural island with a low population, Gozo had better rations and was relatively free of bombing, which might allow for an uninterrupted night's sleep, should sleep be on the couple's agenda.

'Isn't Gozo one of your pal Homer's islands, Number One?' asked Jack as the cabriolet pulled away, to rowdy cheering and marginally restrained ribaldry.

'Aye, sir, it's where Odysseus indulged in seven years of hanky-panky with the nymph goddess Calypso.'

'Well, Fletcher's got three nights.'

'Clichéd ending, though, don't you think, sir?'

'How so, Number One?'

'It's like one of those saccharine novels the lads enjoy reading.'

'What is?'

'Fletcher. A heroic tale of derring-do that ends with a wedding. Painfully romantic and oh-so predictable.'

'I hadn't thought of it that way, Jannie.'

'Neither poetic nor original, sir.'

'Would you have it any other way?'

Van Zyl thought for a moment, then smiled and said, 'No, Jack, I wouldn't.'

GLOSSARY

AB — Able Seaman

Abwehr — German Military Intelligence

airy fairy — derogatory term for a person serving in the Fleet Air Arm

the Andrew — nickname for the Royal Navy

AOC — Air Officer Commanding

ARP — Air Raid Precautions warden

Arrows! — exclamation of congratulation derived from the game of darts

AS — anti-submarine

Asdic — an early form of sonar used to detect submarines by the reflection of sound waves

bag shanty — naval term for a brothel

banana boat — affectionate term for an escort aircraft carrier

Bangalore torpedo — an explosive charge fitted to the end of a long tube that can be extended

Bells, Smells and Yells — sailors' nickname for Malta

black drizzle — diarrhoea

black gang — stokers who worked in the engine room, so called because of the soot, grease and coal dust that blackened their skin

Bosun or **Boatswain** — usually a petty officer, responsible for the efficient seamanship functions of the ship

braai — barbecue

Bunts — signalman specialising in visual signals such as flags, lights and semaphore (literally 'bunting tosser')

a cable — one-tenth of a nautical mile (185 metres)

Carley float — a form of invertible life raft used mainly on warships

chin-strapped — to be down on one's chin strap with exhaustion

C-in-C — Commander in Chief

corned dog — tinned bully beef

cox'n or **coxswain** — senior petty officer responsible for steering and discipline aboard a small ship

Crown-and-Anchor — an illegal gambling game popular on RN ships

DAF — Desert Air Force

DFC — Distinguished Flying Cross

DSO — Distinguished Service Order

E-boat — the Allied name (E stands for enemy) for the Kriegsmarine's fast attack craft (*Schnellboot* in German)

erk — slang for aircraftman; all non-commissioned airmen below the rank of corporal

firilla — a traditional Maltese fishing boat

flat top — nickname for an aircraft carrier

flimsy — very thin paper

fo'c'sle or **forecastle** — the forward (often raised) deck of a ship

gigglegogs — sailors' name for any bacteria and cocci they didn't know the proper name of

give the ferret a run — sexual intercourse

gunwales under — drunk

gyppy tummy — diarrhoea (gyppy being short for Egypt, which is where many service personnel developed the ailment)

HE — high explosive

horse's neck — brandy and ginger ale, a traditional wardroom drink

HMS *King Alfred* — training depot in Hove, Sussex, for officers of the Royal Navy Volunteer Reserve

HMSAS — His Majesty's South African Ship

housey-housey — bingo
IF amplifier — Intermediate Frequency amplifier
josie — Maltese person
Kriegsmarine — the Navy of Nazi Germany
kye — sweet hot chocolate, often served on board at night
leg over — sexual intercourse
LL minesweeper — a ship designed to detect and destroy magnetic mines
logbook stamped — sexual intercourse
LS — Leading Seaman, also referred to as 'killick'
Luftwaffe — the Air Force of Nazi Germany
M&V — meat and vegetable ration
Mae West — an inflatable life jacket, the nickname suggesting that someone wearing the inflated jacket might look as busty as the actress Mae West
MAS boat — the *Motoscafo armato silurante* (MAS) was a fast, torpedo-armed motorboat used by the Regia Marina
MGB — motor gun boat
MTB — motor torpedo boat
MV — Motor Vessel
NAAFI — Navy, Army and Air Force Institutes
NCO — Non-commissioned Officer
neaters — undiluted (neat) rum, as opposed to grog (water added)
NOIC — Naval Officer in Charge
NQOC — Not Quite Our Class
Number One — the first lieutenant; the second-in-command of a warship
the old man — affectionate nickname for the captain
oppo — chum, special friend, buddy (literally your 'opposite number', the person on watch when you are off)
PO — Petty Officer

PRU — Photographic Reconnaissance Unit

pusser — Naval slang for anything that is military-like or service issue

RAF — Royal Air Force

rating — a member of the lower deck; anyone below officer rank

the rattle — disciplinary action; kept in confinement

RDF — Radio Direction Finding was the original name for radar in Britain during World War II

Red Caps — military police, so named because of the red covers worn on their caps

Rediffusion — the relaying of broadcast programmes by cable from a central receiver (Rediffusion Malta was a radio broadcasting company)

Regia Aeronautica — Royal Italian Airforce

Regia Marina — Royal Italian Navy

RN — Royal Navy

RNR — Royal Naval Reserve

RNVR — Royal Navy Volunteer Reserve

R/T — radio-telephony

SAAF — South African Air Force

SAS — the Special Air Service was a British special forces unit formed during World War II to conduct raids behind enemy lines

SAWAS — South African Women's Auxiliary Services

SBS — the Special Boat Section was an elite British unit formed from the Commandos that specialised in beach reconnaissance, sabotage and covert operations in the Mediterranean and other theatres during World War II

Scotch egg — nickname for a hand grenade

scuttlebutt — naval slang for gossip or rumour, derived from the nautical term for the cask used to serve water

SDF — Seaward Defence Force; forerunner of the South African Navy

shitehawk — an enemy reconnaissance aircraft operating out of gun range (also a nickname for a seagull or any seabird)

Snoektown or **Snoekie** — sailors' nickname for Simon's Town

Sparks — radio operator; telegraphist specialising in wireless communication

SS — Steam Ship

tin fish — torpedo

Uckers — a game similar to Ludo, popular in the RN

up the duff — pregnant

vangs — a pair of lines attached to the peak of a spritsail that steadies and controls it from the deck

WAAF — Women's Auxiliary Air Force, women's branch of the RAF

A NOTE TO THE READER

Dear Reader,

Thank you for taking the time to read the fourth Jack Pembroke naval adventure. I do hope you enjoyed it. In this series, I will be tracking Jack's story through World War II and although each novel may be read as a stand-alone, it will follow on directly in time from the previous novel, just as *Malta Inferno* picks up Jack's story in the months after the events of *Hell Run Tobruk*. Book five in the series will tell the tale of Jack returning to South Africa, where he will prepare his ship to take part in the bloody Madagascar campaign of 1942.

In this series, I have chosen a British hero and placed him on a South African ship initially stationed in a Royal Navy base at the southern tip of the continent. It has provided me with the opportunity to marry parts of my own background: my time in the South African Navy as a citizen-force officer, my university education in England, and my love of the Cape … and of the Mediterranean.

Since I was a boy, I have adored nautical yarns and grew up reading the likes of C. S. Forester, Alexander Fullerton, Nicholas Monsarrat and Douglas Reeman. But I always lamented the fact that none of these naval adventures were set in my home, the Cape, despite the presence of an important Royal Navy base in Simonstown. The Jack Pembroke series is an attempt to bring the South African maritime story of World War II to life.

Although I did serve as a citizen-force naval officer, I spent little time on warships, but I have been an enthusiastic delver into archives, libraries, museums and the arcane maritime bilges of the internet.

For an understanding of the role of South Africa's 'little ships' during the war, I'm indebted to K. G. Dimbleby's *Hostilities Only*, R. Eriksen's *The Sea Was Kind to Me*, G. Young's *Salt in my Blood* and especially to J. Duffell-Canham's *Seaman Gunner Do Not Weep* and J. Tennant's *The Red Diamond Navy*. In addition, *Proud Waters* by E. Brookes and *Trawlers Go to War* by P. Lund and H. Ludlam gave me a better grasp of the activities of 'little ships' further afield.

For the story of South Africa's naval war, I found the following books most helpful: J. C. Goosen's *South Africa's Navy*, H. R. Gordon-Cumming's *Official History of the South African Naval Forces during the Second World War (1939–1945)*, C. J. Harris's *War at Sea*, E. Kleynhans's Stellenbosch doctoral thesis, *The Axis and Allied Maritime Operations Around Southern Africa, 1939–1945*, and L. C. F. Turner, H. R. Gordon-Cumming and J. E. Betzler's *War in the Southern Oceans 1939–45*. The South African Naval Heritage Trust's regular *Naval Digest* publications, as well as those of the Simon's Town Historical Society and Cape Odyssey also proved invaluable.

To learn about the war in the Eastern Mediterranean and Malta, I consulted *Siege: Malta 1940–1943* by E. Bradford, *Senglea During the Second Great War 1940–1944* by E. Brincat, *Red Duster, White Ensign* by I. Cameron, *The Maltese Cross* by D. Castillo, *249 at Malta* by B. Cull and F. Galea, *Tattered Battlements* by P. Davies, *Raiders Passed* by C. B. Grech, *In Perilous Passage* and *Six Victories* by V. P. O'Hara, *Operation Pedestal* by M. Hastings, *Malta* by G. Hogan, *Fortress Malta* by J. Holland, *The Raiders and the Cross* by P. Larsimont, *I Wish I Had Your Wings* by A. Mansfield, *Unbroken* by A. Mars, *The Kappillan of Malta* by N. Monsarrat, *Between Hostile Shores* by M. J. Pearce (ed.), *The Siege Within the Walls* by S. Perowne, *The Crucible of War* by B. Pitt, *185: The Malta Squadron* by A. Rogers (ed.), *Malta Convoy* by P. Shankland and A. Hunter, *Red Tobruk* by F. Gregory-Smith, *Supreme Gallantry* by T. Spooner, *Images of War: Malta GC* by J. Sutherland and D. Canwell, *Sniper of the Skies* by N. Thomas, *Our Name Wasn't Written* by C. Vernon, as well as contemporary copies of the *Times of Malta* newspaper.

To gain a better understanding of escorts, submarines, torpedo boats and commandos, I read E. Bagnasco's *Submarines of World War Two*, B. Cooper's *The Battle of the Torpedo Boats*, J. Lambert's *The Fairmile 'D' Motor Torpedo Boat*, J. Lodwick's *Raiders from the Sea*, C. Messenger's *The Commandos 1940–1946*, D. A. Rayner's *Escort*, L. C. Reynolds's *Motor Gunboat 658*, T. Robertson's *Walker R. N.*, W. Seymour's *British Special Forces*, R. C. Stern's *Battle Beneath the Waves*, A. Watts's *The U-boat Hunters*, D. E. G. Wemyss's *Relentless Pursuit* and E. Young's *One of Our Submarines.*

Nowadays, reviews by knowledgeable readers are essential to an author's success, so if you enjoyed the novel I shall be in your debt if you would spare a moment to post a short review on **Amazon** or **Goodreads**. I love hearing from readers, and you can connect with me through my **Facebook page**, **Instagram**, **Twitter** or my **website**.

I hope we'll meet again in the pages of the next Jack Pembroke adventure on the high seas.

Justin Fox

SAPERE
BOOKS

www.ingramcontent.com/pod-product-compliance
Lightning Source LLC
LaVergne TN
LVHW091111080826
845145LV00008B/1872